Advance praise for

THE MAGDALEN GIRLS

"A haunting novel that takes the reader into the cruel
world of Ireland's Magdalen laundries, *The Magdalen Girls*
shines a light on yet another notorious institution that somehow
survived into the late twentieth century. A real page-turner!"

—Ellen Marie Wiseman, author of *What She Left Behind*

The
MAGDALEN
GIRLS

V. S. ALEXANDER

KENSINGTON BOOKS
www.kensingtonbooks.com

KENSINGTON BOOKS are published by

Kensington Publishing Corp.
119 West 40th Street
New York, NY 10018

All Kensington titles, imprints, and distributed lines are available at special quantity discounts for bulk purchases for sales promotion, premiums, fund-raising, educational, or institutional use.

Special book excerpts or customized printings can also be created to fit specific needs. For details, write or phone the office of the Kensington Sales Manager: Kensington Publishing Corp., 119 West 40th Street, New York, NY 10018. Attn. Sales Department. Phone: 1-800-221-2647.

Kensington and the K logo Reg. U.S. Pat. & TM Off.

eISBN-13: 978-1-4967-0613-3
eISBN-10: 1-4967-0613-7
First Kensington Electronic Edition: January 2017

ISBN-13: 978-1-4967-0612-6
ISBN-10: 1-4967-0612-9
First Kensington Trade Paperback Printing: January 2017

10 9 8 7 6 5 4 3 2 1

Printed in the United States of America

PROLOGUE

The nuns convened near the doorway like a swarm of black flies. Some giggled with nervous anxiety. Some clutched the crucifix that hung by their side and stared at the three young women who lay supine before them.

Sister Anne, the Mother Superior, had arranged them in the manner of Golgotha, much like the crucifixion depicted in a Renaissance painting. A punishment should never leave a bruise or draw blood. To do so would defile the body and bring disgrace upon The Sisters of the Holy Redemption. No, it was better to make the penitents realize their mistake through the love of Christ.

No crimson, royal purples, or azure blues adorned the three on the library floor. The composition was artfully arranged, the troublemaker with the most to regret, Teresa, pretty and blond, taking the place of Jesus. Her head was above the other two girls to the left and right, her compatriots in sin. The afternoon sunlight filtered through the room, catching the motes that swam in the air like beaded jewels in the convent's old library. Seeing the girls in their plain uniforms, their arms spread in supplication, their bodies as stiff as the boards they were supposed to be nailed upon, gave Sister Anne modest pleasure. She didn't want to hurt them; she wanted them to realize how much pain they had brought to the Order. She couldn't tolerate insubordination and vain camaraderie from those who had sinned. Rehabilitation and penance were never far from her mind, nor was love.

The nuns craned their necks through the doorway to get a better look. They had seen punishments before from Sister Anne, but this was a new twist. A few clucked in anticipation of the admonishment the three penitents deserved. The Mother Superior towered over them like the Holy Ghost and marveled at the thought of the love flowing through her to them.

Sister Anne crossed herself. "Penance." She pronounced the word slowly, accenting the two syllables distinctly, but barely loud enough for the girls to hear. She lowered her tall, thin body and knelt above Teresa's face.

The girl stared at the ceiling and then closed her eyes. Monica, the dark-haired one, to the right of Teresa, seethed with anger, her gaze full of hate. Lea, white and slender, to the left, was already in prayer. Sister Anne didn't want to punish Lea, because, of the three, she was *the good girl*. However, she had to break the bond between them.

"You know why you are here," Sister Anne said. "Don't speak. Just listen." Her eyes flickered with irritation. "You have hurt us, damaged our Order with your words and deeds. You cannot defame the Lord, go against His will." She wondered if the penitents were paying attention. Of the three, she judged Monica to be the most attentive, but that was only because she was angry. Why did these girls try her so?

"You will lie here, in the position of the Cross, until you learn your lesson," the Mother Superior said. "You must understand what Jesus suffered. You will not eat, nor drink, nor soil yourself." She rose to her feet. "When the evil has been removed from your spirit, you'll be able to join us. I do this out of love, so you will know Christ and His ways."

Teresa didn't speak. Lea muttered silent prayer. Monica spat at the Mother Superior. The spittle fell on the hem of her habit. The nuns gasped. Sister Anne called for a towel. One of the obedient Sisters ran to her side and wiped away the offensive fluid.

"You have much to learn." Sister Anne's jaws clenched. She knelt by Monica's extended arm and withdrew a straight pin from her sash. The girl's eyes flashed in terror as the metallic sliver descended toward her palm.

Monica sat up. "Don't you dare!"

The Mother Superior called to Sister Mary-Elizabeth, who came to her aid. "Hold her hands against the floor."

Monica struggled, but the nun was as stout as the granite that made up the convent. She gave up, exhausted by her fight.

The Mother Superior ran the pin over Monica's palms, tracing the outline of the cross with its sharp point. "If I hated you, I would drive this into your flesh to show you what Christ knew," she said. "His persecutors reviled Him. They wanted Him to suffer, and suffer He did. I don't want you to die a sinner. I want you to be resurrected into heaven." She clasped her crucifix. "Sister, stay with them. It's almost time for prayers."

The nuns in the doorway dispersed. Sister Mary-Elizabeth sat in a chair near the window and watched over her three charges. Sister Anne called out, "Remember what I told you. I love you." She turned and disappeared down the hall, her heels clicking against the stone tiles.

CHAPTER 1

The red rose pinned to Teagan Tiernan's dress looked out of place. She fussed with the closed bud, avoiding the thorny stubs her mother had clipped off the stem, and repositioned it on her left shoulder. It hung there for a moment, giving off its soft fragrance, but then drooped above her breast. After an hour at Father Matthew's, the rose would be as wilted as her perspiring body, and it wasn't even three o'clock yet.

She was tempted to throw it on the bed with the sweater her mother wanted her to bring to the reception. There was no need for it on this unseasonably hot day.

Teagan thought of a million things she'd rather be doing on a Sunday afternoon than gathering at the parish house to welcome a new priest. She could be taking a spin on Cullen Kirby's motorbike, or spending the afternoon with him at the River Liffey, enjoying the cool breeze off the water.

Her mother had picked out the white satin dress. Teagan protested, saying it made her look like a schoolgirl, too immature for a sixteen-year-old, but her mother insisted it was appropriate for a church gathering.

"Come on, all of you, or we'll be late." Her father's anxious footsteps echoed downstairs. His words were directed at Teagan, and at Shavon, her mother. "Me whiskey's getting warm. The punch will be gone by the time we get there. When that crowd starts drinking, it disappears fast."

Teagan sighed. What did it matter? Her father always

brought his own flask to social events, no matter the occasion. She grabbed her brush, swiped the bristles through her hair, and glanced in the mirror over her dresser. She fluffed the hair behind her ears.

Outside, thick clouds drifted near the sun. Teagan squinted at the bright dot that hung like an incandescent bulb in the surrounding blue. If only she could turn it off and extinguish the heat—but she had no more power over the sun than she did getting out of this meeting. She gathered her sweater from the bed and opened the door.

Her mother caught her by the arm in the hall. "Turn 'round and let me take a look."

Teagan swiveled on her low white heels and rolled her eyes.

"No exasperated looks," her mother cautioned, while brushing imaginary lint from her daughter's shoulders. She inspected her from head to toe. "You look like a princess, love. Your father will be proud."

She wrested herself away from her mother. "I look like a fancy girl. Do I have to go? We went to Mass this morning. I'd rather take a walk by the river."

"No getting out of this one." Her mother smoothed the lapels on her new dark suit. "And I know why you want to walk by the river. I imagine it has something to do with Cullen Kirby. He'll just have to wait. Come on, now. It's important to meet the new priest, and we don't want to make your father mad."

Teagan looked down at her dress. She would die of embarrassment if Cullen or any of her school friends saw her in it. It looked as if she was off to a formal dance. There was only one good thing about it—it showed off her breasts. They were too small, she felt, and the tight fabric lifted them into pointed cones that accented her slim figure.

She never felt she could compete with her mother, who always looked feminine, neat, and composed, whether she was going to the market or off to play bridge. Today was no exception. The suit fitted her mother's form perfectly, contrasting with her fair skin. Her mother had pulled her black hair into a tight bun at the base of the neck to accommodate her hat.

"For Christ's sake!" Her father's voice bleated up the stairs. "Do I have to come up there and drag you two to the car?" They started down the steps, Teagan first, her mother following. Cormac stared up, turning his fedora in circles. He took out a handkerchief and swiped at the sweat beading on his forehead. "I'm sick of this heat wave. It's hot as hell itself, and now we'll be late. I can understand my daughter having no respect for manners, the way children are these days, but you, Mother, should know better." He wore a blue suit, a bit too heavy for the day; however, it was his favorite, the one he wore most to work and church.

Her mother looked sour. "There'll be plenty of booze, don't you worry. You'll get your fill. Father Matthew makes sure it doesn't run out. You could compliment your daughter."

Cormac grunted, then ushered his wife and Teagan out of the house with an agitated wave. He locked the door. They followed him to the small space where their black sedan sat in front of the row house. The car windows were rolled up, the seats baking in the sun.

She climbed into the back, punched by the stifling heat. Her father seemed more than irritated by the hot day. She wondered whether her mother and father were happy, but quickly brushed the thought aside. She was lucky to live on the south side of Dublin, away from the poverty and tenements of the north side. Ballsbridge didn't suit her mother, however. She always lamented that they lived too close to Donnybrook and its working-class neighborhoods.

She didn't have much contact with the outside world. Her father forbade most everything that was fun. He was a bureaucrat, a pencil pusher, and although Teagan had an idea what he did as an aide at Leinster House, the parliament, she had never been to his office. She always pictured his as an exciting life, dealing with important people, but he constantly complained about the job and how little money he made. But the nuns at parochial school always told her to count her blessings. A tidy home, food on the table, and a car awaited her, when many in Dublin had few luxuries.

The car jerked away from the curb and turned north toward St. Eusebius Church. It was only a five-minute drive. The warm air streamed into the car, tugging at her hair. The elms lining the road provided patchy shade as they drove. Shavon fussed in the front seat, arranging her new pillbox hat, while her father lit a cigarette with a free hand.

"Shit!" Her father pounded the steering wheel as they neared the church. "We have to park a field away—and in this heat. That's what we get for being late. Who the hell holds a reception in July?"

Teagan protected her hair with her hands and peered out the window. A row of vehicles, shimmering in the sun, lined the road. The church's car park was already filled.

"Watch your language, Cormac," Shavon said as they pulled curbside, a few blocks from the church. "Teagan, take your jumper."

She scowled at her sweater. "It's so hot. I'll look like a dunce."

"Hang it over your arm. A lady should carry it just in case. Manners, you know."

Cormac snickered. "Oh, let it stay in the car. Manners won't get you into heaven."

Her father rarely took her side, but in deference to her mother she would carry the sweater; after all, they had an understanding. It wasn't that she hated her father, but for as long as she could remember, she and her mother had forged a bond. They kept each other afloat when her father was drunk, or when he made strict demands that strained the household. She picked up the sweater and placed it over her arm.

Her stomach knotted as she stepped out of the car. She didn't want to be here—few social situations with her parents were pleasant. She already knew how the afternoon would go. Her father would drink too much; her mother would criticize his drinking and throw disapproving looks his way. Teagan would have to make small talk with lots of people she hardly knew and really didn't care about.

Too bad Cullen wasn't Catholic. As a Protestant, he wouldn't be at this reception. Her parents didn't approve of her boyfriend, but Teagan didn't care. She saw him when she could, mostly on the sly. Cullen was her business and not her mother's. If she could get through this excruciating gathering, maybe she could call him. They might be able to go for that walk after all.

Two times at St. Eusebius in one day was enough—Mass and now this. The parish church loomed in the distance like a granite prison. Teagan had always thought it didn't have much going for it, except for the tall belfry. In the afternoon sun, the church seemed forbidding and hot.

Her father walked ahead of them, eager to get to the punch bowl. Teagan and her mother followed, fanning the heat away. He led them down a path on the north side of the church, through a garden sheltered by tall trees. Laughter spilled out of the open parish house door. Teagan took a deep breath before diving into the crowd. The room was so tightly packed she could barely move. Body heat washed over her like warm bathwater. Cormac waved to a group of men standing across the room and pushed his way to the drinks table. Her mother joined a group of ladies standing near the door.

Teagan spotted Father Matthew, the parish priest, standing near a table holding the punch bowl and several open wine bottles. A framed photograph of Pope John XXIII hung above it. The Pope, attired in a white skullcap and crimson robes, smiled upon the festivities. Father Matthew's face reddened as he joked with the parish men who lined up for drinks. Teagan heard her father ask for punch. After getting a glass, he shuffled off, keeping his back to the crowd. Teagan knew what he was doing. She saw his elbow bend after he reached into his pocket.

Cathy, a girl she knew from school, shouted from across the room. Teagan thought of her satin dress and blushed, but waved back and took a glass of punch for herself. She had started to make her way through the throng when a man in the center of the room caught her attention. He had to be the new priest. He was dressed like one, wearing the clerical collar, dark shirt, and pants, but unlike Father Matthew, he was handsome and young, with solid arms and shoulders like some of the athletic boys at school. The parish women, young and old alike, circled around him like birds pecking at feed.

The women hung on his every word. When he smiled, his cheeks folded into dimples. He laughed and swept back his wavy black hair with his fingers. His sky-blue eyes stopped Teagan in her tracks. Had she imagined it, or had he looked at her with more than an expression of interest? A few women eyed her. One in particular, Mrs. O'Brian, seemed to be taking notes on the new priest.

But he was watching *her* walk toward him. She hadn't imagined it.

Mrs. O'Brian studied them both, her hawklike eyes beaded into dots.

Teagan pushed into the inner circle, ignoring Cathy for the moment. The priest grinned as she snaked her way through the crowd. Was he smiling at her? A tingle washed over her body. She liked the feeling, particularly coming from so handsome a man. Something about him—she couldn't put her finger on it—excited her. Was it the thrill of meeting someone important and new? Or was it his good looks? She stopped short of introducing herself, but stood close enough to hear him answer questions about his new duties. Someone accidentally nudged her from behind. Her arms broke out in gooseflesh as she brushed against the priest.

"Excuse me," she said, without looking directly at him. "Someone pushed me."

The priest's eyes twinkled. Apparently, he was no stranger to adoring crowds. "No apology necessary," he said, and resumed his conversation with the others.

She broke free of the circle as embarrassment rose in her chest. Cathy grabbed her by the arm when she came within reach. "Isn't he gorgeous?" she gushed. "You got close to him! What did he say to you?" Cathy pushed back her glasses so she could focus on the priest. "Father Mark," she said languorously. "I'd love to share my confessions with him."

Teagan scoffed. "You can hardly get to him for all the swooning women. All we need are the other Apostles—Father Luke and Father John—to complete the set."

Laughter erupted from the corner where her father had joined his pals. He was probably on his second whiskey by now.

"I think Father Mark fancies you," Cathy said. "I saw the way he was looking at you." Her friend stared at her. "My, you look dolled up today."

"My mother made me wear this dress—and carry my jumper." Teagan sighed. "I told her it was ridiculous, but she wouldn't listen. And you're daft. Father Mark is old enough to be my da—at least thirty." Her shoulders drooped at the thought. "And even if he did fancy me, what future is there with a priest? None." She was happy Cathy thought she was attractive enough to capture a look from Father Mark.

Cathy squinted at the young priest. "Maybe you could convince him to give up his vows of celibacy."

"Don't be silly." Teagan fanned her face with her hand. "My God, it's hot. I wish we could get air-conditioning here like my aunt Florence has in America. She tells my mother about all the luxuries they have in New York City."

"Let's go to the table and stand by the stairs," Cathy said.

"Stairs?"

"Father Matthew has a wine cellar. I helped him and Father Mark bring up some bottles. It's cooler by the steps." They made their way to the table and the stairs that led below.

Her mother walked to the group of ladies gathered around Father Mark. In the corner, her father leaned on one of his friends, sharing the contents of the flask.

They had only been at the stairs a few minutes when Father Mark broke through the crowd and started toward them. Cathy nudged Teagan in the ribs. "Get ready. Here he comes."

Teagan slapped her friend's hand. "Quit it! I don't want him to look at me."

He stopped in front of them and extended his hand to her. "I've met Cathy, but we haven't had the pleasure." He had no Irish accent and Teagan wondered where he was from. She took his hand, warm to the touch, and shook it. A thrill shot through her, and she pulled her fingers away. She stared at the priest. He filled out his clothes like no other priest she had met. A question popped into her head: *Why would such a good-looking man become a priest?*

"It's very hot and I'm looking for a particular bottle of wine," he said. "I think a drop or two would do me good."

"Teagan will help you," Cathy offered.

She shot her friend the evil eye. "I'm sure Father Mark can manage by himself."

"No, go ahead," Cathy said.

"I don't mind company," the priest said, as he breezed by Cathy. He started down the stairs. Cathy shoved Teagan after him.

She scowled at her friend, grasped her sweater, and clung to the wall as she felt her way down. It was like being a child again, she thought, struggling against the feeling that she was doing something forbidden by following this handsome man. He was so different from Cullen. His maturity and charm captivated her.

Father Mark disappeared for a few moments. A flash of light flooded the stairs. She saw the priest halfway across the room standing under the glare of a naked bulb. The room smelled of must and generations of damp walls. Several dilapidated chairs sat in a corner near a writing desk with a broken leg. A large travel trunk with old books piled upon it filled another. Father Mark scrutinized the wine bottles laid out in a wooden rack against the wall.

He lifted one, read the label, and without looking back, asked, "What's your name?"

"Teagan Tiernan."

"A pretty name." He turned and studied her. His blue eyes bored through her in the close quarters. "Your parents are parish members?"

"Yes. They have been for many years." The intensity of his gaze made her nervous, but she found it hard to look away.

Something like sorrow flitted across the priest's face and then vanished. He flipped the wine bottle in the air and caught it in his hand. "This is what I'm looking for. A nice claret. It's almost a sin to drink it on so warm a day." He reached for her with his free hand.

Teagan instinctively raised her sweater.

"I'm sorry," he said. "I wanted to look at the red rose on your dress. I love roses. They're symbols of purity, you know, especially white ones."

She nodded and cupped her hand over the flower, which had flopped forward. The rose was close to her left breast, which the dress accentuated. Her nerves got the better of her. "Maybe we should go upstairs."

Father Mark smiled. "In a minute. I'm tired of shaking hands and answering questions. Let me ask a few." He leaned against the wine rack. "It's awfully hot to be carrying a jumper."

"My mother made me bring it. She thinks a young lady should always carry one no matter how hot it is."

"Do you know anything about wine?"

Teagan shook her head. "My da drinks it once in a while, but he prefers whiskey."

"Take a look." Father Mark held out the bottle.

She placed her sweater over the books on the trunk, took the bottle, and examined it. "It doesn't mean much to me." She handed the wine back to him.

Raucous voices and laughter poured down the stairs. She wondered if her mother might be looking for her. The thought of being alone with the priest made her stomach flutter, although she wasn't doing anything wrong. So what if she was caught in the wine cellar with him? He didn't seem to be too concerned about their meeting.

"Where are you from?" he asked.

"Ballsbridge, near Donnybrook," she replied, and found herself embarrassed to say so.

"I'm from Dublin—north side," he replied matter-of-factly.

"You don't sound it." she said. "At least not like any north-sider I've ever heard."

"I was educated in London. I worked very hard to get rid of my accent and speech patterns. I was ashamed of where I grew up. . . ." He leaned against the wine rack.

She had only met a few people who lived north of the River Liffey, but she knew life was different there. "You shouldn't be. You've done well for yourself."

He tilted his head. "I've learned you can't erase the past no matter how hard you try." He looked at her with a softness she hadn't expected.

She lowered her gaze.

"You have beautiful hair," he said. "It's almost blond, special in Ireland."

Teagan fought back a blush. "My grandmother on my mother's side was German. I don't remember her. She died shortly after I was born—"

"Teagan . . . Teagan?" Their conversation was interrupted by the slurred speech of her father. He called her name successively, each "Teagan" louder than the next.

"Well, it's been a pleasure, Miss Tiernan. I suppose we'd better go up." Father Mark pulled the string hanging from the lamp and the cellar plunged into darkness.

Her father's calls came in violent outbursts, sending a shiver through her.

"Let me go up first." He brushed past her, the wine bottle in his hand. Teagan followed. The priest stopped in front of her father, who stood surrounded by his friends.

Her father's eyes shone red in a drunken rage. He reached past the priest and grabbed her arm. The room grew quiet.

"I've been lookin' for yeh," her father said, his words slurred. She knew he was angry when his accent burst forth from too much drink.

Her mother put a hand on his shoulder. "Stop it, Cormac. Don't make a scene."

"A scene? I was looking for me daughter." He knocked her mother's hand away and bellowed, "What's to be done when you can't find your own flesh and blood?"

Father Mark put the bottle on the table and extended his

hand to Cormac, but the friendly gesture wasn't returned. Her father glared at the priest.

Father Mark lowered his hand. "I'm afraid I'm to blame, Mr. Tiernan. I asked Teagan to read the titles on some of the holy books in the cellar. I'm not much good without my glasses."

Her father shook as the priest smiled at him. He pointed a finger at Teagan. "She's good at reading, but slow at other things, such as learnin' about life."

"Da, please," Teagan said. She used the only term of affection she knew that might cool her father's anger.

"Yes, daughter, please your 'da.'" He spit out the words and then slumped against the table.

Father Mark caught him before he could knock over the punch bowl and the wine.

"Get your hands—" Her father shook the priest off and grabbed the edge of the table. Father Mark backed away.

Shavon clutched her purse and stared at her husband. "I think we should go."

"It's been a pleasure to meet you," the young priest said to her mother. Father Matthew, who had been entertaining a group of older parishioners across the room, walked with wide eyes toward the new priest.

"Yes, let's go," her father said. "But not before I've had another spot of whiskey." He held up his thumb and forefinger in a pinch.

Father Matthew's cheeks turned a bright red. "I think you've had enough for one afternoon, Cormac."

"All right, then." He hiccupped and his feet shifted unsteadily beneath him.

"I'm sorry," Teagan whispered to Father Mark. "Sometimes he drinks too much."

"No, I must apologize," he replied. "Get home safely."

Her father muttered incoherently and leaned on her mother as they trudged toward the door.

Her mother offered to drive, but her father would have none of it, declaring that he was "sober as a church during Mass." The ride home was quiet except for a sniffle now and then from Teagan's mother. Every time she blew her nose, her father pounded the steering wheel with his fist. He did seem remarkably sober despite the number of drinks he'd had. She had heard one of her friends talk about "functioning drunks." He was one, on many occasions.

When they arrived home, her father exploded. "How dare you embarrass us like that—disappearing with a priest! In the name of all that is holy, what were you thinking?" He swaggered, red-faced and sputtering, toward her. The sour whiskey smell on his breath burned her nostrils and she wished she was anywhere but home. Why couldn't she be with Cullen walking along the river? Her father was so angry she felt as if she would never get out of the house again.

His hand came up, as if he was going to strike her. He had spanked her when she was a child, but had never threatened anything as brutal as a slap.

Her mother shivered on the couch.

"It wasn't my fault, Da," Teagan pleaded. "It was like Father Mark said." But she knew the priest had lied about the holy books and wondered why. Perhaps he didn't want her father to know they had gone to the cellar to pick out wine; after all, she wasn't old enough to drink. She suspected he was covering for her so she wouldn't get in trouble.

Her father leaned toward her, the saliva from his angry words splashing across her cheek. "Don't lie to me. I know what you were thinking. Your slutty behavior will get you into trouble, mark my words. Do you hear me?"

She nodded her head in shame, and tears welled in her eyes. "I didn't do anything wrong. Ma, tell him!"

He raised his hand again.

Her mother screamed, "Stop!"

The shrill sound startled her father. Teagan raced up the stairs to her bedroom.

"And don't come down until you can apologize," he shouted after her. "For Christ's sake, me own daughter tempting a man of God."

She collapsed on her bed, crushed a pillow against her, and

cried until she gasped for breath. The room, hot from the sun, swam around her. She hadn't done anything but be nice to a priest. What was so wrong about that? She threw the pillow across the room, sat up, and looked out the window. If only she were with Cullen, instead of banished to her room. The floral curtains barely moved in the heat.

After about an hour of thinking about what she should do, she decided an apology to her father was in order—not because she was wrong, but to keep peace in the family. To give in was easier than fighting. His drinking seemed to be getting worse each year, his thinking more irrational under the influence of alcohol. She knew how much there was to lose. A few vague memories came back to her—ones she didn't care to remember—shouting matches that ended with her mother in tears. She had been aware of it when she was young, but had managed to shove the hurt aside. Her mother had never been able to stand up to her father when he was drunk. At least today she had screamed rather than sit like a lump on the couch. Her mother was as frightened as she was that a confrontation might tear the family apart.

She also thought about Father Mark. Was he thinking about her?

She got up and looked in the mirror. Her eyes were red and puffy, her coiffed hair a frazzled mess. The rose had withered, the stem broken. She reached behind her neck to unclasp the hooks of her white dress and then sank again on the bed. Her jumper! She had left it in Father Matthew's cellar. Her mother would be furious about her carelessness, not to mention the expense of replacing it. How could she get it back? She'd have to ask Father Mark to return it, and that would require a phone call. She would have to be cautious about approaching the priest. But she wanted to see him again, if only to find out why he had lied to her father.

CHAPTER 2

Pearse McClure jiggled the door at Nora Craven's small apartment. He found it odd that it was bolted. Usually it was unlocked, because Nora's mother, Agnes, was always at home washing, mending, or cooking.

"Who is it?" The question from inside was followed by a round of hacking coughs.

He recognized Agnes's gravelly voice on the other side of the door. Her greeting was like a suspicious interrogation rather than a pleasant salutation.

"Pearse." He braced himself for the reply he suspected would come.

"Off with yeh. She's not here. And if yeh see her, don't send her crawling back to me. I've no use for her unless she mends her ways. She needs to pull her weight in this house."

He knew better than to argue with Nora's mother. A peace offering would be much better. "I brought a pack of fags for you. The brand you like." He held the Player's cigarettes up to the window.

The curtains split and a worn face peered through the wavy glass. Pearse, who had seen Nora's mother at her worst, was still shocked by her appearance. Her black hair, streaked with gray, was disheveled, her face bloated and devoid of color. "What's the matter? You look like death warmed over."

Agnes opened the door a crack and stuck a bony hand out for the cigarettes. "I'm less than chipper, but I suppose these will cheer me up." She grabbed the Player's and closed the door. The curtains fell across the glass.

"That's the thanks I get?" Pearse asked.

"I don't know where Nora is. Try the alley. And keep your nob away from her. She's in enough trouble as it is."

He headed down the walk littered with paper and broken beer bottles. "Thanks for nothing, old crone. How did you manage to squeeze out your beautiful daughter?" He flipped two fingers toward the house and set off to look for Nora. He had a good idea where she would be.

Nora Craven sat in her favorite spot on the north side of Dublin, along a wooded trail in Phoenix Park. She never tired of leaving the tenement behind. She escaped to the park as often as she could, where her only distraction was the sound of the breeze curling through the trees. The shade of a large elm comforted her on this hot July morning. She'd had enough of her mother's nagging. *Nora, hang out the wash. Nora, stitch this. Nora, mend that. Nora, scrub the floor.*

Her home life was worse than being in a prison camp. She wondered if her mother had ever been sixteen and pretty like she was. The pictures in the family album had been snapped in happier days, before her mother got married and became a drudge. They showed her stretched across the couch, a cigarette in one hand and a beer in the other, or at a party, leaning on friends, smiling like a goof. Why couldn't she be as relaxed now? Nora understood life was hard and work could be harder, but wasn't there time for play?

Her blood boiled every time her mother barked an order, and there had been plenty of them lately. She tried to brush them off, but they made her angry, like the ones this morning that caused her to storm out of the house. It wasn't the first time, and she doubted it would be the last. Nothing could be worse than a life lived like her mother's. Little money and hours of housework weren't part of her future. Thank God she didn't have to go to church today. Her mother was sick and her father was working an odd job to bring in a few extra pounds.

Nora reached for the cigarettes she had carried on her bus ride to the park and then reconsidered. She didn't want to become old and wrinkled before her time; however, life was for the young and now was the time to smoke. If she didn't live now, what memories would she have when she was old? She pounded the pack against her fist, took one out, and then reconsidered lighting it.

She leaned against the wrinkled bark of the tree. The dappled lawn, the warm breeze, tempted her to doze off and forget her troubles. The air smelled clean, free of the exhaust fumes that swirled on the road in front of her home. She was in a peaceful netherworld, half-awake and half-asleep, when she heard her name.

Pearse walked toward her, his hands stuffed in his jean pockets. At eighteen and of sturdy body, he had no right to be so damn sexy, she thought. He embraced the "Teddy Boy" look with his slicked-back pompadour and Elvis style. His white T-shirt showed off his broad chest and strong arms. Nora had actually swooned when they'd met at a girlfriend's house on a cold January night. She hadn't fallen on the floor, but Pearse's eyes, with the hint of the devil in them, had made her legs wobbly and taken her breath away. The party turned into more than a Saturday night "steal-a-kiss." They had fitted themselves into a tight corner and petted their way to oblivion, and by the time they broke apart, Nora felt as if she had made love for the first time, at fifteen going on sixteen. He had pressed against her and instinctively commenced a sexy bump-and-grind, which Nora welcomed. That evening was bliss like no other. Since then, they had seen each other when they could—going on six months— and Nora was ready for more.

"I knew I'd find you here," Pearse said.

"You're being smart." She lit a cigarette and handed it to Pearse, who took a drag and sat down beside her.

"Your ma's in a foul mood today."

"She's always a bitch, more so when she's knackered." Nora took the cigarette from him. "She wanted me to do all the housework and I told her it was too hot—and a Sunday to boot. It's a day of rest, for God's sake." Nora laughed.

Pearse rolled his eyes. "You're so religious."

"I told her I was going for a walk to cool off. We don't exactly live at a fancy hotel with air-conditioning." Nora took a hair band from her pocket and swept up her dark brown locks in a long ponytail so the breeze could get to her neck.

He stretched out beside her and took her hand. "So, we have a Sunday. What'll we do?" He winked and crawled closer.

She understood his not-so-subtle advance and said, "You know my answer. Not until we get away from here."

He let out a long sigh. "Be a good girl and give me a puff."

"Here, have your own." She handed him the pack.

Pearse sat up, lit a cigarette, and leaned against the tree. "I could use a drink to calm me nerves. I get all worked up, and you turn me down every time. As well you should, me being a gentleman, and you being a young lady."

Nora snickered, clenched her fist, and punched it against his arm playfully. "And I will until me and you can get out of this dump." She softened a bit and stroked her hand up and down his leg. "I don't care where we have to go, even if it's to London. Just so we have a better life."

"I understand, darlin', but I've got me little job here and me parents."

Nora batted her eyes. "Wouldn't you give up that piddling job and your parents for me?"

"I'm serious, Nora. I'd do it if I could. But starting over with everything new? We'd be lost. What kind of life would we have in London? I don't know a soul there."

"This kind of life." She leaned over and kissed him. Kissing Pearse was the same every time for her. Their lips melted together in a soft heat, their tongues encircled in passion.

He moaned.

Nora pulled away as the bulge below his belt tented into a mound. "That's what you'll get, and more."

Pearse pointed to his crotch. "Ah, me willy. You're torture,

Nora, sheer torture. You bring out the raging soldier." He cupped her face in his hands, pulled her close, and kissed her hard. "There's nothing I wouldn't do for you and you know that. Give me a couple of days to get things together. Let me figure it out and then we'll be off. Me brother in Cork might find us a cheap place to stay until we can get our feet on the ground. Maybe he can get me some work. He has a good job with the brewery there." He rubbed his stomach. "A man can always use a stout!"

Nora's spirits lifted. "Pearse! You really mean it. We can leave Dublin? Start a new life?"

"I'll do what I can."

She leaned back against the tree and sighed. His promise had shattered the anxiety filling her. "Let's walk, Pearse." Nora got to her feet and pulled him up. "I'm so happy I could burst. There's no one in the world but we two right now."

They walked toward the Wellington Monument obelisk, where the afternoon crowds had begun to gather. Although Nora had walked the spacious lawn where it stood a hundred times, the monument held new meaning today. Its sparkling granite spire jutted into the sky as if it were guiding her onward and heavenward. She was sure no one in the park felt the way she did—liberated from a life she could no longer abide.

Nora hovered by the phone the next few days expecting a call that didn't come. Every time it rang she jumped, hoping to hear Pearse's voice on the other end. Instead, it was the butcher, the grocer, or some ridiculous neighbor asking for her mother. Pearse didn't visit the house, either.

"What's yer problem?" Agnes asked one afternoon. "I'm no eejit. Yer looking for a call from Pearse, aren't yeh? Looks like yeh may have scared him off. That's what happens when a girl gets too forward."

Nora scowled. "You don't know a thing about it."

Her mother cupped her hand over her right ear. "What's that, missy? I think yer getting right uppity for a Ballybough girl. Yer father thinks so, too."

She held her tongue, but her mother could surely see the flush rising in her cheeks. She swiped the sweat from her brow and went back to ironing. How long would she have to endure this craziness called a home? She was sixteen after all, almost an adult. All she needed was a fresh start. Pearse's call couldn't come soon enough.

Her father opened the door a few hours later looking for tea. Agnes and Nora had finished eating, knowing he'd make a late-afternoon stop at the pub before coming home. He took off his sweat-soaked shirt and threw it on top of the wringer washer. Clad in his undershirt and work pants, he plopped in a kitchen table chair, his ample stomach and beefy arms propped against the dinette. Nora hoped her father had doffed a couple of brews to take the edge off. He was happier after a few drinks.

Her mother set a plate of cold chicken in front of him. He grunted and said, "Hauling lumber isn't for pansies."

Nora took dirty dishes to the sink. She could feel her father's eyes following her across the room. She grabbed a brush and scraped bits of food from the plates into the wastebasket.

"What's that boy of yers do?" her father asked between bites.

She put in the sink stopper, turned on the hot water, and poured in green dish-washing liquid, purposely keeping to her task. "You know what he does—takes tickets at the car park. He's learning to fix cars, wants to go on to a garage."

Her father sniggered. "Hardly enough to buy a sandwich, isn't it? But I guess there'll be more money in the automotive line."

Nora turned, glowering. "He's going to make a lot of money—you wait and see—enough to take us away from here."

Her parents burst into laughter. "What makes yer think yeh can pull yourself out of here, Miss High-and-Mighty?" her father asked.

Agnes said, "Yeh make me laugh, Gordon," and then broke into a sidesplitting cackle.

"It takes money to leave yer home," her father added, as if to pound the point like a stake into Nora's heart. "Yer ma and I have never been able to do it. What makes yeh think yer so special?"

"I'm not special." Anger rose inside her. She looked at the butcher knife on the counter and considered grabbing it because she wanted to do something awful. Her hands shook at the thought. The bloody scene she had in mind disgusted her, and she fought back the hate filling her head.

"What good are yeh?" her father goaded. "Have yeh thought about leaving yer home and what that means, or is there only one thing yeh care about?"

"Stop it! You've no right to talk to me that way!"

He rose like a rumbling giant, halfway out of his chair, and pillared his beefy arms to the table. "I'll talk any way I like as long as I'm paying the bills."

Nora turned back to the dishes and plunged her hands into the soapy water. The warmth and bubbles felt good against her skin. She wished she could immerse herself in a tub of bubbles in a fancy hotel far away from Dublin.

Nora saw her parents' reflection in the window over the sink. Agnes touched Gordon's arm, as if to say *"enough for one night."* Did they truly think that obliterating her dreams would make it easier to live with them? Was this their way of letting her down, lowering her expectations, berating her into submission?

Her father sat down. "I deserve some respect, Nora. I never get drunk because I promised me wife that. A couple of spots now and then, but that's all. . . ." He spoke in a softer tone.

He was fishing for a compliment, and Nora knew he spoke the truth. She had never seen him drunk. "So?"

"Some men spend a pretty penny on drink and it loosens their lips. They should learn to keep their traps shut."

She turned, suds dripping from her hands, and stared at her father. She hated the glint in his eye. Was he talking about Pearse and her dream of leaving Ballybough?

The following Monday, the telephone rang. Her mother had gone off to the Moore Street markets to buy fruit and vegetables. Her father was at work.

Nora dropped her dust rag and answered quickly. Her heart

pounded as she listened for the voice she wanted to hear. Finally, Pearse responded sheepishly.

"Where are you?" Nora said. "You could have called or come by. I've been waiting more than a week. It's been hell here."

Nora fidgeted with the cord, pacing as far as the line would let her go. "Well? What's wrong? I thought several times of coming to your flat."

"Is your ma home?" he asked.

"No. She's shopping." Nora looked at the small clock on the end table. It was after 2 p.m. "She always catches the three-thirty bus."

"I'll be over in a few minutes." The phone clicked.

She didn't even get a chance to ask him why he wanted to come over. Should she start packing for Cork, or was his call a sign of bad news to come? She sat on the couch and looked at the dingy walls that felt like a prison. They never seemed to come clean, no matter how much she scrubbed. Her mood had already been darkened by a leaden sky and a steady rain that splashed against the windows. She picked up a magazine and tried to leaf through it, but couldn't concentrate. She got up, walked to her room, and looked in the mirror. Her hair needed a good brushing, her face a touch of makeup. She fussed for a few minutes with lipstick and powder and then returned to the living room, where she peered through the window.

She spotted him a few houses away, sprinting through the rain. He looked sad. Not a good sign. He knocked on the door. Politely, she thought. She pulled him into the living room and, like a wounded child, threw her arms around him.

"Me jacket's a mess," he said and broke away from her grip. He brushed the damp from his hair and then stood stiffly against the door.

"I don't care if you're wet. I won't melt." Nora pointed to the couch.

Pearse shuffled to it and positioned himself as close to one arm as he could get. She snuggled next to him.

"Thank God you're here," she said. "I've been burning up inside."

He looked at his hands and sighed. "I should be out with it—I've got some bad news. Me brother in Cork won't have us." He looked at the floor. "I tried, Nora, I really did, but nothing seems to work out for me. His wife's expecting, and he doesn't have room for us for even a day. There're no jobs at the brewery."

She felt as if she had run into a stone wall, but decided to downplay her feelings for his sake. She straightened and said, "We can go later, or find someone else to stay with. It doesn't have to be today. After all, we're in love and we've got each other. Just as long as we make it work. We'll get out of here someday . . . soon."

Pearse stared at her, his eyes as dull as the day. "That's what I want to talk about. I've been thinking about us the past week. Are you sure you're in love with me? It's only been six months."

She crashed into another wall and her heart crumbled. She took a deep breath and shivered against him. "What're you saying? Of course I love you. Don't you love me?"

Pearse took too long to think of an answer. He turned away, unable to look her in the eyes. "Yeah, I love you, but I'm a man and I need to find me own way. You're young and you've got your whole life ahead of you."

Nora could barely move. After a few moments, she crept away and found herself halfway down the couch. The last thing she wanted to be was scared and bitter, but how could she be any other way? "That sounds like something a boy would say, not a man." Her hands trembled, and her eyes grew hot with tears.

"For God's sake, I'm only eighteen, and you're *sixteen*," Pearse said. "What would you have us do, Nora? Run away to nothing? Your parents wouldn't buy it and neither would mine." He turned and faced her straight-on. "Look, the truth is, I met another girl and I want to see her, too. She's older."

She swung her hand toward him, but he caught her wrist before she struck his face. Tears rolled down her cheeks. "Too? There's no room for two. When did you meet this girl?" She lowered her hand in resignation.

"At the pub. It doesn't matter when."

"The pub?" She dug her fingers into the couch, ready to pounce. "I've been waiting here all week, and you spend your nights boozing with some tramp? Was that all it took to dump me?"

"She's not a tramp." His jaw stiffened. "I don't like how you're talking. It's not fair. I better go." He started toward the door, blurting out, "And you've got some nerve, the way you threw yourself at me. Look in the mirror!"

Nora caught him by the arm and pulled him back. She grabbed his belt buckle and he struggled against her in surprise. "Is this what you want? Is this what she gives you?"

He shoved her away. "Keep your hands off me. You make me crazy for sex, but so do other women. You scare men. Did you ever think of that?"

"I'll show you crazy." She grabbed his shoulders and pulled him toward her. She tightened her grip as he fought to wrench free. Nora positioned her right leg under his left and pulled with all her might. They tumbled over the tea table onto the couch. Her hands clawed at his back, as he landed on top of her. There was more than one way to get a man to change his mind, she thought. Sex was as good as any.

Nora didn't hear the door open.

An umbrella popped inside and shook. "It was raining too hard, most of the vendors . . ." Agnes gasped at the sight before her. "Oh me, Christ!"

Nora kicked Pearse off and he tumbled to the floor.

"Get out of here, yeh pervert!" Agnes brought her umbrella down on his shoulders with a few whacks.

Pearse wrenched it out of her hands and tossed it across the room. "You better look to your daughter before you go thumpin' me." He got up and faced Agnes. "I'm too much of a gentleman to say what happened. Let's just say it's over. I hope you're happy, Nora." He brushed past Agnes and out the door without looking back.

Agnes threw her wet things on a chair and sneered at her daughter. "What the hell have yeh done, you little bitch? I'd believe that boy before I'd believe yeh. Yer father warned you about throwing yerself on men. Now see what yeh did? When yer father finds out—oh, I don't want to see it with me eyes. Get out of me sight!"

She wanted to run out the door after Pearse, but she knew it was useless to pursue him. Instead she howled in pain, ran to her room, and slammed the door.

Nora cried on her bed for hours, until she could cry no more, her stomach knotted in anger. She'd heard the apartment door open with a rough call from her father about an hour before, but the house had been mostly silent since then. Her room, at the back of the flat, was as dark as a moonless night because it had no windows. A sliver of light from the living room glowed under her door. She smelled her mother's cooking, a slab of meat being fried. The odor made her realize how hungry she was.

Something scraped against the knob, like metal jangling. Her father called out, "Yer not going anywhere. What a disgrace. Tumbling in our house with a man! If you have to go to the toilet say so, but yer mother will take you. I don't want to look at yer divil face."

Nora ran to the door, fear strafing her chest. The door gave a little and she saw the glint of a chain and lock connected to a small linen closet nearby. She shook the door but it wouldn't budge. "You can't do this," she yelled. "I'm not evil. You can't cage me like an animal!" She pounded against the wood, but no one seemed to hear. Sobbing, she collapsed to the floor.

Her father's shadow shifted in the hall. "Yer going away, where they'll teach yeh right from wrong. It won't be long 'til we're rid of yeh. No more of yer laziness, yer tricks, and draining our money."

The shadow evaporated. When she stopped crying, the house was quiet. She wanted to die—if only she could kill herself. That would teach her parents; she hated them so much. But were they really sending her away? Perhaps a new home would be better. What could be worse than living with them?

CHAPTER 3

Teagan called the parish house and Father Matthew answered. He hesitated when she asked to speak to Father Mark.

"He's not here at the moment," Father Matthew said. He volunteered to find the new priest and have him call her back.

"Please don't bother," Teagan answered. "It's a private matter."

Father Matthew responded with a tepid, "Oh, I see."

"If you can you get him to the phone, I'll call back in a half hour," Teagan said. Her father was at work and her mother was playing bridge with friends a few blocks away.

"I'll see what I can do," the priest said.

Father Matthew sounded suspicious and his tone concerned her.

She walked to the living room and looked at the objects that had been part of her life for so many years. The firescreen was set in place for July. Her grandmother's antique clock ticked on the mantle. Books were shelved in alphabetical order by author. The Chinese lacquered cups, the export porcelain her mother collected, were artfully arranged around the room. Red and blue dragons and yellow chrysanthemums burst forth from the white plates—animals and flowers that had captivated her as a child.

But she wasn't a child anymore and life was changing, often too quickly for her sensibilities. She was growing up and emotions didn't always make sense. Cullen was always around if she needed him, but the experience of having a "crush" on a boyfriend was new to her. He seemed more infatuated with her than she did with him. She didn't want to say they were in love, because she wasn't sure what that meant. In fact, she wasn't sure what love was supposed to feel like. Maybe it was like loving your home and the things that made you happy. She remembered a time once when she was happy. For a few years, when she was about ten years old, her father had stopped drinking. Those were the best days. The world seemed bright and full of life.

She looked at the mantle clock and then made her call. A half hour had passed. The new priest answered.

"I'm sorry to bother you, Father," Teagan said, "but I need to ask a favor."

"No trouble." He sounded in good spirits, happy to hear from her, a pleasant change from the older priest.

"I left my jumper in Father's cellar. I was wondering if I could get it back."

"Oh, I haven't been down there since the party." His voice was relaxed and smooth. "It's only a few days until Sunday. Do you want to pick it up then?"

She had already considered how to respond to that suggestion. "I'd rather not. It's an expensive jumper and my parents don't know I left it at the parish house. My mother will be upset if she finds out I don't have it. Maybe I could come by and pick it up?" She was prepared to walk to St. Eusebius to get it.

"Nonsense," the priest said. "I'll drop it by. How about tomorrow morning?"

Her father would be at work again, her mother might be shopping. She absolutely didn't want her da around if Father Mark was here, but her mother might welcome a visit from the new priest. At least she would be civil to him.

"All right."

At ten the next morning, Father Matthew's well-worn black sedan pulled into the drive. She panicked for a moment thinking it might be the older priest, but Father Mark opened the door.

Teagan saw him through the living room window and was again taken by his athletic form and handsome features. Though he wore black-rimmed glasses, he looked like a movie star from *Photoplay*, only dressed in a priest's clothing. He emerged with her sweater hanging over his arm.

She primped in the living room mirror and smoothed her dress. Her mother and father were both gone, as she hoped they would be.

She met the priest at the door. He greeted her warmly, extending his hand. He smelled faintly of citrus, perhaps an aftershave. Teagan led the priest to the living room and invited him to have a seat. Before he did, he removed his glasses and handed her the sweater.

"Thank you for bringing it," she said. "My mother is quite crazy about this jumper."

"Mothers can fixate on the strangest things. It was lying on the books where you left it."

She winced, remembering the lie he had told. "Whenever we go out—which isn't that often—she makes me carry it."

He smiled, showing perfect white teeth. He folded his hands and leaned back in the chair, as respectable as a priest could be. "I'm glad to know there are mothers who still value good breeding."

She nodded. *Out with it. It won't get any easier.* Her stomach fluttered as she contemplated the question she'd wanted to ask. It took a few moments for her to gather her courage. "Why did you lie to my father?" She looked at him with an uneasy glance.

Father Mark leaned back in his chair, the warmth disappearing from his face.

"You told my father you wanted me to read book titles because you didn't have your glasses," she continued. "That was a lie. We went down for wine."

He rested his elbows on the chair, and raised his fingertips to the bottom of his chin. "Sometimes it's better to lie than to tell the truth. Haven't you ever lied because you didn't want to hurt someone you loved? The truth isn't always clean."

"But you're a priest. You're not supposed to lie."

He looked down for a moment and when his eyes met hers again, they displayed an intensity that chilled her. "If only the world were that simple. Think of the things I know—the confessions, the crimes, the horrors that men and women perpetrate, the lies that protect us. I think God knows that lies are often needed, despite what He might think of them. I wouldn't be a good priest if I had to tell the truth every time a situation arose."

"But the Bible says God hates liars."

"Certainly in terms of bearing false witness, as written in the Commandments."

For a Catholic school project, Teagan had completed a study of Proverbs. She remembered one in particular. "I was thinking of Proverbs six. The things the Lord considers an abomination—one is a 'lying tongue.'"

"I can't dispute that." He lifted his hands in capitulation. "Perhaps I won't end up in heaven. You've obviously studied the Bible. You must excel at winning arguments."

She shook her head. "I don't win many around here. My father never lets my mother or me win."

"I've noticed that about Irish fathers. Quite a few seem to have a chip on their shoulders, as if it's been passed down from generation to generation. Of course, I'm not a father, so I don't suffer from that curse."

"We women are supposed to bear children and cook. I guess that's it, but I have bigger plans."

"Really, what?"

Considering how to answer, she looked out the window for a moment and then back to Father Mark. "I think women should do more than just cook, clean, and have babies. I want to continue my education, so I can contribute to the world. That's what living is about, isn't it? Getting better? I don't want to be like . . ."

Father Mark's eyes sparkled. "You don't have to finish your thought. I understand and admire your thinking. You're quite progressive for an Irish girl, in the vanguard, so to speak. How old are you?"

"Sixteen. I'll be seventeen next March."

He pulled back his sleeve and looked at his watch. "I must get back to church. We have a pastoral meeting in twenty minutes." He stood and offered his hand to Teagan.

His fingers lingered on hers longer than they should have for a good-bye. Father Mark's touch sent a shock through her body. She loved the mature, masculine look of his hands. For an instant, she wondered what he looked like out of his dull priest's clothes. She fought back a blush.

"I hope to see you again—in church," he said. He started toward the door and then turned. "By the way, don't worry too much about lies, at least the ones that don't hurt anyone. The truth can be deadly. That's why I said what I did—so you, or your parents, wouldn't be hurt."

Teagan watched as Father Mark put on his glasses, got in the car, and pulled away from the house. Lonely and out of sorts, she wandered back to the living room. Something about him bothered her, but she couldn't put her finger on it. He was so unlike a priest. Maybe that was it. He was more like a man than a man of God, and in her years of attending parochial school and church she had never met anyone like him. His statement that he might not get into heaven struck her as a novel idea. Why would a priest say such a thing? Father Mark was so different from Cullen. Her boyfriend seemed immature compared with a man who held complicated thoughts and emotions. She found it hard not to think about the priest until her mother returned home and needed help with cooking.

Father Mark lay awake in his small bedroom at the back of the parish house. Father Matthew snored in great rumbles in his room across the hall. The younger priest wrenched himself over on his stomach and pulled a pillow over his head. Each time he was about to fall asleep, another snort in Father Matthew's breathing shook him awake.

But there was something else that disturbed his sleep. Teagan Tiernan floated through his mind in a manner not befitting a member of the clergy. Father Mark had no reservations about being a man; in fact, he was proud of his body and the way women were attracted to him—he could say truthfully they fawned over him. He enjoyed it, and always had, since he'd been a youth.

If it hadn't been for his parents' prodding, he wouldn't have become a priest. They were proud of his older brother, who had led the way to the priesthood, and his sister, who had decided to become a nun and entered a convent as a postulant. He couldn't escape the Church, and had given in, mostly against his better judgment. He chalked it up to youth, inexperience, and a limited worldview. Now there was no way to escape it. The priesthood was part of him.

Any man might have similar thoughts after meeting an attractive young woman. But to Father Mark they were damning. Teagan was bright and beautiful. He saw her in daydreams, but also in the dark when flashing points of light and angels' wings fluttered in the blackness behind his eyelids. His world had been turned upside down by Teagan in less than a week. God was not fair. He played games. Teagan came to him in a blue crushed-velvet dress, which she delicately stepped out of, revealing her naked figure. She called to him like a siren, ready to drown him under waves of passion. She was as voluptuous and fatal as the female vampires in *Dracula*. His body ached with a passion he wanted to be rid of.

It was not the first time he had fantasized about sex with a woman, let alone acted on those fantasies. He had fought the "devil's passion" for years until it had overcome him. In London, he had slipped out of the seminary, his coat wrapped tightly over street clothes, and roamed seedy byways looking for prostitutes. With his good looks and breezy demeanor, he was an easy mark. One in particular found him a refreshing change. He enjoyed her weekly until his conscience got the better of him.

She carried his child. At least that's what she announced the last night he saw her, for he never returned to see her again. He thought it a ploy to keep him coming back—a tactic for more money. How could she know it was his child when she entertained men night and day? Yet he worried she might be right, for several times she asked him not to use protection.

"You're the first woman I've had sex with," he told her when they met.

"You're daft," she said. "A looker like you? A virgin? You're not one of those ginger boys, are you?"

He laughed, embarrassed at his confession. He sat on the bed and stroked her long hair, which fell in brown swirls down her back. A cheap dresser with a mirror sat across from them. Father Mark thought their reflection looked like something from the dirty postcards a school chum had shown him when he was a youth—forbidden, but at the same time intensely erotic. He marveled that she was a whore by societal standards. However, she was also a woman to him—attractive, bright, and full of life. When they fell to making love, she stripped off the condom he had brought along.

"What about . . ." He didn't have the nerve to complete his question.

She understood his objection. "Syphilis? I get myself checked regularly. I'm no fool." She convinced him through her touch how much better sex would feel without it. After she fortified him with a few shots of whiskey, he took the risk. He constantly checked himself for a sexual disease after his time with her, but he never contracted one. However, his anxiety about venereal matters, the lies he told about his whereabouts, and the possibility of fathering a child kept him away. As much as he wanted to see his paid lover, he couldn't.

He hated his two sides: the one, carnal, fueled by erotic pleasure; the other, pious and reverential. After his experiences in London, he vowed he would serve only God and hoped that the Creator, in His wisdom, would deliver him where his contact with temptation would be limited. But God had tested him, sending him to Dublin, a city bustling with wanton women. He hated suppressing desire. There had only been casual glances until he had been introduced to Teagan. Satan cursed him with infatuation.

Could he resist temptation? He was ashamed he couldn't control his sexual fantasies. Why had God placed this girl before him? For heaven's sake, she was only sixteen, not even of legal age. Why was he being tortured with these thoughts?

His hips ground against the mattress. He wished that she were with him right now, so he could run his hands over her smooth body . . . No! He despised himself for having such unclean thoughts about the girl. How could he admit this secret to anyone, even to someone he trusted, like Father Matthew? A confession would be too risky. What if the Church delved into his past? What if his unholy life in London was revealed during an investigation? He would be ruined and his family shamed.

He turned over and stared at the ceiling, aware of the aching arousal in his groin. He grabbed the sheet covering him and balled it up in his fists. There was only one solution.

Despite the risk, he must get over his paranoid thinking, talk to Father Matthew, and get these fantasies off his chest before they turned into an obsession. It was the only way he could end the sin. And he would shun Teagan Tiernan.

Father Mark spotted the older priest the next day in the parish house. Father Matthew sat in his worn recliner, smoking a pipe and sipping a glass of wine. He looked as if he was about to fall asleep. The heat had broken. A cool evening breeze stirred through the room. Father Mark sat across from him on the couch.

Father Matthew's eyelids fluttered. "Are you prepared for Sunday?" He positioned his pipe in the ashtray. The smoke drifted toward Father Mark. It had a somewhat pleasant cherry smell.

"Yes," Father Mark said. "As prepared as I'm ever going to be."

"I'll take it easy on you—at least in the beginning. Just follow my lead." The older priest smiled and lifted his glass.

Father Mark sighed.

"Is something wrong?"

"Yes . . ." He couldn't figure out how to say it, but he had to get it off his chest. "It's a bit of a delicate matter. I don't want you to think it's a confession of any sort, but I need to talk about it."

Father Matthew, looking concerned, put down his glass.

"I've been having thoughts," Father Mark said.

"Thoughts? What kind?"

"Sexual." He looked down at the floor.

Father Matthew lowered the recliner. "Go on. You can tell me. And I won't consider this to be a sacred confession between two priests—just a friendly talk between two men."

Father Mark leaned back. "Thank you. That makes me feel better. You don't know how I've been agonizing over this the past couple of days."

"Just a couple of days?" The older priest tilted his head. "Does this have something to do with a girl in our parish?"

He knows. How the hell did he figure it out already? Father Mark didn't say anything, wondering how much he should reveal. "I'd rather not say. My thoughts have been tormenting me and I feel like a foolish sinner for having them."

Father Matthew turned over his pipe and knocked the burned tobacco into the ashtray. "All men have thoughts. It's natural. It's only if we act on them that the devil enters our spirit."

He wanted to stop, to go no further. He clenched his hands. It was a mistake to bring the whole matter up, but the torment was too much. He needed to talk. Perhaps God was punishing him for his sins with the London prostitute, or for leaving an unwed mother with a bastard child.

"You don't have to tell me. I can put two and two together." Father Matthew stuffed fresh tobacco into the pipe and lit it. The smoke blew through the room in large puffs. "What were you doing in the cellar with Teagan Tiernan, and more importantly, why did she want to talk to you?"

Heat rose in his cheeks. The old man did know! He took a deep breath. "Nothing of importance happened. She's a very sweet girl. She was goaded by a friend into coming downstairs with me—to help pick out a bottle of wine. She left her jumper in the cellar. I returned it to her the other day. That's where I went with the car."

"Her da was furious with her." Father Matthew removed the pipe from his mouth and thrust it toward him. "Cormac's a loose cannon. Drinks too much, but the family has been part of this parish for generations. We wouldn't want to cross him. He works for the government."

"I didn't say this was about Teagan." He wanted to crawl away. "There are lots of beautiful women in Dublin—many of them came to our party."

Father Matthew guffawed. "Not one that I saw! But there are some young women who could tempt a priest."

Father Mark stood up. "I wanted to acknowledge that I'm a sinner and that some of my thoughts have been unclean—as one friend to another. That's all."

The older priest leaned back in his recliner. "And you've done that. There's nothing to worry about. I'm sure this will blow over."

Father Mark nodded. "Thank you for listening. I'm going to turn in now."

"Good night." Father Matthew puffed on his pipe.

He felt the older priest watching him as he walked to the hall. He turned. Father Matthew was looking at him and smiling like a man who had more on his mind than smoking. The priest waved to him. Father Mark walked down the hall and stopped at his door. He opened it, wondering again why he had ever become a priest, and wishing he'd never met Teagan Tiernan.

She arrived at Mass on Sunday with her mother and father. They always sat in the third pew; her mother liked to be among the first for communion. Teagan nestled between her parents, making a point to carry the sweater Father Mark had returned to her. She was happy to have it spread across her shoulders. The heat had disappeared. The granite stones picked up the chill from the foggy day.

Looking solemn in their vestments, the two priests entered

the chancel. Father Mark took a seat near the lectern parallel to the pulpit. She had a childish impulse to wave, if only wiggle her fingers, but thought better of it. The younger priest kept his eyes focused on Father Matthew as the service began and rarely looked out on the parishioners. Even the older priest, who usually had a benevolent smile for everyone, avoided eye contact with her. Only for an instant did Father Mark, with a deep sadness in his eyes, look at her. He turned his head quickly away.

Later, Father Mark assisted with communion. When her turn came to take the sacrament, he ignored her.

The older priest whispered in her father's ear as he presented the wafer. Teagan thought it odd because Father Matthew never leaned in to talk with anyone during communion.

When the Mass ended, her father stood at the end of the pew and said, "Wait for me here." Father Mark walked past them to stand at the church entrance. Her father and the older priest went through a side door leading to the parish house.

Teagan wondered what Father Matthew was up to. She thought of her secret meeting with Father Mark and her heart raced.

Her mother shook her head and tugged at the pearl buttons on her gloves. "I don't know. Perhaps Father Matthew is getting on your father about his drinking last week."

The laughter and talking at the back of the church faded. The doors closed behind them. Still in the pew, Teagan looked back. Everyone, including Father Mark, was gone. The doors opened again. A caretaker stepped inside with his broom and, humming a folk tune, began sweeping the floors. He swept each aisle until he finally came to them.

"Stay put," the caretaker said, urging them not to get up. "It's no bother." He went on about his business.

A few minutes later, her father opened the parish house door. The color had drained from his face. He looked like a man attending a wake as he walked toward the pew. Teagan couldn't tell if he was angry or sad. She saw the red rims of his eyes when he stopped, as if he had been crying.

"Let's go," he whispered in a husky voice.

"Da, what's wrong?" Teagan asked. Her mother echoed Teagan's question, but her father gave no answer. He walked slowly to the back of the church and crossed himself as he passed out the doors.

When they arrived home, her father took off his suit jacket and hung it on the hall tree. "I'm going out. You should both be in bed by the time I get home."

"Cormac? Please tell me what's wrong." Her mother took his hands and pleaded for an answer.

He kissed her on the cheek and said, "It's nothing. We'll get by. You'll see." He shook his head, as he walked past Teagan.

Her mother collapsed on the couch, tears coming quickly to her eyes. "I don't know what I've done to displease your father. What could it be?"

Teagan settled next to her, the lovely atmosphere of the room transformed into anxiety. The objects that she had looked upon so fondly before Father Mark's visit—the sentimental reminders of her childhood—seemed useless and insignificant now. Dread filled her as she thought about her father's strange behavior. She wasn't sure how, but she knew her life was about to change. Her nerves had tightened as they sat in church waiting for her father. Now they threatened to overpower her, to bring her to her knees in distress.

"I don't think it's you," Teagan said. "It must be me."

Her mother, shocked, stared at her. "How could it be you? You've done nothing wrong."

"No . . . unless thoughts are impure."

Her mother took off her gloves and threw them on the couch beside her. "We all have thoughts, but . . ." She squeezed Teagan's hands. "What happened last week in Father Matthew's cellar? Tell me the truth."

"You know the truth—"

"—What? Tell me!" Her mother gave her a pained look.

Teagan took a breath. "Father Mark lied. He didn't ask me to read the titles of holy books. We went to the cellar to fetch a bottle of wine. My friend Cathy was standing at the top of the stairs and she shoved me after him. We were only gone for a few minutes." Father Mark had been right about the truth hurting people. She could tell from the sadness on her mother's face. She wouldn't say any more about what happened. "You know Da, and his moods. I didn't want to cause trouble."

Her mother rose from the couch. "I've got to keep busy. I'll make tea for us. Who knows when your father will be back?" She struggled to get the words out.

The afternoon and evening hours seemed like days as they waited for Cormac, who didn't come home for tea. They ate mostly in silence. Her mother picked at her food. Teagan knew something terrible was happening. Her father never missed a meal unless he was called away by business.

They watched a couple of hours of television and then went to bed.

She was drifting off, when she heard her mother's muffled sobs from across the hall. She wanted to comfort her, but the door the bedroom door was closed. To drown out the painful sound, she turned on the transistor radio her father had given her as a birthday gift and listened to a Dublin station. She heard records by Cliff Richard, Elvis, and a melancholy new song by Ray Charles, "I Can't Stop Loving You." As she shifted in bed, she felt as if she were living on another planet. Her brain commanded her limbs to move and they did—in slow motion. Sadness weighed her down. The Ray Charles hit ran through her head as she tried to fall asleep. She thought of Father Mark, and then Cullen, and wondered if love always had to be painful. The tune seemed appropriate for the night.

Teagan's door burst open at 4 a.m. She sprang upright in bed, staring at the shadowy figures in the hall.

The blurred picture transformed into her father, steadying himself against the wall. Her mother stood behind him. The light cast stark shadows across their bodies.

"Get dressed," her father ordered.

Teagan stared in disbelief. Were her ears playing tricks on her? She rubbed her eyes and then pulled the sheet down. "What?" she asked meekly.

"You heard me. Get dressed! And be quick about it." Her father's voice rose angrily with each word. She smelled whiskey on his breath. "Your mother will be waiting for you." He slammed the door, leaving her in darkness.

She wanted to shout at her father, but she knew that tactic would backfire. The only way to get through to her father was to be kind. *Obsequious.* She had learned the word in school. When Sister had written its definition on the blackboard— *fawning, subservient, obedient*—her father came to mind.

Why was he so angry? Father Matthew must have had something to do with it. She pulled on a white blouse, jeans, and a pair of tennis shoes. She trembled as she opened the door, her stomach churning.

Her mother, attired in a nightgown, stumbled toward her. Teagan gasped. Her mother's eyes were puffy, her face pallid, drained of life.

"Why didn't you tell us?" Her mother struggled to get the question out. She clutched at the door to keep from falling.

Teagan rushed to her, but her mother turned away. "Tell you what? Ma, please tell me what's wrong!"

"Why did you lie? Why didn't you tell us that Father Mark was here, that . . ." Her mother, shaking uncontrollably, burst into sobs.

"I was afraid you'd be mad at me. I left my jumper in the cellar at the parish house. Father Mark returned it."

"Oh God," her mother said and wrung her hands.

Teagan's admission made her mother's sobbing worse.

Her father appeared from the shadows and pushed his wife out of the way. He held the car keys in his hand. "We're going for a ride."

Panic consumed her. Was she dreaming? She expected to wake up at any minute and find herself snug in bed. How could seeing a priest be so egregious a "sin?" Her survival instinct kicked in. She slammed the door and locked it, barely missing her father's fingers. She shook from the adrenaline coursing through her body.

He pounded the door and screamed at Teagan. Her mother

wailed in the hall. Then, the screaming stopped and the sobs faded. The house was quiet for a moment. Teagan cowered on her bed as the clock on her nightstand ticked off the seconds.

The door shook in its frame several times before it shattered, sending splinters of wood flying into the room. Cursing, her father fell to the floor from the force of his momentum. He grabbed Teagan by her legs and pulled her off the bed.

"Listen to me!" His voice cracked with rage, and the veins on his temples swelled as if they were about to burst. "I don't want to make this any harder on your mother than it is. You can either come quietly, or I'll pick you up and haul you out of this house."

She pushed back sobs and managed to say, "Yes, Da."

"Don't call me 'Da.' I don't have a daughter anymore."

Her mind reeled. Her father's words and actions were incomprehensible. What had happened to her father to cause this horror?

He pulled her up from the floor and led her into the upstairs hall. As she passed her parents' room, Teagan spotted her mother on the bed, her head buried in her hands. Her moans filled the room. Her father choked back tears as he guided Teagan down the stairs. He grabbed his suit jacket from the hall tree and put it around her shoulders.

"Whatever you've been told, it's a lie," she said. "Nothing happened with Father Mark."

"Priests don't lie," her father said, and then swore at the ceiling. The sour smell of whiskey filled the air.

"He does!" She pulled up short. "Where are you taking me? I've always done everything you wanted."

Her father stopped and grabbed her roughly by the shoulders. "You're the biggest disappointment of my life."

Stunned, she could think of nothing to say.

He pushed her to the car, and before she knew it she was headed to an unknown destination.

Her father, who seemed to know where he was going, didn't speak.

Teagan looked out the window in silence because she was

afraid to ask him anything. She had heard about kidnappings and abductions from news reports, but they were always perpetrated by a criminal who wanted money, never by a parent. The roads they traveled were mostly unknown to her, although she recognized St Stephen's Green when they passed by. Rows of houses came into view, some with lights on in the early morning.

The sun's pink rays had begun to streak the clouds when their car pulled up to a large gate. The sign on it read THE SISTERS OF THE HOLY REDEMPTION. Down the lane, the granite walls of the convent towered out of the half-darkness. The black roof careened at odd angles over what hinted at a larger complex of buildings. A sudden chill enveloped her as she viewed the somber sight.

Her father rang a buzzer and an elderly man came to the gate and opened it. "Right on time, five in the morning." the man said as he leaned toward the window. "The Mother Superior is expecting you. The Sisters don't let any grass grow under their feet."

"Thank you," her father replied.

The man motioned the car forward. "Pull in, straight ahead. Follow the curve."

The low branches of a line of oaks passed over the car as they drove down the lane. The trees looked like gigantic sentinels shielding the deserted grounds. The car's lights cut through the dawn as it climbed a small hill. A bank of terraced steps, leading to the heavy doorway, came into view. A nun, clothed entirely in black, stood like a statue at the top of the steps. She had no visible arms or legs, only a round face protruding from the habit; she was like a dark monolith in the lingering darkness.

Her father parked the car at the bottom of the steps, but left it running. "I'm not coming inside." He got out and opened the passenger door for his daughter. He led her around the car and up the steps to the waiting figure. "Sister Anne?" her father asked. "Mother Superior?"

The nun nodded, but didn't speak. Teagan studied the imposing figure, still uncertain why she had been taken to The Sisters of the Holy Redemption.

"This is my daughter, Teagan," her father continued. "I believe Father Matthew has told you about our situation?"

Sister Anne's eyebrows lifted, as if agreeing with his question.

"The papers are in the car. My wife and I signed them." He left for a brief moment to gather an envelope.

The nun withdrew her hands from her habit and motioned for Teagan to follow her to the door. The last thing she wanted to do was go inside this dark building with a nun she had never met. Her father handed the papers to Sister Anne, who pressed them against her chest.

"Da!" Teagan cried out.

"I'll be off now," he said, as his daughter clung to him.

The nun reached for her arm, but she shook her off. "Don't do this to me, Da!"

"Good-bye." He wrenched Teagan from his body and ran to the car. Sister Anne grabbed her and the envelope fell to the ground. The nun forced her toward the door as her father raced away.

Teagan collapsed in tears on the stone terrace.

Sister Anne picked up the envelope and bent over her like a dark angel. "You'd best come inside, unless you'd like to spend the rest of your life on the grounds. I wouldn't suggest it."

Teagan knew she had no choice as she watched the nun climb the steps to the door.

It creaked as Sister Anne pulled it open. "Welcome to your new home—for as long as is necessary to expiate your sins." Teagan crawled to her feet, studying the woman who now lorded over her. A long corridor lay in a dark, endless stretch before her.

CHAPTER 4

For a split second, Teagan considered running away. She followed the nun, but then froze at the door in utter desperation. What good would it do? St Stephen's Green was the only landmark she recognized, and it was a good distance from the convent. And what of the nearby houses? Who would answer at this hour? What would they think of a disheveled girl clad in jeans and a white blouse? They would turn her over to the Guards, who would haul her back to the convent. Her parents had committed an unthinkable act, signing papers committing her to The Sisters of the Holy Redemption. One thought, a million thoughts, raced through her head in a dizzying buzz. Her legs wouldn't budge.

Sister Anne's eyebrows raised—a questioning look, but also one of haughty disdain—as if this same scene had played out many times. The Mother Superior seemed the type who would be the eventual winner, Teagan thought, no matter how long it took.

There was nowhere to go, no place to run. The truth crashed down as solidly as the granite walls that made up the convent. As she stared down the hall, a memory popped into her head. It was about an Irish war hero who had died in gaol. She'd read about him in a history book. The dark walk in front of her reminded her of his prison.

"Come along now." Sister Anne coaxed her forward. "I have more important tasks to attend to than listening to the morning birds with a sinner."

Sinner! The word shocked her, like a splash of cold water.

Perhaps that was the way back to her family. A *misunderstanding* had gotten her to this place, not a sin. She could clear up this mistake if the Mother Superior would listen. She'd done nothing wrong and proving it would be easy. She would only have to tell Sister Anne the truth.

The nun held the door open as Teagan trudged past it into the shadowy hall. A square panel of light fell upon the stone tiles from a room midway down. The door closed with a *thud,* and the corridor darkened to a thick twilight.

The dense air was filled with odors: the rocky smell of granite, the smoky scent of burning candles, and the must of ancient wood. They wrapped around her throat like strangling hands. But other faint smells drifted through the hall. Teagan recognized the stinging bite of bleach, the clean scent of detergent. Above her, she heard stirrings—steps echoing across the floors, the rush of water through pipes.

Sister Anne led the way in a determined march of flowing black. The nun turned left into the lit room. Teagan followed and found herself in a sparsely decorated office. The Mother Superior sat behind her large wooden desk. She motioned for Teagan to sit in one of the wing chairs placed in front of it.

She sat and studied the nun's face. It was unlike any she had ever met. The Mother Superior's fine, thin nose and high cheekbones, reminded her of a Renaissance sculpture. However, the narrow band of her mouth seemed menacing, the eyes calculating, unyielding in their dominance.

"This is all a—"

Sister Anne cut her off with a wave of her hand. "Do not speak unless spoken to."

"But I can explain."

The nun rose like an intimidator from her chair. "Apparently, you don't understand instructions. What did they teach you in school? Have you no shame, no respect for your parents or your superiors?"

It was no use talking to this woman. Teagan sighed. If that was the way the Sister Anne wanted to play it, she would go along with it for a little while.

"I'll give you time to ponder those questions as I review your paperwork." The nun resumed her position behind the desk and opened the envelope Teagan's father had given her.

Teagan looked around the office. Aside from the brown desk and the two chairs in front of it there was little furniture. A small bookcase sat near the door. On her right, a gold-framed painting of a prostrate woman washing the feet of Jesus hung on the wall. Three windows were cut into the same granite, but no natural light came in. The shades were pulled down behind parted blue curtains. She wondered what was beyond those windows. Perhaps a way out?

Four wooden children's blocks sat on Sister Anne's desk. They spelled out *LOVE* in carved letters of yellow, blue, red, and green. How odd! She doubted the nun had ever loved anyone a day in her life—at least it seemed that way from her strict demeanor.

Sister Anne took her time reading the papers, turning each page with measured precision. Finally, she finished them and gazed at Teagan. "Do you know why you're here?"

She knew the nun was delivering an accusation, not a question to be answered. She shook her head and wondered if it would be better not to talk at all.

The Mother Superior placed her elbows on the desk and folded her hands like a steeple. "Let me explain. You are a Magdalen, along with the others who will live beside you."

The nun knew she had no idea how the name applied. She could tell by the Mother Superior's smug look.

Sister Anne pointed at the painting of the woman washing Jesus's feet. "Are you familiar with the meaning of the picture?" The nun continued before she could answer. "The painting depicts Mary Magdalene—a fallen woman who devoted the final days of her life to our Lord. He cast out the devils from her soul. She became His follower and witnessed His Crucifixion and Resurrection. We wish the same salvation, the same path to grace for the girls and women here, who come to us as fallen."

The nun shook a finger when she started to speak. "You are here because you have sinned. Many arrive because they are about to succumb, but you have committed a mortal sin, a deliberate and deceitful act, which requires your expiation."

She heard the nun's words, but they didn't make sense. *What mortal sin have I committed? Whom have I sinned against?* She sunk in her chair, crushed by those disturbing questions.

The nun took the papers from her desk and pointed them toward her. "Not the least of your sins is the disparaging lack of honor you have displayed to your father and mother through your lies. I can tell you are headstrong and spoiled. Our way is no *Life of Riley*. I expect you will remain here for many years." Sister Anne dialed a number on a black desk phone and then spoke into it. "Tell Sister Mary-Elizabeth to come to my office immediately."

Teagan stared at the nun, who looked as if she dared her to speak. "I've done nothing wrong," she blurted out.

Sister Anne opened a desk drawer, reached inside, and pulled out a burnished metal rod with a leather handle.

"I'll warn you once more. Speak when you're spoken to." Sister Anne pointed the rod at the blocks on her desk. "I don't like to use corporal punishment, but at times, I have no other choice." Her tone softened. "We are redeemers here. We believe in love."

Teagan fought a bitter urge to laugh as she sunk further into a deepening gloom. *Oh, I see how much you love. Spare the rod, spoil the child!* How would she ever break free from this hellish place if she couldn't defend herself? She had gripped the chair so hard her arms were numb. A horrible emptiness permeated her; even tears refused to fall.

The nun turned the rod toward her and it flashed, coppery in the light. "We have no need for physical adornment here. Give me your earrings and ring."

"What?" She couldn't believe she was being stripped of her possessions. They were so much a part of her she'd forgotten she had them on.

"You are a penitent, unclean before our Savior and the Church. Your body must be naked before God. Hand them to me."

Teagan hesitated before wrenching her fists free from the chair.

Sister Anne stiffened in her chair. "Don't make a fuss. I'll have them taken off you if you don't comply."

She pulled the backs off the pearl earrings her mother had given her when she was fourteen. They had gone to a local jeweler on a blustery day. An old man had pierced her ears with an instrument that looked like a pair of pliers. After a stab of pain in both lobes the ordeal was over. Her father didn't notice the small studs at first. A few days later, he did and yelled at her mother for making a decision about *his* daughter without consulting him. Teagan was certain he would make her take them out, but her father scoffed and said, "The damage is done."

That Christmas, her father gave her a pearl ring with silver band to match the earrings. He told her the ring represented purity and he quoted Bible verses—"The kingdom of heaven is like a merchant who seeks fine pearls," and then words from the Sermon on the Mount, ". . . nor cast your pearls before swine."

She tossed the ring and earrings on Sister Anne's desk.

The nun scowled as she scrambled to retrieve them.

Teagan touched her naked earlobes and noticed the lighter skin on her finger where the ring had been.

The Mother Superior swept the jewelry off the desk into the envelope Teagan's father had given her.

A portly nun appeared in the doorway. She nodded, half-bowed, to Sister Anne and then turned to Teagan. A hint of a smile creased the nun's fleshy cheeks, and Teagan leaned forward, grateful to see a touch of humanity in the gloomy atmosphere of the office.

The nun folded her arms and stood before her. "I'm Sister Mary-Elizabeth, here to show you the 'rounds."

"Sister Mary-Elizabeth will take good care of you," the Mother Superior said. She placed the rod and envelope in the desk, withdrew keys from her habit pocket, and locked the drawer. "I'm off to morning prayers. Sister, you are excused to be with the penitent." She got up from her chair. "Be kind to our newest charge. Show her the true meaning of redemption." Sister Anne started toward the door, but turned before she reached it. "Say your name," she ordered.

"Teagan Tiernan."

Sister Anne pursed her lips and studied her from head to toe. "Now you will be called—'Teresa,' a good Christian name. I doubt you will ever emulate the saint of Avila." She stepped into the gloomy hall and disappeared.

Sister Mary-Elizabeth asked, "Are you hungry? You must be this time of the morning."

Eating was the furthest thing from her mind. She shook her head.

"I've got a mouth on me, and you don't want to see me vexed," the nun said.

Teagan was surprised. The nun sounded as if she had walked in from a working-class Dublin neighborhood. She knew what she meant: Sister Mary-Elizabeth was hungry and if she didn't eat soon she'd be cranky.

"May I speak?" Teagan asked, more at home with this nun than with Sister Anne.

"Of course, child. We're not all cut from the same mold as the Mother Superior." She chuckled and her cheeks jiggled. "But don't get your hopes up. We play by the rules. Come now, I'll show you the laundry before your breakfast, and then there's a whole list of things to do. I'll shrink to nothing if we don't get moving."

The nun took her by the arm and led her from the office. They turned right in the hall and walked to a stairwell near the convent entrance. Sister Mary-Elizabeth stopped. "Thank the Lord, I don't have to accompany a new girl every day. And you should thank your lucky stars we could take you. Sometimes we get petitions for more girls than we can handle. If that was the case today, you might be living in the park." The Sister flipped a switch and a string of bulbs illuminated the stone steps, which led down to a passageway.

Teagan stayed rooted to her spot. "Why am I here?"

The nun's face darkened. "I don't know—and that's no fib. That's between Sister Anne, whoever sent you here, and God."

"My father brought me here, and I'm sure he was talked into it by a priest." The thought made her heart ache.

"It's none of my business, but there must have been a good reason. Your parents have given you up in the name of the Lord." She snapped her fingers and started down the steps. Teagan followed.

Sister Mary-Elizabeth stopped at a metal door at the end of the passage. It contained a small rectangular window cross-hatched by chicken wire. The nun took out her keys, opened the door, and flipped on the light. "It'll soon be time for work. Here's where you'll be spending many of your days."

The smells of bleach and detergent that Teagan had detected when she arrived filled her nostrils. The long rectangular room contained sinks, washers, dryers, laundry baskets, ironing boards, and washing supplies. Rows of fluorescent lamps hung from the ceiling in their tent-like enclosures and cast their harsh light on the appliances and tile floor. A large bank of barred windows, some partially belowground and overlooking a trench, ran the length of the room. Through them, she saw the edge of a verdant lawn and the ashen trunks of old trees.

"This is where I'll be?" she asked, hardly believing her eyes. She stepped inside, taking in the rows of white industrial washing machines and dryers that stared at her with their round, solitary eyes of glass.

"Here and in the lace room," The Sister opened her arms in a grand gesture. "You're lucky—you'll have two jobs. But I admire most those who work in the laundry. There's something cathartic about sticking your fingers in hot water. Getting clean, ridding your hands—and your soul—of dirt . . ." She rubbed her palms together. "Wash away your sins in the name of the Lord. We'll put you to the sorting bins first, to break you in."

Teagan covered her mouth with her hands. The Sisters of the Holy Redemption already had plans for her. How horrific could this nightmare become? Her dreams of university, of making a life for herself, lay in tatters. She had always helped her mother with the laundry when she was a child, and had done her own now that she was older—but a lifetime of this? Had God deserted her and condemned her to unending servitude?

The nun stood behind her, putting a strong grip on Teagan's shoulders. "Believe me, there's no use pitching a fit. I know. I used to work here."

Teagan turned. "You worked in this horrid place?"

The Sister took Teagan's hands in hers. "The laundry was the best place for me. I was such a scalawag before I came here. It took me about a year to realize I wanted to be a nun." Sister Mary-Elizabeth looked around the room with reverence. "Let me give you two pieces of advice. First, don't fight it. It's best if you try to fit in. I've seen all kinds of girls here and the happiest are those who get along. Do what the Mother Superior tells you and don't get into trouble by concocting schemes or listening to others who offer bad advice. If you run away, the Guards will bring you back.

"Second, don't give up. Something good will happen if you allow it. Maybe you'll accept that this is your place in life. It may be a struggle, but it will happen. Or maybe someone will come for you when your sins have been washed clean and you'll walk out of here a good woman. In my case, it was God who saw fit to change my life. Repent and a new life is bound to happen."

Teagan's legs buckled. Convulsing, she collapsed against the nun.

Sister Mary-Elizabeth wrapped her arms around her and repeated, "Now, now," like a lullaby. The nun's unexpected compassion soothed her until she was able to pull herself together. "Let's have something to eat," the nun said. "We could both use some sustenance." Sister Mary-Elizabeth led her through the passageway and upstairs to the hall, now filled with a dull morning light from overhead windows. As she walked behind the Sister, Teagan railed against the reality of her new home—a holy prison filled with hard work and penitence. The odors of bleach and detergent lingered on her clothes. She didn't deserve to be here, but she had to get along until she could figure a way out.

At the end of the hall, Sister Mary-Elizabeth climbed the

stairs to another corridor with a number of rooms off each side. One was the breakfast room. The nun seated Teagan at an empty chair near the end of a long oak table. "Eat quietly. Don't speak. I'll be back after I'm done with breakfast."

Nearly a dozen girls and women, each attired in a gray dress and white muslin apron, sat at the table. Teagan assumed they were Magdalens—the ones Sister Anne had said would live beside her. They had a sunken, defeated look about them. Some slumped over the table, their backs bowed like the arched branches of trees; many lifted their spoons in a shaky manner as if they were old women, despite their young age. A few, whom Teagan judged to be old, might, on further speculation, be young. The deep wrinkles and dark circles under their eyes had obliterated their youth.

An elderly woman, a cook, served Teagan her breakfast: a bowl of watery oatmeal, a piece of burned toast, and weak tea. The woman acted as if the Magdalens didn't exist as she set the food on the table. None of them spoke, although a few mouthed silent prayers.

The plates, cups, and utensils were pitted and scarred from years of use. Teagan had no appetite for any of it and sat staring at the others. She counted ten; she was the eleventh, and they weren't all girls. There were women here, as well; some, Teagan estimated, in their thirties and forties, if not older. *Prisoners, we're all prisoners.* She could think of no better word to describe their condition. *Inmates, perhaps.*

For the most part, the others avoided any eye contact with her, as they did with each other. All had short, clipped hair, except for one, who had somewhat longer black tresses pulled up by bobby pins. When the girl leaned back from the table, Teagan spotted the swollen belly of her pregnancy.

The room was stripped to the minimum: straight-backed oak chairs placed around a table battered with gouges and scratches. A single crucifix affixed to a wall was the only decorative object. The room faced east. The warm July sun fell through broad windows in pleasant splashes. The shadowy waves of leaves quivered on the floor.

Breakfast plodded along for a gloomy half hour. Teagan lifted her spoon and dragged it through the oatmeal. Beige chunks of oats floated in the tepid water. She put the food in her mouth and gulped it down, likening the taste to a packing box. The toast came next. She knew her stomach would be growling if she had nothing to eat. After a few bites, she put the rest back on the plate as the blackened particles of bread stuck to her tongue and the insides of her cheeks. The tea was no better, cold and lacking in taste.

Sister Mary-Elizabeth appeared at the door a half hour later and motioned for Teagan to follow. The others remained at the table. She suspected the Magdalens would soon head to the laundry.

The nun led her up a third set of stairs to the top floor of the convent. Here, the hall narrowed to a point. There were two sets of doors at the end of the passage, a double door to the right and a smaller one to the left. The nun pushed open the larger doors and showed Teagan a large garret containing six beds against each wall. The plain wooden floors and walls had been dulled by the years. It seemed the garret was an afterthought to the stone that made up most of the convent. The ceiling vaulted above her, but any sense of open space was lost in the gloom.

"You get the bed at the end," the Sister said. She pointed to a mattress lying on top of a metal frame supported by four legs. The bed sat to the right of the doors, on the west wall, near the lone window.

"I suppose no one wants it because it's close to the window—too cold in winter, too hot in summer," the nun said. She looked around the room and patted a bed halfway down the left wall. "This is where I slept for a year. It's a middling place, but you'll get used to it. The jacks is across the hall, another reason your bed's not taken—too far to walk in the middle of the night to the toilet."

She wondered how to respond. Rather than antagonize the nun, she decided to be polite. "I prefer the window." She walked to the bed and pushed her hand into the mattress. It sunk under the pressure from her fingers. The bed was small. How silly, she thought, to worry about such a trivial matter. Her toes would hang over the edge in the winter. There were no screens around the beds, nothing to offer any privacy.

A small chest sat in front of it. She lifted its cover and looked inside.

"Your dress and apron, along with your nightgown and sheets, are already there," Sister Mary-Elizabeth said. "You can store the clothes you're wearing."

Teagan looked down woefully. Her white blouse was wrinkled; her jeans had lost their crisp feel. She reached inside the chest and pulled out a gray dress that hung like sackcloth in her hands. It had been patched in several places and obviously passed down from one girl to another. The apron had been bleached so often it felt like a stiff board.

"I'll have a sit while you get into your dress," the Sister said. "Whew. It's hardly past Lauds and I'm already knackered." The nun plopped herself down on another bed and watched as Teagan unbuttoned her blouse.

She kept her back turned to the nun as she undressed, carefully folding her blouse and jeans and placing them in the trunk. The dress slid on over her bra and panties and fell limply over her figure. Only a few days ago, she had complained about wearing her white satin dress to Father Mark's reception. It seemed a lifetime had passed since then. The apron settled upon her, as stiff and solid as a suit of armor.

Sister Mary-Elizabeth got up from the bed and stood behind her. "Let me help you. It needs to be tied at the back. You'll soon get the hang of it. . . ."

The nun deftly tied the strings into a tight bow, but her touch unnerved Teagan. Few women had put their hands on her back. Her face flushed. "Won't it be hot in the laundry? We have to wear aprons in the summer?"

Sister Mary-Elizabeth turned her around and examined her from head to toe. "Of course, you don't want to get bleach, or something worse, on you. You'll be thankful to wear it in the winter. Summer is the worst, but the body adjusts." She patted Teagan's arm. "It's good you got the window." The nun closed the trunk lid and said, "You'll find your way, especially if you're a good girl. Come on, I want to introduce you to someone before you get your hair cut."

She instinctively raised her hands to her head. She hadn't thought about losing her hair, but it made sense after seeing the Magdalens at breakfast. She stroked the blond strands, which were soon to be gone, cropped close to her head like the other girls. She was a prisoner. In history class, she had read about people who were held in World War II camps. They had been robbed of their identities and their possessions. She shivered at the thought. Much like those prisoners, she was dependent on The Sisters of the Holy Redemption, her captors, for her food, clothing and shelter—until she could escape. The notion smoldered inside her. *Escape.* But Sister Mary-Elizabeth was right about some things. It would be impossible to walk out of the convent. She would have to plan an escape, carefully and intelligently, waiting for the right time.

The nun showed her the "jacks" across the hall, a simple setup with two partitioned toilets and three showerheads protruding from a tiled wall. Teagan suddenly realized she'd had no idea how fortunate she was to have a bathroom at home she could use by herself.

"There's no talking during working hours and after going to bed," the Sister cautioned as they headed down the stairs to the second floor. "I know some of the girls whisper now and then, but you better not get caught, especially by Sister Ruth. You'll be so tired by the end of the day you won't have much time to get into trouble." They passed the breakfast room, now empty, except for a few of the kitchen staff. It was almost eight. "The Magdalens you met this morning have been working for a half hour already. The girl I'm introducing you to starts work at six, after her prayers, sometimes earlier. She won't *talk* to you, but she'll pray with you. If Sister Anne puts you on lace, you'll be next to her. Everyone knows Lea."

They entered a large room with a tiled floor and expansive windows. It was by far the most inviting space Teagan had seen at the convent, but strangely reverential in its feel. She suspected that it must have been a library at one point because of the rows of mostly empty bookcases inset into the walls. Heavy crimson curtains, tied open with braided cord, formed fabric scallops around the windows. A tall girl Teagan hadn't seen at breakfast sat in the middle of the room. She leaned over a drawing table that held piles of papers sitting to her left and right.

Sister Mary-Elizabeth approached the girl. "Lea? We have a new penitent. I'd like you to meet Teresa."

The girl barely turned, but swiveled in her chair. She delicately placed her artist's brush in the inkwell to her side. She moved like a crane stretching its graceful limbs. She looked odd, Teagan thought, a bit off. Maybe that was why everyone knew her. Lea's pale blue eyes had the wide, pulled-open look of someone on the brink of madness. She might have been pretty if she were in a decent dress and had makeup on. Her light brown hair was cropped like all the other girls, except for the one who was pregnant. Her spindly arms and legs were attached to an equally thin body. By far the most unusual aspect of her appearance was her pale complexion. There was something alien, almost translucent, about her flesh. Lea's alabaster skin reminded Teagan of the marble figures she had seen in the National Gallery in Dublin. Only the delicate blue veins that crossed her arms provided some color against the whiteness. Lea moved like a water bird, in long, languid actions that left Teagan feeling unsettled.

With her wide eyes, Lea studied Teagan and then turned back to her work. She said nothing loud enough to hear, although her lips moved continuously. From the side, Lea's mouth looked like that of an old woman whose lips trembled with age. Suddenly, she spoke up: "Our Father, who art in heaven . . ." The first words of the Lord's Prayer sounded from her lips and faded into silence.

Sister Mary-Elizabeth smiled. "We shouldn't trouble her. I told you she wouldn't talk to you, which is what you have to remember, as well. She prays constantly—it does the heart good to see."

Lea picked up her brush and dipped it into a water jar. The girl was copying a photograph—a watercolor of the resplendent Christ in a blue gown and red robe, sitting on a golden throne. Christ was surrounded by blue peacocks outlined in gold, frocked saints and angels, and, around the borders of the picture, ancient Celtic symbols in the form of the letter *e*, fashioned into swirling designs.

The nun's voice dropped to a whisper. "Lea is copying the *Book of Kells* onto parchment as a gift to the convent. This will hold a high place in our hearts when it's done. No other Order will have anything like it." The Sister pointed to a table shoved into a shadowy corner and motioned for Teagan to follow. She pulled back a curtain to let in more light. "This is where you'll spend some of your time, mending, perhaps making, lace. Do you know how to make lace?"

Teagan shook her head.

The nun looked down at the table with its assortment of doilies, tablecloths, and embroidered handkerchiefs and then held up Teagan's hands. "Fine, thin fingers. I imagine that's why Sister Anne thought you could work on lace," She lifted the edge of a delicate piece to display its craftsmanship. It looked like a spider's web in the soft light. "You'll soon get the hang of it. If you can write, you can mend lace. You're lucky you won't be spending all of your time in the laundry."

She wasn't sure that lace mending would suit her, but working in this room with Lea seemed a much better alternative than the laundry.

Sister Mary-Elizabeth put the lace back on the table, and grasped Teagan's arm. "Time to have your hair cut."

Feeling trapped, she pulled away from her grip.

The nun frowned and reached for her again. "It won't do any good to struggle. It's for your own safety. You don't want to get your hair caught in the machines. When those accidents happen they aren't pretty. Your hair will grow back when you . . ." The nun looked away.

"When?" Teagan asked, raising her voice. "When, what? When I leave, when someone comes for me, when I become a nun?"

Lea turned her thin neck and stared at them, her lips still moving.

"Don't resist," the nun whispered. "You can't escape, and, if you try, they'll bring you back and it'll be worse than ever."

She led Teagan toward the hall, as Lea watched them with her intense gaze. Despite the strange girl, she hated leaving the room, a sanctuary against the authoritarianism that dominated the rest of the convent.

The cuttery was set up in a cubbyhole across from the laundry. Sister Mary-Elizabeth had instructed Sister Rose, who cut hair, to take Teagan to her work after the deed was done. Sister Rose had a large, beaked nose and thin hands covered with bulging purple veins.

"Must you do this?" Teagan asked.

"Every sinner who comes to us has it done," the nun replied.

Teagan trembled as the old nun picked up a long pair of silver scissors and cut off handfuls of blond hair. She dropped these fine bundles on the floor like wastepaper. Teagan swiped at her eyes and winced at her reflection in the small mirror tacked to the wall. The scissors flashed around her. The nun's cutting was so uneven that hair sprouted out in chunks from her head.

When Sister Rose finished chopping, she picked up a pair of electric clippers. "Don't squirm. I don't want to cut you." She was all business as she went about her work.

Teagan sat as the old nun buzzed her hair so close she was nearly bald. The tears continued, but she knew they would do no good. It had taken many visits with her mother to the beauty shop to get her hair in the shape she wanted. Cullen would think she looked like a freak. He wouldn't be able to stand her.

When she was done, Sister Rose said, "You'll thank me at evening prayers for saving you from the heat." She removed the cloth from Teagan and shook the hair to the floor. "The Lord's always giving me a mess to clean up." She raised her bony hands. "Now, out with you—to work." She led Teagan down the passage to the laundry, the one she had seen earlier with Sister Mary-Elizabeth.

The smell of suds enveloped her as she stepped into the warm room. Sister Rose went ahead of her and leaned down to talk

THE MAGDALEN GIRLS 61

to another nun who sat on a tufted leather chair near the door. Teagan couldn't tell what this nun was thinking. She was young and stout, but not large like Sister Mary-Elizabeth; she seemed like a woman who would have been good in sports. She studied Teagan like a clinician, raising her dark eyebrows in cadence with her observations, and then whispered something to Sister Rose.

No smile, no laugh, no emotion crossed her lips except for the whisper. Finally, she got up from her chair and spoke over the roar of the machines: "I'm Sister Ruth, and, you are Teresa." She folded her hands in front of her. The rosary at her side swung against her hips. Teagan smelled the mealy odor of partially digested wine on her breath. "There is no talking during work, even when you break for food. Do your job and you'll get along fine with me. You'll start by sorting and go on from there as you are broken in. Don't expect to be at this post forever because it's the easiest. I have no use for slackers."

The nuns bowed to each other and Sister Rose walked away. Sister Ruth led Teagan to the sorting bins. A girl she had seen at breakfast was already working there. This Magdalen was her age or younger, but her face looked careworn in the bright fluorescent light. Beads of sweat clustered over her brow as she stuck her hands into the unwashed piles. The cantilevered windowpanes had been opened, but hardly a breath of breeze filtered through the dank laundry.

"Sort by whites, lights, and darks," Sister Ruth ordered. "Pull out the special items like lace, embroideries, silks, and tablecloths. They go in a separate bin. Watch what Sarah is doing. She's the best we have at it, but she does other tasks, too, like pressing—just as you will. I'll be watching." Sister Ruth turned away, as if she no longer cared to talk, and returned to her seat. She picked up a book and thumbed through it before placing it in an inverted V over her leg.

Teagan watched as Sarah sorted. The girl said nothing; she didn't even look at her. Five large piles remained on the floor to be placed in the tattered bins. Teagan suspected there would be much more laundry to come during the day.

More laundry arrived by the hour—truckloads of it. The nuns were doing a good business. Sister Mary-Elizabeth was right about the warmth of the uniform. As she sorted, Teagan prayed for the heat to be gone and for a miraculous escape from the convent.

She looked around at the girls and women slaving away, some working at old-fashioned wringer machines a grandmother would have used. Others stood like sentinels by the modern electric washers and dryers, pouring in bleach when needed, or pulling the clothes from the heat when they were perfectly dried. Two, near the end of the room, slaved over hot irons.

Saying nothing, she worked for hours sorting dirty laundry, some of it particularly disgusting, spotted with feces and blood. Bulky tablecloths, but some of fine lace, were stained with all manner of foodstuffs: gravy, crumbs, condiments smeared across the fabric. Bits of food. Lipstick. Snot. Sticky candy. At one point, in the stifling heat and humidity, the smell of bleach and detergent overpowered her, and she bent over the bin thinking she would either faint or vomit—perhaps both.

She couldn't imagine working here forever. Some of the women who tended the machines and washbasins were old. How did they stand it? Did their brains no longer function, or had they just given up? Her impulse to flee grew stronger, but she kept thinking of Sister Mary-Elizabeth's warnings. Where would she go? Who would take her in? The Guards would return her to the convent. Unless her mother, her only possible rescuer, came to her senses and left her father, which was unlikely considering her dependency upon him. Teagan would have to bide her time until some chance of escape presented itself. As much as she didn't want to admit it, she was trapped. As the hours dragged on, she fought panic. Only the horrible thought of losing control, making a scene in front of the others, kept her from total collapse.

Dinner, the noon meal, consisted of a strip of leathery beef, lumpy mashed potatoes, and a bite of mushy carrot. It didn't help her mood. Teagan was so hungry, she forced the food down. At least, the room, the same as used for breakfast, was cooler than the laundry. The girls looked drained, washed out by their labors. Again, as at breakfast, there was no talking. She didn't mind because she didn't have the energy to carry on a conversation. The only Magdalen who looked the least bit happy was the pregnant girl. Teagan hadn't seen her in the laundry. Perhaps she was working at another job, or being housed in another part of the convent until she had her child.

After the half-hour respite, work started again—more sorting at the laundry—until nearly seven in the evening. When Sister Ruth wasn't watching, Teagan took short breaks, leaning against the baskets and steadying herself. Sarah paid little attention to her and continued on with the sweaty job. She marveled at the girl's resilience, her ability to handle the dull, backbreaking work.

Tea, the evening meal, consisted of leftover dinner. The nuns ate in a separate room. She imagined their food was more sumptuous than that served to the Magdalens. After eating, the girls were led to a chapel at the far end of the hall from the convent's entrance. The small room was lit only by candles. The nuns, led by the Mother Superior, sat on the left side, facing the altar; the Magdalens took their places to the right. Teagan bowed her head but didn't pray. She was too tired to think of anything but rest. After a half hour of vespers, Sister Anne called for bed.

Sister Mary-Elizabeth led them to the third floor. She helped Teagan make up her bed, but cautioned her not to speak because the garret was to remain reverent as dusk approached, and under the nun's supervision it remained so. Teagan took her turn in the shower, too tired to care that she was the new girl, naked for all to see. She put on her cotton nightgown and crawled into bed. All the girls and women were there, including Lea, who was in the bed to her left. Suddenly, it made sense: Lea was the reason there were twelve beds but only eleven girls at breakfast. She had already eaten and begun her work on the *Book of Kells*. The pregnant girl was nowhere to be seen.

The nun wished them a good night, turned off the light, and

left them in the gloom. The pink rays of the setting sun fell across Teagan's bed. She couldn't have cared less if the mattress was too soft, too hard, too short, or too long. A murmur among the girls faded to nothing as she tumbled into sleep.

In her chamber overlooking the drive and terrace, Sister Anne kneeled on the carpet in front of her bed, folded her hands, and began to pray. The words, even the Lord's Prayer, were hard to come by this evening.

Out her second-story window, looking to the east, a graceful line of leafy oaks and Scotch pines sheltered the entrance and wound down the lane to the gate. Her room was plentifully heated in the winter by steam radiators. An ample stone fireplace recessed into the south wall had been the original source of heat. In the summer, her chamber was usually pleasant and cool because of the shade. She came to this bedroom not by accident, nor by the luck of the Irish. She'd inherited it, passed down to her five years ago when the previous Mother Superior died in the same bed in which she now slept. But the ghosts who lingered here, if any, were nonexistent at best, good-natured at worst. She sensed their presence occasionally on religious holidays or in troubling times, and then only the spectral touch of a gentle, guiding hand. Like sprites, they were with her and then gone. No malevolent being had ever reached its thorny hand into her sanctuary. As far as Sister Anne was concerned, the room was perfect for meditation, rest, and retreat from the world.

Tonight, however, she wished for some good spirit to guide her, for trouble welled up within her. She wanted to pray for the forgiveness of her sins: hardness; the lack of understanding of the Lord's way; and, especially, a hated memory that had dogged her for so many years. To eradicate that horrible night from her mind would be bliss! Even now, she didn't want to think of it as she knelt at the foot of her bed and prayed to the crucifix on the wall.

Dear Lord, why have You troubled me so? Why have You led me to this place? Have You sent this girl to punish me? I have never shirked my responsibilities, nor our conversations—

I have been honest and true—but this is not fair, Lord. What You have given me is not just. I am not Job. You test me to my limit!

She dropped her rosary onto the bed. Darkness spread in lengthening fingers throughout the room. The trees outside were turning to black in the dusk. The Mother Superior folded her hands, pressed them against her forehead, and leaned against the bed. She shuddered as she prayed. *I fear You have unleashed a curse against me. The one person I never wanted to face again has come to haunt me.*

CHAPTER 5

"Off with yeh!" Her father pushed her into the hall at The Sisters of the Holy Redemption.

"You're a right sick bastard, you are! Keep your manky hands off me." Nora shoved her father and he reeled backward toward the door.

Sister Anne grabbed her by the shoulders and held on as Sister Mary-Elizabeth stepped in to help. She struggled against them, but the two nuns, particularly Sister Mary-Elizabeth, had more strength than she anticipated.

"Of all the bloody things to do," she shouted at her father. "And you, who goes to church once in a blue moon. I'll get out of here and when I do you won't be safe." She balled her fists and shook them at her father.

"You little—" The word caught in her father's throat, and he swallowed it with a look of deference to the nuns. "I tried to make nice, but yeh wouldn't have it. I introduced yeh to these two fine Sisters who are going to take care of yeh—show yeh the right way—and this is the thanks yer ma and I get."

"You and Ma don't give a fig about me!" She spat at her father's feet.

"That's it," Gordon cried out to Sister Anne. "Beat the bejesus out of her if you have to."

Nora spat again and pulled against the grip of the stout nun.

"Mr. Craven," Sister Anne said with as much dignity as she

could maintain while wrestling with Nora. "I think long good-byes, in many cases, are unnecessary. This is one of them."

"With pleasure, Mother." He turned and walked out the door, closing it behind him. Nora was thrust into the half light of the hall with the two nuns. She pulled free from Sister Anne and ran screaming toward the door, dragging Sister Mary-Elizabeth along with her.

"Hold on to her, Sister," the Mother Superior said. "I've got the door." She rushed forward, lifting her key ring from her habit pocket, locking it just as Nora arrived.

Nora pounded her fists against the wood and then collapsed in a heap.

Sister Anne let out a breath and flattened herself against the wall. "That was quite a performance. One that will *never* be repeated, I caution you. Now, get up."

Nora flipped two fingers at Sister Anne. Sister Mary-Elizabeth gasped and shook her head in disgust.

"It's all right, Sister," the Mother Superior said. "We know how to deal with such crude behavior. Monica will learn."

"Monica?" Nora's voice curdled into a snarl. "Who the hell is Monica?"

Sister Anne smiled. "Why, you, child. You're Monica, named after a beloved saint. Your hair will be cut, you'll wear a uniform, and you'll say your prayers like a good penitent. I dare say 'Monica' will be an improvement on 'Nora.' Take her to *the* room, so she can see the error of her ways." Sister Anne pointed down the hall.

"Monica's not going anywhere!" Nora plastered herself against the door.

"We'll see about that," Sister Mary-Elizabeth said, and grabbed her by the arm. The stout nun swung Nora around her.

To Nora's amazement, Sister Mary-Elizabeth had forced her arm behind her back. She set her heels against the tiles, but the slick surface prevented her from getting any traction. She screamed as she slid down the hall. She had no idea where she was headed—double doors loomed in front of her as if leading to a chapel. Another door, sunken and heavy in the granite, was set into the wall to its right. Sister Mary-Elizabeth pushed her toward that door as the Mother Superior followed.

"You're hurting me," Nora yelled.

"Sorry," Sister Mary-Elizabeth shouted in her ear. "God will forgive me. I can't say the same for you."

The Mother Superior opened the door. Sister Mary-Elizabeth shoved Nora inside.

"Take time to reflect upon your sins, Monica." Sister Anne said. Her face shone red with anger. Nora wondered if the Mother Superior was so upset she might actually hit her. The door slammed shut, the key turned, and darkness covered her.

Nora's fingers crept over the door. She stood, gulping in air, trying not to panic.

"Oh God," she whispered. Her heart raced and her legs stiffened in fear. "I'll *kill* him when I get out of here. I swear *I'll* kill him."

She stuck out her hands like a blind person and stepped tentatively back from the door. In two steps, her feet struck something that scudded across the floor and then tipped over with a thud. The sound faded and there was nothing more—only the dark and the deathly quiet. She reached down, groping in the void, unsure what her hands would find. They found a round wooden rod, and then two more attached by stretchers. She turned the rods upright and her fingers brushed over a circular wooden seat. She was certain it was a stool, like the one farmers used to milk cows.

For a moment, she pondered whether to sit or stand. How many hours would she be confined in this dank chamber, to stand in the dark with her arms by her side? It wouldn't take long to be uncomfortable. Sitting, with her knees close to her chest, seemed safer, more like huddling against a storm. She lowered her body to the seat, placed her arms under her knees, and pulled up, bending her back toward her legs. She rocked on her feet and stared into the blackness. The darkness never fled. If anything, it seemed to intensify. She moaned and blinked, hoping some light might seep into the room, but, despite her efforts, none came.

* * *

The hours passed—how many, Nora couldn't be sure. It was certainly more than two, but it could have been three or four. Without any way to gauge time, she couldn't tell. Something scuttled past her. She screamed, fearing it might be a rat. No one came to her aid. The silence worked on her imagination. Skeletal fingers emerged from the walls. Thin white bones reached for her. An old crone's face with glowing eyes and yellow teeth leered at her. The faint sound of the nuns' voices in prayer, a singsong melody, drifted into her ears and then evaporated into nothingness. She closed her eyes and prayed, something she hadn't done in years. The fingers receded; the horrible face vanished along with the voices.

Her stomach growled, reminding her that her body had needs. How much more of this torture would she have to endure? Even the nuns must have known that a penitent would have to use the toilet after hours of confinement.

Thoughts of revenge came into her head. How would she kill her father? Poison was too slow, a knife too bloody. *I'll shoot him when I get out!* Her mother would make a fuss, but maybe Nora could convince her it was for the best. After all, her mother had turned into a drudge, a pouty, sullen woman, after she married her father. Nora only had to look at the family scrapbooks to prove that.

She thought about the morning. Her father had grabbed her early, his rough hands leading her to a curbside car. Nora didn't put up much of a fight, because she wanted to get away—to a better life—free from her mother and father. Perhaps her father was dropping her off at Pearse's flat with wishes of "good riddance." Could she be that lucky? Little did she know they were headed to The Sisters of the Holy Redemption.

The waiting car sputtered as Nora climbed in the front seat. The beat-up hulk belonged to a drinking buddy of her father's whom Nora had met a few times. Her family didn't have a car and that added to her shame. Her father's friend, equally as burly as her da, chuckled like an idiot as he drove them to the convent. He played with the radio and puffed on a cigarette.

Nora, pinned between the two men in the front seat, couldn't escape. Her father had offered only two words of explanation as he unlocked her chained bedroom door—"slutty bitch." Nora shook her head. All this was happening because she'd wanted to escape her dreary life.

Soon, she realized they weren't going by her boyfriend's house. As far as she was concerned, Pearse could be damned to hell with the rest of them. If he hadn't jilted her, none of this horrible business would have happened.

In fact, she had no idea where they were going. The car traveled south, over the River Liffey, past Dublin's city center. They drove for what seemed like an eternity until they pulled up at the convent gates and an affable old man let them in. Sister Anne had swooped down upon them when they arrived. Her father signed papers and the transaction was done. His buddy sat like an accomplice in the car smoking cigarettes and listening to the radio. A cigarette! My God, she had no cigarettes and there would be none to be found here. What use was plotting revenge upon her father when she couldn't even smoke, eat, or pee? *Think, think, think.* She needed to come up with a way to get out of this hellhole and fast.

Something scraped against the lock. A key? The door opened, light flooded in, and she shielded her eyes. Strong hands gripped her arms and pulled them away from her body.

Sister Mary-Elizabeth leaned over her. "Have you had enough for one day? I suppose you need to visit the jacks. I hope you didn't wet yourself." The nun shook her head. "Mind you, this is what you'll get if you don't behave. We call it the Penitent's Room."

For the first time, Nora was able to see it, almost square, its four walls only two yards wide on each side. The high ceiling seemed to stretch into infinity. The only thing inside was the stool. Long white scratches cut across the walls, as if the penitents before her had scraped their fingernails against the granite—no doubt from the madness spawned by the room.

"Time to eat," Sister Mary-Elizabeth said. "Don't give me trouble, because I'm in no mood. You'll eat, have your hair cut, and be given your uniform."

"Uniform?" Nora asked. Her back ached and her legs wobbled as she got up from the stool.

"This isn't a holiday camp," the nun said. "You're here to work. I'll give you instructions after you get settled."

Nora looked down the long hall to the closed door at the end—the door her father had pushed her past. How she hated him. She saw him standing there, a grinning apparition, mocking her, blocking her way out. She gave the ghost the evil eye. He had always blocked her from doing anything she wanted to do.

There was no use making a break for it—the door was probably locked. Even if she escaped, she didn't know where to go. She decided to change her strategy. She folded her hands and said, "Yes, Sister."

The nun squinted, looking as if she couldn't believe her ears. "That's more like it." Sister Mary-Elizabeth pointed to the stairway leading to the second floor and then locked the door to the Penitent's Room.

Nora climbed a few steps.

"Hold up," the nun ordered. "I don't trust you as far as I could throw Jesus."

You'd be right about that. Nora smiled at the nun, who quickly caught up with her.

Sister Mary-Elizabeth took her by the arm. "Luck is with you. We had room for one more bed. It's under the eave, next to the new girl, Teresa. You'll like her."

Nora rolled her eyes as they walked arm in arm up the stairs. *Yes, how lucky I am to be next to the "new girl" when I don't give a shit about anybody.*

Sister Rose appeared in the laundry with a penitent who looked as if she had been roughed up by a prison warden. Teagan hadn't seen this new girl at bedtime or at breakfast. The old nun chatted with Sister Ruth as the arrival glared into the room, red-faced and fidgeting with her closely cropped black hair. Apparently, anyone who dared approach her did so at their peril.

She figured they would be working next to each other and turned back to her sorting, occasionally looking over her shoulder. The anger emanating from this girl ignited the air. Teagan could feel the hatred pouring from her across the room. She had always wondered what it would feel like to be really mad, because she wasn't allowed to be angry, particularly when her father was drunk. He was the only one who was allowed to make an ass out of himself. She and her mother had to sit—and take all that he dished out.

She spotted Sarah out of the corner of her eye. Her sorting companion was fifteen, maybe younger, and Teagan had no idea where she came from or how she ended up at The Sisters of the Holy Redemption. Now, she thought, there would be three of them standing at the bins. Or maybe Sister Ruth would move Sarah to a new station because she was the veteran.

After a few minutes, the new girl arrived at the bins. Teagan and Sarah stood behind her while the nun explained how to sort the clothes. "You'll work next to Teresa," Sister Ruth ordered with wine-filled breath. "Watch Sarah carefully because she won't be on the bins much longer. Learn well or you'll get the rough edge of the stick." The nun turned away.

"That's it?" the girl asked.

Teagan looked at the bins.

Sister Ruth turned back. "What did you say?"

The girl didn't have time to answer. Teagan heard a hand swish through the air and the blow of a hard slap.

"You bitch—"

The words were cut short by another slap. "Do you have any other questions?" came the mocking reply.

The girl shuffled next to Teagan and gazed into the bins.

The nun returned to her chair.

Teagan shifted her eyes slowly and looked at the girl to her left. The hardness in her face had fallen away as if it was all a façade. Maybe she wasn't as mean as she seemed. In fact, tears were running down her cheeks.

"Get busy, you two!" Sister Ruth yelled from behind.

Sarah continued her work, ignoring all that had gone on. Teagan rummaged through the pile of clothes on the floor next to her and sorted. She had made a game of her job: W.L.D.S. *Whites, lights, darks, special. Whites, lights darks, special.* She kept repeating those four words in her head as she worked, until she thought it would drive her mad. And it was only her second day! No sane person could endure such monotony.

The girl, unsure what to do, locked eyes with her. Teagan pointed to the bins, picked an article of clothing for each and threw them into the appropriate container. *Whites, lights, darks, special.* One didn't have to be a genius to get the hang of it. The key was to resign yourself to the situation, as Sarah must have done. She'd once read about men who could walk on hot coals by ignoring the pain.

They kept at their sorting for an hour. Sarah and the others ignored them. Teagan looked over her shoulder. Sister Ruth was slumped in her chair, her head hanging over her lap. The wine had worked its wonders.

She turned to the new girl, took a chance, and asked, "What's your name?" She had to talk over the whir of the machines.

The girl looked at her, surprise filling her eyes. She, too, looked back at the nun.

"Nora. Nora Craven," she said, and grabbed a pair of black pants. She rummaged through the pockets and then threw them into the "dark" bin.

"I'm Teagan, although they want to call me Teresa. I'm not having it." She looked at Sister Ruth, who had slipped back in her chair, eyes closed, head snug against the wall. "She has a wine bottle somewhere."

Nora smirked. "Glad there's someone who thinks like me, even if she is a bitch." she said too loudly. Sarah eyed them both suspiciously.

"Ssshhh," Teagan cautioned. "Keep your voice down. I don't want to get a crack on the head. Look busy. Keep sorting." She picked through the clothes.

Nora did the same. "They want to name me Monica because of some saint. They're daft. I'll be damned if I'll be one. Who needs that?" She tossed two white shirts into the bin.

Teagan wanted to laugh. "Let's make a pact, then. We'll use our real names when we talk to each other—Sister Anne can keep her saints to herself."

Nora grinned. "Well, I'm game." She picked up a tablecloth and wriggled her nose in disgust. "Oh, benjy. Smells like horse droppings." She threw the cloth into the "whites" bin. Sarah let out a little squeak.

"Wait, that'll get you in bad with Sister Ruth." Teagan gathered the tablecloth and dropped it in the "special" bin. "That's silk, from some fancy hotel. If it gets washed with the whites, you'd be done."

Sarah nodded and turned back to her work.

"She's a talkative one," Nora said.

Teagan leaned against a bin. "It's like being in gaol and no one seems to care. All the Magdalens are brain-dead."

"I didn't know there was such a *proper* name until I came here," Nora said. "Imagine comparing us to a whore. I guess being horned up is as bad a sin as being knocked up." She looked at Teagan with sad eyes. "What are you in for?"

"I'm not absolutely certain, but it has something to do with a priest."

"A priest!" Nora's voice spiked with excitement. "That's one for the books. You're a bad girl. Doomed to hell, you are!"

Teagan looked over her shoulder in alarm. Sister Ruth napped in her chair. "For God's sake, keep it down. Take a look at the girls here."

Nora nodded. "It's sad, but I don't have to. When that old nun, a poor excuse for a beautician, brought me in here, I saw their faces. All washed out. Dead with nothing to live for. And some of them are old. I don't understand why they're still here? I'm not going to be here until I die and they haul me out in a coffin."

"You can't run away. Sister Mary-Elizabeth said there's no place to hide. She's right. The Guards will bring you back."

"I'll be out of here by the next moonrise and won't anybody stop me."

Teagan reached for the pile next to her feet. A silver crucifix cut across her right hand. She winced.

Sister Ruth glared at her. "That'll teach you. You both deserve it, carrying on like two magpies." The crucifix, hanging from rosary beads, swung from her palm. "I saw you talking. You thought I didn't notice. You won't get away with it, so you better not try. Teresa! Come with me." She put the beads in her pocket, pulled Teagan away from her station, and dragged her toward the chair. "Wait here." The nun shoved her down and walked out.

Knowing Sister Ruth was gone, the other Magdalens stared at her, some tittering at her shame.

Nora continued to sort, but looked back a few times, her eyes blazing.

Several young girls were stationed at sinks. Their scrawny hands worked like pumps, pushing and kneading the fabrics they worked on. A few worked with steam irons. The older women were placed next to the whirring washers and dryers. They stared at the machines, apparently looking for any imperfection in the process. They hardly gave Teagan a second glance.

She looked down at her hand. The cross had opened a thin cut, oozing crimson. It was nothing, really, but in addition to its burning sensation, the wound elicited a visceral reaction. *I hate her.* She shook off the thought, not wanting to accept the voice in her head. She had disliked many of the nuns at school, but everyone loathed a teacher now and then.

She had never hated anyone—not even her father when he was so drunk he belittled her and her mother. The Commandments said to "honor your father and mother." She was a good girl, but her father had often told her otherwise. "You're both no good," he had shouted at them when he was deep in the bottle. But she didn't hate her father; she pitied him. She cringed at the thought of hating a nun. She couldn't believe how twisted her mind had become in only a few days.

Sister Ruth returned carrying a white cloth bandage and a bottle of purple antiseptic. The nun swabbed the liquid over Teagan's hand. A fiery burn settled across the cut, and she clenched her teeth. The nun covered it with the bandage and secured it with medical tape.

"That's that," Sister Ruth said. "Now, get back to your station. And no talking."

She walked back to the bins. Sarah continued to work and didn't look at her. Teagan could feel the Sister's eyes following her every move. Nora said nothing, as well, but caught her attention once in a while. There was a look about Nora, one of rage and indignation, like someone about to explode.

Teagan feared that Nora might do so. She tried to calm her down in a way that Sister Ruth wouldn't notice. She raised her eyebrows and directed her gaze to the bins. They were in enough trouble as it was. They worked, saying nothing, until it was time for tea.

Lightning flared in the western sky. Teagan saw the flashes through the garret window as the sun disappeared behind towering clouds.

So, this is how it's to be. My life—dull as mud—watching storm clouds. At least the rain will wash away the day's warmth.

No one had spoken at tea or prayers. She listened as the nuns whispered their vespers, mouths moving like puppets. Lea, of course, joined in, right at home with the Sisters. After prayers, they had filed silently out of the chapel, up the two flights of stairs to their beds, while Sister Mary-Elizabeth and Sister Rose watched over them like stern parents. Not one girl talked, not even in the showers. The two nuns finally turned off the lights and closed the doors. The room was plunged into gloom.

Teagan heard a far-off rumble of thunder. Her body ached and she was ready for sleep. She lifted the bandage on her hand. The cut hadn't caused much pain during the afternoon and a scab had already begun to form.

Nora crawled into bed. It was crammed into the narrow V where the two walls met to form the base of the convent's spired roof. In a way, Nora's bed would be cozy, Teagan thought, almost like having a little cave to crawl in with no one on either side to bother you.

Nora didn't seem to think so. She huffed and pounded her pillow and then propped it behind her back as if she was going to sit up all night. She looked as if she would murder anyone who came near.

The other Magdalens looked as careworn and tired as they had the previous evening. *They don't have the energy to fight. Everyone is too broken.*

Someone whispered far down the room.

Lea sat up in her bed and arched her swan-like neck toward Teagan. "Did you hear that? Talking in bed can get you into trouble. I don't like to make trouble."

"It's horrible not being able to talk," Teagan whispered back.

"You get used to it." She pulled her long arms from underneath the sheet and folded them across her stomach.

"Used to it, yes, but for how long?"

Lightning flashed through the window, illuminating Lea's face. She looked like a corpse in the white glare. Thunder bounced against the granite walls.

"I don't worry about it," Lea said after the noise died. "Where would I go anyway? I have no home."

Nora crawled toward them and rested her head at the foot of her bed. She was close enough she could overhear what they were saying.

"You're a real hick, aren't you, a real bogger," Nora said. She screwed up her mouth into an ugly smile.

Lea looked at Nora with wide eyes. "Nothing you can say will hurt me. I've already had enough trouble to last a lifetime. Besides, Jesus is my friend."

Another flash of lightning lit the garret. Nora smirked. "Oh brother, not only a bogger, but bonkers, too."

"Hey, shut your holes," a girl on the other side of the room said in a harsh whisper. "Do I have to get Sister?"

"See what I mean?" Lea settled back in bed and pulled the sheet up to her neck.

"Well, I guess she's done for the night," Nora said. "Not sure I'm going to get along with her . . . but then, I'm not sure about anybody here."

Teagan turned and looked out the window. The storm was approaching fast; black clouds hovered over the city. Soon, large drops of rain pelted the window and roof. The arched ceiling magnified the sound, like water plunking into a wooden basin. She wasn't sure what to say to Nora; after all, she knew this girl could be trouble. On the other hand, she seemed to be the only Magdalen who wasn't yet broken.

Teagan decided to take a chance. "I think *we* should make an effort to get along."

"Why?" Nora sounded suspicious.

"Because I'm smart and you've got spunk."

"Are you saying I'm dumb?"

Teagan smiled, but she knew Nora couldn't see her in the deepening gloom. "No, but if I had to choose a cell mate in gaol, you'd be the one. Between the two of us, we might be able to break out of here." She could barely make out the lump the new penitent formed in bed.

Nora fought again with her pillow before whispering, "I think we're going to get along fine."

Lightning stabbed the sky not far from the convent. The flash filled the garret with a harsh light that vanished before a crackling roll of thunder.

Teagan had settled into bed when the door opened. Sister Mary-Elizabeth stood in the hall, her form silhouetted by the lamp overhead. She was dressed in nightclothes. Her face was deep in shadow, but the top of her head and the tight band of cloth that held back her short hair were visible. The nun looked into the room for a few moments and then closed the door. The shaft of light from the hall disappeared. The room grew even darker as the storm thrashed outside.

Someone walked past her bed. Teagan wasn't sure of the hour. She shook off her drowsiness in time to see a pair of legs disappear through the window. It had to be one of the Magdalens. Who else could it be? She yawned and stared into the darkness. A cool breeze, following the storm, blew across her. The air felt good after the laundry's heat.

The latched screen had been opened and its wooden frame pushed out. Teagan peered out the window but couldn't see the girl who had escaped. *Escaped!* It had to be Nora. Only she would be crazy enough to try a stunt like this on her first night in the convent. She looked at Nora's bed. It was empty, although the pillow had been covered with the sheet to clumsily disguise her absence.

Her heart raced, wondering what had happened. What if Nora had escaped? Worse yet, what if she had fallen from the roof? Dread tugged at her. She didn't want to think about losing the one friend who might aid her escape. There was only one way to find out.

She pushed the screen open, crawled out, and found herself on the roof of the story below. From her vantage point, Teagan knew she was kneeling over the old library where Lea worked on her *Book of Kells*. The roof sloped down at a low angle, not enough that one would slip and fall, but precarious enough after the rain. She pressed her hands against the wet slate and forced her heels into the cracks that divided the tiles. At the end of the roof, to the south, she spotted a girl clutching the top of a cornice. Towering above her, a Latin cross was situated at the peak of the garret's roof. Teagan eased her way toward the figure in the white nightgown.

"Nora? Nora!" She called the name as loudly as she dared.

The girl turned.

"Are you crazy?" Nora asked and then laughed. "You could fall to your death from up here."

Teagan sat behind Nora. Her gown had gathered the damp from the rain. "Listen to the pot calling the kettle black. What are you doing out here?"

"Come closer."

"No. I don't want to get close to the edge. I don't like heights."

"Well, I'll tell you then," Nora said and pointed down. "It's a good ten yards to the ground. You know the bank of windows and the trench outside the laundry?"

Teagan nodded.

"From here, it's nothing but air to the bottom of that trench." Nora shook her head. "There's no way down unless you have a rope, or if you wanted to kill yourself."

She grabbed Nora's shoulders. "Don't say that. Remember, we formed a team. We need to be strong for each other."

"I suppose we should look over there." She pointed to the north side of the convent. "But it's too dangerous to slide across these wet tiles tonight."

Teagan shivered. "And too cold. Let's go back."

Nora clucked like a chicken.

"I'm not a coward," Teagan said, and inched backward. "And I'm not daft."

Nora let go of the cornice and climbed back toward the window. She stopped about halfway and said, "Look at the stars."

Teagan tilted her head back. Whitish-gray clouds, shredded by a northwest wind, scudded overhead. In the breaks between them, the summer stars wheeled in a clear, black sky. She had never seen them so bright. "They're beautiful. I feel like I could reach out and touch them."

"They feel so close. That's a sign of good luck," Nora said. "We'll take whatever we can get."

Teagan sat for a moment, gazing out over the city. To the south, the lights fanned out in bright dots until they vanished near the city's foothills. To the north, they brightened to a milky haze over Dublin center. The sight was so beautiful she momentarily forgot her circumstances. She grabbed Nora's hands. "Promise me, swear to God, that we'll remain friends and help each other get out of here."

Nora squeezed back. "After what happened today, I'm not sure I believe in God, but I'll accept your oath—swear to that old man in the sky." She sighed. "I'd like to spend the night on the roof instead of going inside. I'd like to be here in the morning when the sun comes up, rather than in that cramped bed."

"Me, too, but we can't spend the night out here. We'll catch our deaths."

"Don't be a stick in the mud."

Teagan let go of Nora. "If you somehow escape before I do, or vice versa, we must promise each other that we'll return for the one left behind. It's only fair."

Nora nodded. "But let's make a break for it as soon as we

can. You see what's happened to the others. Too much time here and you're dead."

The wind struck her. She wrapped her arms around her body. "Yes, but we need a plan. We can't go about this blindly. Every detail has to be worked out—so nothing will go wrong." She pictured her mother, crying in the living room, her father drunk and threatening. Nora was right in one respect. She needed to get out of the convent as fast as she could, not only for her sake but for her mother's. "We'll work on it."

Nora extended her hand.

Teagan shook it. "Done. Now, let's get to bed."

"I suppose you're right. My nightgown is wet. Don't want to catch my death, as you would say." Nora chuckled. She started up, but stopped short of the window, her face frozen in fear. A figure stood staring out at them. "Oh shit," Nora said. "I nearly wet me gown."

Lea studied them, her ghostly presence filling the frame. She put a finger to her lips and pushed open the screen.

Teagan followed Nora inside, glad to be off the roof.

They sat on her bed. Lea bent down in front of them, her face filled with wonder. "What were you doing out there?" she asked softly.

"Just catching the air," Teagan said, trying to downplay their escapade. "What are you doing up?"

"I wake up sometimes. Someone taps me on my shoulder."

"Oh great," Nora said.

Teagan clutched her pillow. "The nuns said you don't talk—only pray."

"I talk to people I like," Lea said.

"Aren't *we* lucky," Nora whispered to Teagan.

"You're not going to report us, are you?" Teagan asked.

"No." Lea stood and walked to the window. She pointed to the southwest, near the cornice where Nora had sat. "Sometimes at night I stare at the grass for hours. Something's out there."

"What's she talking about?" Teagan asked Nora.

Nora leaned toward her. "Damned if I know. There's not

much to see beyond the grounds. A couple of street lamps down the road. This convent's secluded and surrounded by a high wall." She got up. "I've had enough of the spook story. I'm going to sleep and get warm."

"Me, too," Teagan said.

Nora went back to her bed.

Lea continued to stare out the window, acting as if she were the only one in the room. "Something *is* there. Something's *out* there. You'll see."

She wasn't sure to whom Lea was talking. Perhaps the words were just for her, echoing in her head for her own amusement. She pulled up the sheet and wished she had a blanket to break the chill. The sight of Lea staring out the window was enough to send more shivers down her spine.

CHAPTER 6

After several months, the monotonous routine had drained Teagan. She found it hard to concentrate; energy slipped from her body. Prayers, breakfast, work, dinner, more work, tea, prayers, bed. Day after day. Week after week. Sunday morning Mass with a priest she didn't know. The routine never varied. Nothing changed except the piles of laundry. The washing, the drying, the ironing. Teagan and Nora had tried to get out on the roof a couple of times, but either they were too tired or one of the Magdalens was awake.

Nora seemed to be handling the convent life better than anyone. Most of the time, she smiled and complimented Sister Ruth—as if that would get her anywhere. Teagan wondered whether Nora was being nice because she was planning an escape. Usually, the only chance they had to talk was after the lights had been turned out. Nora admitted that her goal of making a break by the August full moon had failed.

"I'm trying to keep myself sane by being cheerful," Nora whispered to her. "You should try it. Maybe you wouldn't be so depressed."

"It's hard, but I keep dreaming of the day I'll get out of here," Teagan said. She often thought about Cullen and the small luxuries she enjoyed at home.

"I want out of this feckin' dump," Nora said. "That's the plan for now."

Summer faded and shifted into autumn, heralded by a series

of damp, foggy days. The shadows cast on the laundry's floor lengthened as the sun trekked southward. Soon, they might disappear altogether in the depths of winter.

Sister Ruth had told Teagan she would move from sorting to lace-mending duties when the Mother Superior gave the command. Sarah had moved to the washbasins, so only she and Nora were at the bins now. No new girls had arrived at the convent, and the pregnant one she had seen on her first day had disappeared. The veteran Magdalens didn't seem to care what had happened to the girl, as if such cases were commonplace.

Teagan suggested she and Nora develop a sign language so they could avoid Sister Ruth's wrath. Most of the time, apparently sedated by her generous noon meal and several swigs from the clandestine wine bottle, the nun dozed peacefully in her chair. But there was always the chance she might nap with one eye open.

Teagan and Nora formulated their new mode of communication while standing at the bins.

"One finger for 'no,'" Teagan whispered. "Two for 'yes.'"

Nora moved her hand in a wavy motion from left to right to indicate "maybe." A flat, horizontal movement meant "stop." Then came every word they could think of that might be needed for an escape, including: car, rope, stairs, window, run, hide, Guards. Nora raised the two-finger salute on her right hand when the word "parents" came up. "That's the signal that we took it up our arse," she said.

Once, Sister Ruth caught them practicing their signs. She came within a few feet, squinted, and said, "What's gotten into you two? Saint Vitus's dance?" The nun looked at them suspiciously.

Teagan didn't dare smile, but Nora did. They said nothing while Sister Ruth, still keeping an eye on them, returned to her chair.

One drizzly day in late September, Teagan and Nora were sorting when Sister Mary-Elizabeth lumbered through the door. Nora saw the Sister first and got Teagan's attention by pointing to her.

The nun scowled at Sister Ruth, who was dozing in her chair, her head bobbling on her neck. Her hands had slipped off the magazine she was reading. The nun jiggled Sister Ruth's shoulders and the overseer snapped awake. Teagan watched the two nuns confer, when she could.

Sister Ruth appeared behind her. "The Mother Superior wants to see you. You have a guest."

"Me?" She was surprised because she had never seen anyone visit the Magdalens.

"Would I come to get you otherwise?" Sister Ruth shook her head as if she was talking to an idiot.

Nora shot Teagan a look.

Sister Ruth led her to the other nun, who stood blocking the doorway.

"It's Father Matthew—from your parish," Sister Mary-Elizabeth said.

Teagan stopped. Her gut clenched as if she had been punched in the stomach. "I don't want to see him. I can't see him."

"Come now," the nun said, and offered her hand as they left the laundry. "You don't have a choice, in these circumstances. You can't refuse a member of the clergy."

"You're wrong." She stood firm at the bottom of the stairs.

Sister Mary-Elizabeth smiled in that soft way that reminded Teagan of her mother when she was being kind. "Sister Anne says Father Matthew has a letter from your parents."

Another punch, equally hard, hit her. The Mother Superior wouldn't lie about something as important as a letter. She had to see what it was about, despite her loathing of the old priest. If he hadn't started her troubles, he had certainly contributed to them. She followed Sister Mary-Elizabeth up the two flights of stairs to the old library, where Lea sat, bent over her work.

The nun pointed to the lace table. "Sit down. I'll tell Father Matthew you're here." She carried another chair to the table as Teagan took her seat.

A few minutes later, the Mother Superior strode into the room displaying the confidence of a prizefighter. Father Matthew followed like a plump sheep.

Sister Anne stopped in front of the lace table. The priest,

looking as corpulent as Teagan remembered, stood behind the chair. He glanced sideways, watching Lea as she worked—anything to avoid looking directly at her. Most involved with her subjugation wanted to keep their distance. Even the Mother Superior had limited her contact over the two months since Teagan had arrived, as if she was purposely avoiding her. She rarely looked her way and never spoke, except for an occasional admonishment about posture or dress. This time, however, Sister Anne was forced to speak.

"I'm sure you remember Father Matthew."

How could I forget? Even the thought of having to talk to the priest repulsed her, catapulting her disposition into a steely resolve. She nodded.

"He has consented to speak with you, giving ten minutes of his valuable time."

Teagan said nothing and stared at the priest.

"It doesn't surprise me that you are ungrateful," Sister Anne said. "You've learned very little while you've been here—an indication that we have much more to accomplish." She turned to the priest. "I'm sorry, Father, for her recalcitrant behavior. I pray for her every day." She pointed to the table where Lea sat. "And don't worry about her. You can say anything in front of Lea and be assured of complete confidence. I'll leave you two to talk."

Sister Anne left the room.

Teagan continued to stare. He wouldn't get the best of her, not now, not ever.

Father Matthew removed his damp raincoat and placed it over the back of the chair. He squeezed his heavy frame into the seat and clamped his arms firmly on the rests. When he looked at her, his eyes seemed as colorless as the sky outside.

She shivered. Perhaps he was here to tell her about a tragedy; maybe something awful had happened to her mother or father. She clasped her hands and waited for him to speak.

Father Matthew's lips trembled, as if he was considering what to say. "I don't have much time. I'm here at the request of your mother."

She leaned toward him. "Is she sick?"

"No." He swiped a few gray hairs back from his forehead with his pudgy fingers.

"Would you care to ask how *I'm* getting along?"

His eyes widened. "I have no intention of doing so. I would never presume to tell the Mother Superior how to conduct the convent's business. I'm sure you don't have it easy, but it's an obligatory life for a penitent." He shifted, stuck his hand in a pocket, and withdrew a small envelope. He allowed her to study it for a moment and then handed it to her.

Teagan recognized the cream-colored paper and the handwriting on its front. The inscription read: *To My Dear Daughter.* The penmanship was her mother's, but it seemed different, not the facile and loose script of earlier days, but constricted and cramped.

"Your mother wanted to visit, but your father forbade such an action." He pointed to the letter. "A wise choice, I believe, considering the circumstances. It would have caused great family harm."

"Harm!" She couldn't believe what the priest had said. "What do you think I've been going through since I—"

He cut her off with a wave of his hand. "No outbursts, or I'll be forced to leave. No message will be relayed to your mother."

"Even you couldn't be that unkind," she said. Her eyes clouded with tears.

He took out a handkerchief and offered it to her.

She ignored the gesture.

"On the contrary," he said. "I'm far from heartless, but I know when I'm right. By all God's angels in heaven, I've done what is holy."

She threw the letter on the desk. "I don't want any part of your heaven."

"Watch what you say." He pushed the letter back to her. "Read it. Time is short."

She picked it up, forced her finger under the sealed flap, and ripped it open. She grasped the folded stationery, but then hesitated, fearing what might be written. She gathered her courage and read.

My dearest daughter,

I've wept so many nights for you. I hope you're well and adjusting to your new home. My heart cries out in pain as I write these words, but we have no other choice, only to assume that your father has done the right thing in sending you away.

The peace I used to know has departed despite my prayers, and, I think, your father suffers, as well, but he displays it in different ways. He has become sullen and withdrawn of late and spends evenings away from the house, leaving me quite alone for much of the time. My anger, disappointment, and frustration are tempered by the turmoil I observe within him. If only I could reach him, be a better wife, perhaps this agony would end.

Father Matthew has agreed to visit you. I begged him to. At first, he wouldn't consent, but a sufficient quantity of tears eventually melted his heart. Please let me know you are well. I think about you every hour of the day and night. Tell Father Matthew that you think of us.

I miss you, but I know this action must be for the best. Father Matthew has assured me of such, and that we will all be justly rewarded. I will pray for your repentance, as I spend equal hours praying for you to reopen your heart to us, and our family to come together once again.

I love you,
Your mother

Teagan brushed a tear from her cheek, folded the letter, and put it back inside the envelope. She looked at the priest and said, "You've convinced my mother, haven't you? What you should be talking about is how I came to be here. This is about Father Mark, isn't it?"

The priest turned away.

"Isn't it!" She said it loudly enough that Lea looked up from her work.

Father Matthew got up from his chair. "I must be leaving now."

"Nothing happened, and you know it!"

He gathered his raincoat from the chair and stood facing her with a clenched jaw. He glared at her and finally said, "I have one thing to say. What is spoken in confidence between members of the clergy cannot be divulged. Nothing *you* can say or do will change that." He flung his coat over his arm and turned.

Sister Anne appeared at the doorway. "Is everything all right? I heard shouting."

"Everything is fine, Sister," the priest said. He turned back to Teagan, his face flushed with anger. "Do you think I would believe your deception over the words of a man of God? Tell me, why should I do so?" He slammed his fists on the table. "Tell me!"

"Because I'm telling the truth," she said calmly.

Father Matthew sighed. "Do you have a message for your parents?"

"Tell my mother I love her." She picked up the letter and placed it in her apron pocket. "Where is Sister Mary-Elizabeth? I believe we're finished."

"She'll be here shortly," Sister Anne said. "Come, Father, I need to talk to you."

"Good-bye, Teresa," Father Matthew said. "It's doubtful we will see each other again on earth; perhaps in heaven, after your repentance."

She couldn't say the words to his face, but she could think them. *I couldn't care less if we ever meet again, in heaven or hell.*

They walked into the hall and turned toward the stairs.

Teagan smoothed the letter in her pocket and looked across the room. Lea was working on her *Book of Kells* drawing, her mouth moving in silent prayer.

As she waited for the nun to return, her breath faltered. It came in quick, halting gasps. For a moment, she felt as if nothing mattered, as if her life had been taken away. She looked at her hands. Her spirit was wounded, but her body still remained.

One October Sunday afternoon, after Mass and the noon meal, the Magdalens were allowed on the grounds. This "reprieve" happened only when the Mother Superior was in a good mood. Teagan, Nora, and Lea sat on the lawn enjoying the autumn breeze. The other girls were gathered in bunches around them. Some of the nuns sat outside, as well. Sisters Mary-Elizabeth, Rose, and Ruth, their habits billowing in the wind, enjoyed the day, sitting comfortably in their folding chairs.

The sun broke through the clouds occasionally as leaves fell around them. Teagan picked up a yellow leaf and looked at the spidery veins that stretched through its indented blades. A soft brown tinted the edges. She had always hated this time of year, when the days grew short and the sun retreated far to the south. Usually, autumn was gloomy, with only the prospect of bleak winters ahead. She shook off her sour mood, telling herself she needed to enjoy the beautiful day—a respite without the drudgery of the laundry. This was also an opportunity to talk without being punished.

"Tomorrow I begin lace-mending," Teagan said, twirling the leaf between her palms.

"How wonderful," Nora said, her voice brimming with sarcasm. "How did you get that gig?"

"I'm not sure," Teagan said.

"The Mother Superior reserves that task for special penitents," Lea said.

Nora rolled her eyes. "Well, I'll be. Isn't it grand that you'll be ruining your fingers and eyesight because you're special. Isn't it delightful that we are able to learn skills that'll help us so much when we finally leave this hellhole?"

Lea shushed Nora with a finger to her lips.

"Come off your cloud, Lea," Nora said. "Lace-mending and laundering? What good will they do us?" She looked up at the semi-naked branches of the oak they sat under. "Tasks to keep us in our place. Oh, I suppose a husband might appreciate it, *if* a man would ever look at us now that we're tainted." She plucked a stem of grass as yet untouched by frost. "I hate Pearse. I'm beginning to hate men period."

Teagan threw the leaf in the air. "I wanted to go to Trinity College, even though it's not Catholic, but I'd need permission from the Church's archbishop. I guess that won't happen. But women should do more than keep house and have babies, don't you think? My father would disagree."

Nora nodded. "God, I wish I had a cigarette. I may have to pocket some from one of the deliverymen. Ugh."

Lea gazed into a corner of the walls surrounding the convent. "I can get you some."

Nora's mouth fell open. "What'd you say? Get me some fags?"

Teagan laughed. "Lea—a good girl like you? You sell black-market cigarettes?"

Lea ignored their taunts and never took her eyes off the corner. "Do you feel it?"

"What?" Nora looked toward the high stone walls.

Teagan followed her stare, as well. Glass glittered like sharks' fins across its top.

"Smart ones, they are," Nora said. "Every time I see that wall I get angry—broken glass on the ledge so you can't crawl over, unless you want to get sliced apart. I didn't notice it when we were on the roof."

"It was dark, how could you?" Teagan asked.

Lea pulled a few blades of grass and stuck them in her mouth. "Yes, I feel them."

Nora chuckled. "Lea, sometimes I think you're completely daft."

Lea turned to Nora, her wide eyes filled with excitement. "Can't you feel them? They're over there in the corner. Maybe they only want to communicate with me."

The sound of children's laughter drifted across the grounds.

"Are there kids around here?" Nora asked.

"We can't go around the corner." Lea pointed past the west end of the convent. "But I think there's another building at the north end—an orphanage." She paused. "Children. I know they're here."

Nora shook a finger at her. "You're trying to get us, pull a fast one, aren't you? This place is creepy enough without you adding to it. If you keep it up, you'll end up in an asylum."

"No." Lea picked up a leaf and swung it in front of her face like a hypnotist's watch. "I'm not lying. I like you two. You're my best friends."

Nora tapped Teagan's shoulder. "That counts for something, right, Teresa?"

"Please, don't call me that, even in jest. I can't stand it." She touched Lea's leg. "What do you feel? Can you tell us?"

"Tonight," Lea said. "We'll go out on the roof and you'll see them, too." Her eyes glittered. "I'll get you some cigarettes, Nora. Don't worry. You can smoke them on the roof and no one will know."

Nora took in a deep breath of the autumnal air. "Just the thought does me good, but don't forget matches or a lighter. This woman has no fire left."

"I have that, too. An hour after lights-out." Lea got up and walked away, leaving them behind. She stopped in the corner and stood with her back to them, stiff and alone like a sentinel.

"I really think she's mad," Nora said, "but if she can get me fags . . . who am I to complain."

Teagan got up and kicked at the leaves. "Maybe she's not as crazy as we think. What if it's all an act?"

Nora brightened, as if she'd had a sudden revelation. "Yes, I get it. She acts daft, so she'll get out of here. It's the madhouse escape, just like I figured. Now, that's a plan."

Teagan grabbed another leaf and studied its brown edges. Decay made her sad. She let it flutter to the ground. She walked toward Lea unable to shake the strange heaviness that filled her. There were only a few more hours of daylight and little left of enjoyment outside. Tea and evening prayers would come too soon.

*   *   *

Teagan's anticipation of another rooftop excursion made the hours drag by. Tea was less than satisfying, as usual, but she had learned to eat what was set in front of her unless it was utterly disgusting. The evening menu would win no awards as far as she was concerned: a thin strip of tough beef, candied beets, and a few kernels of soggy corn. She managed to eat without gagging. The nuns always ate a more sumptuous meal—in a large chamber on the other side of the breakfast room, adjacent to the kitchen. This information came from Lea, who once ate with the Sisters when she announced her *Book of Kells* project. "The food was much better," she'd said without a hint of irony.

Evening prayers seemed to last an eternity. Lea told Teagan she was excited about going out on the roof. "It's something different," she whispered as they headed to the garret. "I like doing things with my friends."

After showering and getting into bed, Teagan lay back with her eyes open, alternately looking at the rafters and checking to see whether Lea and Nora were asleep. She was about ready to drift off when a "psssttt," jolted her.

Lea, dressed in her nightclothes and, holding something in her hands, stood at the foot of the bed. She reached and tapped Nora's toes. The bed jiggled and Nora started.

Lea motioned for quiet and nodded her head, indicating that the other Magdalens were asleep. She clenched her teeth, unhooked the screen, and raised its frame slowly. It made no sound. A cool breeze wafted into the garret. Teagan grabbed her gray wool blanket in case it was too cold on the roof. They had each been given one when autumn arrived.

Lea led the way, pointing toward the cornice where Nora had sat on her first night. She rested about a yard from the edge and looked at the grounds spread out before her. The convent was mostly surrounded by dark woods; however, a few street lamps adjacent to the property cast their feeble light upon the roof. Teagan and Nora took places on either side of her. A half moon blazed overhead.

Nora put two fingers to her mouth and puffed. Lea handed her a cigarette.

"What the hell are these?" Nora asked.

"You wanted cigarettes," Lea replied matter-of-factly.

"My God, these are Gauloises." Nora pointed to the pack. "They're French, and expensive."

"They didn't cost me anything," Lea said.

"I want your connections," Nora said. "When we get out of here, we'll go into business together." She bent over, the cigarette in her mouth, and struck a match. The tip flared in an orange flash. She brought the flame up to the tobacco and inhaled deeply. The smoke fanned around her body and disappeared in a haze. She flipped the dead match into the air. It flew past the cornice and fell out of sight.

"Be careful," Teagan said. "You'll burn the place down." She looked at Lea. "How do you do it? The rest of us hardly get a decent meal. You've dined with the nuns and work outside the laundry." She pointed to the pack Lea clutched like gold. "And who gives you cigarettes? Aren't you afraid you'll get caught?"

Lea shook her head. "No. Everyone trusts me. I'm a good person." She rubbed her arms.

"Let's wrap up," Teagan said. "That's why I brought the blanket out." She tilted her head toward Nora. "Don't burn it with your fag or I'll be in deep." She handed the corners of the blanket to each of them and they huddled closer together.

"Yes, do tell," Nora said, and held out her cigarette in curled fingers, imitating a rich lady. She continued in a stuffy English accent, "Do give us an account of your black-market adventures."

"My stepfather smokes them. He only spends money on expensive cigarettes. I wanted him to quit."

Nora shook her head, amazed. "No wonder they didn't cost you anything—you stole them."

"Smoking's not good for him. He has a terrible cough."

"Where does your stepfather live?" Teagan asked.

"On a farm, west of Dublin," Lea said.

"I've only been west a couple of times, for a drive in the country," Teagan offered.

"I lived near Celbridge. Not much happens there, including

making a living." Lea stretched her long neck and looked up at the moon. After a few moments, she said, "My stepfather couldn't afford to keep me. I wasn't his flesh and blood, and I wasn't cut out for farming. He called me 'too fancy.' He talked to the parish priest, who told him to send me to The Sisters of the Holy Redemption. That was four years ago."

"Four years!" Teagan immediately regretted her exclamation.

Nora thrust her cigarette into her mouth and pulled the blanket over her head like a hood. "For God's sake, Teagan, you'll have us in the Penitent's Room. Everybody get under and keep quiet for a minute."

They huddled beneath the cover. Nora lifted the corner closest to her to let the smoke out.

Lea sputtered and coughed. "Those are nasty," she said, waving the smoke away.

"Like manna," Nora replied. "Now, keep quiet."

After a few minutes, Teagan removed the blanket from her head. The stars twinkled through a white haze surrounding the moon. She looked back, toward the window, to see whether anyone was there. No one stirred. "I think we're safe."

"Thank God," Lea said and waved her hands frantically in front of her face. "We're going to smell like smoke."

"Oh, don't complain." Nora inhaled with gusto, nearing the end of her cigarette. "Lea's not your real name, is it?"

She shook her head. "Sister Anne named me Lea. I hardly remember my real name it's been so long since I've used it."

Nora stared in disbelief. "Sure." She took another drag.

"My stepfather needed a man to help on the farm, so I was the one who got the boot."

Teagan thought about being taken from her own home. "Don't you miss it?"

"Sometimes, when I want to feed the ducks, or play with the sheep and goats. The air is fresh, and my stepfather is a good cook. He learned from my mother." She paused. "But nothing I did on the farm paid for my room and board. Here I can work on my *Book of Kells*."

"Are you an artist?" Teagan asked.

"I dabbled at the farm, but I didn't really try until I came here. I heard Sister Mary-Elizabeth and the Mother Superior talking about the *Book of Kells* and how beautiful it was. They had seen it. It came to me in a dream that night. God told me I should copy it and give it to them. That way, good things would come to me. So the next day I told Sister Mary-Elizabeth about my dream and she got me the supplies I needed." Lea stiffened with pride. "I'm working on 'Christ Enthroned.' My next picture's going to be of the Virgin and Child. Sister Anne is thrilled with my work and can't wait for it to be done. She said it will be 'the pride of Irish convents.'"

"That could take the rest of your life," Nora said.

"I'll be here. I like the convent. At the farm, I felt useless."

Nora groaned and wriggled closer to Lea. "I want to be sure I heard you, you eejit. I can't believe me ears." The red tip of her cigarette faded to black. She rubbed it against a tile and tossed it off the roof.

Teagan pulled the blanket tight around her shoulders. She imagined Sister Mary-Elizabeth, or one of the Magdalens, looking out the window. What a fright they would get from the scene—three disembodied heads sitting on the roof.

"You're fine if you toe the line," Lea said.

"Yeah, but what if we don't want to," Nora countered. "What if we want to get out? And where do you get off saying we'll be fine if we bow and scrape to the nuns? You don't get cigarettes by being nice to the Sisters."

"I could get more, but they might not be French. People do nice things for me because I'm nice to them. One of the deliverymen gave me chocolates because he thought I was a 'good girl.' I didn't encourage him, and I took them because it made him happy. He'd probably get me cigarettes if I asked for them."

Nora laughed. "Yes, you're a 'good girl,' but he probably wanted more."

Lea scoffed.

"Getting fags—almost anything except a Bible—is forbidden," Nora added. "You're going against the Sisters."

"No one's getting hurt. If I can make someone happy, it's worth it. Weren't you happy to get the cigarettes?"

Nora nodded. "I can't argue with that."

"My mother used to say, 'You can catch more ants with honey than you can with vinegar.' I can get candy if—"

Teagan cut Lea off with a "ssshhh." She looked toward the window and whispered, "I thought I saw someone."

They stared at it for a few minutes.

"We should go in," Teagan said. "We've stayed out longer than we should have."

Lea looked dreamily up to the sky. "It's so nice out. I don't want to go in."

"That's the problem," Nora whispered. "If this was anyplace else we could sit out here and smoke until we rotted. No, we have to go in because we have to get up at five in the morning for prayers and then spend the rest of the day doing laundry. You have it easy because of your *talent*. The rest of us suffer."

Lea smiled. "I was chosen by God, Nora, but I forgive you for mocking me." She gave the Gauloises to Nora.

Nora looked at the pack and then tossed it back to Lea. "Keep 'em. I don't want your forgiveness."

Lea looked hurt by Nora's words. Teagan patted her on the back. "Let's not fight. We need each other."

"I'll keep the cigarettes for you," Lea said. "You'll probably want one in a day or two."

Teagan lifted the blanket from her shoulders and the others did the same. She crawled toward the window. Looking through the glass, she saw a white nightgown speed away in the gloom. One of the Magdalens jumped into bed and pulled the covers over her head.

"I think we've been found out," Teagan said to Nora.

"Who?" Nora asked.

"In the middle, on the east wall. I think her name is Patricia."

"I'll take care of her," Nora said.

"Be nice and see what happens," Lea whispered.

"I have one question for you." Nora's voice wavered on the

verge of a hiss. "If I wanted to escape this prison, would you help me?"

Lea didn't back down; instead, she looked at Nora intently. "I want you to be happy. I like everyone."

"You didn't answer my question."

"Come on," Teagan said. "We don't have time to argue." She grasped the screen delicately, hoping that the hinges wouldn't squeak. They didn't. She held it up as Nora and Lea crawled inside.

When they were all in, Teagan got into bed. She spread out her gray blanket and gagged. Lea was right; it reeked of smoke. She kicked it off her, but it was hard to get the odor out of her nose. She opened the window a crack to let fresh air in. Instead of returning to bed, she walked down the room and looked at Patricia. The girl was asleep—or pretending to be. The other Magdalens seemed to be resting peacefully. There was nothing she could do now.

A few minutes later, as Teagan was about to drift off, Nora whispered, "I'm dying for a cigarette."

Lea tossed her the pack.

The next morning at breakfast, Nora made it her job to keep watch on Patricia. Her target was a slight girl with black hair and brown eyes, but who looked as if she could hold her own in a fight. Nora wondered if she was from North Dublin because she reminded her of girlfriends from Ballybough.

Patricia shot Nora a few knowing glances throughout the meal, taunting her with her blackmail-worthy knowledge. Nora didn't flinch.

One of the nuns, for no particular reason, had baked a large basket of rolls. They were a special treat greedily consumed by the Magdalens. Nora noticed that when the basket came to Patricia, the girl took one roll and then tipped the basket toward her lap. Although Nora couldn't see it plainly, she suspected that Patricia had pilfered several. The girl covered her lap with her napkin.

Good, Nora thought, *I've got her now.*

Teagan sat at the lace-mending table looking at the wide array of items that lay on top of it. She had not been there since her meeting with Father Matthew. She picked up a lacy circle that looked like a large coaster, white with filigree work, and her heart sank. *I will never be able to do this.* Several of the pieces looked like what her mother would have called "embroidery" and "crochet" work.

Sister Mary-Elizabeth had taken her to the old library room, after nearly a full day in the laundry, and told her to wait for Sister Rose. The old nun who had cut her hair was going to be her teacher.

The sun was still high enough in the late afternoon that a few rays filtered through the windows, catching the reflection of the motes, which swam in the air like white jewels. Teagan glanced at Lea, who drew the tip of her brush across her picture. As usual, her friend's lips trembled in silent prayer. She had taken no notice of Teagan and Sister Mary-Elizabeth when they arrived.

She opened a book from the large pile on the table. It was titled: *The History of Lace Making from 1500.* The other books, many with leather covers and musty-smelling pages, dealt with lace-making or mending, as well. She thumbed through several, with their detailed drawings and photographs of the varieties of lace, from needle- to machine-made. Apparently, Sister Rose was serious about her instruction.

She had liked history in school, but couldn't imagine being interested in mending lace, a tedious task at best. It seemed suited for a girl in the early 1800s, whose life consisted of working in a household. She imagined a young servant, sitting in the kitchen, huddled next to the stove, mending the garments of her mistress. The wife of her master, on the other hand, sat in her wing chair, warming herself before the hearth, reading the Bible or the latest novel she could get her hands on.

Her daydream was broken by Sister Rose, whose bony form appeared at the door. Her habit hung like a sack over her ancient arms and legs. The nun carried what looked like a blue pillow covered with a dizzying number of wooden bobbins. They hung by threads pinned to a swirling pattern of lace. She placed the pillow in front of Teagan. The nun was about to speak, when Sister Anne, frowning, swooped through the door like an angry crow.

"Sister," she said to the old nun, "your lesson will have to wait." The Mother Superior pointed to the door. "Please gather the other Sisters, except Ruth, and return here. Sister Mary-Elizabeth is on her way with Monica."

Teagan's heart thumped. *On her way with Monica?* Monica was Nora's assigned name. Something was terribly wrong if all the nuns were to be called to the old library except Sister Ruth, who was supervising the Magdalens in the laundry.

Sister Rose left without saying a word. The Mother Superior stepped toward Teagan as if she were treading upon a grave.

Sister Anne bowed her head. Her veil threw her face into shadow. "You have defied me. I told you I would administer punishment, if necessary. Now you'll see that I keep my promises."

Soon the nuns gathered at the door like a swarm of black flies. Most looked on in apprehension, as if transfixed by what was about to happen. Sister Anne pulled the rod from her long sleeve and slapped the desk.

Sister Mary-Elizabeth broke through the phalanx, holding Nora in front of her. Her friend looked determined, but with a glint of fear in her eyes.

"Lea, Teresa, and Monica, get in the middle of the room," Sister Anne ordered. Lea looked up from her work, but her expression was flat, as if what the Mother Superior said was of no concern.

Teagan joined Lea and Nora in the center. Together, they faced Sister Anne.

The nun pointed the rod at them. "You were on the roof last night." Before they could speak, she blunted any objection. "Don't try to deny it. I have a witness. One of you smoked a cigarette." Her eyes flashed and she stabbed the floor with the rod. "How dare you! You've endangered us all. The convent could have been destroyed by fire!"

She crept closer to them. Teagan shuddered as the Mother Superior's face contorted with rage.

"I can't send the three of you to the Penitent's Room. God knows, I can't send you to your parents, who, for good and holy reasons, don't ever wish to see you again." She tapped the rod against her palm. "No, *here* we work with love. A punishment should never leave a bruise or draw blood. To do so would defile the body and bring disgrace upon our Order. No, it is better to make a penitent realize their mistake through the love of Christ. To suffer as He suffered for our sins."

"Now, wait a feckin' minute," Nora said.

Sister Anne shoved the rod into Nora's chest and sent her stumbling backward.

"Unholy, do not soil our ears with your curses. Teresa, lie on the floor with your arms spread."

Teagan wanted to jump through the window and end it all. A simple crash through the glass, a plummet to the trench below, and this torture would be over. But what good would it do other than to give Sister Anne the satisfaction of her death?

A few of the nuns clucked at the girls' predicament, some giggled in nervous excitement. Many clutched the crucifixes that hung by their sides. Even Sister Mary-Elizabeth, the friendliest of the nuns, eyed her sternly.

She had no choice but to obey and lowered herself to the floor. The stone tiles were cold against her skin.

"Lie back, with your arms out, as our Lord would have done, nailed to the cross."

Teagan complied. Going to the roof was a mistake, and now they were all paying for it.

"Monica—one of the thieves—take your place to the right of Teresa, in the same position only lower."

Nora obeyed, but her eyes bubbled with hate.

Sister Anne placed Lea to the left in a similar position and then turned to the nuns. "Look, Sisters, what we have here. Their dresses hang like sackcloth, arms spread in supplication, bodies as stiff as the board they would be nailed upon. Imagine what our Lord endured to give us His holy love." She spread her arms like a great black bird. "It brings me no pleasure to hurt them, but the penitents must realize how they have hurt the Order. Such insubordination, such vain camaraderie, will not be tolerated from those who've sinned. The sinful bond among them must be broken."

One of the nuns spoke a quiet "Amen."

Sister Anne crossed herself. "Penance." She stood behind Teagan, then knelt near her face. "Do you know why you are here?" the Mother Superior asked. "You have hurt us, damaged us with your words and actions. You have tried us severely." She pointed the rod at Teagan, but addressed them all. "You will lie here, in the position of the Cross, until you learn your lesson. You will understand what Jesus suffered. You will not eat, nor drink, nor soil yourself." She brushed the rod near Nora's face. "When the evil has been removed from your spirit, you'll be able to join us. I do this out of love, so you will know Christ and His ways."

Teagan shifted her gaze to the left, but didn't move. Lea's eyes were closed, her mouth moving in silent prayer. Then she looked to the right, in time to see Nora spit at Sister Anne's feet.

The nuns gasped.

"Sister, get me a towel," the Mother Superior said to Sister Mary-Elizabeth. The nun did so quickly and wiped the spittle from the hem of Sister Anne's habit.

Teagan watched as the Mother Superior turned her attention to Nora. "You have much to learn," the nun said and withdrew a long straight pin from her sash. The thin silver tip descended toward Nora's palm.

Nora got up on her elbows. "Don't you dare!"

"Hold her hands against the floor." The Mother Superior barked the order at Sister Mary-Elizabeth.

Nora struggled briefly, but she was no match for the stout nun.

The Mother Superior traced the pattern of the cross over Nora's palms. "If I hated you, I would drive this into your hand to show you what Christ knew," Sister Anne said. "His persecutors reviled Him, they welcomed His suffering, and suffer He did. I don't want you to die a sinner. I want you to be resurrected into heaven."

A chorus of "Amens" went up from the nuns.

Sister Anne rose, replaced the pin in her sash, and clasped the crucifix by her side. "Sister, stay with them until their penance is through."

The nuns dispersed. Sister Mary-Elizabeth sat in a chair behind them, acting as their warden.

"Remember what I told you," Sister Anne called out. "I love you."

The Mother Superior's heels clicked in the hall until the sound disappeared.

"I hate her," Nora whispered.

Teagan didn't answer. She stretched out two fingers of her right hand to signify the "yes" they had devised in sign language.

Sister Anne closed the door to her office and prayed. *Why do these girls try me so?* Rehabilitation and penance were all she asked. *Why should it be so hard?* The memory she had tried to shake since July roared like hellfire into her mind. She flinched and lowered her head into her hands. There was nothing she could do to be rid of it. The room flashed into her mind: the crib, the baby's toys, the bed overflowing with blood where only days before . . . Yes, her sister was working on lace, just as Teresa would be during her years here.

My sister, my beloved sister, writhing in agony, filled with so much pain, the blood nearly burst forth from her brow. Why did it happen? How could so much evil be visited upon one person?

There were no answers for these questions. She lifted her head and stared at the door, knowing that above her three Magdalens were doing penance. Should she let them get up? *No!* They needed to *pay.* They needed to learn what obedience meant. Placing them in the form of the Crucifixion had given her a small amount of pleasure. Even Sister Rose had told her how beautifully the punishment was presented. She smiled, lifted by the thought.

She knew instinctively that Monica would be the last to come around. Stricter measures might be called for, more trips to the Penitent's Room, longer hours in the laundry, more vigils in the chapel for prayer. She would bend Monica to her will—for the greater good.

Daylight had fled, leaving her in the murk of dusk. She wanted to believe that nothing could be accomplished by dwelling on the past, but her mind wouldn't let go of the hatred. *More prayers. Prayer will solve my problems.* She rose from her desk and headed to the chapel to pray.

It would serve Sister Anne right if I peed on the floor, Nora thought. The room was growing dark. Sister Mary-Elizabeth had lit a candle rather than turn on the lights. Under her watch, no one had moved. Every now and then, Nora had heard a garble from Lea's direction—probably a prayer. She tapped her fingers silently on the floor trying to pass the time.

As night fell, someone stopped in front of the room. Nora couldn't see what had happened, but a silent communication flowed across the room.

A few moments later, Sister Mary-Elizabeth said, "All right, all of yeh, rise and shine." The nun slipped into her accent with a little too much humor and liveliness, Nora thought.

"It's about time," Nora said. "I need to go to the jacks."

"You're about to miss tea, so go, all of you and be quick about it. You'll get a bite—if you're good."

Teagan and Lea pushed themselves off the floor. Nora's elbows popped as she got up. Lea yawned and stretched as if she had been taking a nap. Teagan stretched her arms above her head and looked at her. Nora had never seen Teagan, eyes downcast and mouth pursed, look so depressed. They walked out of the library, Lea bringing up the rear.

"Don't tarry," Sister Mary-Elizabeth shouted after them. "I don't want to come looking for yeh. Ten minutes and then to eat."

They passed the room where the Magdalens ate. Several of the girls smirked at them.

"Are you all right?" Nora whispered to Teagan as they walked up the stairs.

Teagan shook her head and smoothed down her apron. "I've never been so humiliated—and by someone who claims to 'love' us." There was a desperate bitterness in her voice.

"She's a bitch," Nora said.

Teagan stopped on the landing. "There's more to it than that." Lea drew close. "She hates me and I don't know why. I can feel it. She wants more from me than penance. I can feel her cold soul. She'd just as soon see me dead."

Nora continued climbing with her friend to the next floor. "Well, your imagination's got the better of you. She might be a devil who brandishes a pitchfork, but why would she want you dead?"

"Her heart is hard because it's been broken," Lea piped up from behind.

Nora turned, eyes blazing. "And how do you know that? Come to your senses, Lea. I've got a broken heart, too, but I don't go 'round treating people like shit. Well . . . sometimes."

Nora stopped. "You ladies go to the jacks, I've got some unattended business to take care of." She sprinted down the hall and pushed the garret doors open a crack. No one was inside—all the Magdalens were still at tea.

She ran to Patricia's bed. She patted the pillow and lifted the mattress before she spotted the lumps under the blanket. As she'd suspected, Patricia had hidden the extra rolls she'd stolen at breakfast. Nora reached into her pocket and sprinkled a white powder over the rolls. She wiped her fingers on her apron and placed the rolls where she'd found them.

Dusting the excess powder from her hands, she joined Teagan and Lea in the jacks. "What a relief," she said as she pulled up her dress and sat down on the toilet. "Now to wash me hands and get something to eat."

"Sister Anne had the window nailed shut," Teagan whispered to Nora at bedtime. "I can't believe it. How would we get out of here if there was a fire?"

"I don't suppose anyone cares," Nora said and pulled the blanket over her. They said good night.

Later, Teagan awoke to the sounds of coughing and spitting. The Magdalens sat upright in bed, looking at the girl who had created all the commotion. It was Patricia, who, between bouts of gagging, cursed to the air.

Betty, one of the older Magdalens—a woman about fifty years old with gray hair—rushed to Patricia's bed. She could just make out the older woman's dim form bent over the bed. "My God, what's happening?" she asked in a voice loud enough to wake everyone in the room—if they hadn't been already.

"Someone tried to poison me," Patricia sputtered.

"Don't be daft," Betty said. "What are you talking about?"

Nora sat up in bed. Her friend was paying particular attention to the interaction between the two women.

"I'll tell you what I'm talking about." Patricia pulled something from under her sheet and thrust it toward Betty's face.

The garret doors opened and the light blazed on. A gasp rippled across the room.

"What nonsense is going on here?" Sister Mary-Elizabeth stood at the door in her nightgown. Teagan had never seen the nun out of her habit. She was as round as a plum, especially her face, which shone white under the band that held back her cropped black hair. "You're making enough noise to wake the dead." She walked toward Patricia, eyeing every girl as she went. "Believe me, you don't want to wake Sister Anne, who's very much alive. There'll be hell to pay after what happened this afternoon."

The nun arrived at Patricia's bed and ordered Betty back to her own. She held out her hand and Patricia gave her a partially eaten roll. "How did you get this?"

"She stole them," Nora said from across the room.

The Sister swiveled toward Nora. "That's enough out of you." The nun turned back to Patricia. "I want to hear the story from you."

"They fell into my lap at breakfast."

Gales of laughter swept the room.

The nun held up her hand. "Quiet! Quiet! I'm telling you that Sister Anne will have none of this. How many rolls do you have?"

Patricia dug under the sheet and pulled out two additional rolls. "Three." She pointed to the top of one. "Look, someone tried to poison me."

Sister Mary-Elizabeth took a roll, studied it, and then lifted it to her nose. "Borax. Well, you might have had to run to the jacks, but you wouldn't have died. This is laundry soap, put plainly." She looked around the room. "Who did this?"

Teagan knew who had put the soap on the rolls. She gave a sideways glance to Nora, who lifted her eyebrows slightly.

Patricia pointed at Nora. "She did it. I'm certain of it."

"And why would Monica put borax on your rolls?" Sister Mary-Elizabeth asked.

Patricia sighed. "Well . . . because."

"Go on. I'm waiting."

Patricia crossed her arms. "I've nothing more to say."

"I figured as much," the nun replied. "Give them to me."

Patricia handed them to the nun as if she were giving away a fortune.

"I'm not going to say anything more about this—and I'm *confident* this will never happen again. Much ado about nothing." She looked at Nora. "A bit of a power struggle going on? Now, for heaven's sake, go to bed and *be quiet*." Sister Mary-Elizabeth walked to the door and turned off the light.

The room was once again in darkness.

"There's nothing worse than a rat," Nora said aloud. "And you know what happens to rats." A murmur of consent filled the room and then died in the air. Someone said, "Life is tough enough without snitches." The Magdalens settled into their beds with a rustle of sheets and blankets.

Teagan tossed uncomfortably, knowing that Nora had put the soap on the rolls. She was amused and at the same time horrified by her friend's actions, which could have gotten her into deep trouble. However, her revenge made sense. Patricia had spotted them on the roof and reported them. That's how word had gotten to Sister Anne. But Patricia hadn't incurred the wrath of the Mother Superior and spent the afternoon on the floor of the old library, however unfair that might have been.

Teagan leaned toward Nora and whispered, "I can't believe you did that."

"No comment," Nora whispered back.

Teagan heard Nora say, "Oh Christ." She looked to her left to find Lea staring out the window.

Teagan got out of bed and stood behind her friend. "Now what?"

"It's Jesus," Lea said. Some of the other Magdalens heard Lea's pronouncement and rushed to the window.

Teagan, shoving with the others, stared out the glass. Slivers of light cut across the lawn, but the grounds were empty. "There's nothing out there," she said.

All the girls took a look and then, shaking their heads and muttering epithets about Lea's sanity, headed back to their beds.

Lea continued to stand at the window.

"I saw Him," Lea said. "Standing on the lawn. In the corner. He was surrounded by children."

"Sure, Lea." Nora took the index finger of her hand, swirled it around her ear, and shook her head.

The sign language was clear. Lea was going mad after four years at the convent. Teagan didn't want to suffer the same fate. The time had come to plan an escape from The Sisters of the Holy Redemption.

CHAPTER 7

——◆——

October lingered on with many days of gray skies and dreary rain.

Teagan was now entrenched in lace-mending, which she enjoyed much more than laundry work. The hours in the old library were pleasant compared to the sweat house conditions in front of the washbasins. Lea was an amiable, but silent work companion. Nora even expressed some jealousy of Teagan's "easy life." Sister Anne made sure that Nora worked extra hours and said additional prayers after their spat.

Teagan learned mending from the able hand of Sister Rose. The old nun's fingers were gnarled and knobby with age, but still nimble. Sister Rose taught her how to choose the appropriate materials, thread a bobbin, make stitches, and perform other feats with a needle. Her desk was now crowded with scissors, thread, pattern books, and the tools she needed for the trade.

Even Sister Anne stopped by from time to time to study her mending. The Mother Superior never said much, but when she did, it was to point out flaws. Rather than engage the nun, she nodded her head and asked for forgiveness for her sloppy work. Sister Anne acknowledged her contrition with a smirk and a quick exit.

While she worked, she often daydreamed of her parents, her mother in particular. She wondered if her mother spent long days in the living room staring at her Chinese porcelain, or on the bed crying. Her father would be at work on weekdays, leaving her mother at home, except when she left the house to play bridge. It occurred to her that her mother would have to explain her absence. What would Shavon tell her card-playing friends when they asked about her? The ridiculous came to mind. Was she murdered? Had she been kidnapped? Abducted by space aliens?

Of course, her father wouldn't have to account for anything. He would never have to bring up the subject at work, or with his friends at the pub. She could hear him saying, "She's fine," to his Guinness-swilling buddies, if the subject was ever broached. Perhaps a few eyebrows might be raised at church, but the good parishioners of St. Eusebius knew how to keep a secret. Only the most brazen would be bold enough to touch upon so delicate a subject. Perhaps her mother would tell her friends that she was in staying in New York City with her aunt Florence and her rich doctor husband. Yes, her mother could make the most of it if she wished, bragging to her friends about what a good life her daughter was living in America's most vibrant city. Teagan could only wish her life had produced such a fairy tale, as she mended a tear in the white lace sleeve of a dress.

One night, as they had other times when it was possible, she and Nora discussed how they would escape. No easy plan came to mind. They talked so softly they were sure even Lea, in the next bed, couldn't hear. Teagan scrunched in the corner of the eave, as close to Nora's ears as she could get.

"I've tried to make a few friends with the deliverymen," Nora said, "but they're in and out so quick—hardly time to flirt. Even with me extra hours." She turned on her side facing Teagan. "I think Sister Ruth has cut back on her drinking. Maybe the *Mother* caught her napping. Now she's like a cat stalking a mouse—all eyes and ears. Hardly anything gets past her."

Teagan sighed. "I don't have a plan at all." She shook her head. "I sit at my desk, mending lace, and think about my ma and da and Cullen. I even dream about them, and no answers come. I keep hoping something will guide me. Maybe we need to pray for our release."

Nora frowned. "It was God that got us here in the first place."

I wouldn't go looking to Him for help." She pointed to Lea, identifiable only as a narrow mound under her blanket. "If she wasn't so nuts, I'd say she was our best chance. But I don't trust her. She probably knows every nook and cranny of this place and the location of the keys to every lock." Nora smacked her lips. "I can almost taste getting out of here. There's got to be a way. We'll find it."

"I hope so. Sometimes I want to give up and be like Lea or Sister Mary-Elizabeth—accept what life has dealt me. Then I come to my senses, and I want out of here more than anything else in the world."

One of the Magdalens stirred in the middle of the room. Teagan hoped it wasn't Patricia, although the girl had presumably learned her lesson from Nora's revenge.

"Better be off," Teagan said. She grasped Nora's hand and said good night.

One Monday in early November, a light rain, mixed with flecks of snow, fell upon the convent's grounds. Teagan watched the white flakes fall as she scrubbed stains at the laundry basin. One of the Magdalens was sick with a bad cold, and she had been assigned to take her place. Nora was nearby working at one of the washers. Sister Ruth varied their duties because she felt it was good for the girls to "learn as much as you can."

Nora had been right in her assessment of the supervising nun. She was more attentive than usual when the vans arrived carrying their cargo. Except for an occasional look at a magazine, she kept her eyes on the girls. She checked the laundry bags at the door, so the men got only a quick look at the Magdalens before heading back to work. The return laundry was handled much the same. The girls hauled the bags to the hall. Sister Ruth watched as the men picked them up, limiting any interaction with the girls.

About ten in the morning, Sister Mary-Elizabeth walked into the laundry and tapped Teagan on the shoulder. "You're popular," the nun said with mild sarcasm. "Another visitor." She motioned to Sister Ruth, who nodded her assent.

Sister Mary-Elizabeth smiled, but Teagan declined to join in her good mood. "I'll withhold judgment until I find out who it is." Unpleasant memories of her meeting with Father Matthew lingered in her head.

The nun's smile broadened. "It's a young man accompanied by an Anglican priest."

The blood drained from her head. She held on to Sister Mary-Elizabeth's arm as she came to the realization that her visitor might be Cullen Kirby, her boyfriend whom she hadn't seen in four months.

The Sister patted her hand and said, "He's a nice-looking boy with reddish-brown hair."

It had to be Cullen. She was excited now, the most she had been since her conversation with Father Mark at the parish house. She blushed in front of the Sister. *I must look a fright!* She looked at her rough-worn hands, chapped and red from work. She patted her hair and smoothed her apron.

The nun sensed her eagerness and led her up the stairs to the old library. Teagan braced herself as she entered the room. As usual, Lea was working on her book. A tall man in a dark overcoat stood near the drawing table admiring her work. Sister Anne stood in front of another man sitting by the lace table. The Mother Superior turned as Teagan entered the room, revealing Cullen.

Teagan wanted to rush to his side and hug him, but Sister Anne's stern expression tempered her desire. She spoke harshly to her: "I've only agreed to this meeting because the Reverend Conry is in this room as an emissary of the Anglican Church."

The man standing near Lea turned and smiled at Teagan. "Happy to meet you, Miss Tiernan."

Sister Anne frowned. "She should be addressed by the name given to her by the good Sisters of the Holy Redemption—Teresa."

The Reverend Conry smiled at the Mother Superior. "Of course. My mistake." Teagan surmised there was no love lost between the two.

"I think fifteen minutes should be more than enough time to

complete your business," the Mother Superior said to Cullen. "Sister Mary-Elizabeth will be back to see you out." She strode from the room along with the other nun, her habit brushing against Teagan.

"Pay no attention to me," Reverend Conry said to her. "I'm fascinated by what this young woman is doing—imagine duplicating our national treasure!" He took off his coat and wandered back to Lea's table.

Cullen got up from his seat and extended his hand. He was being cautious, Teagan thought. She wouldn't have been surprised if the Mother Superior had laid down rules for their meeting.

Teagan shook his hand and reveled in the warmth of his touch, a shocking surprise on the cold day. Sadness clawed at her as she took her seat at the table. "I'm sorry you have to see me this way." Tears stung her eyes.

Cullen grasped her hand.

She sobbed as his fingers touched hers. "Please, don't. I'm afraid I'll get you into trouble. And I don't want you to remember me this way." She drew her hands away from his and hid her face.

"I don't care about that old busybody," Cullen said. "My God, Teagan, what have they done to you?" He forced the words out, nearly gasping for air. "You're so pale, you look weak. Are you okay?"

She nodded, lowered her hands, and looked at him. He retained the sandy red hair, the ruddy blush, the smattering of freckles on his cheeks that she remembered so well. However, he looked older now, more mature, his brown eyes steely with confidence and his mouth firmly set. It wasn't hard for her to imagine that he was her protector—a prince who had come to rescue her from the wicked stepmother of fairy tales.

He reached inside his coat and withdrew a small package wrapped in Christmas paper. "This is for you," he said, and handed it to her. "From your mother. She thought it would be easier if I smuggled it in. It wouldn't have to pass inspection from the Sisters."

Cellophane tape held the triangular folds on the paper in place. She raised her index finger to open it and her hand shook.

"It's all right," Cullen said. "They're early presents. Your mother told me what was inside. Go ahead." He looked as if he wanted to reveal more, but frowned instead, as if he was scared his words might upset her.

Teagan dug into the package, ripping off the paper. She wondered what to do with it, concerned that the Mother Superior would confiscate the gift. "She doesn't know you're delivering this?"

Cullen grinned. "No. I kept it hidden in my coat. It wasn't easy."

She peeled off the last of the paper, took a pair of scissors, and cut the tape that held the box shut. It popped open and revealed the transistor radio her father had given her, along with a rolled piece of silk. A small earphone lay next to the radio. She could listen to it while falling asleep and not disturb the other Magdalens. Teagan lifted the silk. A neck scarf imprinted with a pattern of red poppies on a green background unfurled before her eyes. She carefully folded it and put it in her pocket.

"Please thank my mother," she said, her voice cracking. "I'm going to hide my presents so no one can get them."

"I'll thank her. Your mother told me to put fresh batteries in the radio. They should last a few months." Cullen looked at the Reverend Conry. He was standing on the other side of Lea now, watching her draw. Cullen moved his chair and leaned closer to Teagan.

She could feel the heat from his body. He smelled clean, not like laundry soap, but of freshly scrubbed skin. She wanted to touch him, to huddle close to him, feel him next to her.

"Do you know why I'm here?" she asked him.

He lowered his head for a second, but then lifted it and looked at her free from pity. No priest, no nun, no boyfriend, not even her father and mother had looked at her the way Cullen was looking at her now. His love traveled from him into her heart. She grasped the table to keep from swooning.

He nodded. "I heard the rumor, but I don't believe it. My

father told me there were nasty words being spread about you. He said the rumor began with your da at the pub. . . ."

"My da is a drunk," she said. Maybe she had been wrong about her father's ability to keep a secret. "Obviously, he has no inhibitions at the pub, but he can barely speak to my mother." She looked down at the radio, remembering the last time she had used it. The song "I Can't Stop Loving You" came into her head.

"Let's pretend we're holding hands," Cullen said. "Touch the ends of my fingers." He reached his right hand across the books and the lacework that lay on the table.

Teagan extended her hand so the tips of her fingers touched his. A charge coursed through her body, and she relished the thrill of it.

"Your mother contacted me," he continued. "We met in secret. The whole business is crazy, but I was willing to do anything to find out what happened to you. I felt like a spy. My mother and father don't even know I'm here. I skipped morning classes." He swirled his fingertips over hers. "I wanted to see you so much that I went to Reverend Conry and asked him if he would help me, because I knew I couldn't get in here by myself. I told him the truth—your mother wanted me to give you a Christmas gift and your father wouldn't let her. I didn't tell him about the rumor. I don't think you need to worry about Anglican circles. I'm doing an early Christmas favor. I had to tell the Reverend something, sweeten the pot for him. Frankly, I think he was more interested in getting a good look inside the convent than in my visit. If I were eighteen, I'd get you out of here—at least I'd try."

Her heart raced, knowing Cullen had taken a huge risk for her.

He inched his fingers over hers. "I heard something happened with a priest. The rumor going 'round is that a girl threw herself at Father Mark. Because you were sent away, you became that girl. One of my mates heard you had sex with him."

Teagan shuddered and withdrew her hand. *Sex?* The joy she'd experienced a few moments before fell away in a dizzying spiral. The rumor was uglier than she had imagined, and her suspicions about why she had been sent to the convent were confirmed. She looked at Cullen. "It's not true—I never had sex with Father Mark." She wanted to say that she had never even thought of such a thing, but that wasn't true. "You can't believe my father or any of his drunken friends."

Cullen's lips parted in a half smile. "I never believed it from the beginning." His smile drifted away. "I didn't know where you were. No one would say anything. It was like you died and there was no burial. It was awful."

She looked at the lace-mending tools spread out across the table. "It's been terrible here. This is my life, but I'm going to get out."

Sister Mary-Elizabeth appeared at the door and addressed them. "I'm sorry, but you'll have to leave now. Teresa is needed at her duties."

Cullen nodded, got up from the table, and whispered, "I'll come back for you. Count on it."

Teagan smiled, but her heart wasn't in it. Any hope for happiness seemed far away.

The Reverend Conry walked toward them. He extended his hand and said, "It was nice to meet you"—he lowered his voice—"Teagan."

"Thank you, Reverend," she said. "You, as well."

The nun escorted them out, leaving her alone with Lea. She hated her strange friend at that moment. *Look at her, scribbling on her papers as if nothing in the world is wrong!* She wanted to wrench the brush from her hand and smear it across her precious "Christ Enthroned." What good was her artwork? What difference would it make to the world? It was nothing but busywork, concocted to appease the Mother Superior and keep Lea out of the laundries.

Sister Mary-Elizabeth reappeared and motioned for Teagan to follow her back to the laundry. Teagan placed a large piece of lace over the box, with the gifts still in it, and brushed past the nun. The stout nun gasped in surprise and clambered after her. Teagan darted down the stairs toward Sister Anne's office.

Sister Mary-Elizabeth trundled after her. "Come back!"

Teagan neared the door.

"Teresa! Don't!"

Sister Anne lifted her head as she rushed in. The nun gave her a cruel smile, as if she enjoyed seeing her penitents crumble under intoxicating draughts of freedom. She raised her hand, signaling her to stop. "Whatever you have to say, I've no time to listen. Don't waste your breath."

Teagan slammed the top of the desk with her hands, sending the *LOVE* blocks skittering across its top.

The Mother Superior's eyes flared with anger. "How dare you! Another outburst and it'll be the Penitent's Room for you—overnight and without tea."

Teagan stepped back from the desk, as Sister Mary-Elizabeth rushed in behind her. After a few deep breaths, she said, "You're holding me through a veil of lies fabricated by a priest." She tried to remain calm. Maybe Sister Anne would listen if she showed some restraint. "Let me clear my name. I've done nothing wrong. Let me phone my mother, it's the least you can do."

"Sit," Sister Anne ordered.

Teagan took a seat in front of the desk.

"Sister Mary-Elizabeth, leave us and close the door. I'll return Teresa to you in a few minutes." The Mother Superior repositioned the *LOVE* blocks as the other nun slipped out of the office. Sister Anne folded her hands.

"Hear me out," the Mother Superior said. "Your parents want nothing to do with you. I have papers signed to that effect."

Teagan started to object, but thought better of it. She knew her mother missed her and wanted to see her, although the letter did ask for her repentance. If she showed Sister Anne the gifts as proof of her mother's concern, she was certain they would be taken away.

"I have it in writing, and by word, that you are here because you seduced a priest. You had carnal thoughts regarding him, which led to actions—"

"What actions?"

The Mother Superior held up her hand. The sleeve slipped from her wrist, revealing the underside of her arm. Red slashes cut horizontally across her white skin. Sister Anne grappled with her habit. She glared at Teagan, daring her to defy her again. "Touching, initiating intimate conversations, inducing erotic thought . . ."

Teagan blanched at the Mother Superior's words, but refused to cower; instead she said, "If I must, I'll go to every authority I can to secure my release from The Sisters of the Holy Redemption."

Sister Anne laughed. "Who would take the word of a Magdalen over that of a priest? The Archbishop? The Holy Father? Write to the Pope, see how far you get. And in case the thought has crossed your mind, don't try to escape. You'll have no place to go, no one will hide you. When you're found—and you will be found—the Guards will return you to the convent. You'll be back, but in worse shape than when you left." She pointed to the *LOVE* blocks on her desk. "Once you stop struggling, life will go much more smoothly."

Something snapped inside her—a distinct *pop* and the world went red. She grasped the arms of her chair, for what she really wanted to do was crawl across the desk and strangle the Mother Superior. She forced herself to remain sitting long enough that her vision began to clear. Sister Anne's form reappeared surrounded by a reddish haze. Despite the Mother Superior's admonishment, she would write the letters, and if those failed, she would escape with Nora.

Sister Anne leaned forward and, in a chilly voice, said, "Your attitude is atrocious. Back to work."

A series of loud knocks interrupted them. They had an urgency, as if the matter could not wait.

"Come in!"

Sisters Mary-Elizabeth and Ruth, looking pale and drawn, stood at the door.

"What's wrong?" Sister Anne asked.

Sister Ruth stared at the floor. "It's Monica, Holy Mother."

"Well, go on," Sister Anne said, exasperated.

"She's gone," Sister Mary-Elizabeth said. "She's escaped." Sister Anne hissed and sank back in her chair.

A wave of despair, like a cold dampness, washed over Teagan. She brought her hands to her face. Her best friend at the convent, the one most likely to escape with her, had vanished. Now she was alone and, worst of all, she had doubts that Nora would ever fulfill her promise to return. She sat, silently, shaking in her chair.

CHAPTER 8

Everything around her was gray. She couldn't believe what she had done. She'd seized the opportunity, taken the chance, and now she was—she didn't know exactly where—on the byways of Dublin.

Nora imagined Sister Ruth's shame, Sister Anne's anger at her escape. The Mother Superior would be furious with Sister Ruth, who had drifted off reading a magazine when the hotel delivery van arrived. It was one of those Hollywood gossip magazines, filled with handsome movie stars and buxom starlets in glittering low-cut gowns. *What I wouldn't give to be there now—away from Dublin, away from me stupid ma and da, giving Pearse the two-finger salute across the Atlantic. Think of it! On the Pacific shore, drinking champagne and smoking cigarettes, having a date with an actor who was starring in a picture. There must be millions of them to choose from.*

The van hit a pothole. The jolt knocked Nora's head against a shelf. She stifled a cry, hoping to keep her presence a secret. She knew the driver didn't see her sneak inside. The tablecloth she'd pulled over herself slipped, allowing her to see the road out the rear windows.

Nora gave herself a mental pat on the back. How kind she had been to step up and help when Sister Ruth was indisposed. The nun had been strict lately, but this mistake was going to cost her. Nora had put a finger to her lips and urged the driver not to wake the slumbering Sister Ruth. "She's had a rough night," she told the short man with thinning hair, who looked bored with everything around him, including the Magdalens. "Female trouble." The man was unmoved. Perfect, Nora thought, he couldn't care less about the goings-on at the laundry.

As Sister Ruth snoozed and the others went about their business, they ignored Nora when she helped the man pull the return laundry down the hall and onto the truck. He was happy for the hand. All she asked for in return was a cigarette, even though she had Lea's stashed in her apron pocket. He gave her one at the delivery door, and when he climbed into the cab, she opened the back, crawled in, and hid under a clean tablecloth. The cab was separated from the rear of the van by a metal partition. He could neither see nor hear her.

From its movement, she knew the van had turned left from the gate. That was good, because it was headed north, toward her home. She'd heard Mr. Roche, the old caretaker, say goodbye. Now that she was a safe distance away, she planned to get out of the van, before it made any more stops. Sister Anne would have the Guards searching for her within minutes of the discovery of her escape.

The day was draped with rain and spits of snow. The gray cocoon formed by the tablecloth was oddly comforting, almost like being in a warm cave. She peered through the windows. Unfamiliar buildings swept by on both sides of the road. The van stopped. She heard the driver cough.

The vehicle began moving again, then turned right and swung Nora back toward the shelf. He was now headed east, toward the sea. Time to get out.

She stuffed the tablecloth in a bag, crawled to the rear, and waited for the van to stop.

When it did, she opened the doors and stepped out, much to the surprise of the driver behind, who honked his horn and smiled broadly. She closed the doors, ran to the nearest footpath, and, looking up, found a road sign mounted on a wall. She was in a residential tract on Northbrook Road, an area of older homes with wide stairs and arched doorways. Instinct told her to hurry back in the direction from which she had come. When she was a good distance from the van, she slowed down. The cold air bit at her, but it was good to breathe outside, away from the stifling atmosphere of the convent.

She reached Charlemont, a busy road with residences and some businesses. She peered in windows, trying to act nonchalant, but people were staring at her. *Eyes. Eyes everywhere.* Everyone was looking at her—a girl in a plain gray dress covered by a white muslin apron. *And, my hair.* What must everyone think of her prison-maid bob? The few women who had ventured out in the cold carried umbrellas and wore heavy coats to stave off the elements. Their hairdos were perfect. Pert cuts with tips curled behind the ears, or layers of hair piled upon their heads. She shivered and rubbed her palms over her arms. She hadn't had time to grab a coat during her quick escape. A blast of wind flung rain against her body.

The realization of what she'd done hit her. She was without money, without a change of clothes, and a good distance from home. She darted into an alley, plastered herself against a damp wall, and took a few deep breaths.

Teagan. Teagan would hate her, as well, thinking that she had broken her promise. However, she'd made a vow and she would keep it. How and when that would happen she didn't know.

Sirens sounded in the distance, and she kept out of sight in the alley. Perhaps they were already after her. She peered down the road and spotted two Guard cars weaving through traffic, blasting their way past her. She waited a few more minutes before stepping out of the alley and then walked on the footpath that led north.

People stared at her. A few snickered; most raised their eyebrows in derision as if they had seen a circus freak. Then she saw a man sitting next to an iron grate for warmth. His legs stuck out into the sidewalk, forcing passersby to step over them. He wasn't old—probably in his twenties—but his face shone beet red from drink and the cold air. She wondered if he might be drunk and approached him tentatively.

"Pardon," she said.

He pushed his wool cap back and stared at her with drowsy, bloodshot eyes.

"I'm in need of food and a change of clothes," Nora said. "Is there a mission nearby?"

In a thick brogue, he answered, "Yer in luck, me lay-dee." He pointed north, gave her a few simple directions, and then asked for money. Nora laughed, not in condescension, but at the irony of his request. She was as broke as he was.

She left him sitting there, his head lolling. A few blocks away she found the mission.

The printed sign over the door read HOME AND HEARTH in bright yellow letters, cheerful on the raw day. The building was narrow but long, and near the back, Nora saw a score of men and women eating at a table. She opened the door and a bell overhead tinkled.

A woman with an angular face and silver hair looked up from her tasks. She neither smiled nor gave a greeting. She looked at Nora as if she was expecting her next crop of indigents to walk in the door at any minute. The shelter was warm and smelled of damp coats curling by the steam pipes. The aromatic odors of a spicy beef stew also drifted through the air.

The woman sat stoically behind her desk. Something in her eyes gave Nora a chill. It was hard to tell what it was, but if she had to guess it was recognition. The woman knew, or suspected, where she came from. Only her need for a change of clothing kept her from running out the door.

The woman dropped her pencil on a pile of papers and eyed her with distrust. "May I help you?"

"I ran into a man down the road. We're both homeless and he directed me here."

"Really?" the woman countered. "How long have you been homeless?"

"Going on four months."

The woman opened a card file on her desk. "What's your name?"

Almost without thinking, Nora said, "Monica." There was no reason to give her real name.

The woman tapped the file. "Last name?"

"Tiernan." She said it straight-faced and with no hint of guilt.

"Monica Tiernan." She flipped through the file, stopping at the "T" and inspected the cards behind the divider. "I have no record of a Monica Tiernan. I know every needy person in the neighborhood. We make it our business to know everyone, you understand. We don't serve those of low moral character."

Nora understood the implication. Home and Hearth was no sanctuary for drug dealers, drunks, pimps, prostitutes, or others of questionable morals like the Magdalens.

"Oh, believe me," Nora said. "I'm of high moral character, just fallen on hard times. Me parents died and I lost me home." The truth of her statement was enough to bring a teary glaze to her eyes. Nora hoped the woman would notice.

"Do you have identification?"

"None," Nora replied. "Not even a bag to put anything in."

"That's an unusual dress you're wearing," the woman said.

"Found it and the apron in an alley not long ago. It was better than what I had on, and warmer, too, which is the reason I'm here. I need a change of clothes and I'd like to eat a bite."

"Where did you find this clothing?"

"On Northbrook Road, not far from here."

The woman pursed her lips and handed Nora a card. "Fill this out. We need some information for our mission. You're welcome to food. I'll look for clothes. I think we might have something in your size."

As she filled out the card, Nora made up the answers to the questions as she went along, all the time keeping an eye on the woman. There was only one telephone in the room that she could see, and it was on the front desk. She feared the woman might call the Guards.

The woman returned with her arms piled with underthings, a plain blue dress, and a warm gabardine coat. Nothing about the outfit was fashionable, but she accepted it gratefully. Everything she wore could now be changed, except for her shoes, the black flats the Magdalens wore. They weren't really suitable for the weather, but they would get her by until she could find a suitable pair.

"You can change in the ladies' room in back," the woman said, "then have something to eat."

"Thank you," Nora said, and exchanged her card for the clothes. The woman took it, sat again at her desk, and read the information.

On her way to the ladies', the powerful smell of the stew called to her stomach. She opened the door to the toilet, and kept it slightly ajar as she changed. She left her old clothes in the corner. Through the crack, Nora saw another woman, who looked as if she worked at the mission, approach the desk. The two looked over the card and conferred.

Nora took a few minutes to change, making sure to take the cigarettes from her apron. Unsure when her next meal would come, she scooped up a large bowl of stew and a piece of bread. She sat with other men and women, but said nothing as she ate, positioning herself so she could watch the two women.

As Nora gobbled up her meal, the second woman left the desk, seemingly satisfied by her conversation with the woman in charge. An old man in a shabby coat sat next to Nora, slurping his soup and chomping bread with dentures, which slipped in and out of his mouth. Two one-pound notes stuck out of his coat pocket. They would be so easy to lift, she thought.

She eyed the notes and then moved her hand toward the man, making sure no one was watching. The woman at the desk fiddled with her pencil, never giving her a look.

She touched the top of the notes, feeling the woven texture of the money. The man shifted and she withdrew her hand. Seconds later, she pulled the money out in a quick move and transferred it to her gabardine coat. *This will get me a taxi home. Forgive me, but I need this more than you do.* She knew that might be a lie; however, considering the hand that her parents and God had dealt her lately, petty theft and guilt were the least of her concerns.

The woman at the desk dialed the telephone.

Nora spooned the remainder of the soup into her mouth and finished her bread. Instead of feeling warm satisfaction, she froze in fear at what the woman might be doing. Was she calling the Guards? Did she suspect Nora was a Magdalen? Rather than risk being taken back to the convent, she decided to get out. Her stomach was full enough.

She stood up, leaving her bowl behind, and rushed to the woman. "Excuse me, can I use the phone before you make that call?" She thrust out her arms, seeking pity. "I need to call my aunt. She might take me in!"

The woman put her palm over the mouthpiece. "Can't you see I'm using it? You'll have to wait a few minutes. Sit down. Are you sure you've had enough to eat?"

"More than enough," Nora said and then bolted for the door.

"Stop!" The woman dropped the telephone and rushed after her.

Nora turned north toward the city, running as fast she could. The woman screamed at her to come back. "I know what you are! You're a dirty, filthy Magdalen! I've called the Guards on you. They'll get you!"

The woman's voice faded away as Nora ran. She turned a corner to flee from Charlemont and, panting, collapsed on the stairs of a brick home. The day was growing darker, an ashen sky shifting from slate to black. Behind her, the warm glow of lights filled the windows. How wonderful it would be to have a home again, to feel the true warmth of a family—to experience the love she never felt she had—to be together on St. Stephen's Day. To be secure.

She clutched her coat and wrapped it tightly around her neck. Tears gathered, but she was determined not to let them fall. Rather, she pushed them back and let the anger swell within her to drive her forward. She would return home, face her parents, and make them take her back. She hadn't been the best child growing up, but she didn't deserve this. If they'd only listen to reason and not brand her as a whore, she'd repent and live like a good girl.

She walked on, staying close to the footpaths in case she was spotted by the Guards, but the greater the distance she traveled from the mission, the less she feared being captured. Soon, she was close to Charlemont again and headed north toward the River Liffey. A taxi sat on a corner, exhaust smoke billowing in gray clouds from the pipe. She fingered the notes in her pocket and then opened the back door. She crawled inside and said, "Ballybough."

The driver nodded and pulled away from the curb. She leaned back in the seat, enjoying the warmth, watching the buildings flow past her.

I am so alone. And no one cares whether I live or die.

Sister Anne fought against the rage building inside her. How many times would she have to kneel in prayer to expiate the sins of the Magdalens? How would God punish them? He would not be as magnanimous as she. Kneeling, she placed her elbows on the bed. They sank into the soft coverlet her mother had given her years before she entered the convent. It always reminded her of home and the beautiful things her mother and sister could craft with their hands. She hadn't been as gifted.

Jesus, on the Cross, looked down on her with His wooden eyes. *Oh Lord, hear my prayer.* The silence in her head also reminded her of home, of the father who had deserted them after her sister was born, the mother who scraped, saved, and struggled to keep the family clothed and fed. Winters were often harsh, sometimes with little to eat and no heat to keep the family warm.

The sleeves of her habit slipped down her arms, the red scars revealing a history of painful suffering inscribed in flesh. How easy it would be to walk across the room to the bureau, open the top drawer, and withdraw the blades that had been her friends for so long. It had been several months since she had cut herself; she thought she had conquered the obsession that thrilled her, and at the same time, robbed her body of will. She deserved to be cut. The feeling, she suspected, was much like that of heroin addicts, who slipped into an endless lethargic maze of highs and lows, knowing they couldn't escape the drug.

She clenched her hands and prayed harder, hoping for an answer. The question of what God would do sat like a boulder upon her soul. But this time, after a few minutes, a confident voice in her head told her what to do. How did Satan tempt Jesus in the wilderness? *You must offer them something and then take it away. He offered our Lord all the kingdoms of the world and their splendor.* That was the answer. They must refuse the offer, but still they would pay. *I must teach them a lesson about the consequences of sin and its effect on their salvation. The wages of sin is death.*

A sudden fury raged inside her about Monica's escape. She rushed from her bedroom and called for Sisters Mary-Elizabeth and Ruth. They would aid her. She found them eating with the other nuns in the private room apart from the Magdalens. The anger in her face must have shocked them, for the nuns both jumped from their seats and ran to her.

"Gather the girls and take them upstairs," Sister Anne commanded.

"They've not finished eating," Sister Mary-Elizabeth said, wiping a few crumbs from her mouth with her napkin.

"Just do as I say. Bring a plate of warm biscuits from the kitchen, a candle, and matches. See if Sister Constance has baked any of her gingersnaps."

Sister Mary-Elizabeth wrinkled her pudgy face.

She was shocked, Sister Anne thought. *Well, they'll be more shocked when they find out what I have in mind.*

The nuns wasted no time. Habits billowing behind them, they flew to the room where the Magdalens were eating. Sister Mary-Elizabeth shouted, "Everyone out. Follow the Mother Superior."

Sister Anne stood near the door, gauging the girls' expressions. *Teresa has the look of a hunted animal. Good.*

The others dropped their utensils and, eyeing the Mother Superior, got up without speaking and filed into a single row.

"Upstairs," Sister Anne ordered and led the way. "Now!"

The Magdalens sprinted up the steps to the third floor with Sister Ruth following behind. The Mother Superior raised her hand, and the girls stopped in the hall between their sleeping quarters and the toilet. This lesson would be brilliant, a living parable of good and evil. She instructed them to stand single file and then walked down the line, judging, hoping to ascertain who might have participated in Monica's escape. The girls were mum. There were no expressions of remorse or guilt, only anxiety manifested in their clenched fists and tight faces.

The Mother Superior spoke in a measured tone to reinforce the punishment they were about to receive. "Monica has left The Sisters of the Holy Redemption without permission. Did any of you have a hand in this?" A gasp rose from the group. Most of the Magdalens looked down at their feet. She gazed down the line. No one raised a hand.

Sister Mary-Elizabeth arrived carrying a full plate of warm ginger biscuits, the candle, and matches. The nun took her place by Sister Ruth, who also stared at the floor. Under Sister Ruth's watch, Monica had escaped. Sister Anne would deal with her later.

"I hope for your sake you are telling the truth," Sister Anne said, "in the name of our Lord, because if I find any of you've helped this penitent in her escape, your punishment will be strict and severe." She opened her arms as if to welcome them back to the flock. "But even if none of you helped Monica, there is a lesson to be learned." *They look like lost dogs.* The voice prodded her. *Get on with it. Let them know how sinners are punished.*

"Our Lord's followers were ostracized, punished for their loyalty and devotion. Many of you may think your life unfair, your trials as a penitent undeserved. Nothing could be further from the truth. The Lord died, with love on His lips, for your sins. I want you to know that love."

She took the biscuits from Sister Mary-Elizabeth and walked down the line, holding the plate under each girl's nose. Some of them groaned as the warm odor of baked ginger entered their nostrils.

"Who among you would rather have one of these than listen to me talk about love and the graces of our Lord?"

Without hesitation, Patricia, the girl who had stolen the rolls, grabbed one of the biscuits. The others recoiled, astonished by her action. Lea grabbed Patricia's wrist and tried to force the prize back on the plate.

"No, I'm starving," Patricia said. "I didn't get to finish me meal."

Sister Anne squeezed Patricia's fist until the biscuit crumbled in her palm and fell in pieces to the floor. She tilted the plate and, one by one, crushed them under her feet.

Patricia's chest heaved. "It's not right, to make us suffer."

"You have no willpower," Sister Anne said. "All will be punished because one has sinned. Our Lord knew He must give up all temptations from Satan to attain heaven. You have failed." The girls watched her as they stood in line in the hall.

"Do you know how hell has been depicted over the centuries?" She directed the question at Patricia, but she wanted all of the Magdalens to learn the answer. The girls watched her every move and stood like statues in the hall. Patricia wiped tears away and shook her head. "By fire and by ice," she continued. "You'll experience it tonight because of my love for your salvation." She pointed to the candle that Sister Mary-Elizabeth held. "Hell is either eternal fire or deathly cold. There will be no prayers tonight, only penance, because one of us has lost her way. Sister Mary-Elizabeth, light your candle and hold it out." The nun did as she was told. "Each of you will place your hand over the flame until you feel the tortures of hell. Then you will strip off your clothes and plunge into icy waters." She pointed to the showers. "Sister Ruth, make sure the water is cold and the penitents are cleansed."

Betty, the older woman, was the first to hold her hand over the flame. With a faint sneer on her lips, she looked stoically at the Mother Superior. Sister Anne knocked her hand away when the woman's eyes closed in pain. Betty took off her clothes, left them in a pile on the floor, covered her genitals with her hands, and ran to the shower. She screamed as the icy water hit her.

Patricia took her turn next, placing her hand over the flame until she winced and cried out. The Mother Superior was tempted to pull the girl's hand back, but was satisfied she had learned her lesson. Patricia took her plunge into the cold water.

Sister Anne studied Teresa as she approached. What was she thinking? The girl's eyes showed little emotion except for a brief flash—what was it? Hatred? Resentment? Fear? No, resolve. *She hasn't been broken. By the grace of God, I will break her, make her pay. She is a friend of Monica's.*

Teresa stood firm as the candle seared her flesh. Sister Mary-Elizabeth's eyes widened as the penitent, unblinking, took the punishment. The nun moved the candle away from Teresa's palm, but Sister Anne stopped her.

The flesh bubbled and Teresa's eyes rolled back in her head. She stumbled and Lea caught her in her arms.

"Enough," Sister Anne said. "Get to the shower."

Teresa coddled her reddened palm, and then stripped off her clothes.

Sister Anne said to Sister Mary-Elizabeth, "Make sure her hand is bandaged. I don't want infection. She needs to work. Continue until all have been punished."

She left Sisters Mary-Elizabeth and Ruth in charge. As she walked away, some of the girls screamed as the punishment continued. The sounds died as she retreated to the silence of her room. The Magdalens continued their penance. She took solace in that thought as she knelt at the foot of her bed for more prayers. After a few minutes, she received another message from God. *You have done well. Through you they have learned the meaning of salvation.* What further trials would she have to endure for their sakes? Tears came to her eyes as she bowed her head and pressed her folded hands against her face. *Thank You, Lord.*

Teagan's palm burned as if she had placed it on a hot stove. The only time she had suffered a similar burn was when, as a curious child, an ember had landed on her foot. A friend of her father's was clearing the ashes from a stove and she had gotten too close.

Even Sister Mary-Elizabeth seemed taken aback by Sister Anne's punishment. She had carefully cleansed Teagan's palm, run cool water over it, slathered a healing salve on the blistered skin, and wrapped it in a gauze bandage. With that she sighed, patted her on the shoulder, and sent her off to bed.

The garret was so chilly Teagan could see her breath. After

the lights had been turned out, she, along with many of the other girls, crawled into each other's beds for warmth. Lea, shivering from the cold water, threw back the blanket and invited her to snuggle as they struggled to get warm. She settled next to Lea, side by side, taking care not to brush her burned hand against anything. The slightest touch brought the fire back to her palm.

"Sister Anne is a witch," Teagan whispered. She wanted to use another word, but didn't out of deference to Lea. Nora, wherever she was, would have had no qualm about using the word. Maybe that was why Nora was free and she was still imprisoned in the convent.

Lea turned and faced her. The shadows made Lea's wide eyes appear even broader than in daylight. Teagan felt as if she were sharing a bed with an alien, a Venusian perhaps, with a long neck, and eyes that could see through you.

"She's only trying to teach us to be good," Lea said.

Anger surged through her. "Stop defending Sister Anne! Nora was right to escape. I'd leave in a flash if I had the chance."

Coughs and sneezes echoed through the room.

Lea frowned and stroked Teagan's arm. "I didn't mean to upset you. The Mother Superior only wants to make sure we get into heaven—she wants what's best for us."

"By burning us and sending us to frigid showers? We're likely to catch cold, or get pneumonia. Sister Mary-Elizabeth was even shocked at Sister Anne's tricks."

"Sister Mary-Elizabeth does what she is told. What choice does she have? I want everyone to be friends—happy here and in heaven."

Teagan groaned. Lea's naïveté made it impossible to reason with her. She knew Lea was far from normal and couldn't grasp the severity of their situation. In fact, many of the girls shared a mentality that Teagan didn't understand. They were like lambs being led to slaughter. Didn't they know they had a choice?

"Speaking of tricks, do you want to play a game?" Lea said. "It'll take your mind off your troubles."

"A game?" She wondered what crazy idea her friend would come up with next.

"Yes, get your blanket. I don't want to disturb the others."

Tegan crawled out of bed, still nursing her burned hand. She looked back to see Lea leaning over the bed, her head thrust under the frame. Only her backside was visible underneath the covers.

"What are you doing?" Teagan whispered when she returned. Lea lifted her head and put a finger to her lips. Fortunately, the girl next to them had buried herself under her blanket.

She watched in amazement as Lea silently lifted three wooden planks and placed them on top of each other. Her friend dug around with her right hand, her arm disappearing into the darkness underneath her bed. A few moments later, she withdrew her hand. Teagan couldn't see what was in it, but she knew one thing. This would be the perfect hiding place for her Christmas gifts, which were still concealed on the lace table downstairs. She would smuggle them up tomorrow.

"Crawl in," Lea whispered.

Teagan got in bed beside her, both sitting with crossed legs. They arranged the sheet and the two blankets over them as if they were playing like children, building a fort in the bed. Lea switched on a black penlight and their cozy space lit up with a flash. The brilliance blinded her for a moment, and she closed her eyes until her pupils adjusted. When she opened them, she saw a deck of cards by her knees.

"Tarot cards," Lea said.

Teagan's jaw dropped. "You're totally mad, Lea. If we're caught using these cards, our previous punishments will seem like a Saturday night dance. Sister Anne will view this as witchcraft." She remembered the time Father Matthew, the parish priest, had lectured some of her school friends about the evils of witchcraft and Satanism when they were caught playing with a Ouija board. She had refused to join them because she held a slim belief that the board might work. The thought frightened her.

"That's silly," Lea said. "This is fun—only a game. I used to play with the cards at home." She took out the deck from its package and shuffled. Some of the large cards were split and torn from use.

"How did you get them?"

"They were my mother's. I rescued them after she died. My stepfather was going to throw them away."

Lea shifted the penlight so the beam fell on the space between their legs. She placed seven cards, facedown, on the bed, and pointed to them. "You draw first."

A thrill raced over Teagan, raising the hair on the nape of her neck. "I don't want to." She shook her head. "It's bad—wrong."

"The spirits are never bad or wrong—only if you *allow* them to be. And *we* don't want that." Lea ran her fingers over the cards.

The small voice inside told her not to touch them, but she couldn't help but wonder how her life might turn out. She brushed her fingers over the cards and a charge of static electricity sparked from one of them. She jumped as the jolt shocked the end of her finger.

"See! What did I tell you!"

Lea giggled and pointed again.

"Oh, all right." Her eyes were drawn to the fourth card on her right. She picked it up and turned it over. Lea shone the light on the card. It showed a regal woman sitting on a throne. In one hand, she held a gold scepter.

"The Empress," Lea said solemnly. "A trump card in the *Major Arcana*."

"What does it mean?"

"You're going to get pregnant."

Teagan resisted the urge to scream. "Pregnant?" she asked in a voice as soft as she could make it. A sudden heaviness wrapped around her legs and groin.

"The Empress is the nurturer, the mother of all creation."

"I suppose that means I'm getting out of here. That's the only good thing."

"It's a good card," Lea said. "It means you will have a long and fruitful life."

Teagan took the card and studied it. The woman looked royal, a *Mona Lisa* smile on her face. "Lea, this is silly. I don't believe in this stuff."

Lea held the light up to her face and blinked. "Then don't. But the cards never lie. I'll draw a card for Nora."

The mention of the Nora's name made Teagan shudder.

Lea took the seven cards, shuffled them, and placed them on the bed. She rubbed her long fingers in circles over them and picked one. It was The Empress again. "How odd," she said. "Nora will have a family, too."

"I'm happy for that," Teagan said. "It means Nora and I will both escape this horrid place." She wondered where Nora was and hoped that her friend would remember their promise to help each other escape. How glorious it would be to live out their lives free from the Sisters.

Lea returned the card to the six others, shuffled them again, and hesitated. "Now I'll draw." She placed the cards on the bed, spread her fingers wide across them, and mouthed a few words Teagan couldn't understand. She picked the card at the right end and lifted it so only she could see it.

"Well?" Teagan asked, eager to find out what Lea had picked.

Lea dropped the card between them and shone the light on it. It was The Hanged Man, a figure suspended upside down by his feet from a tree branch.

"It looks frightful," Teagan said. "I hope it's nothing bad."

"It's not the death card." The sparkle disappeared from her large eyes. "You can interpret it two ways. It may mean I'm happy just where I am, my life is 'suspended.' Or it could be a card of . . ." She turned it over and returned it to the deck.

"What?"

A frown spread across Lea's face, its darkness settling upon her like a weight.

"Sacrifice . . . martyrdom." Lea gathered the cards and placed them in the pack. "I think you should go back to your bed."

Teagan wanted to soothe her. "I'm sure it's not as bad as all that. Anyway, I don't believe in these cards. It's silly stuff for children."

Lea turned off the penlight and their makeshift cavern went

black. She lifted the blanket and cold air rushed in. Teagan shivered and made her way out of Lea's bed.

She lay in her own for a long time, cocooning the blanket around her. She was too cold and then too hot. The images on the tarot cards lingered in her head, especially The Hanged Man. She wondered what it meant for Lea, and then she shook her head, thinking how silly it was to believe that a card could predict your life.

She wondered how Nora had escaped. Had she climbed over the wall? That would have been too dangerous, and surely someone would have seen her. How had she done it? Had she slipped out a door or hidden in a laundry bag? She clutched the side of the bed until her burnt palm hurt. *Damn. Damn her to hell.* She rarely used curse words, because her mother had told her that only the "lower classes" used them, but she found herself berating the Mother Superior and Nora. Her friend had deserted her like a traitor, and not only she, but all the Magdalens had paid the price. However, when she considered what her friend had gone through to escape, she admired her courage. Nora had taken a chance and succeeded. Most likely, she would have done the same.

She dabbed at her eyes with her sheet. She couldn't beat her fists against the wall or slam a pillow on the bed because she would wake up the others. There would be hell to pay.

She remembered her vow to write to Father Matthew, or maybe even the Pope, to tell her side of the story. What sin, what transgression had she committed? Someone in the Church had to believe her. She would make them believe it! She forced herself to relax and released her grip from the bed. Her respite was short-lived, however, and her body soon succumbed to tension.

She pondered a question: *What good will it do to mail any letters?*

And then a more disturbing thought struck her. *Who would mail them for me?*

CHAPTER 9

The taxi dropped Nora several blocks away from her home. The driver, uninterested in Ballybough, collected his fare, wished her a good evening, and sped off, the exhaust twirling in the cold air.

She stood looking at the row houses that had been part of her neighborhood for as long as she could remember. Her time at the convent had twisted her perception. It seemed so long since she'd been gone, yet it had only been a few months. The doorways, the cars, even the garbage bins were the same, but the view felt different, somehow distorted as if seen through a lens.

The road lamps came on as dusk fell. Drizzle fell in white drops through the light. She pulled up her collar and kept it close to her face. She didn't want anyone she knew to recognize her. That chance was too likely. At one point, she even ducked into an alley to avoid a woman who lived down the road from her parents. She was glad she had eaten, because going into a shop was too risky.

The cold kept the roads quiet for the most part. She walked for an hour, smoking a few cigarettes, and then stood under a lamp, staring at the door she knew so well. The droplets on her coat reflected the light like tiny, sparkling diamonds.

My old home. It seemed like years had passed since July. A turbulent well of emotions bubbled inside her. Her insides tensed, yet a strange sense of relief came with the knowledge that she at least had a chance to talk to her parents. She swiped at her eyes, her wet fingers cold against her cheek.

She wondered what to say, what to expect, after she had gathered enough courage to knock on the door. The anger she directed toward her parents dissipated with her anxiety. She had vowed to kill her father for what he had done. But reality was different. How could she confront them—possibly anger her parents—when they were all she had? Perhaps it would be best to beg for mercy. If they would accept her apology, she could start over again.

What had she done to deserve this punishment? She had gone over the question a thousand times since her father had dropped her off at the convent. It came back to her again and again. Maybe it didn't matter, but standing under the lamp, she took an inventory of her sins. She had been vain, thrown herself at Pearse and fantasized about him and a few other boys. She hadn't always been kind to her father and mother. She avoided housework and didn't study as much as she should. Was she so different from other girls? Didn't they think about boys, and wonder what it would be like to hold them and kiss them and someday make love? Perhaps her major sin was pride. She thought she was better than her parents, better than the neighborhood, even better than calling Ireland her home when it came down to it. Her parents couldn't abide that sin. *Pride.* It had gone before her fall.

She walked to the door, lifted her hand to knock, and then stopped. Her fingers, suddenly heavy, froze a few inches from the wood. A combination of exhaustion and despair fell upon her and she gasped for breath. Shivering, wet, cold, she forced her fist to the door. With each knock she gained a bit of strength.

A light flashed deep behind the closed living room blinds. From where it was situated, she knew it came from her parents' bedroom. A grumble filled the small house. Then she heard her father's rough voice. "Hold your horses, for God's sake. Can't a man rest?"

The door yanked open, spilling the light upon her and the

walk. He stared, taking her in from top to bottom and his mouth opened. No words came out.

"Gordon, who is it?" Her mother appeared in the bedroom door wrapped in her heavy green bathrobe.

"Da," Nora said. "Please let me in." For the first time, she wondered if she had made a mistake.

"How did yeh get here?" he asked.

Her mother took a few steps, and then, recognizing Nora, covered her mouth with her hands.

"I ran away."

"Our daughter is dead." He slammed the door.

The force knocked her back on her feet. "Oh my God," she whispered. Her anger kicked in. She hadn't come this far, taken this risk, to be stopped. He hadn't even listened to her. She needed to get inside to—what? What did she want to tell them—apologize and ask them to take her back? She'd be a good girl and do everything they demanded. If they would only listen, she could convince them she had changed. She never wanted to be sent away again.

She pounded on the door. The last knock faded.

Her father yanked the door open again. This time a blistering rage covered his face. He spit at her. "Go away, whoever yeh are. Didn't yeh hear me? Me daughter is dead."

"Da, please listen." She thrust out her arms. "I've changed. I'll never cross you and Ma again. I promise. Please let me come inside." She stepped toward him.

His hand rocketed toward her. It struck hard against her left cheek and sent her reeling onto the sidewalk. She landed on her rear with a *plunk*.

The door slammed again.

Behind it, her father shouted, "Go away. Our daughter is dead. I'm calling the Guards." She could hear her mother yelling, as well, indistinguishable beyond the door, her strangled voice filled with hostility.

She pulled herself up and rubbed her bottom. Her cheek stung as if little needles had been poked into it.

Her father lifted a slat on the blinds and swore at her again. The slat dropped and the house went dark. She knew her father would call the Guards.

She hadn't prepared herself for their reaction. She had wanted to believe that her parents would listen to her, even welcome her into the house. *Stupid.* Whom could she turn to? *Pearse?* He lived a few blocks away. Maybe she could convince him to come to the door, at least talk to her, but after this confrontation she wasn't prepared for another. *Cold.* A cup of tea would do her good.

She hobbled down the road, to the east. Soon, houses would be decorated for Christmas and families would gather to celebrate. There would be lights and song and parties to break the dark. Her home was dead. She strode toward Pearse's flat, despondent that she would never be part of her parents' lives again and angry that she was alone.

He has to let me in. After all, he caused all this trouble in the first place. If he'd taken me to Cork like he promised, I wouldn't be in this mess. She would show Pearse what a mistake it had been to desert her.

She slowed as she came near to a row of homes much like her parents. Everything was cold, black and gray. Headlights flashed behind her and she shifted to a casual walk, to allay suspicion. She didn't dare look back. Her body shifted from anger to anxiety as a chilly fear encased her. The car rolled up beside her, traveling even with her, disappearing and reappearing between the autos parked on the road. She spotted the blue panel on its side and knew immediately it was a Guard's vehicle.

The car sped up to an empty space ahead and pulled over. The Guard rolled down his window and peered out. "Get inside."

Nora stopped, leaned toward the officer, and smiled. Maybe he would leave her alone if she cooperated. "What's wrong?" Her nerves, tightly strung, sang in her head.

"You might be who I'm looking for. We got a call about a woman trying to get into a house. A man reported his daughter should be taken back to The Sisters of the Holy Redemption, where she's been living for several months. That's a long way from here. Do you know anything about that?"

Nora shook her head.

"I think you do, so why don't you get in the car and it'll save me the trouble of getting me shoes wet."

It was no use. Her father had called the Guards and they had her now. She dropped the smile and studied the officer. He was young, raven-haired under his cap, with a strong chin and intense eyes that scrutinized her under thick black brows. She could do worse than this man, she thought.

"Crawl in the passenger seat," he ordered. "Lucky I dropped me partner off an hour ago. He's got a divil of a cold. Won't be out tomorrow, neither."

Nora stepped into the road, around the car. She opened the door and slid inside. The warm air from the heater blew under her coat, knocking the chill from her legs.

"So, are yeh Nora Craven?" He knocked a cigarette from a pack with his knuckles and lit it. A smoky haze filled the interior.

Relishing the smoke, she breathed in deeply. She leaned toward the officer and asked, "Do you mind if I have a fag?" Why use her own?

He tipped his cap back and shook his head. He knocked another cigarette out, handed it to her, and opened his lighter. When he did, she cupped her hand around his.

She sat for a moment, enjoying the pleasure of the cigarette. It occurred to her that she could lie, but she knew the Guard would be smart enough to take her to the station and question her there. A quick call to The Sisters of the Holy Redemption would reveal the truth. In no time at all, she would be back, facing the wrath of the Mother Superior. On the other hand, she could relax with the officer, maybe even have a little fun before being returned to her holy prison sentence. *Why not?*

"Would you believe that I'm eighteen and my name is Molly Malone?"

The officer laughed. "Yer dress isn't cut as low as hers is, I wager."

"No." The heat was rising in the car. Nora opened her coat

and exposed her plain blue dress. She hoped the officer would take note of the ample curves under her less-than-sexy outfit.

The Guard smiled. "How old are yeh?"

"Eighteen. Just turned." One lie led to another. She would turn seventeen in February, but the way her life was going she didn't care if she told a little white one. *Everyone thinks I'm a slut anyway. Isn't that why they sent me away? Because I'm a tramp?*

"Yeh look older," he said, "maybe twenty-one."

"If I were with anyone else, I'd slap them. You never tell a woman she looks older than she is." She wondered if he was right. Maybe her time with the Sisters had done something awful to her face, or maybe it was her cropped hair. She hadn't time to think about such details.

"Gordon Craven said his daughter is a Magdalen. I've heard of them before. We took a couple of them back to a convent about a year ago. They were bad girls. Always looking for the thing that made their families send them away. Are yeh like that?" He took off his cap and placed it in the seat between them. His raven hair, wavy and full, came into view.

She looked down at his left hand. There was no ring on his finger.

She nodded and immediately felt sad. She knew what the Guard was after. Maybe if she let him have his way, she could convince him to let her go. Then she could find Pearse.

How stupid! Pearse wouldn't want me if I have sex with another man. I know it. Oh, what's the use! He'll never want me—I'm damaged goods.

The Guard threw his cigarette out the window, pulled the car away from the curb, and headed southeast. At first, she thought he was taking her to the station, but as they drove farther away from Ballybough, past the Royal Canal and then on to Dublin Port she began to worry. The radio crackled and he picked up the microphone. "No sign of her," he reported. "Still looking. Broadening the search." He signed off.

He seemed to know where he was going. Nora rolled down the window and threw out her cigarette. The car passed rows of brick warehouses on deserted dismal roads. Fog lowered its misty hood over the lamps and hung on the tops of buildings like wet gauze. The officer slowed at a dull road and pulled in between two parallel rows of trucks near a wharf.

He stopped the car and turned off the lights. The dashboard still emitted a feeble glow. He slid closer to her and placed his arm over her shoulder.

"What would yeh do to keep from going back to that awful place?" He looked into her eyes.

Sex was not supposed to be this way. She had no illusions about a white gown, a perfect wedding, and a blissful honeymoon night with her new husband. However, intercourse in a Guard car at a deserted quay wasn't the picture she had imagined for an ideal first time. The Guard was right. The convent was an awful place and she didn't want to go back, but was it worth the cost? Her eyes clouded over as she thought about the choice she had to make. Was it really a choice? Her parents considered her dead. She had no one to turn to. A man was offering her a bit of solace in exchange for pleasure. What could be wrong with that? As far as she was concerned, she had no other plan for the future. The voice inside her head screamed: *I'll get even with them for throwing me out!*

She took a deep breath. "Almost anything."

"Good." He unbuckled his belt. Nora turned her eyes away when she heard the zipper crackle. "Want another cigarette?"

She shook her head. "Maybe later."

"Okay." His hand moved to the top of her head, forcing her face downward.

She surrendered any resistance and the world turned black.

Someone shook Teagan's shoulders, waking her from a sound sleep. She was too comfortable under the covers to move.

"Wake up," the voice insisted.

She recognized it as Lea's and said, "Go away." She opened one sleepy eye and gazed toward the cold and vacant window. As far as she could tell, dawn was many hours away. She had no idea what time it was.

Lea shook her again. "I have to talk to you."

Teagan rolled over under the comfortable warmth of her blanket, rose up on her elbows, and tried to make out her friend's face in the dark. Only the lamplight from the far ends of the grounds traced into the room. The garret was brighter now that it was winter. In the summer and fall the light was obscured by oak leaves.

"What is it?" she asked, irritated by the interruption of her sleep.

Lea sat on the edge of the bed. "Something's happened to Nora. Something bad."

If she had been anywhere else but the convent, Teagan would have laughed, but her intuition told her she should pay attention to what her friend was saying. "What?" She pulled the covers up to her neck.

"Something she'll regret."

Teagan scoffed. "You don't have to be a fortune-teller to know that. She's in a load of trouble. There'll be hell to pay if she gets caught." She withdrew her arm from under the covers and pointed at her. "You're paying too much attention to hocus-pocus—with the tarot cards, seeing things at night. I'm beginning to think you *are* daft."

Lea put her hand on Teagan's shoulder. It was warm on the cold night. "I'm not mad. I have a gift. I've had it all my life. My mother, God rest her soul, passed it on to me. My stepfather didn't understand my power. He wouldn't let me use it."

"Now you're talking nonsense."

Lea bent over and a shaft of light cut across her eyes. The effect made her look as if she were in a 1940s detective movie.

"I saw it again last night," Lea said. "This time I knew it was real." Her voice dropped to a whisper. "Sisters Anne, Mary-Elizabeth, and Ruth. I couldn't see the faces of the other nuns, they were in shadow. Mr. Roche was digging a hole. It was small and they placed something, wrapped in white, inside it. Mr. Roche took off his hat and Sister Anne and the others dropped to their knees and prayed. Then they covered the ground with fresh sod."

A shiver skittered over Teagan and the hair rose on her arms. "What are you saying?"

"They're burying things in the corner. The same plot where I've seen Jesus, where I know spirits live. The nuns have been out there with Mr. Roche. I've seen them at least five times. At first, I wasn't sure of what I was seeing, but now I know why these visions come to me, and why I keep staring at the grass. Spirits live there—all holy."

Teagan sat up. "You're telling me that Sister Anne and the others are burying 'things' on the grounds and no one knows about it?"

"Yes." Lea lifted her head and the light fell across her mouth. Her lips were firm and straight with determination.

"Well, it's probably not gold or treasure, and it can't be adults," Teagan said. "Sister Anne isn't the kindest person in the world, but I don't think it's black magic. This isn't some satanic ritual. If they're small and wrapped in white . . . they're burying . . . children. What else could it be?"

Lea nodded. "I knew it inside, but I didn't want to accept it because it's so horrible. I wanted to rid my mind of what I saw. It makes me cry—all those poor babies buried in a mass grave without so much as a headstone or a cross. No church burial. Nothing but the cold earth. That's why Jesus is there—to give them comfort."

Teagan lay back, suddenly heavy and tired. Lea's admission had exhausted her with grief. "It's late. Let's try to get some sleep before we have to get up."

Lea rose from the bed. "What do you think we should do?"

Teagan grabbed her arm before she got away. She was concerned that her friend's revelation might go too far and cause all the Magdalens a great deal of grief. "I'm glad you told me, Lea, but let's keep this to ourselves. I'd rather no one else knows about this for the time being."

Lea lifted a finger to her lips and slipped into bed without a sound.

Teagan turned over and looked out into the dark. She couldn't see the southwest corner Lea spoke of, but she knew where it was. If she got out of bed and stood in front of the window, she would be able to see it. The world outside was cold, uninviting in the fall, and she thought about the babies, buried under the damp earth. In the winter, their unmarked graves would be covered by frost and snow, in the spring and summer by wildflowers and fresh grass, and in the fall by yellow oak leaves. No one would ever know what rested under the ground. Except the nuns.

She stared out the window, hoping to fall asleep, but rest did not come easy. A few stars shone brightly enough to be seen. How far away were they? Did the planets that circled them hold beings who suffered as much as earthlings? Speculating on such thoughts was foolish. She closed her eyes and imagined a letter she would write to the Pope asking for her release. She hadn't harmed anyone; she had been sent to the Sisters by a vengeful priest. And if those words did no good, perhaps she would have to describe a plot of ground that held the bodies of many innocent children. Perhaps the Pope would be interested in knowing what horrific events had occurred at the convent of The Sisters of the Holy Redemption. Perhaps he would send someone to investigate.

Nora learned his name was Sean Barry and he'd been a member of the Guards for two years. She'd found this out when he'd dropped her off at his one-room Ballybough flat after midnight. He still had several hours to go on his shift, and then he would need to go to the station to check in. He told her to take a shower and make herself at home. "Whatever you do," he said, "don't go out." Mrs. Mullen, the landlady, he explained, was a force to be reckoned with and did not take kindly to girls being entertained by single young men. "I worked too feckin' hard to get this place, and I don't want to be down and out."

Nora promised to do as he said.

"Help yourself to whatever's in the icebox." He left her alone.

The flat, if you could call it that, was a bit ragged, but it was warm with a comfortable bed in the middle. The blinds were pulled on the lone window that looked out on the road. A shower, sink, and toilet were tucked behind a blue curtain off to one side. A hot plate and tiny refrigerator rested on a counter across the room. A battered old television with a bent silver antenna sat on a cheap metal stand near the window. The only other piece of furniture was an overstuffed armchair with shirts and trousers tossed on it.

Nora took off the clothes she had been given at the shelter and threw them on the bed. She stood in her bra and panties and felt self-conscious about being nearly naked in a man's flat. But what difference did it make after what she had done to save herself from being sent back to the convent?

She stripped and fled to the shower. Cold air smacked against her skin. The steam heating pipes hissed across the room. Some of the stall tiles were missing, and a ring of black mold circled the drain. Sean's housekeeping habits were of little concern to her, although her mother would never have let her family live this way. She turned on the hot water and luxuriated in its warmth as it streamed down her body. She took his soap and shampoo and showered thoroughly. Even though it wasn't as nice as her bath at home, this old shower was much nicer than the one at the convent. "Never look a gift horse in the mouth," her mother had told her repeatedly. She now understood what that old adage meant.

The hot water ran out. She stepped out of the shower and grabbed the towel hanging from the rack. The small oval mirror above the sink was fogged. She rubbed her fingers over it, and before it clouded over again, she caught a quick glimpse of herself—a girl with short black hair and heavy eyes who looked much older than she should.

She slipped back into her bra and panties and crawled into bed.

Sean awakened her several hours later with a kiss on her forehead. He slipped out of his uniform and snuggled his lean body against hers. They had sex twice before they fell into a deep sleep.

In the afternoon, they woke up together. Nora fried potatoes and a cut of beef, and they ate together on the bed, watching television. They didn't talk much. The situation reminded her of her parents when they would eat out of the kitchen. She and Sean had gotten so intimate, so comfortable, in so short a time, yet she hardly knew him. Was this what growing up, finding a man to marry, was like? The circumstances seemed odd, off-kilter, because the specter of the Sisters hung over her like the Holy Ghost, prodding and poking at her conscience.

After they ate, Sean showered and dressed for work.

She watched him put on his uniform and asked, "What did you tell them at the station?"

"About what?"

Nora shifted uncomfortably on the bed. "About me?"

He shook his head. "Nothing. I said I didn't find no woman." He tossed her a pack of cigarettes. "I bought these for yeh. Amuse yerself while I'm gone, but don't smoke them all. Fags are expensive."

"What am I supposed to do?"

"Stay easy. Make yerself pretty for me, so when I come home we can tear up the bed."

She pulled a cigarette from the pack. "Thanks. How long is this supposed to last before I go crazy, or you decide to toss me out?"

He put on his hat and gathered his coat from the chair. "As long as it lasts—as long as it works. I'm a good man, trying to do a girl a favor." He put his hand on the doorknob and then stopped. "Yeh can leave anytime, but where would yeh go?" He opened the door and stepped into the dark. She heard the bolt fall into place.

He was right. There was no place to go until she figured out what to do.

For two nights, she sat on the bed, watching the telly and smoking cigarettes. She finished the Gauloises Lea had given her and part of Sean's pack. Occasionally, she took a nip from a bottle of Irish whiskey he had tucked under the counter. The sex was okay, but the isolation of another prison was getting on her nerves. She found herself checking the locked door, counting the cracks in the plaster, cleaning the bathroom and the hot plate, hoping for a jaunt in the daylight.

On the third night, she walked to the blinds and peered out. The drizzly weather of the past few days had ended; the sky looked black and clear above. The window glass felt cold on her fingertips. She thought about what she wanted to do. She turned off the lights and quickly raised the blind. No one was out except a black cat who sat licking itself on a trash bin across the road. Sean had good maps of the city and she knew where she was. The flat was only a fifteen-minute walk from Pearse's.

She tested the window lock, and it opened without any trouble. There was no screen, nothing to get in her way if she decided to leave. She lowered the blind, sat on the bed in the dark pondering her fate. Sean wouldn't be home for hours. She could leave the window unlocked, go out, come back, and he would never know. At least, that's what she hoped. She didn't think he was a violent man, but he had warned her not to leave.

Sitting was driving her mad. Nora put on her blue dress and bundled up in the gabardine coat. In a few minutes, she was walking among the few people on the road. She passed a store with a tall case clock in the window. It was about ten minutes after eight. Most everyone was home eating dinner, or at the pub knocking back a pint. A cold wind from the northwest stung her face. As she got closer to her destination, the shops, the roads themselves took on a familiar look. Still, the neighborhood seemed strange, different. She wondered again if it was she who had changed and not the surroundings.

She came to the whitewashed door with the brass number 17 tacked onto it. She lifted her hand to knock. He heart thumped so hard she could hear it in her ears, feel its frantic beat in her chest. The same sensation had filled her when she had knocked on her parents' door a few days before. Would Pearse have the same reaction? What if he slammed the door in her face and refused to talk? Why would he have anything to do with her? What would she do, walk away? The whole idea was crazy. Still, if she thought about it, he was the one who had gotten her into this mess by not taking her away. If only she hadn't thrown herself at him, and instead let things work out naturally. Maybe there was still a chance that Pearse would do what she wanted. Was there no way out of this horror? She would never know unless she tried.

She took a deep breath, tightened the muscles in her face, masking her fear, and knocked on the door.

Someone was at home. A television blared in the background—a British comedian's jokes and audience laughter echoed in the room. She knocked again, this time louder.

The door opened a crack and a young woman peered around its edge. "Yes?" was all she said.

Nora took a step back.

The woman opened it a bit more. She was pretty, but looked tired with purple half circles under her eyes. Her hair was sandy red, the color of a fall sunset, and fell loosely about her shoulders. She wore blue jeans and a large men's shirt. When she opened the door fully, Nora saw why she wore the white shirt. The woman was pregnant.

The sight took her breath away. She forced the question out "Is . . . is . . . Pearse here?"

"Who wants to know?" the woman asked.

"I'm . . . an old friend."

"He's working late at the garage. I'll tell him you called. What's your name?"

She said the first name that came into her head. "Monica."

"Monica?" The woman, narrowing her gaze, stepped back behind the door. "He's never mentioned a woman named Monica. I know he had girlfriends before me. I'm his wife."

Nora stared at the woman, unsure what to say. After a few uncomfortable moments, she backed away. "I'm sorry I bothered you."

The door closed and she was alone on the road again. *It figures,* she thought. *Every door closes in my face. The bastard deserted me and married the woman he met at the pub. She's the one who took him away! I hope to God he didn't talk about me so much she recognized me!*

She hurried back to Sean's. The flat was dark. She opened

the window, crawled through, and locked it behind her. She fell
on the bed, with her clothes on, and cried. She had never felt
so alone in her life. Only Sean could keep her away from the
Sisters. There was nothing else to do.

Sean had the night off two days later. Something seemed to
be troubling him, but Nora couldn't tell what it was. She asked,
but he shrugged off her questions.

"Let's go for a walk," he told her after tea. "It'll do us both
good to get out of the house."

She agreed—it was the first time he had suggested they go
out together. He put on his jacket while she grabbed her coat.
She was still wearing the same blue dress she'd gotten from the
shelter because she owned nothing else in the world.

They walked to the east, in an area that Nora hadn't been in
before. She tried to start a conversation—about where they were
walking—but Sean only shook his head and grunted, "I don't
know." He was in no mood to talk.

When they rounded a corner, Nora saw a man standing in
a derelict doorway about halfway down the road. His right leg
was casually bent, his heel propped against a brick wall. He saw
them coming and lit a cigarette. The flash lit his face and she
recognized Pearse. He looked more grown-up than she remembered. His black hair was slicked back, but his face was harder,
his frame heavier than before. He wore a leather jacket over a
white T-shirt and jeans.

She turned on her heels, ready to run, but Sean grabbed her
arm and dragged her along the footpath toward the door. Pearse
smiled as she struggled against him.

"I'll take over from here, boyo," Pearse said.

"Thanks," Sean said, and pushed her toward Pearse.

"Let me go!" Nora thought about calling out for the Guards,
but that would achieve nothing. She was already in the custody
of a man who could deny everything she said.

"Men have to stick together," Pearse said, and took hold of
her arm. "When you have a woman like this—"

Nora slapped Pearse as hard as she could. His head swiveled

from the force of the blow. Pearse lifted a fist, but Sean held him back.

"Remember what we agreed to, *boyo*," Sean said. "No rough stuff. She'll have enough to deal with when she gets back to the Sisters."

"I'll make sure of that." Pearse rubbed his jaw with his free hand.

"She left you with a going-away present," Sean said. "Four fingerprints on your cheek."

"I hope you got what you wanted." Pearse puffed out a little. "She wanted it from me, but didn't get it."

"Yeah, fine," Sean said. "I'm off now. Yeh'll make sure she gets delivered?"

Pearse nodded.

Sean walked a few steps, but then turned back to Nora. "I can't believe yeh took advantage of me. Ate me food, drank me whiskey, smoked me fags. Yeh lied about yer age. A man can get in big trouble for that." He stalked off, leaving her alone with Pearse.

"Want a fag?" Pearse fumbled with his jacket. "Maybe your last?"

"Yes."

He struggled to hold on to her and take a cigarette from his pocket. "I'll let you go, if you promise not to run."

Nora sighed. "I won't run. Where am I going to go? I don't even know where we are."

Pearse offered her the cigarette. "I can outrun you anyway, even if I've put on a stone."

Nora backed up to the door, which led to an abandoned secondhand furniture store. A broken table, a few old chairs still stood in the grimy windows on either side of them. She felt like the furniture—used, discarded, unable to do much of anything except rot.

"So your wife ratted on me."

Pearse took a drag on his cigarette. "How could you be so stupid? I married her after you left. Did you think I was going to desert my pregnant wife for a brasser, for a rock 'n' roll, just because you'd come back? I'd have to be off me nut. Your da did me a favor."

"I thought I loved you," Nora said. "Now I see who you really are."

"You only wanted to get out of Ballybough." Pearse stomped out his cigarette on the footpath and looked at his watch. "They should be along any minute now."

"Who?"

"The Sisters."

Nora inhaled and then puffed the smoke in his face. "I'll get out again, and when I do, I'm not coming back. As far as I'm concerned you're all dead." She shoved her back against the door to keep from shaking.

"When me wife told me, I knew it was you. I went straight to the Guards and found out you were missing. My inquiry got back to Sean. He was more than willing to let you go when he found out how old you really are." He stood in front of her. "My God, Nora, how far will you stoop to have a man?"

"Not as far as you to ruin a woman."

He spat at her feet. "You're lucky I paid any attention to you at all."

Headlights cut through the night. A black Ford pulled over to the curb and settled into idle. Nora could see the driver through the side window. Mr. Roche, the caretaker, leaned over the steering wheel, peering out the glass.

The passenger door opened.

Nora recognized the walk, the tall, erect posture of the nun who climbed out of the car. There was no mistaking the Mother Superior.

"Thank you, Mr. McClure," Sister Anne said. "I'll take over now. I assure you this won't happen again. You'll never have to worry about this penitent bothering you again. Come along, Monica."

Pearse looked at Nora, his brows furrowed. "Monica?"

"One of the delightful benefits of living with The Sisters of the Holy Redemption." She stepped toward Sister Anne. "It's been a pleasure seeing you, *Mr. McClure.* Drop by for a visit anytime. I'm sure you'll be amused."

The Mother Superior grabbed her arm, but Nora pulled away. "Don't touch *Monica. Monica* may get upset and make a big fuss."

Sister Anne's lips parted in a thin smile. "I doubt it. Sister Ruth is waiting for you in the backseat."

Nora shot Pearse a withering look, then walked to the car and got into the backseat. She slid next to a scowling Sister Ruth, as the Mother Superior shut the door.

Sister Ruth held on to Nora with her muscular arms. "*You* ruined all my plans for the evening."

"Nice to see you, too," Nora said and pushed back in the seat. "I'm sure what you had planned wasn't as important as this."

"Little—"

"Now, Sister," the Mother Superior chided from the front. "Be nice to Monica. She's going to be spending time in the Penitent's Room." She turned and smiled at Nora.

Mr. Roche pulled the car away from the curb, and it sped toward the convent. As the houses of Ballybough slipped by, Nora realized she'd given herself to a man and got nothing for it but a return trip to The Sisters of the Holy Redemption. Sean had lost his cigarettes and whiskey, but she had lost something much more important. She could never get it back again.

CHAPTER 10

———>○<———

Sister Anne changed out of her habit and into her nightclothes. Monica continued to surprise her. She had ridden to the convent without saying a word; she had even stepped into the Penitent's Room without resistance. Perhaps she was learning repentance after all. Perhaps her venture back in the world had softened her to the possibility of a life without sin.

She knelt in front of her bed, her usual location for prayer, and wished she were somewhere else in the convent. The windows were closed against the cold. The radiator rumbled and clacked in the corner. She breathed deeply, the semi-moist air filling her lungs. In the Penitent's Room all would be black, soundless, now that evening prayers were over in the adjoining chapel. She wished she had the courage to be with Monica, holding her, giving her the comfort and love she needed during her time of penitence. Good Mother Superiors might do that, but her time alone with God was more important than prayers with a Magdalen.

Sister Anne bowed her head and prayed with a reverence and fervor that shocked her. She spit out the words, saying them almost to the point of a scream. *Our Father, who art in heaven, hollowed be Thy name!* She stopped. Did God hear her prayers? Was He listening?

She looked back to the bureau and thought about the blades, clean, silver gleaming, cold, waiting to slice the soft skin. How many hours had she spent in the Penitent's Room herself trying to exorcise the pain? Her fellow Sisters never knew she was there. Most of the time it was late at night, long after the others had gone to bed. She had taken the blades with her. No one could see the blood smeared into the wall by her fingers. The ancient rock absorbed it like clay absorbs water.

So many times she had prayed there—the Lord's Prayer, Hail Mary's, desolate prayers of absolution. So many times she had sought relief from the despair sluicing through her soul like a rampaging river.

She never understood why her mother hated her so when it wasn't her fault.

"Why did your sister have to die?" her mother kept asking. "You have conversations with the Lord every day. You are a godly person. Why didn't He save her? Couldn't you have saved her with your petitions to God?" Anger scorched her mother's voice.

The questions kept coming as her mother's depression deepened. Sister Anne expected her to ask one day, "Why didn't He take *you* instead of her?" It wasn't her fault her sister died in childbirth, but she had been in the room, praying for her, already having assured her mother that she would live, by the grace of God. She prayed so hard her head hurt, but her sister died despite her pleas. The baby lived, but it wasn't enough. Her mother withered like a dead rose, the red blossom turning to brown, drying to dust. Then there was no family at all.

The guilt, the recrimination, continued until Sister Anne was forced to put the baby up for adoption, while she started a new life at The Sisters of the Holy Redemption. Her mother died a few months later in an asylum. Sister Anne had visited her once after she was admitted. Her mother didn't recognize her, and she couldn't wait to get away from the smell of shit and urine, and the constant moaning and chattering of the insane. She returned to the convent, stripped, and stood under scalding water for an hour. Her skin flushed red with heat; she could barely breathe, and her lungs stung from the hot vapor. That was the first time she cut herself.

Prayers tonight seemed to stop at the ceiling. She thought

of Monica and wondered what she was doing. Did it hurt being alone in the Room? She knew it did. Sometimes it was
more painful than anyone could bear. Was Monica hungry? Of
course, but the penitent must bear up against the punishment.
The only way to get stronger was to let it come to you, absorb
it, make it part of you.

She rose and walked toward the bureau. Time slowed, and
each step felt like she was in another woman's body, walking
on a spongy mattress. She reached for the drawer. The fingers
crawled, touched the oak knob—smooth and rounded by a half
century of use. She pulled it open and the blades came into view,
the cool metal calling to her. *Press them against the flesh. Let
the penitent bleed.*

She took one out, turned it over in her hand, being careful not to let it cut. She pulled up her sleeve and looked at the
scarred ridges on the underside of her forearm. Just one, another one, would make the pain go away.

Not wanting to indulge in the vanity of her condition, she
avoided the mirror over the dresser. A blue delft washbasin sat
on its oak top. She held her arm over the basin and ran the blade
across her skin. A crimson trail followed the cut, forming a thin
line at first, then swelling, running in droplets down her arm.
The blood fell into the bowl turning the water a smudgy pink.

A shock, akin to adrenaline, rushed through the cut. Her
arm relaxed as she watched the blood run and the water finally
turn red. A cool haze crept over her; she imagined the feeling
was like the infiltration of opium into the lungs. Nothing much
mattered—not the convent, not Monica, certainly not her pain.
Euphoria filled her body. She dipped her arm into the water and
then gingerly lifted it out. A clean white towel lay nearby. She
wrapped it around her arm to staunch the wound. She would
add it to the laundry items tomorrow and no one would be the
wiser.

She knelt again at the end of her bed and looked up to the
crucifix. She began her prayers, this time relaxed and earnest.
Jesus was looking down upon her and she knew He was smiling.

* * *

Sister Mary-Elizabeth opened the door and peered in at Nora. A smile formed on the stout nun's face, not exactly welcoming, but as close to a friendly greeting as she had seen in months.

"You had a rough time, I hear," the nun said and handed her a plate with a cup of tea and toast. "That's all you get until you're out of here, so you better enjoy it. I'll be back in an hour to take you to the jacks for the night."

She stared up at her, defeated, exhausted from her escape and return, unable to think about the future. Even the thought of tea and toast repulsed her. She took the plate and placed it on the floor. "Do you ever get tired, Sister Mary-Elizabeth? Tired of living?"

The nun frowned. "Don't talk like that. All you have to do is cleanse yourself and all your problems will be solved—just as they were for me. I can't think of a better life than serving God. You'll come around."

She chuckled at the irony of the nun's words. *Cleanse yourself and all your problems will be solved?* Stuck in a black cavern, reduced to eating toast until she was released, then what? A life in the laundry until someone—anyone—came to her rescue. A knight riding a white horse seemed an unlikely scenario. She couldn't trust men, she couldn't trust women, whom could she trust?

As if reading Nora's mind, Sister Mary-Elizabeth piped up in a joyful voice. "You have to come to terms with yourself. That'll get you by. Don't let anyone rule your life except God. He'll talk to you."

"Thanks for the advice, but right now I don't have any friends, real or imaginary."

"Oh, what's the use talking to a girl like you? Use this time to think! Find yourself." The nun moved the door a bit, about to plunge Nora into darkness, but stopped. "Truly. Find God and your life will change."

Before the darkness overpowered the light, Nora saw the scratches on the walls she had noticed during her first time in the Penitent's Room. She slumped on the stool and her head sank heavily on her chest. Her mind was as blank as the room.

It felt good not to think of anything at all, to let the blackness encase her, seep into her soul. *Maybe that's how I should cope. By thinking of nothing at all.* Even the room felt good. No dampness, no cold. She was sinking into emptiness and she liked it. Maybe Sister Mary-Elizabeth was right. If her parents wouldn't save her, if Pearse and a man like Sean would have nothing to do with her, maybe she should turn to God. The thought gave her a temporary lift, before she closed her eyes. She was too tired to think. The dark swallowed her and, along with it, her thoughts of God.

She had never felt so alone since Nora had run away. Sister Anne had strictly reinforced the "no talking" rule and had chastised all the nuns, particularly Sister Ruth, for their lax behavior. Teagan couldn't even speak to Lea—not that there was much to talk about—because she had been moved out of the old library and back to the laundry to take Nora's place. They were both so tired, they said little before they crawled into bed. Before her reassignment, she had managed to smuggle her Christmas presents to the hiding place under Lea's bed. Her friend was shocked that someone cared enough to give her gifts and offered to keep them safe.

For days, her job had been *WLDS* again. *Whites. Lights. Darks. Special.* It was grinding work, sorting, lifting, a few days at the washbasins, and then back to sorting with nothing to break the monotonous routine. The burn from her punishment the night Nora escaped had healed to fresh skin, but red splotches covered her hands from contact with bleach and detergent. Her shoulders ached each night as she crawled into bed. Even Betty, one of the older Magdalens at the convent, commiserated before lights-out about how "morose" the girls had become. "Christmas is coming," she lamented. "Couldn't we have a bit of joy in our lives?"

The Magdalens heard that the Mother Superior had punished Sister Ruth harshly for Nora's escape. The athletic nun had accepted the blame for falling asleep. Rumors also circulated that Sister Ruth had spent time in the Penitent's Room, but none of the gossipers could swear to it. However, shortly after her dressing-down by Sister Anne, Sister Ruth appeared to have given up her clandestine drinking on the job. Now the nun sat upright in her chair, never reading a magazine or book as she used to, rarely letting her posture slip. It was as if she had a board attached to her back that kept her stiff and out of sorts. She took her punishment out on the Magdalens by barking orders all day and running the laundry as if she was a warden. All the laundry packages entering or leaving through the delivery door were now inspected, without hesitation, by Sister Ruth.

One night, Teagan borrowed Lea's penlight, and under cover of the blankets, wrote the letters she envisioned. She wrote longhand, painstakingly, on a plank taken from under Lea's bed. Even the paper, pen, and two pilfered envelopes were "borrowed" from her friend's desk in the old library. Lea never asked what the items were for. As always, she wanted to help Teagan.

She agonized over every word. After all, one of these was being addressed to the Pope, the other to Father Matthew. When it came down to it, her careful planning, her organized thoughts, were thrown out when the black ballpoint touched the paper.

Her tone was conciliatory, yet firm in her understanding of the situation. She had been wronged, and the Church should recognize her "parents' misunderstanding" that sent her to The Sisters of the Holy Redemption. As she understood it, her "relationship" with Father Mark was "mistakenly" blown out of proportion by Father Matthew. The conditions at the laundry were deplorable and should be corrected. The answer to her problem was simple—an immediate release and an apology from the Church. In order not to cloud the issue, she never mentioned the supposed dead children. That would suffice. She wrote for two hours before signing them both.

She returned the light, the pen, and the board to Lea, who concealed them like a master thief. Her friend moved without making a sound, her stealth uncanny when called for.

Teagan didn't sleep well that night, wondering how she would get the letters out. Sisters Anne, Ruth, and Rose were no good, for they couldn't be trusted. Her only chance at getting them posted was through Sister Mary-Elizabeth, who had displayed goodwill toward the girls now and then.

Teagan found the nun the next morning after breakfast. The odd meal, creamed corn with sugar, toast, and watery tea, upset her stomach, which was already on edge from her decision to mail the letters.

Sister Mary-Elizabeth, carrying a serving tray with toast and tea, rushed down the hall with the Magdalens, who were headed to the laundry. Teagan caught up with her outside the Penitent's Room. The nun placed the tray on a small table sitting between the chapel and the room, and then lifted the key chain that hung from her sash. She stopped when she saw her.

"Get along now, to work," the Sister ordered. "I've got business here that's none of yours."

"I won't be a minute," Teagan said. She looked up the stairs and then down the hall as the girls filed past, making sure that no Sisters were watching. "Could you please post these letters for me? I'd be so grateful." She pulled them from her apron pocket.

"Two letters. You have been busy. Pens, paper, and envelopes are scarce around here." The nun eyed them suspiciously. "Who are you writing?"

Blood rose in her face. Of course, Sister Mary-Elizabeth would want to know. Did she really think that the nun would blindly post the letters without looking at them?

"To my parents," Teagan said.

The nun frowned. "Contact outside the convent is forbidden, unless there's an emergency. Is this an emergency?" She forced a smile. "You seem healthy enough to me."

She returned the letters to her apron pocket. "I wanted to tell them how much I loved them and how well things are going here."

"Isn't that nice," Sister Mary-Elizabeth said with a hint of sarcasm. "I don't believe it for a minute."

Teagan said bluntly, "One is to the Pope and the other to Father Matthew. That's the truth."

The nun stared at her in surprise. "Now, what would *you*

be wanting with those two fine gentlemen? Best be rid of those. Now, get along, or they'll be a boatload of trouble for both of us."

She strode down the hall, wondering if the nun would tell the Mother Superior about her letters. Any path veering from "normal" was a risk at the convent. This was one she was willing to take.

As she turned to go down the stairs to the laundry, she saw Sister Mary-Elizabeth open the door to the Penitent's Room. Someone was sitting inside—a girl in a blue dress. Her face was covered in shadow. Was she a new Magdalen, already being punished for her transgressions?

The day dragged on for Teagan. Sister Ruth stationed her at a washbasin near the front. Her job was to work on the delicate fabrics, to make sure all the stains were treated and out before hand-washing. She made sure her letters weren't ruined by detergent and water splashing onto her pocket.

Sister Ruth was her usual watchdog self and kept a close eye on the day's work. Several times, vans rolled up to the delivery door. She was waiting for the right moment to hand over the letters. Some of the men looked familiar from her days in the laundry, but no opportunity presented itself.

After the noon meal, she resumed her station at the washbasin. Sister Ruth returned to her chair in the middle of the room and, with that, no chance of getting the letters out.

About three in the afternoon, a brown van pulled up to the door. Sister Ruth inspected the parcels as a middle-aged man and his young assistant shoved them inside. Near her chair, the nun exchanged greetings and papers with the older man, ignoring the dark-haired youth who couldn't have been much more than eighteen.

While the two adults were distracted, Teagan decided to act. She sneaked away from her station, winked at the young man, and handed him the letters. "Please post these as soon as possible," she whispered. "Don't tell anyone. It's important. I'll pay you back for postage, and more, when you come back." She winked again.

He broke into a wide smile. "More?" He looked at her from head to toe.

She raked her hand through her hair and swung her hip to the side. "More. As much as I can give." It pained her to act like a tramp, but if it got the job done. . . .

He winked back at her. "I've heard about you girls. Me boss told me. I'll be looking for more."

Sister Ruth was finishing up. Time was running short.

"Remember. Not a soul." She blew a kiss and hurried back to her station.

The young man stuffed the letters in his back pocket and waited for his boss. As he was leaving, the young man looked back and grinned. The two disappeared into the van. Teagan hoped she had made the right decision, but as with all of her actions these days, she had little choice.

At tea and evening prayers, Teagan asked God's forgiveness for what she had done. She had acted like a tease and lied to the young man. If He listened, she hoped God would forgive her. She'd worry about the boy later. Her prayers were sincere, the most they had been in months. Perhaps the Creator had better things to do, bigger problems to tackle, than to pay attention to a penitent at The Sisters of the Holy Redemption. After all, in October, the world had teetered on the brink of nuclear war when the United States and the Soviet Union sparred over missile bases in Cuba. Even the nuns had prayed for peace.

That night, after lights-out, she talked quietly to Lea about what she had done—how she had written the letters to the Pope and Father Matthew and asked the young deliveryman to mail them.

"I even offered him favors," she said, thinking her words would shock Lea.

Her friend seemed unconcerned. "It happens all the time. The country boys always wanted something from me. When they were young they saw what animals did. They wanted to experience it, too. It was natural they should be so curious. I told them no—I was keeping myself a virgin for God and the Saints. All I had to say was 'God and the Saints' and they kept their hands to themselves. My stepfather would have murdered them if he'd found out what they were looking for."

Teagan laughed too loudly and Lea shushed her. Her friend put a finger to her ear and ducked under the covers. Teagan did the same when she heard the footsteps in the hall.

The door creaked open and a shaft of light pierced the room.

Teagan opened her eyes and peeked out from under her blanket. A nun—it could only be Sister Anne, as tall as she was—held an electric torch. Its beam cut through the air and bounced off the beds in the room until it came to Nora's.

A girl who looked like Nora followed the Mother Superior, but this penitent didn't have the swagger or confidence of her friend. In fact, she looked broken: head down, arms hanging at her sides. She shuffled like an old woman a few paces ahead of the nun. Teagan wondered who the new Magdalen was.

As the girl drew closer, she recognized the face, the black hair scruffier than when she had seen it last. It was Nora! In a blue dress like the one she had seen on the girl in the Penitent's Room.

Her friend collapsed into bed. She said nothing as Sister Anne pulled the blanket over her and switched off the torch. The room went dark until the Mother Superior opened the door and disappeared in the hall.

"Nora. Nora," Teagan whispered, and sat up in bed. It didn't matter to her whether the others heard her or not. She was sure they were as curious as she was.

"Teagan?" The question was weak, the voice watery with exhaustion.

"Yes. You're back!" Her friend had returned, but not in the shape she had expected. How could she be angry at her for her desertion? "What happened?"

Nora rustled under the bedclothes. "Tired. Too tired." The voice drifted away like a whisper lost in the air.

"Are you all right?" Teagan asked, but there was no answer.

"Leave her alone." Lea appeared at Nora's bed, staring down at her. "I told you something bad happened. I was right."

Teagan, worried that Nora had been hurt, lay back as Lea returned to her bed. She wanted to go to sleep, but she also wanted to hear what her friend had to say about her escape. Dispirited and exhausted, she had ended up back at the convent. She had been the girl in the Penitent's Room. Teagan looked at the silent figure under the blanket. *If she couldn't escape, how can I?* The thought fell like a weight upon her. She was dying to hear Nora's story. The morning couldn't come soon enough.

CHAPTER 11

The cold air on Christmas Day stabbed into the lungs. Snow had fallen during the night, turning the ground a milky white. Teagan and the Magdalens, happy to be out of the frigid garret, watched from the window of the breakfast room as it fell from the slate sky. Betty said snow always gave her a good feeling about the holiday. She remembered the last time it had snowed on the day—1956. Sister Rose, looking frail, came in to announce a special Mass for the Magdalens after they ate. The rest of the morning and most of the afternoon, excluding dinner and evening prayers, would be devoted to games in the old library.

"No work today," Sister Rose said to elation around the table.

The nuns had draped the convent walls on the first floor with colored lights. A live tree stood at the end of the hall near the Penitent's Room. When she had the opportunity to pass by, Teagan watched its vibrant red, blue, and green lights blink, the colors reflecting off tinsel. The tree with its heady scent of pine reminded her of past holidays and evening gatherings around the fireplace at home. She had thought of those as good times, but now she wondered. Away from her parents for so many months, she was able to put into perspective what family holidays had been like. Her father would begin drinking about noon—any excuse was a good excuse—and wouldn't stop until it was time for bed. The hours would drag by as she and her mother watched her father slide into a boozy oblivion. Her mother would sip a few drinks, as well, to appease her husband, but always ended up guiding him upstairs. If it was a two- or three-day holiday, the process would begin again the next morning with a "spot of the hair of the dog that bit him." Her experiences at the convent and at home bore psychological similarities. The Mother Superior, however, was a different matter. Her physical abuse was different from her father's threats. Here, she was learning to take care of herself, to guard against it if she could.

After breakfast, the Magdalens were herded down the stairs, past the tree, and into the chapel, which, despite a number of lit candles, was not much warmer than the garret. Teagan took her place in a pew about halfway back from the small altar. Nora slid in next to her.

They'd had little time to talk since Nora's return, even though Teagan was bursting to hear about her time away from the convent. Nora had never wanted to discuss it, as if she had been a different person from the one who had managed to escape. A lot of the fire that Teagan admired had vanished. The color in Nora's cheeks was slight and she often wiped sweat from her brow on the coldest days. Talking to Nora was like talking to a middle-aged woman whose life was reduced to a humdrum existence, much like the picture Nora painted of her mother in Ballybough.

Teagan turned to her friend. Nora's lips parted and she took Teagan's hand in hers. There would be no chance to talk now.

The nuns filed into the room in a silent cadence. The chapel's stillness was broken only by the rustle of their habits as they took their seats in the first two rows of pews. Three priests walked behind the Mother Superior, who stopped near the altar.

Teagan gasped. A priest she didn't recognize led the way, but he was followed by Fathers Matthew and Mark. The men didn't look at the Magdalens. They stared straight ahead, walking as solemnly as the nuns, and sat in chairs placed on opposite sides of the altar.

Sister Anne held up her hands. "We gather on this blessed day to celebrate the birth of our Lord."

Nora looked at Teagan as Sister Anne spoke. "What's wrong?" she asked, whispering.

"That's Father Matthew on the left and Father Mark on the right, the one who got me in trouble . . . well, you know what I mean."

Nora craned her neck to look at Father Mark. "He's a nice-looking priest. I can think of worse men to get in trouble with."

Betty turned from the pew in front and scowled. "You better hold your tongues or you'll get the rough edge of Sister Anne's."

Nora frowned at the older woman, but Teagan was too upset to care about Betty's comment.

"Our special guests today are Fathers Matthew and Mark from St. Eusebius," Sister Anne said. "They are most concerned with your well-being on Christmas. As a holiday gift, they have brought along Father Anthony, who is visiting here from Italy. He will hold today's Mass. Give him your attention."

The tall priest with deep-set eyes began the Mass in Latin. Teagan paid little attention to the words because she was scrutinizing Fathers Matthew and Mark. Neither of them appeared interested in the girls. Father Mark turned his handsome face toward Teagan once, and then looked quickly away. Had he seen her, or was he gazing at the group?

She trembled on the cold, hard pew. She wondered whether Father Matthew had received her letters. Was that why the priests were here? The thought rocked her and she pressed herself against the hard backrest. She wanted to scream at them, proclaim her innocence in front of the Magdalens and plead for her release. But a vision appeared in front of her face—a hand. It was her father's hand, threatening to strike her if she caused trouble. The fingers in front of her were enough to dispel her anger. Her rage simmered into sadness.

"Are you all right?" Nora asked and gripped her hand harder.

Teagan nodded and took a breath. It would do no good to speculate. The priests were here for Christmas and probably nothing would happen.

Father Anthony conducted communion behind the small altar. Each of the Magdalens filed up after the nuns, taking the host. Father Matthew held the wine. Father Anthony smiled at Teagan and blessed her as he placed the wafer on her tongue.

Father Matthew wiped the cup, but neither smiled nor spoke to Teagan as he lifted it to her to drink. She wondered whether he even recognized her. Father Mark sat motionless across the room.

The Mass ended about forty-five minutes after it began. The priests and Sister Anne left first, leaving Sisters Mary-Elizabeth and Ruth in charge of the Magdalens' exit.

Teagan crowded her way forward to look at Fathers Matthew and Mark. They were racing after Sister Anne, as if they were in a hurry to escape the girls. The Mother Superior turned and held out her arm. The sleeve of her habit hung like a black drape as she ushered them into her office. She followed them inside and shut the door. They were gone. The vague sense that she might have a conversation with the priests evaporated.

Sister Ruth clutched the railing as she led the girls to the old library. Sister Mary-Elizabeth took up the rear. Teagan held back on the stairs until Nora caught up with her. They climbed up side by side.

"Maybe we can sit together," Tegan said. "We'll have a chance to talk."

Nora puffed, her face turning red with each step.

"Are you ill?" Teagan asked. She wrapped her arm around Nora's waist. "You haven't been the same since you got back."

"I'm all right," Nora said, swiping her hand across her brow. "I think I got a bit of a cold in the Penitent's Room. I was there for a day and a half."

"For so long?" She remembered seeing the girl in the blue dress. They were at the top of the stairs now. Teagan let go of her as they walked to the library. "That's horrible."

Nora nodded. "It really wasn't so bad. I let myself go. I know it sounds strange, but it was like I became the room. I blended into the walls, became part of the darkness, part of the rock. I was sad when the door opened because I had to eat my toast, or go the toilet, and deal with this nonsense again."

A warm glow filtered out of the library door. The Magdalens filed inside in silence. Teagan hadn't been inside the room for a week because she was needed in the laundry. Colds were going around, and, depending on their severity, some of the girls were confined to bed.

The nuns had decorated the room with candles and red and green crepe paper. A long table had been set up against the wall near Teagan's lace-mending desk. A punch bowl and two rows of round, individually wrapped, packages sat on top of it. Four round tables with folding chairs were set up in the center.

Sister Mary-Elizabeth clapped her hands. "Girls, today is Christmas. Remember to give thanks when you open your gift. Count your blessings you're able to live here, doing meaningful work, and you're not out on the streets fending for yourself like poor, miserable unfortunates." She pointed to the table. "Help yourself to punch, without any kick from the divil." A few of the Magdalens laughed and the nun smiled. "Your present is marked with your name. Enjoy it with Christ's blessings. And you may talk until evening prayers!"

A cheer arose from the Magdalens. Teagan held on to Nora as the other girls chatted away in good spirits. "Let's go to the back of the line so we can talk," she said with anticipation about an event that at any other time would have been ordinary— Nora's foray into Dublin. "Tell me everything that happened."

"I'm completely knackered." Nora sighed and leaned toward Teagan. "You can't tell anyone, not even Lea, but I think I'm knocked up."

Teagan gaped at Nora.

"Shut your mouth and look normal," Nora said. "Don't give the nuns any ideas."

"You're pregnant?" she asked as quietly as she could.

Nora walked a few steps. "I think so. I shagged a Guard while I was out. He turned out to be a bit of a tool. That's to be expected—most men are. But I've not been meself lately. Me breasts hurt and I've been feeling nauseous in the morning. I've been keeping this under wraps."

"Oh my God, Nora. What're you going to do?" Teagan covered her mouth as soon as the words were out. "I'm sorry. What a stupid question. There's nothing you can do but have the baby."

Nora looked down, red-faced. "I don't really want the baby, but I can't have an abortion, so I'll carry me little bad egg to term. There'll be a new Craven in the world come next August, give or take a week."

Nora's news shocked Teagan. All the happiness and planning that would go into having a baby were pointless here. She watched as the Magdalens ahead of them went about their Christmas Day, getting their little gifts, when much more important news was happening around them. If Nora were in love with this man and they intended to have a child, they would be celebrating her pregnancy with cake. Everyone would be talking about their life together. Here, all Nora had to look forward to was having the baby and putting it up for adoption. Teagan wondered whether her friend had even thought that far ahead. She knew that as the baby grew, it would be harder for Nora to leave the convent, so any escape they might make together would have to be made soon. Time would grow shorter with each day.

Teagan clasped her hands. "I don't know what to say. Congratulations?"

Nora smiled. "I wouldn't go that far. I suspect, but I'm not sure."

"When will you tell the nuns?"

"I've been thinking about that. If it's true, I'll keep it a secret as long as possible and then tell Sister Mary-Elizabeth. At least she won't hit me." She looked down at her stomach. "Not showing yet."

The punch bowl was in front of them. Nora took a cup, poured a full ladle into it, and took a sip. "Umm, grape." She smacked her lips.

Teagan did the same. She searched for her gift on the table, only a few were left. She came to a circular package bound in white Christmas paper and red ribbon. *Teresa* was marked on the top in pen.

Nora found hers and sniffed it. The other girls were unwrapping their presents—they were all the same.

"Chocolate biscuits," Teagan said. "I suppose it's better than nothing. We never get dessert." She wondered what her parents were doing this Christmas morning. What about Cullen? Was he thinking of her? Her stomach turned over.

"Yeah, biscuits." Nora said and rubbed her belly. "I already got my present." She rolled her eyes.

Teagan laughed and held on to Nora as they looked for Lea. She was sitting at one of the tables and munching on her present. No one sat with her. Most of the Magdalens avoided her because they thought she was so strange. Teagan and Nora joined her at the table, ate their snacks, and looked forward to a day without work. Sarah soon joined them for a card game of Authors.

The more Teagan thought about Christmas Day, the angrier she got. She knew the priests were at the convent for a meeting with Sister Anne, and she intended to find out why. Something else bothered her, as well. If she and Nora were to escape, they would have to do it within the next few weeks, not months later. A plan needed to be devised soon. She wondered whether Nora had changed her mind.

A few days after Christmas, Teagan returned to her table in the old library. Now that Nora was back and the colds had died down, she was no longer needed in the laundry. She had begun work on mending a lace tablecloth when Sister Anne came to the door and motioned for her to follow. The Mother Superior led her downstairs to the office, closed the door, and told her to have a seat. The *LOVE* blocks were arranged in a different position from the last time she had seen them. They were directly in front of Sister Anne, so anyone sitting in the chair couldn't miss the message.

"I'm trying hard to control my anger," the nun said. "How dare you do this?" The Mother Superior pulled two letters from the desk drawer and shook them at Teagan's face.

She blushed, but rather than making her feel bad, her embarrassment energized her. She held on to the chair and leaned forward. "How *dare* you do this *to me* when I've done nothing wrong? You're angry because you know I'm right."

Sister Anne dropped the letters on the desk and reached for

the rod. It appeared near the folds of her habit. She thwacked it against her palm. "I ought to beat you for what you've done. Do you realize the mess you could have created if these letters had gotten out? Fortunately, the delivery boy you bribed with sexual favors turned them over to his boss. The man has been doing business with us for years and knows how foolish you girls can be. He was right to give them to me." She slapped the rod against her desk. "Fool! Petitioning the Holy Father and Father Matthew because *you* have been wronged? Who would take the word of a slutty girl over an ordained priest?"

Teagan swatted the *LOVE* blocks and sent them flying across the desk and onto the floor. "*You* don't have any idea what love is about. All you care about is keeping your prisoners in line and making money."

"Pick them up *now!*"

Teagan shook her head. "There's no love in this place."

Sister Anne grasped the rod horizontally between her clenched fists and rushed toward her.

Teagan fell back as the rod neared her throat. It barely missed her, catching on the chair's wings.

Sister Anne shook as she spoke. "I could kill you for the hurt you've caused me." The nun pushed harder against the chair. The rod inched closer to Teagan's neck.

She grabbed the rod and pushed back. "Kill me? Is that what you want? Is that your idea of Christian virtue?"

Sister Anne dug her feet into the floor, pushing harder, until the rod came to a stop against the chair.

She gulped, managed a quick breath, and said, "Kill me, then. You'll be doing me a favor."

Sister Anne stopped, her stern face turning ashen. She retreated, rod in hand, behind her desk. She returned it to the drawer and walked to the scattered pile of blocks. She knelt and picked them up, gently, one by one. She looked at Teagan, her eyes watery yet still flashing anger. "Fathers Matthew and Mark have denied any wrongdoing. Your accusations against the convent have wounded me and the Order greatly." She gathered the letters and arranged them on her desk.

"That's why the Fathers were here, isn't it? You wanted to show them the letters?"

Sister Anne nodded. The Mother Superior leaned over her desk like a wounded bird, unsure of itself, fluttering, not knowing what to do as the body faltered. Teagan had no sympathy for her.

"If you persist in this madness, I'll have no choice but to send you away," Sister Anne said.

"What do you mean?"

"To an asylum—where you will be cared for until it's deemed you are well."

Teagan shook her head in disbelief. The Mother Superior would stop at nothing to ruin her life. "I'm not daft."

"Aren't you? False accusations. Infatuation with a priest. Thoughts of suicide."

"Suicide?"

"You want to die, don't you? You asked me to kill you. That's what you want. I know much more about these things than you do."

"You know I'm innocent. That's all I have to say." She left her chair and walked toward the door.

"Stop," the Mother Superior ordered. "I should send you to the Penitent's Room, but in light of your confused emotional state, hoping for death, I don't think it's a good idea. I'm calling for Sister Mary-Elizabeth." She picked up the telephone and turned her head so Teagan couldn't hear the conversation.

Gasping for breath, Sister Mary-Elizabeth arrived less than a minute later. "I came as soon as I could," she told Sister Anne.

"I want all in this room to see what I'm doing, so there is no question about what happened to these letters." She lifted the first and tore it into pieces, and then did the same to the second. She gathered the scraps in her hands and gave them to Sister Mary-Elizabeth. "Burn them," she ordered, "and make sure no more are written."

Teagan opened the door without looking back.

Sister Anne yelled as she walked away. "Remember what I said about your future! I'll fulfill my promise if I have to."

Teagan turned into the hall, not wishing to address Sister Anne directly. "I'll remember," she muttered as she climbed the stairs to the old library. She took a seat at her desk but couldn't work. Her hands shook as she watched Lea. Now there was something else to worry about. What if the Mother Superior made good on her threat?

Sleep did not come easily to Teagan for weeks after her confrontation with Sister Anne. Most nights she fluffed her pillow, fussed with the blanket, and tossed and turned in every possible position to get comfortable, but hardly anything worked. Often she stared at the ceiling, trying to force endless plans of escape out of her head. When sleep came, she dreamed of running free on Dublin roads, walking along the banks of the River Liffey with Cullen, even planting flower boxes at her parents' home. The euphoric feelings of freedom were extinguished when she awoke, leaving her exhausted and nervous.

In January, she was forced to work in the laundry again because another round of colds was circulating through the convent. Fortunately, she and Nora had escaped the virus. When they could, they used their hand signals and plotted how they would escape. There were few moments when they could talk. Escaping through the delivery door, as Nora had done, was out of the question now that Sister Ruth had been fooled. "Once, a fool; twice, a murderer," the nun had cautioned all the Magdalens with a glare in her eyes. The nun watched them all day, her gaze rarely interrupted. Each ensuing week their escape became more critical because of Nora's pregnancy, although the signs were not obvious yet. Teagan noticed a small swell in Nora's belly after she pointed it out, but no one else seemed the wiser. Not even Lea knew.

One day in early February, Teagan returned to the library to work at lace-mending. No one was around in the afternoon, since the Sisters trusted Lea, so she took the opportunity to speak with her friend. Lea was bent over her parchment, putting the finishing touches on "Christ Enthroned."

"What do you think?" Lea asked, as Teagan approached.

She leaned over the table and studied the drawing. "The colors are beautiful. You've done a wonderful job." Teagan looked toward the hall to make sure no one was near. The lights blazed overhead, although the day was fairly sunny. Any bits of snow had melted, as the sun rose higher and the days lengthened.

"I have to talk to you," Teagan whispered. "It's important."

Lea looked at her quizzically. She put her brush in its holder and turned to Teagan.

"You're our friend?" she asked Lea. "You want what's best for us?"

Lea nodded, looking perplexed by her questions. "I want us all to be friends. All of us—even the nuns."

Teagan blanched at Lea's assertion that they could be friends with the nuns, but decided to ignore the comment. "Remember when we played with the tarot cards?"

"Yes. The Empress card came up for you and Nora—long life and fruition."

The old nun, Sister Rose, walked past the door, but didn't glance inside. The nun's presence startled Teagan, and she stepped back from the table. Sister Rose disappeared down the hall, probably too consumed with thoughts of cutting a penitent's hair to notice a conversation in the library.

Teagan stole back to the desk and put her hand on Lea's shoulder. "That's right, and that means we're going to get out of here."

Lea scrunched up her mouth. "I suppose."

"*You* told me the cards never lie. Nora and I need your help."

Lea looked at her mournfully. "*My* help? What can I do?" She shook her head. "I don't want to lose my two best friends in the world."

Teagan grabbed Lea's hands. "Then leave with us. The three of us can make a go of it. We'll help each other."

Lea slumped in her chair. "I don't think I could ever leave here. What would I do? Draw pictures? No one will pay me for them. I can't go back to the farm where I'm not wanted. I don't have any other talents."

"You can read fortunes," Teagan said, grasping at anything to sway her friend.

Lea laughed. "Most people think fortune-tellers are frauds. I'd probably get arrested."

"Think how wonderful it would be to live in the world again. To smell fresh air—to be in the country with the ducks and geese—to be away from the stench of this place."

Lea tilted her head.

"If you want us to be happy, help us," Teagan pleaded. "The nuns trust you. You're the best friend we have. The convent's doors are always locked, the keys are protected by Mr. Roche, and the grounds are gated. Help us come up with a plan."

Lea's eyes filled with tears.

"Help us, please."

Lea wiped a trickle away from her cheek. "I want you and Nora to be happy."

Teagan hugged her. "And we want you to be happy. But Nora and I won't be until we get out of here." She paused. "I know this sounds odd, but can you get me a hammer and a bit of machine oil?"

Lea's face brightened. "I think Mr. Roche has those things in his office."

"Good. I'm going to come down with a fever this afternoon. Somehow get them to me between tea and prayers. Do your best. If it can't be done today, see if you can do it tomorrow." She walked toward the door.

"Where are you going?"

"I'm getting sick. Remember?" She sneaked up to the toilet and ran hot water over her face. Then she looked for Sister Mary-Elizabeth and found her standing outside the Mother Superior's office. Sister Mary-Elizabeth promptly sent her to bed because of her "fever."

A few hours later, Lea crept into the garret with a hammer and a small can of sewing machine oil in her pocket. She had taken a chance before tea and entered the open caretaker's cubby across the hall from Sister Anne's. The Mother Superior's office door was closed. "I needed a hammer to work on a shaky leg on my desk," Lea told her. That was going to be her excuse if she got caught.

As soon as Lea left, Teagan went to work on the window near her bed, taking out the nails that had been used to secure it. She oiled the window tracks and raised and lowered the sash until it made no noise. She stored the hammer, oil, and nails under her bed in case she needed to nail the window shut again. Her only regret was that she had missed tea. Her stomach growled. Tomorrow, she was certain, her health would return.

"I'm going out on the roof," Teagan whispered to Nora and Lea after Sister Mary-Elizabeth turned out the lights.

"Are you mad?" Nora asked. "Don't be a fool—you'll freeze to death."

"I'll only be outside for five minutes."

"Why?" Lea asked. "What if you get caught?"

"I'm going out there in a couple of hours. I'll tell you why after I get back. Now, be quiet."

She covered up and fell asleep under the warmth of her blankets. Her nerves, tingling with excitement, rocked her awake sometime after midnight. The garret was quiet; no one was stirring. She crept out of bed and walked to the garret doors, as if headed for the toilet. In the murky light, she could see the girls were sleeping, a few even snoring. The constant and familiar sounds of sleep would aid her plan.

She returned to her task and eased the sash up without a squeak. She unlatched the screen, crawled outside, and lowered the window quickly so an unwelcome blast of winter air wouldn't wake up the Magdalens.

The cold cut through her nightclothes. She sat on the tiles, judging whether it was safe to walk. It might be better to crawl. The winter snows on the west side of the roof had melted in the February sun. It seemed safe enough. She ran her fingers over the slate—no ice that she could feel—but in the dark it was hard to tell. She decided to crawl to her objective—the northwest corner of the convent, on the opposite side of where Lea, Nora, and she had congregated before.

There was little wind. Once her body adjusted to the temperature, she found the cold bearable. The moon drifted in a cloudless sky adorned with a blaze of stars. The lights of Dublin swam in the haze to the north.

She tested each tile before crawling farther toward the precipice, the length of the convent away. Its dark line beckoned her like a primitive explorer who longed to find the flat edge of the world. It took longer to get halfway across the roof than she thought. At this pace, she would be outside at least a half hour. She crawled faster, hoping to get to her goal sooner.

Her nightgown caught on the edge of a tile. She hitched her gown past her knees and carried on, like a dog on all four paws. Her left foot slipped, but she saved herself by clutching the tiles with her hands. It was a long way down. She would have fallen north of the laundry, somewhere around the chapel, onto the grounds. Another surprise appeared as she closed in. The north section of the convent was joined to a longer extension of the building, like a T, going west for some distance. It was only one story, with a flat roof, and past it, a row of lamps lined a deserted road. This structure had to be the orphanage that Lea had talked about, where some of the nuns the Magdalens occasionally saw lived and worked.

She reached her destination, over the chapel, panting from her exertions. She lay flat on the sloping tiles, hooked her fingers over the edge, pulled forward, and peered over the side. Her heart raced at what she saw.

Below, a spiked iron fence rose from the ground less than a yard from the foundation. The drop to the earth was three yards at most. An escarpment swelled up to the wall, making an escape difficult but much more likely than from the south side of the convent. The fence was a problem. One had to avoid the spikes and swing far enough out to land on the slope leading down to the road. A Latin cross stood at the peak of the roof. It looked solid enough. A plan came to Teagan's mind and she couldn't wait to tell her friends.

Teagan looked west over the low building and marveled that the orphanage was so secluded from the main convent. The only way into it had to be through a north entrance, or perhaps the small west door in the chapel. She had wondered where it went to. She shuddered, thinking of the children who might have died there.

She took her time crawling back, savoring the fresh, cold air on her skin. The feeling was so unlike the heat and humidity of the laundry and the often stale atmosphere of the library. If she had to stay here forever, she could imagine spending her life on the roof. The calm, the beautiful dark, filled her with a sense of peace. A serenity that she had experienced only a few times in her life filled her. She knew she was making the right choice, convinced more than ever that she and her friends had to escape this sacred prison.

The next morning, Teagan was bursting to tell Nora about her plan. The other Magdalens were scurrying about, the garret awake for the day, so she had to remain silent. The moment to talk presented itself as they walked to the breakfast room.

"I made a discovery last night," Teagan said discreetly.

Nora held on to the handrail as they descended.

"I'll talk to Lea this afternoon." She smiled at her friend. "I believe my plan will work." The other girls were close behind, so talking was difficult. In particular, she didn't want Patricia to hear. The girl had been an enemy since Nora had sprinkled her rolls with borax. "That's all I can say."

Nora reeled toward the wall and clutched the rail. Teagan let the others pass.

Teagan held on to her. "Are you all right? You look pale."

"I'm fine, but I think the time has come to divulge the secret."

Teagan balked, wondering how the nuns would react to Nora's pregnancy. What if they sent her away? "Oh my God, we have to get you out of here! We *all* have to get out of here!"

Nora held up her hand. "I won't be going anywhere, feeling like this. What use would I be to you?" She hitched her thumb toward the roof. "And if it involves gymnastics, you can count me out. Besides, I've had time to consider what happened when I left. What life do we have outside this convent?"

Teagan felt as if Nora had punched her in the gut. "You're not giving up, are you?"

Nora shook her head and inched down the steps. "No, but I'm pregnant, for God's sake."

She helped her friend down the stairs. "I won't let you give up. We can make this work—together. Lea is different—maybe she should stay here—but you and I need to get out."

She and Nora joined the other Magdalens in the breakfast room. There was no chance of talking now. She looked out the window and sighed. Clouds had rolled in overnight. Dread welled up inside her, as oppressive as the leaden sky. The winter day closed around her. How much could she take before she cracked? Dublin—Ireland—the whole world lay outside these grounds. If she found a way out, she would never come back. She would drown herself in the River Liffey before returning to The Sisters of the Holy Redemption. Forced servitude was no substitute for life.

Her breakfast of lukewarm tea, cold bacon, and toast turned her stomach. It was hardly enough to get a body started on a frosty morning.

Nora sat across the table, picking at her food. Her friend lifted her bacon, put half of it in her mouth, tried to chew, and then spit it out. She turned white and pursed her lips, as if she was holding back a retch.

Patricia raised her hands in alarm as she watched Nora. "Sister—"

"Shut up!" Teagan got up from her chair. "She's fine, aren't you, Nora?"

Nora nodded. "The bacon is bad."

The other girls stopped in mid-bite and looked at their food.

"Thanks for ruining my appetite," Patricia said.

"Anytime." Nora smiled.

The meal dragged on as the girls kept their eyes on Nora. After breakfast, Teagan walked to the library while Nora descended to the laundry. Sister Rose was already at the library door with a basketful of lace that needed mending. The nun dropped the work beside the desk and gave instructions on what to do and how fast it needed to be completed. After Sister Rose left, Teagan gathered her tools and began repairing a tear on a woman's Irish-lace handkerchief.

Before the noon meal, she found an opportunity to talk to Lea. "If we get enough fabric, we can make a rope to lower ourselves over the edge," Teagan explained. "Sometimes things rip apart because they're so old, or they fall to pieces in the dryer. Quite a few of the pieces are solid but the stains won't come out. Sister Ruth marks the inventory book and explains to the customers what happened. The laundry's been doing business for so long, and everyone trusts the nuns, so hardly anyone complains. The girls throw the scraps in a wicker basket that Mr. Roche empties once a day. I've seen it done many times." She leaned in to Lea. "That's where you come in. The nuns trust you more than any other Magdalen in the convent. Everything Nora and I get will have to be stowed under your bed until we have enough to make the rope. Will you do that for us?"

Lea looked undecided, but after a frown, she nodded. "Yes, but isn't it dangerous?"

"It's the only way out of here, unless you know where the keys are kept."

Lea tapped the end of her brush against the table. "Mr. Roche has keys, but I don't think he lets them out of his sight. Sister Anne has a set, but I don't know where she keeps them."

"So, that settles it. We'll have to be careful of the fence. That's the most difficult obstacle to clear. We can tie the rope around the cross and lower ourselves down. There's only a small rose window on the north side of the chapel. We don't have months—or even weeks—because Nora—" Teagan froze.

Lea stretched her long neck like a bird looking for food. "What about Nora?"

Teagan's face flushed. "I can't say."

Lea's eyes bored through her. "She's pregnant, isn't she?" Lea pointed her brush at Teagan. "I knew that would happen. The cards said so, it must be true." She turned back to her table and lowered her gaze. "The cards said you'd both have long and fruitful lives. They don't indicate where, though. I was hoping it would be here with me."

Teagan patted Lea's shoulder. "Nora's pregnant, but no one knows except us." She paused. "You can come, too. You don't have to stay here forever."

Lea shook her head. "My stepfather used to say, 'You can't beat a dead horse.' He was right. I'm not going anywhere. This is my home."

"I promise that after I leave and get settled, I'll come back for you. Cross my heart."

Lea shrugged and then turned back to her work. After a few moments, she said, "We'll see . . . we'll see."

A shadow moved across the floor, dark, flowing like a black river. She turned to find Sister Anne, her face grim as stone, only a few yards away. The Mother Superior said nothing as she walked toward them.

Teagan pointed to Lea's picture. "I think it's beautiful."

The Mother Superior continued her slow walk.

"Don't you think so, Mother?" Teagan asked. "Lea wanted my opinion."

Sister Anne stopped, her hands clutching her crucifix. "Why should I believe anything you tell me? You've proven yourself to be a liar. I suspect you two were conspiring about something." Her eyes flashed. "Teresa, you have a visitor, so come with me. Lea, get back to your painting. If you know what's good for you, you'll have nothing to do with this girl."

"Yes, Mother," Lea responded meekly. The life drained from her friend's eyes.

"Come with me, Teresa," Sister Anne said.

When they reached the closed office door, the Mother Superior stopped. Teagan stood in the hall. "I'm not going in, because your visitor has requested a private conversation. I'll see you when he's finished."

He? Teagan's heart fluttered. Could it be Cullen? No, Sister Anne would never leave her alone in a room with her boyfriend. Another thought struck her: *Maybe it's my father. No, it couldn't be.*

"Well, go ahead," Sister Anne prodded. "Open it."

Teagan opened it. Only the man's legs were visible, extending from one of the two chairs in front of Sister Anne's desk. He wore pressed black pants and a pair of brightly polished shoes. He slowly came into view as she walked toward him. The door closed behind her.

She recognized the curly black hair, the handsome face as it appeared in the wing chair. Father Mark rose from his seat and smiled at her. His expression wasn't insincere, Teagan thought, but it was awkward, a forced smile from guilt and pain. He didn't extend his hand, but instead gestured to the chair next to his.

"Please sit down," he said. "I've come to get something off my chest. A confession, of sorts."

Teagan sat, unsure what the priest was getting at, but she doubted no good could come from a conversation with a man who had driven her from her home.

CHAPTER 12

Teagan had been blinded by his perfection. As her anger bubbled up, she vowed to regard him as a man, nothing more, hardly a man of God. How ordinary he looked sitting in the chair. Sister Anne had opened the drapes, inviting the winter day in. The insipid light did nothing for him. It fell behind him, leaving his face darkened by shadow. His eyes had lost the sparkle they'd held when she first met him at the rectory. What a glorious beginning that had been: a day filled with flirtatious innocence, only to be dashed by alcohol and lies. The creases around his eyes had deepened, as well, making him seem older.

He started to lean toward her, but then collapsed in his chair, as if deflated by the effort to be friendly. He clutched the armrests.

"I don't know how to begin," he finally said. "It's foolish of me to ask how you're doing. I can tell from looking." He studied her, his dark brows coming together. "You look tired, Teagan. Are you getting enough rest?"

She suppressed the urge to laugh, and wondered if, for spite, she should play the part of the unrepentant Magdalen, and answer his question with sarcasm. It was too easy to be slutty, too easy to be angry. And what good would it do to antagonize him?

"None of us gets enough rest, really," she said calmly. "You have no idea what it's like here, do you?"

"I don't think any priest does." He turned away and gazed out the window for a moment. "Nuns handle the operations of the laundries. It's their domain." He looked back and straightened in his chair. "Sister Anne showed us the letters you wrote. Father Matthew was happy that they went no further than the Mother Superior's desk. Everyone agreed no harm had been done."

"I suspected as much."

"Of course, I'm rather shocked by your appearance—your weight, the gaunt look, the extreme cut of your hair. You were thin to begin with."

Teagan smiled at the irony. "You did look me over. I knew you did." She brushed her hand across the top of her head. "Sister Rose, 'The Butcher of Holy Redemption' as we like to call her, keeps our hair short. She cuts it every two weeks like clockwork, so it doesn't get out of hand, even though she's so frail she can hardly hold the clippers. Sometimes the girls bleed from the cuts on their heads." She laughed. It echoed in the room. "We wouldn't want to copy the latest styles, you know. God forbid we had a bouffant, or a flip. I guess such things are for those who live in the realm of the 'worldly.' But you saw me at Christmas Mass. I guess you couldn't stand to look at me."

Father Mark cringed. "I'm sorry."

Teagan knew enough to reject his thoughtless apology outright. She stared at him with an icy glare. "Why are you here? I'm sure it's not to see me. Otherwise, you would have come long ago. Or perhaps you don't want to talk about it. In that case, I'll call for Sister Anne."

"Please . . . please, hear me out." He leaned toward her. "I've been through hell because of this whole business."

"'*I've*' been through hell?" She wanted to slap the priest. She balled her fists and shook them at him. "Unless you can give me a good reason to stay, there's nothing else to talk about. Why don't you go back to your Bible, your rosaries, and your Masses, so you can save the other *sinners* around you?" She got up and turned her back to him. "You disgust me!"

She felt him, warm, against her.

He put his hand on her shoulder. "I wanted to pray for *our* sin, for God to forgive us."

She lurched away. "Liars must earn their absolution."

She heard his breath catch.

As she turned, he reeled backward. A sob burst from his lips as he sank into his chair. He swiped at his eyes. "I'm asking for your forgiveness, Teagan."

She stood, unmoved by his plea.

"Did you hear me?" he asked. "I'm seeking your forgiveness. It was *our* fault. We were both to blame. You know that. *You* felt it, too."

"Then tell the truth about *your* sin. Get me out of this convent."

He shook his head. "I can't do that. We've both sinned and have to pay the price."

Teagan turned and walked away. At the door, she looked back. "I didn't realize how weak a priest could be. You're scared of the truth. I'm calling for Sister Anne—at least she's honest in her hatred. I'm going back to the laundry. When I walk out of here, I don't want to see you again. Do you understand? I want nothing to do with you."

Father Mark got up without a word. His arms hung by his side. He gathered his coat and hat and brushed past her, pausing briefly at Mr. Roche's office. The old caretaker hobbled to the doors and opened them. The priest disappeared down the convent steps.

Too numb to cry, Teagan walked unsteadily back to the chair. The *LOVE* blocks on Sister Anne's desk taunted her with their ridiculous message. Her mind reeled. Now that he was officially an enemy, Father Mark would go about his business, ignoring her forever. Perhaps she had at least made him think, placed the guilt of her circumstances squarely on his shoulders. Was he so vain that he thought he'd be absolved by an admission of her feelings about him?

A few minutes later, the Mother Superior appeared at the door as if she had materialized from the ether. The sight of the smug Sister Anne plunged Teagan deeper into despair. She sobbed, unabashed by the nun's presence. The Mother Superior reached for her, as if in sympathy. Teagan sensed a flicker of compassion in the gesture. The spark was brief and was extinguished almost as quickly as it began.

Sister Anne withdrew her hand, straightened, and said, "I don't know what Father Mark had to say . . ." She faltered. "He spoke to me of compassion and forgiveness. That's all he would tell me."

Teagan lifted the edge of her apron and wiped her eyes. "You wouldn't believe me if I told you."

"I already know the truth."

"Then there's nothing I can say or do that will change your mind."

The Mother Superior harrumphed and clapped her hands. "There's no time for such foolishness in the life of a penitent. Work. Good, hard, honest work is what you need to save your soul. And it shall be done. Back to your mending." She pointed to the door.

Teagan's legs felt as if they were weighted with chains as she trudged back to the library. Lea, bent over her desk, ignored her as she resumed her work on a lace handkerchief. She wondered whether her friend had taken Sister Anne's words, *"Have nothing to do with this girl,"* to heart.

No one celebrated Nora's seventeenth birthday in February. She decided not to mention it to anyone, not even to Teagan. Her baby was the most important thing on her mind.

A few days later, her hand slipped on the slick porcelain of a basin. She caught herself with the other as pain stabbed her stomach. *My God, I'm going to have the wanker on the spot.* She looked over her shoulder at Teagan, who stood near a dryer. Another afternoon in the laundry for both of them. There was no escaping it. Sister Ruth was preoccupied with an incoming delivery and hadn't seen her slip. The girl closest to her, Sarah, eyed her with concern.

She looked down at her hands—rough, raw, with reddish welts from the hot water and bleach. The sight of her blistered hands, the acrid smell of the laundry, suddenly turned her stomach and she bent over the basin.

Sarah rushed to her side. "Are you okay?" Her eyes were wide with fear. "Should I call Sister Ruth?"

Nora looked at the stout nun bending over a laundry parcel near the entrance. She wanted nothing to do with her, despite the fever building in her head and the blue dots prancing across her vision. "No." She clutched the basin's edge with both hands. "The smell is doing me in. Give me a minute."

She stepped back from the sink and swayed into Sarah's arms. The slight girl caught her, but Nora's weight was too much. They both ended up on their knees on the floor.

"Sister Ruth! Sister Ruth!" Sarah's screams rang out over the roar of the machines.

Nora closed her eyes and sank against Sarah's chest. The sensation of settling against the girl was oddly comforting, like having a good friend who understood all your problems. She wanted to close her eyes and take a long nap; and, when she awoke, everything would be better.

"What's the matter with you?" a stern voice asked.

Nora opened her eyes and found Sister Ruth staring into her face. Teagan looked over Sister Ruth's shoulder.

"Get back on your feet this instant!" the nun demanded. "This is no time for a nap, not when there's work to be done." From her tone, it was obvious that Sister Ruth still held a grudge against Nora for escaping.

Nora held out her hand to Teagan, who tried to lift her. She flopped back against Sarah.

"Oh, for the love of God," Sister Ruth said. "Give me your hand." Her thick fingers extended from the black sleeve of her habit. Nora reached up, but she slipped from the nun's grasp and landed against Sarah again. Sister Ruth leaned down and grasped her under the arms. In a dead lift, the nun grunted and wrested Nora to her feet. Sister Ruth half-carried, half-dragged her to a secluded corner in the north side of the laundry, away from the washers and dryers. Nora called out for Teagan, but Sister Ruth waved her away.

"What's gotten into you?" Sister Ruth said and lowered her head even with Nora's. "You look like the divil himself. Sit down."

Nora slid into a plastic folding chair that had been placed in the corner. It felt cool against her hot skin. She wiped her forehead with her hand.

"I'm off," Nora said and forced a smile. "It's those horrible breakfasts you serve us. Makes me sick to me stomach."

"Nonsense," Sister Ruth said. "None of the girls are complaining about the food, except you." She ran her hand across Nora's forehead and then shook her fingers in the air. "Your head's as damp as castle walls in spring. You've got a fever." She looked at Nora from head to toe a few times, then her gaze stopped at Nora's belly. The nun's eyes blazed.

"Stand up," Sister Ruth ordered.

Nora got up from the chair, shaky on her feet, but steadied herself by holding on to a wall.

Sister Ruth put her hand on Nora's stomach and nodded her head. "Let me tell you what's going on—if you don't mind me grabbing a bit of Sherlock Holmes." She smirked. "You were gone for nearly a week, you're sick to your stomach, and your belly's got a bump." The nun thrust her hands on her hips. "You're pregnant."

Nora wondered how she should respond. She hadn't wanted any of the nuns to know until she had told Sister Mary-Elizabeth, the one who might soften the blow to Sister Anne. Perhaps she could bluff Sister Ruth.

"That's ridiculous. I'm not feeling well." She sat in the chair. Her head swam as if she were on a carousel.

"No, my little lass, you're turning green, and it's not from envy. I'm getting Sister Anne. She'll decide what to do with you." She stormed away, her habit flowing behind her.

As soon as Sister Ruth had gone, Teagan ran to Nora and knelt down in front of her. Her friend grabbed her hands. "I'm done for," Nora said. "She's gone to get Sister Anne."

"You told her?" Teagan asked.

"No, but Sister Ruth's not stupid." The room spun around her, and she lowered her head. "I really feel like I need to barf. You'd better get back to your station or you'll be in trouble."

Teagan stood. "Okay, but I'll be watching."

Nora slumped in her chair as the minutes ticked away. She gulped in air and closed her eyes, hoping to stem the circles rotating in front of her eyes. Sister Anne would be furious; she could feel it in her bones. Who knew what the Mother Superior would do? Maybe she'd send her away for the length of her pregnancy to someplace more comfortable, like a hospital. She thought of herself resting in a room, reading a magazine in bed, a nurse serving her tea and breakfast in bed.

That bubble burst when she opened her eyes. The Mother Superior glared at her. Sisters Ruth, Mary-Elizabeth, and Rose stood on either side of Sister Anne, their strict gazes falling upon Nora like rays from an ominous black sun.

"Get up," Sister Anne said and tugged on Nora's arm.

"I don't feel well." She grasped the Mother Superior's arm.

"I've had enough of this! Get up! I want to see for myself."

She steadied herself against the wall and hitched herself up.

Sister Anne leered and pointed to Nora's stomach. "In plain sight for all to see but the blind. Come along."

She pulled at Nora, who stopped a few feet from the chair. "I'm going to be sick."

"Don't be—"

Nora's throat convulsed, and a stream of greenish bile flew from her mouth onto Sister Anne's habit. The Mother Superior skittered back, her lips tight and her eyes filled with disgust.

"Oh, Mother!" Sister Ruth hurried to get a towel from a laundry bin.

"Fool!" Sister Anne stepped forward as Nora slumped. "You'll be mopping this up for the rest of the afternoon. Not only your mess, but the rest of the floors." Sister Ruth rushed back with a towel and dabbed at Sister Anne's habit.

"Stop it," Sister Anne said and pushed the nun away. "I'll have to burn this one. Spawn of the devil upon it."

Nora's stomach felt better, although her head was still swimming. She clutched the railing that ran alongside the long bank of windows.

"Can't you see she's ill?" Teagan shouted above the tumult.

"Shut up!" Sister Anne's voice was shrill, enraged by the question.

"I will not shut up. She's sick. She needs care or she might lose the baby."

Sister Anne swung at Teagan, slapping her hard on the left cheek.

Teagan gasped and stumbled backward. Sister Anne's face reddened as she raised her hand again.

Teagan said nothing, but turned her other cheek to the Mother Superior. The color drained from Sister Anne's face. The nun strode toward the door, calling back, "Take Monica to the Penitent's Room for the night, where she can consider the consequences of her actions." She turned and gave a defiant look to Teagan. "Teresa can clean up this mess, and when she's through here she can scrub every hall in this convent. Don't let her stop until she's finished." She disappeared up the stairs.

Sister Ruth pointed to Teagan. "You heard the Mother. Get busy. Mr. Roche will give you a bucket and a mop."

Sister Mary-Elizabeth took Nora by the arm and led her through the laundry to the stairs. "Looks like you've gotten yourself into a big mess this time. Didn't anyone teach you the rules of the game?"

Nora nodded. "I guess I've never played fair."

The nun shook her head. "And look where it got you—another night in the Penitent's Room."

Nora clutched the railing as they walked up the stairs. "Would you be good enough to get me a glass of water before you lock me up? I'm feeling parched."

"I suppose I could do that," Sister Mary-Elizabeth said. "No need to punish the baby."

They stopped outside the door to the Penitent's Room. Sister Mary-Elizabeth unlocked it with her key. Nora stepped inside and sat on the stool. The door closed, sealing the darkness over her. She flicked the vomit from her caked lips. It wasn't so bad in the Penitent's Room anymore, she thought, as she waited for the nun to return. *Maybe I'm getting used to it. I'll be spending the rest of me life in the dark.* She patted her stomach and made a vow: *Whatever happens, I want you to have a better life than me. I'll do me best for you.* She closed her eyes and thought of a cooling draught of water.

Sister Anne stripped off the habit and threw it at the door. This one would have to be thrown out, like the old ones that had fallen apart. She opened the wardrobe, found a clean habit, and slipped it on. She sat at her desk and gazed out the window, looking at the bare branches of the oaks and the dull sky, the light slowly decaying everything to monochrome. Spring could not come soon enough. When she was a child, she had dreamed of going to the Caribbean or Bermuda to spend winter days on sun-splashed beaches, with nothing to do but swim in the cerulean waters and watch the puffy clouds slip by. But that dream had never been fulfilled. Family circumstances had made it impossible to take a holiday outside of Ireland. Even a few days off in Dublin were a luxury for the family.

She tried to empty her mind of thoughts about the penitent. Monica was no good. She deserved her time in the Room, to consider her sin, even though she was pregnant. If her sister had considered her sin, perhaps she wouldn't have died in childbirth. God's punishment for the sinner could be harsh. *Contemplation. Contemplation is good for the soul. At least the Buddhists, with their hideous excuse for a religion, got something right.* She would release Monica in the morning after a night of "contemplation."

She didn't feel like praying, and instead she picked up a book of religious verse. She thumbed through the book, thinking it would calm her nerves, but another voice called to her. *Another cut and the pain will be gone. The deeper the cut, the better you will feel.* She slammed the book on the table and shouted,

"No!" Her cry rattled against the window and dissipated in the emptiness of the room. The blades were no good today; the thought scared her. What if she cut too deep?

A feeble knock broke her daydreams. Sister Anne stood up, straightened her habit, and turned to the door. "Come in."

Sister Rose, looking like an old crane, stepped inside. "Sister Mary-Elizabeth wanted me to tell you that everything has been taken care of before tea, Mother. Monica is in the Penitent's Room, and Teresa is attending to her cleaning."

"Good." Sister Anne pointed to the soiled habit lying near the door. "Take that away and see that it's destroyed."

"Yes, Mother." Sister Rose bowed and then lifted the stained garment. The old nun seemed so brittle Sister Anne thought she might snap in half.

"One more thing," Sister Anne said. "Bring Teresa and Lea to me. I need to talk to them, and be sure to tell Sisters Mary-Elizabeth and Ruth not to let Teresa eat until she has washed all the floors. Is that clear?"

"Yes, Mother." The nun backed away and closed the door.

Sister Anne sat at her desk and waited for the girls. After a few minutes, the same weak knock came. "Enter," Sister Anne said, without much enthusiasm, as she turned her chair. The three entered the room and stood in front of her. She ordered Sister Rose to wait outside until she had finished with the girls.

She studied them. Teresa was still pretty, if not thinner than when she had arrived. Her skin seemed lighter; her color had faded over the months. None of the Magdalens saw much of the sun. Still, she had a defiant look about her. The grim determination set in her jaw, and her erect posture, reminded her of another woman she had known. Lea, on the other hand, looked like a girl who would forever struggle to find a place in the world. Sister Anne knew Lea was smart and artistic—maybe too bright for her own good. She had known people like that. Brilliant students who, when it came to living, couldn't figure out how to light a stove, let alone raise a family. Often they were stunted emotionally by their own pain. Lea, with her large eyes and long neck, gave the appearance of a fragile being, one not meant for this world. A push and she would be over the edge. It struck Sister Anne that Lea's vulnerability was the reason she had liked the girl from the beginning. It was a secret bond between them, but not one to be cultivated, only exploited.

"You must answer me honestly," Sister Anne said. "I will know if you're lying."

Teresa smiled, but a smirk simmered underneath.

"I will ask you only once." She lifted the silver crucifix that hung from her sash. "Did either of you know that Monica was pregnant?"

They stood silent before her. She thought Lea looked perplexed by her question, but wasn't entirely certain of her guilt. The girl could just as easily have been sad that Monica had been sent to the Penitent's Room.

Teresa glanced at Lea. *Now we're getting somewhere.*

"Come now," she coaxed. "You both knew."

Neither answered her. Lea shuffled her feet and looked out the window. Teresa stood silent.

"Talk," she ordered, but neither obeyed. Sister Anne stared at them for a minute, deciding what to do. She didn't want to put them in the Penitent's Room with Monica. Lea was a hopeless case, a child really. But Teresa was another matter. She doubted her innocence, but she had no firm evidence. The Mother Superior called out for Sister Rose.

The elderly nun opened the door.

"Take them back to their work," she ordered.

They left her room, and soon she was sitting alone as dusk encircled the convent with its indigo light.

She lit a fire to break the chill. She had hoped to sever the bond between them, to ascertain the father of Monica's child so she could report him to the Church. But it was no use today. She was sure of one fact, however: Neither girl had spoken, so neither one had lied.

Nora couldn't see the glass in her hand, but she could feel its cold slickness after she drank the water. Sister Mary-Elizabeth had been kind and brought her an apple, as well. She put it in her apron pocket to eat later when she was sure she'd be hungry. She stared into the dark. Swirling patterns of lights and stars formed in her eyes. The faces of her friends, Teagan and Lea, popped out of the wall. Both smiled at her in a silly way and she grinned back, although no one was there to see her brief happiness.

Would death be easier, more welcome, than sitting in this torturous room? Or was death like this? She shivered, as if a cold hand had grasped her shoulder, and she jerked backward expecting to see the Grim Reaper, but the void that stretched behind her was black.

She took the last sip from the glass and ran her fingers over its surface once more. Sister Mary-Elizabeth had made a mistake, one that could be fatal. Sister Anne would be furious if a Magdalen committed suicide in the Penitent's Room. She could toss the glass against the granite, take a shard, and cut deeply into her wrist. By the time the nuns found her, she would be dead. But her child would be dead, too. Her baby didn't deserve to die because of what she had done. Nora placed the glass on the floor and closed her eyes. She needed sleep.

Sister Ruth had spat at her as Sister Mary-Elizabeth led her away from the laundry. *"Cast out the harlot from your heart!"* The words rang in her ears as Sister Ruth's contorted mouth spoke them over and over again in her head: *Harlot, harlot, harlot! I must be one.*

She slapped herself and shook her head. *What is happening? I can't give up. I won't let them beat me.*

A sickening wave of exhaustion washed over her. She scooted back on the stool, slumping against the rocky surface of the wall. A twinge hit her stomach. Did the baby just kick? It could have, although she was only three months into her pregnancy. Maybe she had imagined it.

A tiny point of light formed in her eyes, and like the other swirls and stars she had seen before, she expected this one to vanish. It grew, however, from a dot to a spreading aura that filled her eyes. She blinked, hoping to rid herself of the uncomfortable glare—it was blinding—creeping toward her from the door. Instead of fading, it grew brighter. She held her eyes open, thinking her vision had somehow been compromised by the darkness, but the light was there, growing, filling the room with its power. The walls came into focus, even the white scars, the scratches of the penitents before her. The glass that Sister Mary-Elizabeth had given her lit up like a prism on the floor.

The room exploded in a rainbow of color.

She closed her eyes for a moment. When she opened them, she gasped. A beautiful lady was standing before her, weeping, tears flowing from her eyes. The lady was dressed in a brilliant white gown, and she held a white rose in her hands. A blue veil covered her head and fell in silky waves down her sides.

Nora opened her mouth to speak, but no words came out. The woman's tears fell upon her apron and their warmth spread throughout her body. She felt as if she were sitting in her favorite spot in the park on a warm spring day, the sunlight enlivening her, filling her with joy, vanquishing the winter cold. Fear drained out of her as the woman held out her hand. She wanted Nora to take the rose.

Nora grasped the flower and felt its firm, thorny stem, the downy softness of its white petals. A shock coursed through her right arm and shoulders before settling in her heart. She thought it would explode with happiness—but the feeling was more than happiness. *Ecstasy.* She knew the word, but had never experienced it, had never truly known what it meant. Every nerve in her body was on fire with joy. There was no pain to be found anywhere, in the glowing room, in the convent, perhaps nowhere on earth. All was peace and happiness. She luxuriated in its love.

The lady smiled and the tears stopped. Nora took the woman's hand, kissed it, and the room swirled away. She closed her eyes and sank into a whirlpool of light.

A strange feeling struck Lea at evening prayers. She viewed her time in the chapel, after four years, as a meditation rather than a supplication before the altar. Instead of praying, head bowed, legs on the kneeler, as most of the Magdalens did, she would focus on the candles in the room and let her mind roam free. She didn't consider it an escape, but a chance to relax from her art. The room comforted her with its wavering yellow light, the smell of burning wax, the murmur of muttered prayers.

But this evening was different. Something extraordinary had happened in the Penitent's Room, next to the chapel. She knew it as resolutely as she knew those small bundles had been buried in the yard, as certainly as she had seen Jesus on the lawn. The feeling crept over her as she thought of nothing in particular, the sensation of a force so powerful it could rend open the heavens. It wasn't ominous or evil; on the contrary, joy crawled up her spine, and gooseflesh prickled her arms. It was a woman, the Virgin, garbed in white, crying for her friend Nora. The vision stayed with her for about a minute and then disappeared into the vapor, leaving Lea spent but tingling in ecstasy.

She walked with the others after prayers, all the Magdalens headed to their sleeping quarters above. Sister Mary-Elizabeth led the way this evening. The usually affable nun seemed out of sorts to Lea, with little patience for the girls. The nun scowled when she touched her arm. Lea was uncertain whether she should bother her, but decided to recount her experience in the chapel despite the nun's mood.

"What is it, child?" The nun stared at her, irritated.

"Did you feel anything at prayers, Sister Mary-Elizabeth?" She felt foolish asking the question.

"Outside of my usual lumbago on these cold evenings, no." She stopped on the landing to let the Magdalens pass. "Let me tell you, I've had my fill of this day, to be sure. I'm ready to put you all to bed and crawl into mine." She shook her head.

"Who's in the Penitent's Room?" Lea asked.

Sister Mary-Elizabeth held her hand to her forehead in disgust. "What's it to you? Has she done something else I should know about? She gets into such trouble." The nun relaxed a bit and lowered her hand. "Oh, that's right, you don't know anything about what went on today in the laundry. Well, good for you, but your friend Nora—Monica—is in the room."

The other Magdalens disappeared into the toilet or the garret, leaving Sister Mary-Elizabeth and Lea standing under the glare of an overhead light.

"I have a confession to make, Sister," Lea said.

Sister Mary-Elizabeth rolled her eyes and shook her head. "I'm a nun, Lea, not a priest."

"No, it's not that. Sometimes I see things that others don't."

The nun smiled. "Is that all that's bothering you? We know you do, even the Mother Superior—we've come to expect it." She turned and started to walk away.

"I've seen the children buried in the yard. Sometimes I see them at night when everyone is asleep. They wake me up."

The nun stopped abruptly and turned to her. The Sister's face was rigid, her eyes searching for an answer. "What do you mean?"

Lea walked toward her. "What I just said. I saw you and the other nuns burying bundles in the yard with the help of Mr. Roche. But that's not all."

Sister Mary-Elizabeth crossed her arms, her hands fitted into the opposite sleeves of her habit. She stood like a black monolith. "Go on."

"I've seen Jesus and the Virgin."

"Watch what you say, child." The nun pursed her lips. "There's a large divide between reality and blasphemy. I've seen the Virgin, too, many times, in the Bible, in paintings, in my dreams, but I would *never* say I saw her in person."

Lea tilted her head. "I saw the Virgin today. She wore a white dress and carried a white rose. She visited Monica in the Penitent's Room. She was crying."

"Monica?"

"No, the Virgin. She was sad for Monica."

The nun grabbed Lea by the shoulders. "I think we've had enough of this foolishness. Time for bed." She walked with her down the hall. "It's the emotion of the day. There's been too much trouble this afternoon at The Sisters of the Holy Redemption. That's what's affecting you."

Lea stopped by the garret doors. She pushed it open gently and peered in. The other Magdalens, including Teagan, were getting ready for bed. She let the door close. "I know babies and girls have died here. I know it as sure as I'm alive."

Sister Mary-Elizabeth, her eyes dark, lowered her head. She said slowly, "The convent has seen many a tragedy. Some have succumbed from disease and neglect—but not caused by the Sisters. Their families have neglected them or they've neglected themselves. In some cases, we were too late to save them. It's a sadness that weighs upon us all." She lifted her head and managed a weak smile. "But we mustn't dwell on these things. That will do no good."

"Have some girls tried to escape by the roof and died?"

The nun shook her gently. "You are full of it tonight, a gobsmack full." She opened a door and shoved her inside. "Lights-out in ten minutes! Go to bed and forget all this nonsense. No wonder you're an artist. You make things up in your head."

The door closed, leaving Lea to wonder whether she was crazy to go out on the roof tonight as she had planned.

After the lights were turned out, Lea told Teagan about seeing the Virgin, and her conversation with Sister Mary-Elizabeth. "You see things all the time," Teagan snapped. "No one takes you seriously."

Her friend muttered a terse account of her afternoon interaction with the Mother Superior, including the slap across the face. Apparently, Teagan was still smarting from her run-in with Sister Anne.

"I have to get out of here," was Teagan's telling response before she pulled the covers over her head. She settled like a lump under her blanket. Nora's bed was empty.

It had been too long since she had been outside, Lea thought, as she gazed out the window. No one had discovered that Teagan had taken out the nails and oiled the runners. The black panes were icy with cold. In reality, the temperature outside was probably no more frigid than when she had to run from her bed to the toilet on a chilly morning. She had grown up in winter cold and summer warmth, a country girl who could handle the weather. How wonderful it would be to breathe fresh air again, maybe for the last time on the roof, because once Teagan and Nora made their escape she was certain the window would be secured with more than nails, maybe even be bricked up.

The faraway stars shone as hazy blobs through the window. All she had to do was lift the sash, unhook the screen, and crawl out. She wanted to do this for her friends. They were so unhappy here and, frankly, the convent had been turned upside down since they came. All the other girls seemed to fit in—they didn't cause much trouble or antagonize Sister Anne. There had been run-ins before, but nothing of the sort that was going on with Teagan and Nora. Perhaps the world was changing—for the worse. There was rock and roll and other modern things she had paid little attention to. *I want no part of it. I won't be going home. All I want to do is finish my drawings and be comfortable until I die. Then I'll meet Jesus and the Virgin.*

So far, Teagan and Nora's plan hadn't progressed too far. Storing old bits of sheets and tablecloths under her bed in the hope of making a "rope" to lower themselves to the ground was harder than they'd thought. They had only gathered a few pieces longer than arm's length, and she wasn't sure those would hold their weight. She chuckled inwardly. And her friends thought *she* was daft!

Lea slipped from under her covers and stood at the window. None of the other Magdalens would suspect a thing. Many of them had seen her standing in the same spot, looking out on the grounds. The cold air penetrated the glass and her nightgown, causing her to break out in chills. Now was the time.

She lifted the sash, undid the latch, crawled out, and lowered the window, a process that only took a few seconds. The cold shocked her, but she breathed in deeply, relishing the icy air that plunged into her lungs. She held on to the frame and lowered herself to the tiles. The cold burned her skin and her feet skidded on a slick coating of frost. Teagan had told her how she had crawled to the north face of the convent to scout out the planned escape route. That was where she was headed, too.

The going was slow and slippery, but she managed to get to the far end by forcing her fingers and toes into the ridges between the tiles. She looked over the roof. The ground did slope up toward the end of the chapel, just as Teagan had told her. The spiked iron fence was a problem. The girls would have to swing over it by rappelling like a mountain climber on a descent. If they could manage that, it would only be a short drop to the ground. Even if they cleared the fence, they might swing back into it. If so, they could simply climb down by positioning their feet against the bars. But there was the problem of attaching the makeshift rope.

Lea looked across the sloping roof to the cross positioned above her. It looked sturdy enough, attached to the apex. More material than they had currently gathered would be required to run a rope from the cross to the ground—she estimated at least ten yards.

A sound, like an animal scratching, rose from below. She held on to the roof's edge and looked over her shoulder. Something was in the yard. She couldn't quite see it, but an aura, bright and white, lit the corner where the chapel connected with the low building that stretched west. The light crept up the walls, rising from the ground.

Sister Mary-Elizabeth's voice came to mind. *"No wonder you're an artist. You make things up in your head."*

The air seemed colder as the nun's voice grew louder: *"There's a large divide between reality and blasphemy. I've seen the Virgin, too, many times, in the Bible, in paintings, in my dreams, but I would never say I saw her in person."*

Lea clutched the tiles and tried to turn around. Her fingers slipped and she slid a bit from her perch. Was it Mr. Roche with an electric torch? Did he know she was on the roof? If he did, she was in serious trouble.

She studied the light. Its brightness had spread. It wasn't confined to the corner; the grounds seemed to be lit by some kind of preternatural glow. Lumps of white, globules of powdery light, were bouncing from the earth, getting higher and higher up the convent walls until they nearly reached the three stories to the roof.

Then she saw the fingers, arching, with dirty nails, grasping at the tiles. Then a head—a little boy with no eyes at all, dark sockets in a glowing white face, leering at her. Another blob appeared, a child too young to tell if it was a boy or a girl, as it drifted in the light toward her. It was crying, its tiny arms thrashing in the air. More and more of them came up the side of the building. Children covered in tattered blankets with bodies blackened by dirt.

She uttered a prayer. She had seen these children buried and done nothing about it. Now they were out to get her. They cried out silently, admonishing her to reveal their secret to the world.

"No!" Her legs slipped on the tiles.

They were coming closer.

"I can't tell. They'll hate me! They won't believe me, they'll send me away!"

The boy with no eyes touched her foot. Her leg turned to ice under his touch.

They were rising from the grave because she knew their secret. Their faces were all around her.

She stiffened as they closed in. The cold swallowed her. Her fingers and toes went numb.

The white faces leered at her as she fell.

Teagan shot up in bed at the sound of the scream. She turned toward Lea's bed and her stomach knotted.

The Magdalens rustled in their beds.

"What was that?" Patricia asked in a groggy voice.

The overhead lights snapped on, and Sister Mary-Elizabeth stood in the doorway, her face twisted in a look of horror. "That was the most bloodcurdling shriek I've ever heard, loud enough to wake the dead. What's going on?"

Teagan said nothing as the Sister ambled toward the end of the room. The nun covered her mouth with her hands when she saw Lea's empty bed. "Oh my God." She peered out the window into the night.

CHAPTER 13

The shrill cry entered the Penitent's Room. Nora shook, thinking she'd had a nightmare, but it didn't take long for her to
realize that the sound was real. The voice seemed alien, un-
earthly, and the scream had set her shivering. Her back ached
from sleeping against the rough stones. She dragged herself off
the stool, fumbled in the dark, and found the door. She put her
ear to it. There was commotion above. Odd, she thought, considering it must be the middle of the night.

Shouts. Women screaming.

*Oh my God. What if there's a fire? I'd be burned alive and
nobody would remember until I was a pile of ashes.*

Sister Anne's muffled voice yelled instructions. "She needs
medical treatment! Carry her inside!" Footsteps sounded on the
stairs.

When she realized she might be left in the Penitent's Room as
a catastrophe unfolded outside, she panicked. She pounded on
the door, yelling for help. No one seemed to hear. The commotion in the hall continued unabated.

Nora screamed and kicked the door, trying desperately to get
someone's attention.

Finally, the key scratched against the latch. She blinked as
Sister Mary-Elizabeth's harried face appeared in the light.

The nun shook her head. "I haven't got time for you now. I'll
get to you in the morning."

"I need to use the jacks," Nora said. She didn't really, but she was willing to use any excuse to get out of the room. "What's happening?"

"Nothing to concern you. Can't you hold it for a minute? We're in trouble here." The Sister started to close the door.

"I've seen the Virgin." Nora blurted out the only response that she thought would get the nun's attention.

The nun froze, her forehead crinkled in amazement. "You?" she asked incredulously.

"Yes. The lady in white carrying a white rose."

The nun took a deep breath. "Oh, my Jesus. You and—" Sister Mary-Elizabeth pulled Nora out of the room, slammed the door and locked it.

Nora blinked in the light. She looked up and saw a line of Magdalens, including Teagan, peering down the staircase.

"Get back to bed—all of yeh," the nun said and flicked her wrists to shoo them away. "This is too much." She turned to Nora. "You get up to bed with them. Tomorrow we're going to the Mother Superior and tell her what you saw." She rushed off down the hall.

The girls backed off a bit, but still hovered near the landing.

The front doors were open. It was the first time Nora had seen them so since the good weather in the fall. A crumpled body, the clothing stained with blood, lay near the door. The Mother Superior and several nuns, including Sisters Mary-Elizabeth, Ruth, and Rose, were bent over it.

The nuns didn't notice Nora creeping closer to the girl. Lea lay pale and limp on the cold marble, her eyes closed. Her night-gown was pulled up on her right leg, exposing a deep red cut. Blood oozed from her flesh to the floor.

The nuns were wrapping towels around Lea's leg. Sister Rose knelt behind the girl and cradled her head in her lap. The old nun took a handkerchief from her gown and wiped it across Lea's forehead. Sister Ruth folded her hands and prayed over the body.

Soon, a siren echoed in the hall, followed by lights arcing up the drive. Two men in white uniforms hurried into the convent with a stretcher. The nuns watched as the men bent over Lea, attending to the wound and checking her pulse. As they lifted Lea's body onto the stretcher, Nora joined the other girls at the landing. She stood next to Teagan.

"What happened?" Nora asked.

Teagan walked away and motioned for Nora to follow. They walked up the stairs to the garret before Teagan spoke. "Quick, help me." She pointed to Lea's bed. "Find the loose planks underneath. I've got to get the nails and hammer out from under mine."

Nora rushed to Lea's bed, got down on her knees, and reached under it. She pounded the floor until the sound reverberated as a hollow *thud*. She tugged on one of the boards and it came up easily in her hands. "I've found it!"

Teagan was at her side, handing the nails and hammer to her. Nora had just replaced the board when the other girls appeared at the door. She and Teagan returned to their beds. They sat quietly as the others skulked into the garret.

"What was she doing out on the roof?" Patricia asked before plopping on her bed. "I thought the window was nailed shut."

"I thought so, too," Betty answered. "But she took a nasty fall, that's for sure. Better her than me. Someone's going to pay the piper for this." The older woman turned to Teagan and looked at her with accusing eyes.

"I have no idea what she was doing out there," Teagan said.

The Magdalens broke into chatter among themselves, but everyone hushed when the Mother Superior and Sister Mary-Elizabeth were spotted down the hall. The girls crawled under the covers and pretended to sleep. The nuns ignored the other Magdalens and walked straight to Nora.

"I want to talk to you after prayers and breakfast," Sister Anne said. "Sister Mary-Elizabeth has reported a serious matter." Her lips quivered. "I'll get to the bottom of this—there will be no blasphemy in this convent." Her eyes bored into Nora and then shifted to Teagan. "If I find that you two had anything to do with what happened tonight—I'd think you'd know better by now." She turned to the window, lifted it, and shook her head.

"Sister, as of tomorrow that window will be barred. I'm sorry it has come to this." She closed it and walked away.

"All right, Magdalens, lights out," Sister Mary-Elizabeth said. She stopped at the door and flipped the switch, then left the room. Once again, Nora was in darkness.

Nora crept out of bed and whispered to Teagan, "Lea fell off the roof?"

"We're to blame," Teagan said.

"*We?*"

"She was helping us plan our escape." Teagan's blanket rustled as she wrapped it around her body, and then asked Nora, "And why are you having a private meeting with Sister Anne?"

"I saw the Virgin in the Penitent's Room."

There was a long silence before Teagan whispered, "Now who's crazy?"

Lea was absent from the convent for several days. True to her word, Sister Anne ordered bars placed across the window the day after the incident. Teagan continued her lace-mending while Nora worked the laundries. One evening after prayers Teagan was finally able to convince Nora to recount her "visitation" by the Virgin.

Sister Anne had met with her and Sister Mary-Elizabeth in her office. Both nuns kept a skeptical distance from any admission that Nora had seen the Holy Mother of God. Sister Anne was stern and demanding, asking Nora to renounce her vision; Sister Mary-Elizabeth sometimes chuckled at the "vivid imagination" of the penitent.

"The room does strange things to a person," Sister Mary-Elizabeth said.

"We are not here to encourage hallucinations," Sister Anne stated. "We are here for penitence and absolution."

Teagan scratched her head and came to a realization about the sightings. "Did Sister Mary-Elizabeth mention that Lea saw the Virgin at the same time you did? You were in the Penitent's Room and she was next door in the chapel."

Nora gasped. "No. I guess that proves I'm not daft."

"It proves nothing—an example of mass hallucination or, at least, a dual vision." Teagan wanted to believe, yet she couldn't force herself to accept what her two friends had reported.

"I can't wait to talk to Lea," Nora said. "Sister Mary-Elizabeth must have thought that something crazy was going on. I was by myself and Lea was in the chapel. We couldn't talk through the walls." She shivered. "It gives me the shakes."

The next morning, the convent doors opened and voices echoed up the stairs. Teagan rushed to the library door in time to see Lea, aided by two nurses, hobbling up the stairs. Her friend looked frail, as if the fall had disabled her. Her hair shone almost silver in the light; her face sagged as she gingerly lifted her leg to walk. Lea looked even more like someone who was from another world, Teagan thought, a delicate crane-like creature with fragile sensibilities.

Lea was absent from work, dinner, tea, and prayers. Teagan had expected her friend to be in bed early that night, but was surprised to find Sister Mary-Elizabeth sitting in a chair at Lea's bedside.

As she readied herself, Teagan watched the nun, who sat reading her Bible, glancing occasionally at Lea, who looked like a blanched corpse covered by a blanket. She marveled at how quickly plans, and life, could change. Now that Sister Anne had barred the window, there was no chance of escaping from the roof. Without Lea's help there would be no collection of scraps for their rope. Something else would have to be done.

Teagan approached Sister Mary-Elizabeth, walking tiptoe to the chair. "Pardon me, Sister, I wanted to ask a question before lights-out. . . ."

The nun closed her Bible and looked at her with dull eyes. "Yes?" She sounded defeated.

"Is Lea going to be all right?"

The nun placed her hands over the book. "It was touch and go. She hasn't spoken since she fell. The nurses managed to get some soup down her." She looked at Lea, whose chest rose and fell with shallow breaths. "The doctor told us she got an infection—blood poisoning. She nearly lost her leg. But they told Sister Anne they got the nasty business cleaned out." The nun looked as if she was about to cry. The Sister took a handkerchief from her pocket and wadded it in her fist. "And to think that she saw the—" She stopped, unable to continue until she had composed herself. "That's the Lord's business. Anyway, I and the other Sisters are on duty—twenty-four hours a day. We're praying our little Lea gets better."

"I can help, Sister, if you'd like." Teagan moved closer to the nun.

The nun's face brightened. "That's very kind of you, Teresa. I'll bring it up to the Mother Superior."

"I imagine Monica wouldn't mind watching, too, if you need the help."

The nun's smile faded. "Sister Anne will have her own say about who should watch over Lea, but thanks for the offer. Now, I suppose we should all get to bed."

"Where are you going to sleep?"

"In this chair." She patted her Bible. "I'll be fine."

Lea suddenly rose up on her elbows. "I see the lady in white! I see her!" Sister Mary-Elizabeth reached for her and Lea recoiled, her eyes stony and fixed in delirium. "I'll come back to the Sisters and live out my life. Come back—my life!" Lea shut her eyes and collapsed onto the pillow.

The nun dabbed Lea's forehead with her handkerchief. "Poor thing. Think what she's going through. It's madness."

Teagan nodded and walked back to her bed. Sister Mary-Elizabeth turned out the lights, and Teagan heard the nun trundle back to Lea's side.

When Sister Ruth turned on the lights the next morning, Sister Mary-Elizabeth was fitted tightly against Lea's side. She got out of bed with the rest of the Magdalens as Sister Ruth took her shift in the chair.

The bedside vigil continued for Lea over the next several weeks. The nuns never asked Teagan to watch over her friend, although she volunteered to sit when the Sisters had to be somewhere else for a short time. Work continued unabated, as her routine shifted from the laundries to lace-mending depending on what jobs needed to be done. Even Nora held Lea's hand sometimes at night before going to bed.

Sister Rose, the nun who cut their hair, now had laundry duty most of the time. That was the only benefit to come from Lea's illness that Teagan could see. The old nun wasn't as strict as Sister Ruth. Nora continued to work, although her belly bulged like an inflated football. It was no secret anymore to the Magdalens that she was pregnant. Sister Anne continued to make her disdain known by singling out "Monica" in evening prayers. The Mother Superior had cut back Nora's extended work hours, however. It was as if she knew Nora wouldn't try to escape. She would risk injuring herself or her baby if something went wrong.

One day in the laundry, under the lesser supervision of Sister Rose, Teagan detected a change in Nora's attitude. Her friend, who usually had a sarcastic remark for the nuns and most of the Magdalens, was humming as she worked at the sorting bins. Teagan slipped away from the washbasin and walked toward Nora, who was digging through a soiled pile of laundry. Her friend looked thin except for her stomach, but there was color in her cheeks and a good amount of energy in her efforts.

Teagan stopped beside her and sorted clothing to allay any suspicion on the part of Sister Rose. The smells here were different from the washbasins where detergent and bleach permeated the air. The sorting bins were a stomach-churning feast for the nostrils. The odors of rotten food, feces, stale cologne and perfumes wafted from the piles. Despite that, Nora hummed happily.

"Why the good mood?" Teagan asked.

Nora glanced at her and then went back to her work. "I know it sounds strange, but something's changed. I'm not as sick as I used to be in the mornings." She patted her stomach. "I'm getting used to this child inside me."

Teagan lifted a pair of dirty jeans out of the pile and shoved them into the "darks" bin. "It sounds like you're getting comfortable with being a mom. A few weeks ago, I didn't think you wanted to have the baby."

Nora smiled quizzically, as if she knew something that Teagan didn't. "What happened to Lea has made me think about life. I don't want to die, and I want my child to live. I know the nuns are going to make me give it up for adoption, but at least it'll have a life—and it might have a good one if the right family adopts. It's not great here, but it beats living on the street, and the nuns will take care of my baby."

Teagan was astonished by her friend's words, and she felt her mood darken. "You've had a change of heart. You sound as if you want to stay here now. What happened to 'hellhole' and 'prison'?"

Nora's eyes displayed an intensity that had been reserved for her displeasure with the Sisters. "What choice do I have? It's hard for a pregnant woman to hide. I want to have my baby, and now that that's been decided, I'm going to play the game for a while."

"Well, I'm disappointed, to say the least, but I understand. Maybe we can—"

A hand came to rest on Teagan's shoulder. She jumped and turned to find Sister Mary-Elizabeth standing behind her. Her broad frame obstructed any view into the laundry.

"Follow me, both of you." She directed them to the corner of the laundry where Teagan had had her confrontation with the Mother Superior. Nora sat in the same chair while Teagan stood beside her.

Sister Mary-Elizabeth held a bulging laundry sack in her hands. She stuck it out. "I've left Sister Ruth with Lea and hauled meself down the stairs. Look at this."

Teagan looked at Nora, wondering what they should do.

"Well, go on," the nun urged. "I haven't got all day."

Teagan took the bag by its rope strings, placed it on the floor, and opened it. The bag's wide mouth revealed the clothing scraps and the tattered sheets that had been collected and stored under Lea's bed. A deck of tarot cards, Mr. Roche's hammer, sewing machine oil, the nails used on the window, and

Teagan's Christmas gifts rested on top of the fabric. Teagan's hands trembled as she looked up from the bag. She didn't want to look the nun in the eyes.

"You both should get down on your knees and thank Jesus that *I* found this, and not one of the other Sisters," the nun said. "I doubt Lea had anything to do with this."

"We were planning to escape," Nora said. "Lea was helping us."

Teagan couldn't believe her ears. "Nora!"

Sister Mary-Elizabeth shook her finger at them. "I don't want to hear any more about it. Polluting the mind of an innocent girl like Lea . . ." She pointed to Nora. "You're in no condition to try such a thing, and you—" Her fiery eyes pierced Teagan. "I'm surprised, but when I think about it, I should have figured you were in on such nonsense. You're the fancy one in the group. How about bed checks every night? Is that what you'd like?"

Teagan started to object, but the nun wouldn't have it. "If Sister Anne had found these things—and these cards—I shudder to think what would have happened. Imagine, satanic worship going on under our noses."

"How did you find them?" Nora asked.

"That's me business, but if something from a Magdalen is pitched under the bed and you have to go looking for it . . ." Sister Mary-Elizabeth closed the bag and lifted it. "I'm going to return this hammer and oil to Mr. Roche and destroy the rest of these items."

"The radio and the scarf are my Christmas presents from my mother," Teagan said. "I didn't get to use them."

"And how did they get here?" the nun asked. "You know such things are forbidden."

She thought of the sad day at the lace table when Cullen had given her the gifts. "Someone who loves me delivered them."

The Sister sighed. "I'll ask the Mother Superior to keep them, but I can't guarantee it. I don't want to see or hear of any such nonsense again." Her voice dropped to a whisper. "If I'm forced to act as a watchdog, I will report you to Sister Anne. Mind yourself." She turned and left them in the corner.

Nora stood. Teagan plopped in the chair. Sister Mary-Elizabeth conferred with Sister Rose at the other end of the laundry.

Nora placed her hand on Teagan's shoulder. "You look beat."

The urge to give in to the nuns, to cry, to break down, had never been stronger. She felt as if her insides had turned to lead. What was the use of fighting such a force? It was more than she could handle to take on The Sisters of the Holy Redemption, let alone the Church. If she couldn't win the battle here, nothing she could do, no letters she could write, would ever succeed in freeing her from the convent.

Teagan looked at her friend. "We were going to be a team. We were going to get out of here together."

"I know," Nora replied wistfully, "but I've made my bed, and now I have to lie in it. I'm sorry." She leaned over and whispered, "I'll help you in any way I can."

Teagan shook her head. "No. You're in enough trouble as it is. I can take care of myself." She looked out the large bank of windows at the bare March trees. "Did you know that today is my birthday?"

"No," Nora said. "Happy birthday. Mine was last month."

"It's glorious being seventeen, isn't it?"

Nora managed a chuckle.

They continued their work in silence until it was time for tea.

After prayers, Teagan and the other Magdalens filed into the garret. Patricia, the girl who had reported them for being on the roof months ago, smiled smugly at Teagan as she walked past on her way to bed.

Teagan glared at her, and in a voice loud enough that all the Magdalens could hear, said, "I'll make your life a living hell if you ever rat on anyone again."

Patricia recoiled with a look of mock horror, holding her hands up to her face. "I don't know what you're talking about." She eased back against her pillow. "If I were you, I'd think carefully about what you say from now on, or you'll be the one living in hell."

She wanted to spit in Patricia's face. Instead, she walked away as the girl called out, "I'm going to be a nun. I'll pray for you."

A few of the Magdalens chuckled.

Later, Sister Mary-Elizabeth settled in the chair beside Lea, but not before checking under all the Magdalens' beds. Teagan looked at Lea, still unresponsive, and Nora, who had covered her head with the blanket. For the first time since Nora had arrived, she knew she was alone in her quest to escape the convent.

The weather shifted in late April, and although the days were mostly cool and damp, the sun often shone on the grounds with the radiance of spring warmth. The winter grass, which had retained some of its color, deepened to its rich Irish green as the weeks progressed.

Lea had recovered her strength and was well enough to hobble about the garret. The nuns brought her food daily, so she wouldn't have to walk downstairs. Sister Rose hauled in part of a broken school desk, along with paper and paints, so Lea could continue her work on the *Book of Kells*. She still spent most days resting with her leg elevated, but the nuns' bedside vigil had ended. So had Sister Mary-Elizabeth's nightly bed checks, much to Teagan's relief.

One night, Teagan told her friend that their plot had been discovered.

Lea sighed with relief. "We should never have planned an escape." She pointed to the heavens. "See, it was never meant to be. God was looking after us. We'll all be happy here."

Teagan grasped her hand, but cringed inside, knowing Lea's alliance with the nuns was assured. *I can't believe there's no way out. I won't believe that.*

One Sunday afternoon, Teagan, Nora, and Lea sat outside enjoying the day. Teagan couldn't remember a more beautiful spring day. The sun's rays bathed her, coaxing the winter chill out of her bones. The warmth felt glorious on her face and arms. The other Magdalens, spread across the lawn, luxuriated in the day, as well, happy to be out of the laundry's confines. Even the nuns enjoyed a special freedom because the Mother Superior was out of town on Church business. Sisters Mary-Elizabeth and Ruth sprinted across the yard in an impromptu game of shuttlecock. The white plastic "birdie" flew high into the sky. Sister Mary-Elizabeth was worse at the game than Sister Ruth and missed the shuttlecock on most tries, her large arms jiggling underneath her habit.

Teagan lay back on the warm ground and thought again about escaping from the convent. On such a beautiful day, it was hard to focus on a suitable plan. She kept drifting off while Lea and Nora talked about babies. Her eyes had fluttered shut when a shadow blocked the sun from her face. Sister Rose bent over her, the nun's long fingers stretched toward her.

"An Anglican priest is here to see you, Teresa," Sister Rose said with extreme formality. The nun straightened as Teagan jumped up from the ground. Her heart beat fast; it had to be the priest who had come with Cullen before Christmas. Who else could it be? The only news she had gotten about her family had come through her boyfriend. Was the priest alone?

She followed the nun, who strode toward the door in long, rigid steps. "He wants to talk with you. I wasn't sure what the Mother Superior would do, so I made a decision," the Sister said. "You can meet him in the library—with the doors open. I'll sit on a chair outside until you're finished."

The priest was seated at Lea's desk when they arrived. It was the same man. Teagan struggled to remember his name. Sister Rose nodded to the man and excused herself.

"I'm Father Conry," the priest said. "I hope you remember me."

"Certainly," Teagan replied. "It's nice to see you again, Father. Please, sit down."

He sat in the chair in front of the lace-mending table, stretching his long legs in front of him. "Thank you. It's a rather awkward arrangement here at the convent, but we have no other choice. . . . Sister Rose told me the Mother Superior is gone today, so I feel we can speak freely."

It was odd having a man, a priest, so close to her. He made her a bit nervous; after all, her experience of meeting with another priest last summer hadn't been good.

"Cullen is sorry he couldn't be here," Father Conry said.

"He's very fond of you, you know." He looked at her sadly, as if he felt an unrequited love existed between Cullen and her.

The blood rose in her cheeks, and she wondered why she had such an emotional reaction. In this case, it didn't stem from a forbidden attraction she felt for her boyfriend, but from embarrassment. Why would it be so uncomfortable seeing Cullen? Last July, she would have given anything to be with him. Had months of the Sisters' influence crept into her head and heart? She felt dirty thinking about a boy she'd once liked and desired, and about being alone with this priest—as close as she would ever come to a man these days. These thoughts made her question her commitment to leave the convent, and she tamped down a shudder. *No! I won't stay here!* She struck them from her mind and looked at the priest. He had a kind, caring face, masculine in its width; there was no dainty femininity to his features. She might be able to talk to him about anything, if she felt up to it.

"I'm certain he would hope for the same from you," he said.

Teagan lowered her gaze. "I'm sorry. I'm surprised by your visit—I . . . we, rarely get visitors."

He leaned back and crossed his legs. "I don't have good news, unfortunately."

She leaned forward in anticipation of his words.

"Your mother requested a meeting with me, which was a much wiser course of action than calling Cullen." He took a breath. "I do believe your mother likes Cullen, even though he's not Catholic. She was happy he delivered your Christmas gifts."

Teagan winced at the memory of her gifts. She didn't know whether they had been destroyed.

"Your mother is concerned—concerned enough that she wanted to talk to a member of the clergy; however, not one of your parish. She knew I was here with Cullen in December." He fixed his eyes upon her, and Teagan braced for bad news. "Your father's drinking has gotten worse and your mother . . ." He intertwined his fingers. "I'm sorry . . . it's difficult enough to say to anyone, but especially to a young woman in your position."

"Please, tell me."

"Your mother is depressed. I believe it's because she has lost her daughter, and she's about to lose her husband."

"What do you mean?"

"She thinks your father can't be saved from his alcoholism. He may harm himself."

Teagan closed her eyes.

Father Conry reached across the table and touched her hand. "Don't despair. There may be hope yet. Perhaps he can work himself out of this. Your mother is trying to get help for both of them, for the first time in their lives."

The old anger came back to her, an inner tirade against her father and what he had done to their family. She calmed herself as best she could. "I know my father. It will take a miracle to get him to quit drinking. Even Father Matthew has told him more than once that he drinks too much." She remembered the day she met Father Mark and how her father had exploded in rage. He'd had enough to drink then, which Father Matthew had pointed out. "I hope he doesn't hurt my mother. If I were out of this place, I'd convince my mother to leave him. . . ."

"Cullen was brave enough to tell me your story." He let go of her hand. "Between you and me, I don't believe the rumors. You're a kind girl, who I think has been mistreated."

Teagan choked and fought back tears. At last, someone believed her, but what good would it do?

"Unfortunately," the priest continued, "my hands are tied. I have no legal standing over you, and even less influence with the Catholic Church."

She sat back, trying to take it all in. Was there nothing Father Conry could do? Probably not, but she was cheered by the possibility that he believed in her.

"There's something else—" His face reddened. "I wouldn't say it, were it not for your situation, but you're old enough to know." He looked around the room. "One can see a library like this and believe it's all peaches and cream at The Sisters of the Holy Redemption. I'm not convinced. I believe innocence can be lost in the houses of the holy as easily as in the dwellings of evil."

Sister Rose appeared at the door, craning her neck to see what was going on.

Father Conry waved to the nun. "A few more minutes, Sister." He turned back to Teagan. "I'll get on with it. There's a rumor that Father Mark—the young priest at St. Eusebius—has gotten a girl in trouble. Mind you, it's just gossip, and nothing has been proven. I think the diocese is in a bit of an uproar, however."

Drained by his words, Teagan slumped in her chair. "Oh, Father, I don't know what to think. If it's true, people may believe he's not the man of God he says he is, and I might be vindicated. On the other hand, they may think I set him on this course."

The priest nodded. "I thought you should know. Such news may work to your advantage in the future. Please do me one favor, however. Don't mention that you heard this from me. I'll keep my ears and eyes open, and if there's anything I can do, rest assured I will." He got up from his chair and smiled. "I sincerely hope all turns out well. I'll give Cullen your best."

Teagan shook his hand. "Thank you, Father. Your words have given me the most encouragement I've had in months. I'll go to sleep tonight with hope. Yes, do give Cullen my best."

He turned and called out, "Sister, I'm ready to leave."

The old nun appeared in the doorway. She escorted Father Conry to his car. Teagan followed them out to the green lawn shimmering in the bright sunshine.

The priest drove away toward the gate. She knew Mr. Roche would be waiting there to let him out, a thought that struck her with some force.

"Aren't you the fancy one," Nora said as Teagan rejoined her and Lea. "You get all the visitors—priests, boyfriends, Anglicans—while Lea and me sit on our bums."

Teagan didn't respond. She plopped down, snatched a blade of grass, and stuck it in her mouth. Her attention was focused on the car moving toward the gate.

CHAPTER 14

Teagan was startled from her sleep one early morning in late June. Heart pounding, she sat up to find Sister Anne kneeling in front of her bed. The nun's head was bowed, her body forming a black triangle, illuminated from behind by a single candle. Its yellow rays flickered, spreading a ghostly light through the garret. The flame quivered, and Sister Anne's hands, folded in prayer, emerged from the darkness.

The nun lifted her head, and in the faint glow, Teagan saw the sagging mouth, the sallow skin, and tear-streaked eyes. The other Magdalens were silent in their beds. Teagan wondered whether she was having a nightmare. But the nun raised a finger to her lips and began to whisper her prayers again, sounding a soft mantra. This was no dream. Sister Anne went on for several minutes, while Teagan, legs stiff, arms plastered to her sides, stayed rigid in bed. The other girls seemed to have been under a spell.

Finally, Sister Anne looked up. "I'm praying for myself, but I wanted to see you. Do you know the pain you've caused me?"

"Why? What have I done to you?" Teagan managed to eke out the question.

The nun shook her head. "It matters little now. What's past is past, but the memories remain. When I look at you, I look into the blackness of my soul."

Her words made no sense. She couldn't force the Mother Superior to reveal her pain, and she didn't want to scream at her. The others might think that Sister Anne was praying at her bedside to exorcise some demonic spirit. The Magdalens would never look at her the same. So she closed her eyes and kept quiet as the nun continued her prayers. *Enough! Enough!* She tried to remain calm as the nun's prayers drifted into her ears: penitence, forgiveness, redemption.

Nora and Lea were of no use to her now. The escape plan had been thwarted when Sister Mary-Elizabeth discovered the scraps of fabric under Lea's bed. Her friend had nearly lost her life because of her scheme. Looking back, it seemed a desperate idea. Nora was only concerned with her baby. She pictured herself at Betty's age, still mending lace or tending the laundry, day after day, week after week, year after year. The monotony, the penance, would chip away a bit of her soul each day until there was nothing left but a robotic shell of a woman who prayed continually to God but who had no life, no real reason to live.

All throughout May and June, she'd prayed to be delivered from the convent, but no opportunity presented itself. Sister Ruth stood guard like a bulldog over the laundry. An escape like Nora's was out of the question. Since her fall from the roof, Lea seemed scattered and confused. The trust between them had dwindled. The window was barred, so there was no chance to escape from the roof anyway. She didn't want to give up hope; if she did, she feared she would lose her sanity. She understood that fear was a certainty, as sure as her heartbeat.

Teagan opened her eyes. The light of dawn filtered in the window. She looked at the foot of her bed. Sister Anne was gone. Was she ever there? She inspected the blanket covering her feet. Nora and Lea slept peacefully in their beds, their dreams undisturbed by a night visitor. She threw off the covers and walked to the spot. Nothing—no wax, no disturbance of any kind, indicated that the Mother Superior had been there.

However, the scent of smoke, as if a candle had been extinguished, lingered in the air. The door to the garret stood ajar. Teagan scurried to it and looked down the hall. All was normal in the unfolding dawn, but for a slight haze, perhaps the smoky drift from a smoldering wick.

* * *

By early August, the Magdalens were sweltering in the laundry again. The bubbling washers and electric dryers magnified the summer heat and humidity. Teagan wondered whether Nora would make it through the remaining few weeks until her delivery date. The child grew inside her, puffing her out so much that the nuns put her on "light work," which meant standing next to the equipment to make sure all the cycles were completed. Sarah was in charge of transferring the loads between machines, while Nora, hefting her swollen belly with her hands, supervised.

One afternoon, Nora slumped against a washer. Teagan and Sister Ruth rushed to her.

"I'm going to have the baby," Nora panted. The color drained from her face; sweat poured from her forehead.

"Nonsense," Sister Ruth said. The nun grabbed Nora's left arm and held on, trying to steady her. She glared at Teagan. "Get back to your work!"

Teagan stood firm. "She's my friend, and I want to help."

"It's me own baby, and I can bloody well tell when it's coming." Nora attempted to step away from the washer, but her legs went out from under her instead. Sister Ruth held on to Nora's left arm while Teagan caught the right. It took both of them to lift her up.

Nora shook her head as if to shake off an ache. "See, what did I tell you?"

"You're not due," Sister Ruth said. She frowned, but then called out to Sarah. "Tell Sister Mary-Elizabeth to call for the doctor."

Soon, Sisters Mary-Elizabeth and Rose were in the laundry along with a few other nuns, whom Teagan believed must have come over from the adjoining orphanage.

One, whom Sister Ruth called Sister Immaculata, a nun with prominent dark eyebrows and piercing blue eyes, examined Nora while Betty brought over a chair. Nora thanked her and sat, looking like a lost child, but pleased with all the attention showered upon her.

Sister Immaculata poked Nora's stomach with her fingers

and then moved them under her distended belly. The Sister put her hand on Nora's forehead. "Tsk-tsk." She nodded her head and proclaimed, "I would say this penitent needs medical attention. She may be having the baby."

The nuns lifted Nora from the chair and whisked her away. Teagan had no time to wish her luck or say goodbye. She was left standing by the chair as her friend, caught in a whir of black habits, disappeared out the door.

Nora had escaped again, but this time under the watchful eye of the nuns. Teagan wasn't sure when Nora would be back—if ever—or what would happen to the baby. She walked with measured steps toward the basin where she had been working. After more than a year of penance, the time to leave The Sisters of the Holy Redemption had come, no matter the cost.

Nora had escaped the first time in a delivery van. Since Father Conry's last visit, Teagan had paid careful attention to small details, including delivery schedules and the nuns' routines. Now that she was back in the laundry, she kept mental notes but didn't share them with anyone. It became increasingly clear that Nora's escape had been a single instance of good fortune. Teagan had no plans to escape by that means. Sister Ruth, even the other Magdalens, were more aware now. Teagan had formulated a new scheme and the time had come to put it in action, but she needed the aid of another person, a girl who might have access to, or at least the knowledge of what she sought. Lea knew where to find everything in Mr. Roche's office.

She got her chance two days after Nora had been taken away. Rain poured upon the convent after vespers. The messy night made her plan even more plausible. *Who would think a Magdalen would try to escape on a night like this?* The rain would provide good cover.

After going to the toilet, she spotted Lea standing in front of the garret window before lights-out. The other Magdalens were getting ready for bed. Lightning flared outside, illuminating the room and outlining her friend's form in an eerie white flash. She stole up behind Lea, attempting to ascertain what had captured the girl's attention.

"Look." Lea pointed to the plot in the southwest corner where the children had been buried. "They're out tonight." She clapped her hands. "Enjoying the weather."

Teagan squinted, looked past her friend's shoulder, but saw nothing, only the sodden ground and the dark veils of rain. She was tempted to crawl into bed, but reminded herself that she had to act. "Yes, I see them, too."

Lea turned, her eyes narrowing. "You're joking. Don't make fun of me."

"No, really, I see them." She stepped beside her friend. "There in the corner."

"What do you see?"

Teagan tried to remember how Lea had described them. "*White bundles*" popped into her head. "Two figures bathed in white, one a little boy, the other a little girl, I think. It's hard to see because it's raining so hard."

"That's what I see, too! But what about the other one, hidden in the corner?"

"Yes, I see him, too."

"*Her*." Lea folded her arms and looked into the rain. "They're calling to me to come outside—more than ever. They were trying to talk to me the night I fell. Would you like to come with me?"

Teagan started at her friend's suggestion. The only way Lea could talk to the children was to go outside. They couldn't get outside without opening a door. The timing was perfect, if she played along. "Of course, I'd love a chat. What do you want to ask them?"

"I want to know whether they're happy. I hope they weren't mistreated."

She couldn't believe her good fortune. The idea was Lea's. No one would suspect because the nuns loved her, despite her odd behavior. Yes, she'd sneaked out to the roof with her friends, but she wasn't a troublemaker who wanted to destroy order at the convent. Lea was happy where she was, as long as she could work on her art and talk to the spirits.

"Don't get into your nightgown," Lea said. "Crawl into bed and pull up the covers. We'll wait a couple of hours after the lights are turned out. When I tap your shoulder, get up, but don't say anything."

Lightning flashed to the west. A sharp *clap* of thunder sounded through the walls.

Teagan turned down her blanket, took off her shoes, and got into bed. Lea did the same.

Patricia yelled from her bed, "Hey, what's up with you two?"

Teagan wondered whether they should abandon their plan, but was surprised when Lea answered, "Modesty—something you don't know much about. Teresa and I have decided to undress in the dark as a penance to God."

"Bollocks." Patricia huffed and shook her head.

"I'm sure Sister Anne would approve, and as a future nun, you could take a few lessons yourself."

"You're both loony birds." Patricia slid under her blanket and turned away.

Lea winked at Teagan. They only had to wait until the lights were turned out.

Sister Mary-Elizabeth, on schedule, appeared a few minutes later outside the garret doors, followed by the Mother Superior. Still clad in their habits, they walked slowly down the aisle, looking at each girl.

Teagan's breath caught in her throat. She wondered why the Mother Superior was with Sister Mary-Elizabeth on her nightly vigil. Would Patricia report them for wearing clothes to bed? However, the nuns passed the girl without a word being uttered. Apparently, her warning about "ratting" had worked.

Exhausted by her work at the washbasins, Teagan soon fell into a sound sleep.

Later, her bed shook. Lea, looking like the thin ghost, stood over her, beckoning her to follow.

She got up, slipped on her shoes, and tiptoed down the aisle to the doors. It was unlikely any of the Magdalens would wake up when they left, because the girls used the toilet at all hours of the night—that was usual behavior they slept through every night.

The hall was dark except for a sliver of yellow light that fell from Sister Mary-Elizabeth's doorway—a room next to the garret she shared with Sister Rose.

"She may be awake," Teagan cautioned Lea.

Her friend seemed unconcerned. "We'll have to take that chance if we want to talk to the spirits. They're still in the corner."

Teagan held on to Lea's shoulder. "You go first. If they see us, I'll say you were sleepwalking and I was trying to get you back into bed." She looked down at her clothes. It would be hard to explain why they were in their work dresses, but she would concoct a reason if she had to.

Lea passed Sister Mary-Elizabeth's room without a glance and headed down the stairs. Teagan peeked in. The nun, head lolling, was asleep, the book she had been reading collapsed in a tent on her stomach. Sister Rose was asleep on the opposite side of the room.

The second floor was in shadow. Sister Anne and Sister Ruth's bedrooms were down the hall, but no one stirred.

"Where are we headed?" Teagan asked.

"Mr. Roche's office. He may have keys."

Soon, they were running past the chapel on the first floor. A cathedral lamp, high above, cast its cold rays on the marble floor. Their shadows loomed large on the walls. The convent's wooden doors rose in front of them. Lea stopped at Mr. Roche's office, across from the Mother Superior's, and ran her fingers over the casement above the door. When she withdrew her hand, she held a silver key.

Lea put the key in the lock and turned it. The door clicked open, revealing a desk and a small chair, a workbench, and a wonderland of grimy tools in a box. A stack of brooms, rakes, and other garden tools stood in one corner.

"How did you know about the key?" Teagan whispered. Her heart hammered in her chest.

"I've seen him put it there."

"You were in here to get the hammer and oil."

Lea stepped inside. "I've been in a few times. Sometimes he's here, sometimes he's not. Mr. Roche likes me."

Teagan didn't want to press her friend, but every step Lea was taking made sense. If anyone would have keys to the grounds, it would be Sister Anne and Mr. Roche. She had never thought to ask Lea about stealing keys from Mr. Roche's office. Teagan doubted that her friend would ever do anything against the Mother Superior, but the caretaker was another matter.

"You could have gotten us out all along—without falling off the roof," Teagan said, irritated. However, her annoyance was tempered by Lea's unpredictable character; she had always been hard to figure out.

Lea shot Teagan an exasperated look. "I don't know whether Mr. Roche keeps keys here. It's only a hunch. He might sleep with them next to his bed. And, besides, you and Nora are the ones who are always planning an escape. I don't make a habit of rummaging through offices. I'm only doing this because of the spirits. Talking to them is what's important."

"Well, let's not waste time," Teagan said.

They attacked the desk together, pulling open drawers, but being careful to leave the contents as they found them. Instead of keys, they found papers, cigarettes, pens, pencils, a girly magazine, and a dented silver flask.

"Nothing," Lea said.

Teagan circled the small office. "Let's not give up. Maybe they're someplace else." She dug into the corner where the brooms, rakes, and hoes stood. She bunched the handles and pulled them away from the wall. A spit of silver shimmered against the granite. A large ring with a dozen or so keys hung on the wall.

"This is what we're looking for," Teagan said, relieved to find them. She handed the ring to Lea. "Now we have to find the right one."

"They're marked," Lea said. She pointed to one that looked like a large black skeleton key. "This one opens the front doors."

Teagan's pulse quickened. The doors were only a few feet away, along with potential freedom. If the gate key was on the ring, she could escape and never look back—except for her promise to Nora. Even so, she was determined not to make her friend's mistakes.

"There's something else we can use." Lea pointed to an umbrella on the other side of Mr. Roche's desk.

Teagan picked it up. "Let's go."

Lea closed the office and replaced the key on the casement. At the convent doors, her friend inserted the large key into a hole surrounded by an ornate metal plate. Lea turned it and the lock clicked. Teagan opened the door. Cool air poured over her like a first draught of freedom. Without hesitation, she opened the umbrella and stepped outside. No night had ever looked so beautiful, despite the rain that spattered on the umbrella. She stuck her hand out and reveled in the satiny feel of the drops in her palm.

Lea rushed down the steps and turned south toward the spirits' corner.

Teagan stopped in the lane.

Lea noticed and turned.

"I'm not going with you." The cool rain fell on her face and shoulders as she handed the umbrella to her friend.

Lea remained steady on her feet, true to her nature, and held out her hands. "I wondered when you would leave. Was this a trick?"

Through the murky light of the convent's lamps, she looked down at the black pavement, unable to face her friend. "If you think tonight was planned, you're wrong. I told you from the beginning I wanted to leave. I've been thinking how to get through the gate for a few weeks now. You made it happen, Lea." She looked up and frowned. "But, I lied. I didn't see your spirit friends—but I believe you can see them. So go talk to them, help them, do whatever you have to do. Then go back in and replace the keys before you get caught. I don't want you to suffer one minute in the Penitent's Room. You don't have to tell Sister Anne a thing. She'll dole out her punishment to all the

Magdalens tomorrow. For that, I'm sorry." She pointed to the keys. "Please let me out."

Lea lurched forward and hugged Teagan, holding the umbrella over them. The faint odor of inks—the colors that Lea used to paint—crept into her nose. The smell was a way to remember her friend.

"I'll walk you to the gate," Lea said. "You and Nora should be happy. The spirits will wait for me."

They huddled under the umbrella and walked in the shadows of the oaks and pines. Teagan wondered what would become of her in the world outside the convent. The thought brought up memories that flashed through her mind like ghosts: her father drunk; her mother sitting sullenly in a chair waiting for him to sober up; walks with Cullen along the river. At the time, she had believed everything was normal, because she didn't know better. Now she knew it wasn't. Then came her chance meeting with Father Mark, a catastrophe that had changed her life in innumerable ways. What waited on the other side of the gate—freedom, or more slavery? If her parents wouldn't take her back, she had no place to go. Which torture—inside or outside of the convent—would be the easiest to endure?

She stopped as the gate came into view. Lea stumbled beside her.

"I don't know if I can do it," Teagan said. Tears formed and she fought against them. "I'm not sure I'm strong enough."

"Why?" Lea asked. "This is what you want."

"I don't know what to do. I can't go to my parents'. I can't go to Cullen's. No one will have me." She collapsed against her friend and sputtered on her shoulder. The umbrella tumbled to the ground.

Lea hugged her and patted her back as they stood in the rain. "God will protect you. If you want this, He wants this."

Teagan wiped her tears with her sleeve. "Are you sure? I've lost my faith over the past year. I don't think He exists."

A lamp flickered down the street. Lea smiled. "Of course He's real. Why do you think He wants you to leave this place? You have other work to do. My job is to talk to the departed spirits—to help them find peace." Lea stepped back. "Go to your parents. Ask them to take you in."

Teagan picked up the umbrella and handed it to Lea.

"No, you take it," Lea said.

"No, you keep it. If it's missing, they'll know I was in Mr. Roche's office. Wipe it off and put it back where it was."

Teagan walked silently to the gate.

Her friend unlocked the padlock and lifted it so the chain wouldn't clang against the ironwork. The gate was locked, too, but soon it swung open.

Teagan stepped on the footpath. Her shoulders were soaked, and she shivered in the damp air.

Lea closed the gate, locked it, and replaced the padlock on the chain with a *snap*. She peered through the gate like a woman saying good-bye to a friend who was off to gaol.

"Good-bye, my friend," Lea said. "I'll miss you. God bless."

Her words touched Teagan. She reached through the gate and clasped Lea's hand. If her friend was right—if there was a God—she needed Him now more than ever. Lea's God was kind and accepting, the kind of God Teagan wanted to know.

She let go and walked north toward St Stephen's Green. She remembered her father driving by the park as he brought her to the convent. It struck her that finding Cullen's house might be easier than getting to her parents'. He lived near Saint Patrick's Cathedral. When they had first met at a party, he had pointed out that he could see the cathedral's spires from his front door. She had been to his home several times.

She picked up her pace, running on adrenaline, wanting to see Cullen, anxious to see her parents, hoping for their acceptance. The road stretched into interminable night, but on each side of it there were lights from residences and shops that lit the way. She would follow those beacons. Perhaps the feeling of hope they provided would last until she found her way home.

CHAPTER 15

Teagan had never experienced such odd feelings before. Dread hung over her like a cloud. Every few minutes she would feel a counteracting rush of excitement. It was as if she had never been free in her life, like a baby bird spreading its wings for the first time. Dublin was big, even larger at night it seemed, and now she was an escapee. The Guards would be looking for her as soon as the nuns discovered her absence.

She tried to get out of the rain, but it was difficult. Some buildings had awnings and overhangs; others didn't. She avoided road lamps. Her apron was soaked, and she clutched herself, shivering. It had protected her dress somewhat, but even it was beginning to get wet. She walked as fast as she could, headed north.

She skirted the greenways of St Stephen's, the park she had passed the terrible night she was brought to the convent.

A twenty-minute walk brought her to a neighborhood that looked familiar. The jutting spires of Saint Patrick's Cathedral, dreary against the night, came into view. She ducked under one of the arches and shook herself like a dog to wick off the water. Standing beneath the sheltered archway of the Protestant cathedral provided a glimmer of hope. Cullen Kirby's house was nearby. She knew that from her visits to his home. From his porch, she had seen the cathedral's spires with their crosses pricking the sky. The hour was late, and she had no place to turn. She would have to somehow get to her parents, in Ballsbridge, in the morning. She had nothing to lose.

Why not? The worst that can happen is I get arrested. The Guards will take me back to the convent, and I'll spend the night in the Penitent's Room.

Her memory served her in this time of need. Except for a wrong turn, which she attributed to the late hour rather than a faulty sense of direction, she was soon standing across the road from the flat where Cullen lived with his parents. His bedroom window was around the side of the building, sheltered by a narrow alley created by an adjacent home. His parents' room was on the front overlooking the road. No lamps were on, except for a small one over the door, which cast a rectangular patch of light.

The footpath to the door was gated, but the alley was not. She crossed the road, sloshed through the grass, and stopped in front of Cullen's window. What if he and his parents had switched bedrooms? His parents would certainly be upset and report a young woman trespassing on their property. The Guards would be called. However, she had to take the chance.

She tapped on the window—so lightly at first she could barely hear the knock herself. The glass was covered inside by thick curtains. She gathered her courage and tapped again. This time she was certain that anyone inside would hear the noise.

The curtains parted. An eye peered out. The fabric fell back into place, and the process was repeated again. The second time they opened slightly wider. Suddenly, they were flung apart, revealing Cullen, his eyes wide with shock. He was naked from the waist up, attired only in his pajama bottoms.

Teagan put a finger to her lips.

He lifted the window and gaped at her. After a few moments, he whispered, "It's really you. At first, I thought I was dreaming."

"I've run away." She was embarrassed to admit it. How sad to be reduced to a girl running away from a cloistered prison.

Cullen shook his head, and his hair shifted like sand. "My

God, where are you going?" He looked back into his bedroom. "Do you know it's after two-thirty?"

She pulled her arms close to her chest. The damp was sinking in now, like a coating of frost on her limbs. "Can I come in? I'm cold and wet."

"Of course, but we have to be quiet. My parents are home. I've never had a girl in my room in the middle of the night." He opened the window as high as it would go and held out his hands. The ledge was slightly higher than Teagan's waist. She grabbed him, while he tugged, and within a few seconds she was seated on the floor.

"Shhhh," he whispered. He searched for his pajama top in the chest of drawers.

"Can I stay long enough to warm up?" Teagan whispered back and shivered again, this time more violently.

He switched on a small lamp attached to the headboard. "Don't be silly." He sat on the side of his bed. "You can't wake up your parents at three in the morning. They'll have a fit. Your da is hardly stable as it is." He patted the mattress, offering Teagan the opportunity to get off the floor.

Teagan shook her head. "I'm fine." She scooted closer and reached for his hands. "I know it's very odd for me to show up at your house like this, but I'm here because you're my best friend. . . ." She studied him, feeling scared that she might do something she would regret later. She wasn't anxious with him the way she'd been with Father Conry. If anything, it was tempting to be with her boyfriend. Any feelings of discomfort dissipated in Cullen's warm bedroom. Her thoughts didn't embarrass her. A spark flashed between them. "I think I'd better stay on the floor," she finally decided.

"What kind of guy do you think I am, Teagan? It doesn't hurt that you're special to me, but I want to help you, not seduce you."

She looked into his eyes. "Thanks. There can't be anything more between us at the moment. I can't even think like that." She wrapped her arms around his knees and savored the feel of his body. His legs were thin, but strong, like a runner's. He'd always been lean, not too muscular, but with a knack for field sports.

"Brrrr. You're cold. You need to get out of those wet clothes." He loosened himself from her grasp and got a blanket from the closet opposite his bed. "You could change in there, but there's hardly room to get in. Why don't you wrap up in this and you can sleep in my bed. I'll take the floor." He handed her the blanket. "You'll have to leave in a few hours because my da gets up early for work. Maybe I can sneak you a piece of toast or something."

"That's nice. I might take you up on it."

Cullen fought back a giggle. "If someone knocks, roll off the bed and get between it and the window. I'll jump back in bed."

How nice it would be, Teagan thought, to take him in her arms and hold him. She pushed the thought aside almost as quickly as she considered it. Hugging Cullen would lead to more than playful caresses. Cullen might not resist, and if pushed, she probably wouldn't put up much of a fight, either. It had been so long since she'd walked with him or held his hand. Even a kiss could be dangerous. Right now, he was the friend she needed. If there had been more time, she would have told him everything about the convent—her struggles and how good it was to be free again.

Cullen turned away as she stripped to her undergarments and wrapped herself in the blanket. When he turned back, she was holding her dress and apron in her hands.

"I'll hang them in the closet for a few hours," he said. "Maybe they'll dry a bit."

He took her clothes, got hangers, and hung them up. He grabbed a pillow and settled on the floor.

Still encased in the blanket, Teagan slipped into bed and covered herself with the sheet. She rolled onto her stomach and leaned over the edge. Cullen peered up at her. "Just one kiss— for thanks," she said.

He lifted himself on his elbows. Their lips met briefly, and a jolt coursed through her. They drew apart, Teagan, at least, sensing that had the time been right, she could have asked him into bed. Now she was warm enough that the blanket was hot and cumbersome. Keeping herself covered with the sheet, she cast off the blanket and dropped it on the floor next to him.

"Hey," Cullen said, "you don't need to do that."

"You'll be cold by morning."

He smiled up at her. "I'm perfect, just perfect."

"Good night." She switched off the light and settled in bed, thinking how fortunate she was to have a friend like Cullen. The house was quiet, and she felt calm and protected in his room. The light from the road lamps cut across the top of the curtains and threw thin slivers of white across the ceiling. She traced her fingers up her stomach, across her breasts, and to her face. She felt more alive than she had in months. When she looked up, the ceiling seemed to drift into the heavens leaving a universe of stars above her.

When Cullen nudged her, she was in a deep sleep that ended too quickly. He sat on the edge of the bed and kissed her forehead, then drew away. "It's nice to wake up with you in the morning." He opened the curtains. The blue light of day flooded the room.

Teagan yawned and rubbed her eyes. She was used to getting up at dawn, but not used to staying out so late.

"My parents will be up in about a half hour," he said, looking out the window. "Do you want something to eat?"

Oddly enough, she didn't feel hungry—she was eager to get to her parents' home as soon as possible. "Don't bother. Why take the chance of waking them up? I'll eat something at home." She straightened under the covers, aware that she only had on underwear.

Cullen coughed. "I'll take a trip down the hall while you put on your clothes. When I come back, I'll open the door a crack rather than knock. Tell me if you need more time." As quick and quiet as a cat, he was gone.

Teagan threw off the sheet and ran to the closet. Her dress was damp, but it didn't matter. She had nothing else to wear. If the sun was bright, it might be dry by the time she got to her

parents'. She dressed quickly, in a hurry to leave. Every minute in the daylight would mean taking extra care, especially if
the Guards were around. The clock in Cullen's room read five
thirty—about the time she would be discovered missing from
the convent.

Cullen poked his head around the door. He sat beside her on
the bed. "Father Conry told me he visited you."

Teagan nodded. "He gave me the bad news about my father.
He also told me about the rumor that Father Mark had gotten a
girl pregnant. I don't know what to think."

He grasped her hands. "Everything will work out. You'll
see—and when it does, remember the friend who took you in."
He leaned over and kissed the side of her head, his red hair
brushing against her face. She loved the soft feel of it.

"I have to go. I don't want the Guards to see me. They'll
question a woman on the street at this hour. I'm leaving my
apron here. Get rid of it when you can."

"I'll take care of it." Cullen padded over to the chest and
pulled a drawer open. He returned with a five-pound note.
"Take this. It's a bit of a haul to Ballsbridge from here, but this
should leave you with some money to spare. There's a taxi stand
at the end of the road."

"That's too much," Teagan protested.

"Pay me back someday." He folded the note into her hand.

She kissed him gently on the cheek and got up to leave. He
raised the window and held on to her as she slid to the ground.
She felt dirty, like a tramp, sneaking out of a man's room at
dawn, even though nothing had happened.

He called out softly, as she walked away. "Remember what
I said." He leaned out the window and waved. "Come back
to me."

She blew him a kiss and then strode to the footpath. She
looked east to the end of the road and saw several taxis queued
up there. The five pounds Cullen gave her would come in handy.

The house looked empty. She leaned forward from the backseat and looked through the glass. Her nerves popped like fire-

works. A lifetime of memories came flooding back as the driver pulled up to the curb: playing in the garden out back, birthday parties, visits from school pals, the meeting with Father Mark. She blotted that dark stain from her mind.

The car was gone and the curtains were closed. Her mother always kept them open unless they were going out. She looked in the post box—it was empty. The anxiety she'd experienced in the taxi lessened somewhat with the idea that her parents might be away. She had hoped that only her mother would be home. They could talk before her father arrived from work.

She didn't want to stand in the yard as the neighbors left their homes. Some nosy person had probably already seen her. Her mother always kept a spare key under the garden gnome at the edge of the drive. She tipped it on its side—but there was no key on the ground. She was about to reposition it when a flash of silver caught her eye. Black electrical tape held the key to the statue's base. She ripped it off and fitted it into the lock.

Nothing had changed. The hall rack sat near the door as it always had. Her father had grabbed his coat from it the night he had taken her away. The Oriental carpet runner on the stairs looked clean and fluffed; the banister glowed with a golden-brown polish. Her mother's Chinese porcelain plates still shone red and white in the living room. However, her portrait had been removed from the mantle. She wondered if every trace of her existence had been obliterated.

One thing was different in the kitchen. A plant stand filled with African violets sat near the back door, in front of the garden window. Her mother had never grown house plants. She had been satisfied to putter with window boxes in the spring. A dozen or more plants rested on metal arms that shot out from the tall stand. The violets bloomed profusely, offering clusters of white, purple, and yellow flowers. The tubular leaves were healthy and green, like soft pillows covered with fine down.

Teagan spotted a note on the kitchen table: *Dear Mrs. Bryde: Thank you for taking care of the plants while we're on holiday. I'm quite obsessed with them these days. You only have to water them on Wednesday and they'll be fine for the week. Please don't get any drops on the leaves.* What day was it? *Wednesday?* The days blended together when you were at the convent. Sunday was the exception.

She only had to turn on the telly or the downstairs radio to find out. She didn't know Mrs. Bryde; in fact, she had never heard her mother mention the name. Would this woman be looking for the key under the garden gnome, too? It was too overwhelming to think about, standing alone in her "home."

She returned to the staircase and walked slowly up. Her parents' bedroom door was open; hers, which her father had broken down, was closed. She put her hand on the knob, dreading what she would see, but twisted it open anyway.

Light flowed into the room from the hall, like the sun trying to penetrate a murky ocean. The curtains were drawn tightly over the window. Everything came into focus in shades of gray. Nothing looked out of place. Her bed was undisturbed. Her books were just as she had left them on her desk. The sweater she had left at the parish house during her encounter with Father Mark hung over the back of the chair. She swiped a finger over her desk and a coating of dust collected on its tip. She wondered if anyone had set foot in her room for more than a year.

The closet was closed. When she opened it, she found her clothes lined up on hangers, undisturbed from when her father had taken her away. The dress she had worn on her fateful meeting with Father Mark still hung, white, shiny, like a troubled beacon before her eyes.

She stepped out of her dress and stood naked in front of the mirror. The convent had few mirrors because they encouraged vanity. The only time she caught sight of herself was when she spotted her reflection in the laundry windows. However, the mirror over her desk didn't lie. She was thinner, her face creased and tired, and she looked much older than a girl her age should. Her cropped blond hair was darker now, possibly because there was so little light in the room, but when she opened the curtains briefly, she realized that the lustrous shine of her youth had evaporated. She was bony and not fit to be seen—all thanks to the Sisters.

She wanted to get out of the bedroom—it brought up too many bad memories. The living room was the only pleasant place to spend a few hours. But what now? A shower, some dinner, and clean clothes? That was the best plan she could come up with. She showered and put on a blue summer dress over clean panties and a bra. The rich, silky fabrics were like heaven compared to the coarse cottons she wore at the convent. She stepped out back, stuffed her old dress into the garbage bin, and covered it with trash. She doubted her parents would ever notice.

They hadn't left much in the icebox because of their holiday, only enough to make a sandwich. Cold water sat in a pitcher. She decided to try a beer from her father's stash in the pantry. She had sipped it before on occasion, when her father allowed, but its taste seemed particularly harsh and bitter today. *Ugh. I don't understand why he likes it.* The foamy brown liquid made her sleepy after half a bottle.

She ate her sandwich at the kitchen table, looked at the plants, then snapped on a small transistor radio her mother had positioned on a shelf over the sink. The announcer dutifully reported the weather for Wednesday. Mrs. Bryde could be here at any time, she thought in a momentary panic. She cleaned her plate, poured the half-finished beer down the sink, and stretched out on the living room sofa.

The sound of the front door opening jolted her awake. Teagan looked sleepily at the petite woman in a floral housedress who stepped into the hall.

"Hello!" she called out.

The woman jumped, dropping the key. She clutched her purse, which was strapped over her right shoulder. "My lord," she said breathlessly, "you scared the life out of me!"

"I'm Teagan Tiernan." She got up from the couch.

"Who?" The woman stepped toward her. She was pleasant enough, Teagan thought, with a bright face and dark hair streaked with gray.

"Teagan." She extended her hand. "I'm Cormac and Shavon's daughter."

"I'm Mrs. Bryde." The woman shook her hand.

"I know. I saw the note."

Mrs. Bryde stared at her. "I've come over to water the violets." Her gaze wandered over Teagan, from head to toe. The woman took a few steps toward the kitchen and then turned back. "I hope you don't think me rude, but this is a very odd situation. Your mother never mentioned to our bridge group that she had a daughter." She fidgeted with her hands, exposing the silver rings on her fingers.

"How long have you been playing bridge with my mother?"

"About a year. She's new to our group in Donnybrook."

So, her mother had abandoned her old bridge partners in Ballsbridge for women who didn't know her. Teagan smiled as an excuse popped into her head. "That explains it. I've been away for a while—living with my aunt Florence in New York. My mother misses me so much she doesn't like to talk about it. I'm only here for a short visit. I hadn't planned to arrive before they got back from holiday."

Mrs. Bryde frowned, apparently not buying Teagan's explanation. "They're not scheduled to be home until Sunday." She clasped her hands. "You'll have a long wait."

Teagan returned to the sofa and stretched out her legs. "Well, please go ahead and water the violets—I'm not good with plants." She laughed. "My mother decided to exercise her green thumb after I left."

The woman looked at her oddly and slipped off to the kitchen. Teagan heard the rush of tap water and the *clang* of the metal watering can in the sink. As she listened, she formulated her answers to the woman's expected questions. Mrs. Bryde returned in a few minutes.

"How long are you staying?" the woman asked.

"I'll be staying with friends the next few nights and then back on Sunday. I came over to check on the house—my mother wanted me to do that."

"It was nice meeting you," Mrs. Bryde said. Teagan could tell she didn't mean it. "Perhaps I'll see you later in your visit."

"Perhaps. Don't bother to lock up. I'll take care of it."

"Good-bye." Mrs. Bryde opened the door. Teagan watched as the woman got into her car.

She shut the door, collapsed against it, and sighed. So that was it. Out of embarrassment and shame, her mother had joined a new bridge group after Teagan had been taken to the convent. That way, her mother would never have to talk about a daughter. Silence was her mother's new fashion. Mrs. Bryde would certainly be curious about finding her in the house and find the circumstances odd, but probably not serious enough to call the Guards. If she called other members of the group, they would be as in the dark as Mrs. Bryde.

Teagan returned to the living room and plopped on the couch. She had exchanged one prison for another. Was there no way out of being a Magdalen? She turned on the television, hoping it would distract her. A long day stretched ahead with nothing to do. A bit more food and then what? She couldn't go to Cullen's or any of her girlfriends'. Everyone acquainted with her knew her story, she suspected. She thought of Father Matthew and Father Mark enjoying a glass of wine in the parish house as she sat a prisoner in her own home. Her parents were on holiday. How depressing. Her father was probably drunk by now, and it was hardly noon.

The telly would have to be her company for the day. Nothing was working. Life was horrible, with the real possibility that it might get worse. Sunday seemed an eternity away. She had planned to keep the curtains closed and most of the lights off after sunset. Just like a gaol. The thought depressed her. The hours crept by.

By the next afternoon, Teagan had had enough. She had slept poorly on the couch, keeping one eye open during the night. Every *pop* and *creak*, every breath of wind, sent her nerves jangling. She expected a Guard to show up at the door at any minute. A cold sandwich and water were her only fare. She missed her mother's cooking: salmon cakes, beef and cabbage, coddle sausage, and potato stew. The imaginary odors filled her head and made her hungry for something more substantial than the dregs she was eating. She still had most of the money Cullen had given her. Perhaps she'd have to go out for food.

As the day dragged on, she found a sheet of her mother's stationery and a pen. She wrote three notes, but destroyed each of them before she found the right tone on the fourth. It was a simple letter explaining her escape from the convent and how she had come back to her home to be reunited with her parents. She hoped they would forgive her and welcome her back. That was what she wanted *more than anything in the world.*

She placed the note on the kitchen table next to her mother's instructions to Mrs. Bryde. Her mother couldn't fail to find it there. As she paced, she thought about returning to Cullen's after dark. If nothing else, it would break the boredom of being alone. Maybe he'd agree to put her up overnight, and together, they could work out what she should do next.

Dusk was falling when Teagan heard a car door slam in front of the house. She lifted a slat on the living room blinds and peered out. A black sedan had pulled up to the curb, and two men in black suits were exiting the car. Both men, lean and long, looked official and stern. She gasped when she saw who was in the rear seat. Cullen, his head cradled in his hands, slumped forward.

She ran to the kitchen, hoping to escape by the back door. One of the men was already on the brick walk leading to the garden. A heavy knock reverberated through the hall. She had to open the front door. What if they broke it down? She couldn't hide. Even if she did, how long could she hold out before they found her?

She smoothed her dress, took a deep breath, and walked down the hall.

Her fingers trembled as she reached for the knob.

The man cocked his head and doffed his hat when the door opened.

"Teagan Tiernan?" His eyebrows lifted.

"Yes?" she asked, as if asserting her innocence.

He introduced himself as a "district detective," flashed identification, and then returned it to his coat pocket. "Please come with me. We're here to take you back to The Sisters of the Holy Redemption."

She peered over the man's shoulder. Cullen was still slouched in the seat. "He had nothing to do with this," she said.

The detective looked at the car. Cullen leaned back, disappearing from view.

"We know," the detective said. "The elderly lady who lives next door to the Kirbys saw you crawl out the window yesterday morning. It took a while for her to tell Cullen's parents, and for him to confess what had happened. He's in no trouble—except with his family. It wasn't hard to figure out where you were."

"Let me close up," Teagan said. The man followed her in as she picked up the key from a living room table. As she locked the door, the other man appeared from the side of the house and got into the driver's seat. She replaced the key under the garden gnome.

The detective took her to the car. Teagan slid into the backseat with Cullen.

"I'm sorry," he said as they pulled away. "My parents wore me down. I lied at first, but then I told them the truth. They were upset you spent the night in my room. That nosy old biddy next door—I could . . ."

She shot him a look. "Don't say too much. Don't worry, everything will be all right." But deep down, she knew she was only soothing Cullen's feelings. The crushing feeling of despair, which had been a part of her life for more than a year, fell over her again. Life had been a shifting terrain. The elation she'd experienced on slipping out of the convent had vanished once she got to her parents' home.

She said nothing on the trip back to Cullen's, other than good-bye. The car sped off to the convent. She wondered what Sister Anne would have in store for her. She dreaded seeing her again. They drove past Saint Patrick's Cathedral and St Stephen's Green, and traveled down a few of the roads that she had walked in her short time away. Mr. Roche was standing at the gate when the car pulled up. He looked at her like a mortified parent, swung open the iron enclosure, and waved them through. As they passed under the oaks and pines, Teagan wondered what her escape had accomplished. Not much, as far as she could see—a brief encounter with Cullen and a heartfelt note to her parents. If her father found the note before her mother, he would destroy it and no one would be the wiser. It would be as if she had never set foot in the house. The only thing her father might miss was the one beer she drank.

When the car stopped, Teagan opened the door. The Mother Superior stood at the top of the steps, in the same spot as their first meeting. Nothing had changed in a year but the thoughts in her head. She looked at the granite façade and sighed. *This will be my home forever. Better get used to it.* Her concession felt hollow. No sense of relief, depression, or elation filled her. Suddenly she felt nothing.

Teagan walked up the steps to Sister Anne. The heavy doors from which she had escaped only a few days ago stood open. Sisters Mary-Elizabeth and Rose stood in the hall.

The Mother Superior's face was fixed in a quiet fury that crackled with anger. The nun said nothing as she walked past. Neither did the other Sisters. Teagan walked down the hall and heard the *clang* of tableware and shifting chairs overhead. The evening meal was being served.

She stopped at the entrance to the Penitent's Room. The door was open, revealing the dark cave of solitude. She had avoided it in her days here, but this time there was no way out. She sat on the small stool. Sister Mary-Elizabeth approached. The door closed, the lock bolted, and she was jolted into nothingness. Her breath fled and she thrust her palms against the walls to steady herself. *Black. Black.* A darkness she had never experienced. The stone felt cold against her hands. After a few minutes, her fingers felt as if they were frozen. She stabbed at the granite as she slumped to the floor.

CHAPTER 16

The sun reflected off the grounds like a bright lantern when Nora arrived back at the convent from the hospital. She wanted to walk through the lush blades and feel the dew splatter against her ankles, but her baby boy clamored for attention. He wasn't sleeping; instead, he pummeled her breasts with his fists and gurgled incessantly. The sound made her happy. In fact, it thrilled her much more than she expected.

He was a strong child, despite being delivered early, but had made good progress once the natural birth occurred. The doctors had kept her a few more days than usual because of his early arrival. She called him Seamus because she'd always liked the sound of the name. She dismissed calling him Pearse, her ex-boyfriend; Sean, the child's father; or Gordon, her father. They reminded her of her problem with men.

She wanted to sit in the sun with her baby and enjoy the sparkling day. He batted his long black lashes and cooed. Seamus had the strong chin of his father. He would be a looker someday, she thought, quite the ladies' man.

The hospital nurse escorted her to the top convent steps and then returned to the car. Sisters Mary-Elizabeth and Ruth waited for her. Both nuns, particularly Sister Mary-Elizabeth, smiled broadly when Nora lowered the blanket from Seamus's face.

"Oh, by the saints," Sister Mary-Elizabeth said and pinched his cheek. "What a fine-looking young man."

"He'll make some family very happy," Sister Ruth chimed in.

The nun's words struck her like ice water in the face. Nora recoiled when Sister Ruth reached out to touch him. She knew what was going to happen to her son. Nothing in the world could change her baby's fate. He would be suckled by her, then by a wet nurse, and later put up for adoption. She had learned through whispered conversations what happened to a Magdalen's child. Even the kind doctors and nurses at the hospital told the truth, telling her she should enjoy her baby while she could. Everyone knew what happened to a child born out of wedlock. Many "deserving" Catholic families would welcome Seamus because they couldn't bear children of their own. Even so, it was tasteless and crass of Sister Ruth to bring up the adoption of her child before she set foot in the convent.

Sister Ruth ducked into the Mother Superior's office and Sister Mary-Elizabeth guided her to a door on the west side of the chapel. Nora had noticed it before at prayers, but had no idea where it went. If anything, she thought it might open to the gated compound surrounding the convent. The portly nun jangled her keys to find the right one. To Nora's astonishment, a bright hall opened before them. A group of nuns Nora had seen only at prayers and meals strode through the long, narrow building. Sister Mary-Elizabeth had taken her to another area of the convent that housed the orphanage. The cries and laughter of children echoed down the hall.

The wing was shaped by a series of connecting granite arches, as if it had been a portico at one time. But unlike the main building, the walls were paneled. Ancient beams, pockmarked by woodworm, stretched across the roof. The building reflected its durable age, a comforting thought. It was somehow inviting, more of a home than the sepulchral chambers in which the Magdalens lived and worked.

Sister Mary-Elizabeth opened a door about halfway down the expansive hall to a small room that contained a chair and table. A glass contraption, a large suction cup attached to a bottle, sat on the table.

"Feed your baby and then give us milk," the nun ordered.

She pointed to the breast-milking apparatus. "The wet nurse won't be available for a few days, so we'll need to get a supply now and then. We want your child to be well-fed. He'll be staying in the orphanage under our care."

"What? Now?" She couldn't believe they were taking Seamus away from her so quickly.

"Don't worry," the Sister said. "He'll be fine. Believe me, it'll be easier for you—the sooner you get used to giving him up. There's no sense prolonging the agony."

"Me breasts are in agony now," Nora said. "He's been a hungry divil." Her nipples were raw and sensitive underneath her uniform. She wanted to take the suction cup and smash it on the floor. That way she would get to see her baby every feeding time.

"Come now," the nun coaxed. "I'll help you with your uniform." The Sister unbuttoned Nora's uniform so it fell open at the back. "If you want privacy, I'll step outside."

Nora nodded, and the nun went into the hall and closed the door. Sister Mary-Elizabeth could still see Nora if she wished, because the door had a glass insert.

She placed Seamus in her lap and wriggled out of her uniform and the shoulder of her cotton slip, revealing her right breast. Seamus looked up hungrily, as if he knew what was in store. He reached for her. Nora leaned over and brought his head up. She winced as his mouth attached to her nipple.

After a few seconds, the pain disappeared and she became one with her child. The feeling was unlike any she had ever experienced. This little creature, so dependent on her, gazed into her eyes with a look of warm helplessness and love. No one had ever loved her so unconditionally. She brushed back his fine black hair and he gurgled happily. The sucking sounds comforted her and filled her with a sense of purpose. She was doing something good for the first time in her life. She didn't want the happiness to end.

Sister Mary-Elizabeth turned, looked in the window, and smiled. The nun pointed to the milking machine and made pumping motions with her hand. "I'll show you how to use it, if you need help," the nun shouted through the glass.

"I can figure it out," Nora shouted back.

Sister Mary-Elizabeth turned to talk to another nun who passed by. Nora was left again with the baby and her thoughts. The feeding lasted until Seamus took his lips away. Nora raised him to her shoulder and patted him on the back. He let out a loud burp.

Nora situated Seamus in her lap, until he was comfortable, and then used the machine. Her milk, a thin white liquid, poured into the container until it was full.

She kicked the door with her foot and Sister Mary-Elizabeth turned. She signaled for Nora to wait. The nun reappeared with Immaculata, the Sister who had sent Nora to the hospital. She took Seamus from Nora's arms and smiled when she saw the bottle on the table. "That will come in handy," Sister Immaculata proclaimed. "He's such a good baby. It's amazing how good things can come from bad." She looked sternly at Nora. "We only need you for milk until the wet nurse arrives. You can return to your duties. I'm sure the Mother Superior will approve."

Nora's stomach turned over. The thought of giving up Seamus made her nauseous. He was already gone! The Sisters wouldn't even allow her a few meager moments of joyous motherhood.

Immaculata walked away with Seamus and opened a door on the left side of the hall. Nora made a mental note of the room's location as she dressed. A plan had already hatched in her mind.

"Time to go back," Sister Mary-Elizabeth said. "How do you feel?"

"A little weak," Nora said, stretching the truth.

"I don't doubt that you're knackered from the birth," the nun said. "You probably need rest before you go back to work. But, knowing you, I'm sure you'll be up and about tomorrow."

Nora nodded, but said nothing as the Sister led her down the hall. When the nun opened the door leading to the chapel, Nora fell forward, dragging the nun inside with her. The door shut by itself. Nora stumbled to a pew and collapsed.

Sister Mary-Elizabeth rushed to her, so consumed with Nora

she forgot to lock the door. Nora had hoped that would happen. "Are you all right?" the nun asked as she hovered over her.

"I'll be fine." Nora gasped a few times for extra effect. "Just get me to bed."

The nun helped her up from the pew. Soon Nora was resting with a grin on her face. She had escaped laundry duty.

She glanced at Teagan's bed. It looked as if no one had slept in it for several days. The blanket was neatly folded at the foot, and the sheets were crisper than the other Magdalens' beds. There was no one around to answer questions about her friend's whereabouts.

Nora dragged herself to tea. Teagan was still missing. At vespers, Nora was thinking about a different matter than her friend. She kept her eye on the door that led to the orphanage. Nothing had changed as far as she could tell. She hoped it would still be unlocked when she came back in the early morning hours.

At bedtime, she questioned Lea about Teagan, but her friend revealed nothing. If anything, Lea seemed depressed, unable to talk. Even the country girl's enigmatic smile had faded, but Nora suspected Lea knew a great deal more than her silence indicated.

Having nothing to do for a few hours, she curled up in bed and slept. A few Technicolor dreams about giving birth and nursing invaded her sleep. One, about suckling, seemed so real she shot upright in bed, her nipple burning in pain.

The garret was dark, and the time was right. The Magdalens, unaware of her, snored and snuffled as she walked to the doors. She stopped in the toilet before she headed downstairs to the chapel.

Its doors, heavy and wooden, echoed the design of the convent's entrance, only on a smaller scale. They were always closed, except during prayers or Mass, but never locked. Her breath caught as she pulled on the carved wooden handle. What if one of the nuns was inside? The thought scared her briefly, but she would lie if necessary. *So sorry to disturb you, Sister, but I felt the need to pray.*

A small electric lamp burned in the corner. It cast a dim light throughout the chapel. All the votive candles had been extinguished, but Nora knew where they were kept, because she had seen the nuns fussing with them so many times. She found them tucked inside a chest of drawers near the back. She took one of the longer candles and a box of matches and headed toward the door that led to the orphanage.

Her prayer had been answered. The door swung open to the orphanage hall. A large cathedral lamp hung from one of the weathered beams, throwing its light, suffused with filigree shadows, over the granite and wood.

Nora glanced at the clock attached to the wall. It was after two, and everything was quiet. She wasn't sure where the nuns who worked here slept, but no one was up. It was long past any midnight feedings. How many nuns, how many children, were here? She had no idea.

She reached the room where Immaculata had taken Seamus. Her heart racing, she gathered her courage and opened the door.

It took a moment for her eyes to adjust, for only the scattered light from a small lamp attached to the orphanage's south wall filtered through the windows. As the room came into focus in dull gray forms, she was able to make out a row of metal cribs in its center, five in all. A desk and chair sat on her left, to the east, while a heavy, mirrored armoire took up most of the west wall. Her nose twitched. It smelled like a baby, with the unmistakable odor of a diapered infant in the air.

She lit the candle and put the matches on the desk. Holding the flame, she tiptoed toward the cribs, then stopped and looked in each, from left to right. All were empty except the last one, near the armoire. She placed the candle on the desk and walked back to the last crib. She uncovered the baby inside and turned the child over. Seamus's black hair and strong chin came into view. The baby sputtered, and Nora put a finger to his lips to quiet him. His arms flailed at his sides briefly, but, as if he had been expecting the comfort of his mother, he closed his eyes and drifted off.

She gathered her baby and sat in the chair, content to rock

him in her arms and watch the candle's flickering shadows play about the room. The thought crossed her mind that she was like the Madonna—caring for the poor child she had brought into the world. She could have been anywhere—her bedroom, a cottage near the Cliffs of Moher, a manger—all equally suitable nurseries for the expression of her maternal warmth. Nothing in the world could take the place of being close to her baby. He slept peacefully, lulled by the quiet and depth of her affection, as she drifted toward sleep.

For what must have been an hour—she wasn't sure how long—she kept watch, savoring her devotion to her baby. She knew sitting with him was forbidden. Sister Immaculata had made it clear that she wasn't to see Seamus again, but her love was greater than the nuns' demands. She wanted to see her baby as many times as she could manage.

Seamus kicked and fussed when she repositioned his body against her chest, and soon, his bawling erupted into whining screams. One of the nuns was sure to hear him cry out. If she was discovered, her time with him would be gone forever.

She ran back to the crib and covered him while he thrashed about. The candle still burned on the desk. A terrible thought struck her; she couldn't blow it out, for the smoke would fill the room. She would be discovered for sure.

The armoire. It was the only place large enough to hide. She gathered the candle and matches, hurried across, and opened its double doors. The cabinet was divided into two sections, with drawers on the left and a tall compartment on the right that was empty except for sheets draped over hangers. Nora ducked inside, the candle still burning, and closed the doors behind her.

Seamus, now fully awake, howled.

Keeping the candle aflame was too risky. She blew it out hoping the wick wouldn't smolder for too long. Smoke churned in the air. She grabbed the edge of one of the sheets as a makeshift mask and breathed through it to keep from coughing. A small spit of orange died on the wick. She placed the candle on the matchbox in the corner of the armoire.

The nursery door creaked open. Footsteps sounded in the room. She heard the bustle around Seamus's crib, a body length away. The nun's voice was muted, but words sounding like *"now, now"* filtered through the armoire doors. For a few minutes, a soft hum, like a song, rose in the air. Seamus quieted and the singer's voice faded. The door clicked shut.

To be safe, she waited a few more minutes before slowly opening the armoire doors. She peeked out. The nursery was dark and empty, except for her baby. Seamus was asleep on his back, a pacifier perched near his lips. It was too dangerous to stay. She had to get back to bed before dawn.

She leaned down, kissed him, and then looked around the room to make sure that everything was just as it had been when she arrived. She closed the armoire, pushed the chair close to the desk, and tiptoed out of the room. The clock read fifteen minutes before four. She made her way down the hall, through the chapel, and back to bed without being noticed.

Screams awakened her as dawn broke.

"Fire! Fire!"

Sister Mary-Elizabeth, dressed in her nightgown, flung open the garret doors and screamed at the Magdalens. "Get out, now! Go downstairs to the lawn. Mr. Roche will see you out!"

Nora shot up in bed, awake to the horror around her. Shouts echoed down the hall. She jumped from bed and looked out the barred window. Balls of thick black smoke, rising from the orphanage, filled the grounds. The roiling clouds billowed into the pink sky.

She trembled at the terrible thought that filled her head: *The candle and the matches! I put the candle on the matchbox and left it in the armoire.*

She sank to her knees in front of the window. "Seamus! Seamus!"

Lea grabbed her by the shoulders and lifted her up. "We have to go outside." Her friend sounded calm compared to the frantic voices around her.

"My baby . . . my baby is in there. Please, let me go."

Lea grabbed her hands and led her toward the door. "I can help."

The gritty smell of burning wood filled the hall as they fled down the stairs. Below them, the nuns screamed. The Magdalens, like a herd of frightened animals, rushed down the stairs in a torrent and out the doors.

Lea kept her hands on Nora, pushing her forward until they were in the yard, running past the front of the convent, then south and west, until they could see the burning orphanage. They gathered in an area normally off-limits to them.

Nora shook violently at the sight of the burning building. "Oh my God! Dear Jesus." Her son was inside—the son she had hoped would have a better life than she. She clenched her hands and brought them up to her temples. The pain was excruciating. How could she have been so stupid? *Please don't let my son die! I can't go on if he dies!*

She collapsed to the ground and buried her face in her hands.

Lea had heard something when she and Nora fled past the chapel. It sounded like frantic knocking from the Penitent's Room. The noise bothered her, but there was something more important in the yard that vied for her attention. She needed to save Nora's child because *the others* told her so.

Their tiny bodies wrapped in burial cloths, they floated above the ground and pointed to the orphanage windows. They cried, especially a little boy with dirty smudges on his face and hands. *Save him. His crib is in front of that window.* The boy stuck a grubby finger toward it. *Go through the chapel.* Lea had been with the nuns in the orphanage a few times when they needed help, but she had never spent much time there.

The Sisters attacked the flames with buckets of water and then fell back from the heat and smoke. Sister Immaculata appeared around the side of the convent, leading a stream of coughing children into the yard.

"Please look after Monica," Lea said to Sister Rose, the old nun who stood watch over the Magdalens. "Her baby is inside the orphanage." The nun steepled her fingers in prayer and nodded.

Lea ran to Sister Immaculata. The orphanage children clustered around the nun's legs.

"Where's Monica's baby?" Lea asked her.

The nun shook her head. "The smoke, the flames . . ." The nun was too shocked to be of any use.

Lea spotted Mr. Roche at the entrance to the convent. He stood on the steps waving his hands through the air as if he could magically remove the smoke from the building.

"I need your keys, Mr. Roche," Lea said.

He looked at her, stupefied, and waved her away. "Go on with yeh. I've no time for yer craziness."

"Someone's in the Penitent's Room. It's locked!"

"Christ Jesus!" He crossed himself, then sprinted, keys in hand, toward the room. Smoke rolled across the convent ceiling, darkening the already dim interior. He thrust the key into the lock, turned it, and pulled on the handle. Teagan, gasping, tumbled against him.

"Get out!" He pointed to the open convent doors. "The orphanage is on fire."

Lea pushed her friend toward Mr. Roche, who was poised to head outside. "Take care of Nora."

Sirens sounded around the convent. The fire service had arrived.

Teagan looked back. "Where are you going?"

Lea ducked into the chapel. Mr. Roche grabbed Teagan's arm and pulled her away. Her friend was yelling, but the words she was shouting made no sense; it was as if she had stepped into a dream.

Regal and serene, He stood in front of the orphanage door, welcoming her, hands outstretched. She smiled because He was so like the pictures she had seen in her Bible and in art books. He even bore some resemblance to her "Christ Enthroned" portrait from the *Book of Kells*. Her mind flipped back to her picture. The face at the door came alive. He was wearing a red tunic and a blue robe, but the colors of His clothes made little difference.

They were diffused by a halo of light that surrounded Him. His brown skin shone in the white light; His luxuriant beard, the color of His skin, came to a point well below His chin. His eyes locked on to hers. She was shocked to see that they were blue, but behind their deep sparkle lay the stars and galaxies of the universe.

He motioned for her to follow. The door flew open, and a thick plume of smoke poured into the chapel as if funneled by a ferocious wind.

She covered her mouth. The smoke parted around her, and she was able to breathe.

She followed Him into the hall. The flames turned to ash where He stepped. Glass broke on the north side of the orphanage, and a column of water flew over her head. The stream struck the burning beams and fell, steaming, back to the floor. Part of the roof collapsed behind her with a crashing *thud*. She continued forward. He held up His hands and the water bounced back as if it had hit an invisible wall. A shower of cool drops fell upon her, knocking back the blistering heat.

The door she'd sought was coming close, on the left. He pointed to the knob, and she turned it. The metal singed her flesh, but she felt nothing except the desire to move into the fire. The water splashed and sizzled behind her. She opened the door.

The thick black smoke parted around her. Through her stinging eyes, she saw firemen running on the other side of the windows. The heat stabbed at her; flames licked at her feet and arms. Her guide was gone. She was alone in a room filled with fire. The little dead boy outside had pointed to the window at the far end of the room. A crib lay across from it. She walked to it, feeling as if the sun blazed around her.

The infant looked up at her, blinking. How beautiful he was. Fine black hair covered his head. Perfectly formed lips complimented the sturdy chin. How handsome the eyes, too. They were blue, like the man's eyes who had guided her in, and they glittered with the same stars. The child held out his arms and she grabbed him.

He snuggled against her.

She held him in her outstretched arms, reaching for the window, trying to get him as far away as possible from the inferno. The furniture blazed, the cribs burst into flame, the walls and ceiling crinkled with heat.

Nora! Nora! Here he is!

"Oh my God!" Teagan stood by Nora, holding her back from rushing toward the window.

The fireman grabbed his ax and smashed the glass. It shattered in a gale of shards. Dense smoke plumed from the window.

The ashen cloud parted briefly. Teagan saw Lea's arms with the baby in her grasp. Her friend's clothes burned upon her as she split the flames.

Nora screamed. The fireman reached inside with his protected hands and arms. He pulled the baby from Lea and placed him on the ground. He dropped over the infant, his mouth upon the baby's. He pushed on the infant's chest, but it did not move. He bent again and again, forcing his breath into the boy.

Teagan ran as close as she could to the window before the heat forced her back. "Get out, Lea! Save yourself!"

Her friend smiled as she had seen her do a thousand times, that enigmatic look of peace, a tranquility that Teagan had seldom experienced.

The wall of fire leapt forward. The orphanage windows crackled.

Lea stood in the flames, quivering, with her arms outstretched from her sides. Her hair burned as she sank into the fire.

"Oh God! No!" Teagan cried out. *You were too good for the world—a saint living on this wicked earth. I'll miss you.*

A blast of water from the opposite side of the orphanage burst through the windows. The room exploded in gray smoke and ash.

Teagan turned to see the fireman still bent over the child.

Nora hovered nearby. Her friend looked blankly at the baby and uttered, "Seamus . . . Seamus." Even the tears had stopped flowing.

The baby lay limp on the wet grass.

The fireman put his hand on Nora's shoulder and shook his head.

Nora wailed and dropped to her knees. Her cries sounded to Teagan as if all the good, all the reasons for living, had drained from her soul.

Teagan knelt and sheltered Nora's body with hers. Her friend stiffened, but didn't cry out. Every muscle in Nora's body shook as she reached for Seamus. Her arms failed her, and she collapsed on the ground. Teagan fell on top of her and cried.

CHAPTER 17

———⇥•⇤———

The girls spent most of the day in the old library, sitting uncomfortably near the whir of gigantic fans that forced smoke out the windows. Teagan found herself staring, with tears in her eyes, at Lea's desk much of the time. The uncompleted *Book of Kells* lay on top, a testament to the convent's loss. Out the window, she could see the firemen, and a few of the nuns, sifting through the charred debris. Sister Anne stood silent, stern, most of the time rarely looking away from the orphanage. Often, she would lower her head and clasp her hands in prayer.

The Magdalens had been excused from laundry duties as the firemen cleared the smoke from the convent. The orphanage had been destroyed. All of the children had been saved except for Seamus. He was nearer the heart of the fire than any of the others. The firemen weren't sure how it had happened, but in the destroyed armoire, they found the remains of a melted candle and the cinders of burnt matches.

Nora huddled in a corner near the lace-mending desk. If Teagan hadn't known her friend was in the room, she wouldn't have spotted her. She was like a trapped animal, hiding, wrapped into a ball, never speaking or moving. When the cooking staff delivered the noon meal from serving carts, Nora refused to eat.

"Please say something," Teagan said to her friend after eating. "I'm sorry about your baby." She struggled to hold in the sadness that swamped her.

Nora stared past her, mute, her gaze like an inmate in an

asylum. Teagan had no idea whether her voice even registered with her friend.

The day crept by with nothing to do. Sisters Mary-Elizabeth and Ruth were always nearby, keeping the Magdalens in check, ordering them to keep quiet, and admonishing them to spend the day in silent prayer. It was hard to say anything over the roar of the fans.

Late in the afternoon, Sister Mary-Elizabeth kneeled on the floor near Nora. She held her hands and prayed for what seemed like an eternity. When the nun turned, she had tears in her eyes. She gathered the other Magdalens in a semicircle in front of her so she could be heard.

"The orphanage has been destroyed," the nun said in a quivering voice. "We believe the fire was started, accidentally or on purpose, by a candle and matches in the newborn room."

The girls gasped. Teagan looked at Nora, who stared straight ahead like a mannequin.

"We're devastated," the Sister continued, "but the damage has been done and it will be months before we can reopen. The fire service thinks the whole wing is unsafe and might need to be demolished. Fortunately, thanks to Sister Immaculata, all of the children escaped the fire alive—except for one." She pulled a handkerchief from her sleeve and dabbed her eyes. "We also lost someone very dear to us—your sister Lea. She now rests in God's arms in heaven. She died trying to save . . . a baby." The nun looked at Nora, who still sat like a rock in the corner. She got no response. "There'll be no work today, but we'll resume our schedule tomorrow with a few changes. You'll sleep here tonight because we need your beds for the nuns who were displaced by the fire."

A groan erupted from the Magdalens, followed by a few grumblings about the lack of comfort.

Teagan glared at the others, incensed that all they could think about was having a comfortable bed, as if those in the garret were any prize. She kept her mouth shut, however, because everyone's nerves were frayed.

Tea was served from the carts, and it was better than most

that had been served in the past months, with a good serving of beef, potatoes, and gravy. Perhaps the nuns and the cooks felt sorry for the girls.

Sister Rose conducted the evening prayers in front of the wide bank of windows in the library. Behind her, the sun set in red-hued splendor. Later, additional mattresses were hauled in by the fire service and a few helpful priests Teagan had never seen before.

After tea, the Magdalens were allowed to use the toilet and gather their bedding and clothing from the garret. Lea's clothes were spread across her mattress, as if she had arranged them for later use. Teagan gathered her things quickly, happy to be out of the room that held so many memories of her friend.

The girls climbed into their makeshift beds. Nora rocked on her heels in the corner. The lingering smell of smoke permeated the air, but had lessened from the overpowering stench of the morning. The fire service had turned the fans to a low setting, creating a constant breeze, which brushed over the Magdalens.

Sister Mary-Elizabeth crept into the room and squatted next to Nora. She attempted to lift her, but Nora collapsed on her side, her legs continuing their restless motion. Frustrated, the nun left Nora and came to Teagan's bed.

"I don't know what to do," the Sister whispered to her. "I'm at me wits' end. I think she should go to the Penitent's Room for her own safety."

Teagan sat up, horrified by the suggestion. "Sister, it would kill her. She's fragile enough as she is. Look at her—I'm not sure she's ever coming back to us."

The nun stared at Nora and then shook her head. "Perhaps you're right, but we can't watch her twenty-four hours a day. If she doesn't come around, the Mother Superior will send her away."

"I'll sleep by her. Let's pull her mattress next to mine. I'll hold on to her, and if she moves, I'll know."

Sister Mary-Elizabeth smiled. "Now look who's showing the patience of a saint? That's an excellent idea—but you know it'll be back to the laundry with you in the morning. You'll be

knackered." The nun pursed her lips. "You'll need another uniform. What happened to it?"

"I left it at my parents' house," Teagan said. She didn't want
to tell the nun that she had left her apron at Cullen's and her
uniform in her parents' garbage bin. She reached into the dress
pocket and felt the bills that remained from Cullen's five-pound
note. They reminded her that there was a life outside of the convent. As far as she was concerned, her escape had accomplished
little except retribution. She had spent nearly two days in the
Penitent's Room, with little to eat and drink. If it hadn't been
for Lea, she might be dead now from smoke. Her friend had
saved her.

Nora needed her now. She couldn't leave now if she had the
chance. She had to help her friend get well, help her grieve the
loss of her baby. *I'll stay for her. No one else. I promised her.*
Teagan looked squarely at Sister Mary-Elizabeth. "I'm no saint,
but Nora needs me and I'll do what I can to help her."

"I'll talk to the Mother Superior. She may have another idea
about how to handle Nora—like the Penitent's Room, or something worse—but I'll try to talk her out of it."

"Where is Sister Anne?" Teagan asked. "She hasn't been here
all day."

"I think she's praying. She spent most of her time wandering
through the wreckage. She's said very little to anyone." The nun
pointed to Nora's empty mattress. "Help me get it next to you
and then let's get Nora . . . I mean, Monica."

They carried the bedding and placed it next to Teagan. They
hooked their arms under Nora's, lifted her to her feet, and
dragged her to the bed. Nora fell on it in a heap and curled into
a fetal position.

"She's like a child now," Sister Mary-Elizabeth said. "You'll
have to watch her like one."

"I will."

Teagan settled beside her friend. Nora whimpered and kept
her hands near her face as if she was protecting herself from a
nightmare.

The nun turned off the overhead lamps, but the stark light

from the hall poured through the open door. The Magdalens seemed restless, Teagan thought, uncomfortable with their new surroundings. They coughed and tossed and turned long into the night. She covered Nora with a blanket and held on to her waist as the hours passed. Sleep was fitful, as she thought about what Nora must be going through. Nothing could be worse than the death of your child.

No doubt remained. She fought the anxiety, the gut-wrenching thirst for revenge that filled her. The brown manila folder's contents lay scattered across her bed like fall leaves.

Sister Anne had dreaded this day, pushed it back at all cost, refused to let it get the better of her. For months, she refused to believe what she suspected, while every instinct inside betrayed her intuition. Why did she have to relive something so terrible?

The cuts from the silver blades ached on her arms, and she fought against the siren call of laceration. Instead, she took a pair of gloves from her drawer, put them on, and bound her wrists with an elastic band. Her fingers could move comfortably.

She sighed and sat on the edge of the bed. She didn't want to believe it—but in her mind the thought had always been there, like the twinkling of a far-away star in the night sky. She had anticipated this nightmare from the beginning. Now it descended upon her like a malevolent spirit, threatening to overwhelm her.

The horrors of the day were too much: the fire, Lea's death, the death of Monica's baby, the destruction of the orphanage, the displacement of her loyal staff. What did these events say about her powers as an administrator? The diocese leaders were sure to wring their hands, wag their tongues, and question her abilities. They might even remove her as the Mother Superior. How could she be trusted to run a convent? Her credibility had been destroyed in one terrible day.

She crossed her arms and held them close to her body to keep from shaking.

After she settled down, she reached with her bound hands for the top page of the report. If she looked at it again, perhaps the type would magically change. A pen, an eraser, a strike across the name with a felt pen and the name would be obliterated. However, no magic, no deletion could change the facts. To conceal the truth was futile. Unquestionably, there were copies of the documents that lay across her bed.

The name cut into her eyes. *Sarah Brennan.* Her sister. Death had come after a long labor and a caesarean that her sister and mother had put off until the last possible moment. Sister Anne had urged them to act sooner, but Sarah had insisted on a natural childbirth, until, of course, her body began to fail. By the time the doctor cut the baby girl out, several blood clots had traveled to Sarah's lungs and then onward to her heart. She was dead within the hour. The drugs were administered too late. *Too late.* Everything was too late! Sarah's face had turned blue, constricted by death. Her mother watched in horror as they pulled the bloody sheet over Sarah's face. Sister Anne cried until she could only sputter, and remembered hating the baby that squirmed nearby in a crib. She wanted nothing to do with the child; she even refused to visit it in the hospital. Her mother withered at home. When the infant was strong enough, she was adopted.

Sister Anne shook her head. The family was named Tiernan. They called the little girl Teagan. A respected Catholic family had adopted her sister's child, and sixteen years later they had met again—resurrecting the memories of her sister's death.

Sister Anne had loved Sarah so much the pain never seemed to subside. Her sister had been the ideal child, a loving and helpful girl who always had a kind word and often wiped away her tears. Their mother was a nervous sort. Sarah added stability to the family when their father deserted them. Losing her sister was like losing a parent.

So much came back to her when she saw Teagan on the steps: the gait; the high cheekbones; the curve of the jaw; the tall, lean form. She knew for certain when the paperwork was presented, but she had wanted to believe there was another Teagan Tiernan, even though the coincidence was too much. For months, she had wanted nothing to do with the penitent, only to punish her when necessary, make Teresa's life as hard and painful as her sister's. But no revenge could ameliorate the toll exacted on Sarah. No punishment would be sweet enough.

She had even decided to put Teresa, as she called her, on the lace-mending table. It was a hobby her sister had excelled at. She would give her sister's daughter a taste of the craft—a torturous pleasure, she hoped.

That was how she felt until today. Now the world was crumbling around her. Her punishments hadn't worked; if anything, they had made a few of the Magdalens, like Teresa and Monica, more unruly. It was true that Patricia, Betty, and a few other girls had found a home with The Sisters of the Holy Redemption, but many had decayed into nothing at all. They might as well have been automatons, tending the laundry, mending lace, saying prayers, eating, sleeping. But that was how duties were conducted at the convent. No one, certainly not the Church, ever remarked on the day-to-day operations.

Sister Mary-Elizabeth had told her what Teresa was doing— sleeping by Monica's side. That was love in its highest sense. She thought of the *LOVE* blocks on her desk, the ones she had taken from the crib in her sister's room. The ones intended for the new baby. They sat on her desk offering a message to all the Magdalens. Until today, she hadn't understood its true meaning. The *LOVE* blocks had been a consequence of her hatred, not affection.

She dropped the page on the bed and got up. The green oaks and Scotch pines outside her window seemed bleak in the encroaching dusk. Every now and then, the itchy smell of smoke entered her nose. She couldn't see the destroyed orphanage from her room. However, the destruction was real, and it would still be there tomorrow when the sun came up. That was a reality, among many, she couldn't deny.

She knelt at the foot of her bed and looked up at the crucifix. Somehow there was more truth in her prayers tonight than there had been in years. Sister Anne lowered her head and prayed that in the morning she would find the strength to exorcise the demons in her heart.

*   *   *

Sister Mary-Elizabeth awakened the Magdalens after what seemed a short night.

Teagan had slipped away from her hold on Nora. Her friend opened her eyes when the nun's early morning call came, but did nothing else.

The nun announced that the chapel was still too smoky, so she conducted a short matins service in the old library, mentioning Lea and the baby. She then ordered the Magdalens upstairs to change for breakfast and work. Not only was there laundry to be done, but the convent needed to be scrubbed, to rid the rooms of smoke and grit.

Teagan remained with her friend as the other girls hurried out. The nun stood over Nora's bedside, a quizzical look on her face.

"Nora. Nora?" Teagan shook her friend's shoulder. Nora's eyes closed and she curled into a ball. Teagan looked up at the nun.

"Leave her be," Sister Mary-Elizabeth said. "There's nothing we can do. She will either come around or Sister Anne will send her to the asylum. She's no use to us here and we can't watch her the whole livelong day."

"But she'll die," Teagan said. "The asylum will kill her. Please tell Sister Anne not to be hasty."

The nun looked down on her, her lips tightly drawn. "You can tell the Mother Superior yourself. She wants to see you after breakfast."

She thought of the two nights spent in the Penitent's Room and how she might have been killed from smoke inhalation if Lea hadn't saved her. "What is this about? More punishment?" she asked, getting up from her mattress.

"I have no idea what the Mother Superior wants." She crossed herself. "I'll pray for your repentance." She bent over, studying Nora's face. "I suppose she'll be all right here. It doesn't look like she's going anywhere. You'd best go along now. Don't keep Sister Anne waiting." She walked away, leaving Teagan alone with Nora.

Teagan knelt beside her friend. "Nora, if you can hear me, please listen. Listen with all your might." She touched her shoulder. "If you don't get up, if you don't move, Sister Anne is going to send you away. You're not going to like an asylum one bit. You're not crazy—just crippled with grief. If you think living here is bad, think about what it'll be like living there." She sighed and brushed back Nora's unruly hair with her fingers. "Unless, of course, you don't want to wake up . . . I have to go. Think about what I've said." She cringed at the thought of Nora dying slowly from physical and mental stagnation.

Many of the Magdalens had taken care of their morning duties and were on their way to breakfast as Teagan trudged up the stairs. As she climbed the steps, she looked down on the Penitent's Room and the chapel doors. Her nose twitched at the smell of charred wood still drifting through the air. The thought of talking with Sister Anne depressed her. The Mother Superior would be in a foul mood after yesterday's events. What did she want? More punishment, penance, an account of her escape? Whatever Sister Anne wanted, she wasn't looking forward to it.

She took off her blue dress and threw it on her old bed. The nun who slept there now would have to deal with it. She showered, got into a clean uniform, which Sister Ruth had provided, and ate breakfast. The room was glum. None of the Magdalens wanted to return to work; their routine had been shattered by the fire. Even the food failed to measure up to the previous night's dinner: lukewarm oats, a charred piece of toast, and a strip of soggy bacon.

Teagan ate as much as she could stomach and then followed the girls down the steps. While the others continued to the laundry room, she turned into Sister Anne's office. The Mother Superior sat at her desk, absorbed in her work, the *LOVE* blocks displayed in front of her. The room was brighter than Teagan had ever seen it. Because of the fire, the drapes and windows were open, letting a fresh late summer breeze flow through the room.

Sister Anne looked up when she heard footsteps. She pointed to the chair in front of the desk.

Teagan sat.

The Mother Superior got up and closed the door.

They were alone now. A queasy feeling struck Teagan's stomach.

Sister Anne sat stiff-backed in her chair and gazed at the files on her desk. She picked up a letter and pushed it across the desk. It had been sent with no stamp or return address. Teagan didn't recognize the handwriting.

"Go ahead, read it," the nun said flatly. "It was delivered yesterday by the sender. He dropped it off at the gate with Mr. Roche." There was no smile on her face, no sarcastic grin; in fact, the Mother Superior showed no emotion.

"I had to read it," the nun explained. "I'm required to read letters that arrive for the Magdalens . . . you understand."

Teagan pulled the sheet of folded paper from the envelope. It was from Cullen.

"The Guards told me you were with him—Cullen."

The Mother Superior was strangely calm, as if her mind was on more important issues.

Teagan nodded. She couldn't deny it. There was no reason to. She opened the letter. Cullen apologized for what he felt was a betrayal, but wrote that he had no choice when questioned by his parents. The neighbor had done them in. He also professed his affection for her and promised that when he turned eighteen, and had the legal means to secure it, he would rescue her from the convent. She blushed and stuffed the letter back into the envelope.

"Marriage is a holy vow between a man and a woman," Sister Anne said. "Not one to be taken lightly. Do you understand the obligations and responsibilities of marriage?"

"Of course," Teagan said. "I also know what it's like to live in a home where marriage is a struggle, a loveless union."

The Mother Superior nodded. "Practically useless except for bearing children."

"I have no intention of having sex, or getting married, if that's what you're worried about." Teagan studied the Mother Superior. The nun's eyes were clouding with tears.

"I've prayed for you, Teresa." Sister Anne looked at her. "I've made it my life's work to eradicate evil, particularly sexual thoughts, from the Magdalens who enter these halls. But no matter how hard I try, it doesn't seem to be enough."

"You're wrong," Teagan said, her voice suffused with anger. "You've beaten any life out of us. Look around you—look at the women who are here, like Betty. What would she do if she was turned out on the street? She'd be like a child, or feel like a prisoner in her freedom, like I did. I felt useless and sad in my own home, trapped by guilt and despair, because that's how I've come to see myself in one year. Useless—a sinner who can never be redeemed."

Sister Anne walked to an open window. "Look how beautiful it is—the grass, the trees in leaf. Ireland can be so lovely in the summer." She put her hands on the casement for a few moments, then turned and asked, "Did you sleep with him?"

Teagan shifted in her chair, taken aback by the directness of the Mother Superior's question. "It's none of your business . . . but I didn't. I've never slept with a man." She paused. "And I've never seduced a man, despite what Fathers Matthew and Mark might say."

Sister Anne walked to her desk and pointed to the *LOVE* blocks. "Would you like to know where I got these?"

Teagan shrugged. She knew Sister Anne would tell her despite what she wanted. The Mother Superior seemed on firmer ground now, more like her old self.

"My sister was to have a baby. She died during childbirth. The blocks were in the baby's crib." She bowed her head briefly. "They were never used, so I took them to remind me what happened. I look at them every day, and sometimes I weep—mostly from anger and hate. I want the anger and hate to disappear, but it's the most difficult task I've ever faced. Demons can be very insistent and tricky, prodding you with their fiery pitchforks."

Teagan didn't know what to say and only nodded.

"I've tried for years to rid myself of the hate I feel for the child who killed my sister. My sister was unmarried. The father of her child was just a boy, on the verge of being a man, who ran away from his responsibility. My mother and sister hid the pregnancy from everyone, even me, until it was obvious. What a great disappointment it was for my mother. It sent her on the road to destruction. She didn't want my sister to end up here, or in a place like it. In hindsight, it would have been better for everyone if she had. At least here, the child would have been attended by doctors and the clergy. The birth wouldn't have been left up to my sister and mother."

"Why are you telling me this?" Teagan asked. "Have I done something wrong? Am I to be punished again?"

Sister Anne picked up the *L* block and turned it in her hands. "The punishment was that you lived and my sister died."

Teagan flinched in her chair. Her eyes widened in slow recognition. What the Mother Superior was professing didn't make sense. She'd misheard the nun. It was monstrous, horrid, to even consider such an idea. She smirked, thinking that the Mother Superior was attempting some kind of perverted joke to make her insane. Perhaps Sister Anne wanted to drive her crazy, like Nora, so she, too, could be shipped off to an asylum. She slumped in her chair, trembling.

Sister Anne replaced the block, aligning it with her fingers, and returned to her chair. A dreary look spread across her face, one opposite of the day outside. "It's true," the nun said. "You're my sister's child—my niece."

"It can't. . . ."

"Let me assure you, it's true." Sister Anne lifted the folder on her desk. "I didn't want to believe it either. You're welcome to look at the papers if you'd like. It's all spelled out here."

Teagan grabbed the file and opened it. Her reading confirmed what Sister Anne said. Her parents had never told her she was adopted. Her thoughts shifted to her father, whom she blamed for keeping the truth from her. It was one of many things unspoken, including his hard drinking, in a family filled with secrets. No wonder he was eager to get rid of her. She wasn't even real flesh and blood.

"When did you know?" Teagan asked, barely aware of the question. She looked through the windows to the green canopy outside. The scene came into focus like a painting. The leaves fluttered in the breeze, their color broken only by the rough gray bark of the trees. The room—the trees outside—nothing seemed real.

"I knew from the beginning, but sometimes the mind doesn't want to accept the truth." The nun spoke slowly, forcing the words out. "There was a strange connection—something in you triggered it in me. Your face, the shape of your head, your walk—they have tortured me. I prayed at your bedside one night. I don't know if you noticed."

Teagan nodded, remembering her memory and the smell of the candle in the hall.

"I had to find out for certain, so I called for my sister's file. Of course, everything I feared fell into place." Sister Anne sighed. "I've hated you since you came here." She clasped her hands and lowered her gaze. "There, I've admitted it. I've hated you and the sin you represented. And I tried to make you suffer, despite love, so you would pay for killing my sister. I hoped that through your suffering—a gift that our heavenly Father gave us—you would become a better woman. But try as I might, I cannot love you. I'm not even sure I can forgive you. It's tragic for one in my position. I'm trying, but I'm not sure I'll succeed."

"You could let me go, so we never have to see each other again." Teagan placed the file on Sister Anne's desk. She immediately regretted the words, as she thought of Nora, immobile, on her bed.

"I wish I could, but I have no authority to do so. The Church would not allow it. You're here until someone takes you away. No matter how many times you escape, you'll be returned to spend your days with us."

Teagan shuddered. It could be years before Cullen could wrangle a way out for her. And what if he changed his mind, or found another girlfriend? How horrible it would be to grow old in the convent, like Betty, withering away until she was a dusty memory.

Sister Anne opened the file and stared at the papers inside. She said nothing for a time and then put the folder down. "Times change. We all change eventually. If nothing else, we die. The fire yesterday taught me something about love. Lea demonstrated it with her willingness to give up her life to save a child. And, in her way, Monica showed me, too. The depth of her love has been demonstrated by her grief."

"Please don't send her away," Teagan said.

"I hope, for her sake, she recovers, but if not . . ."

The hard veil of obstinacy had fallen over the Mother Superior again.

"I think you've said everything I need to hear," Teagan said. "For once, I'm dismissing myself."

Sister Anne didn't raise an objection. "Work will be good for you. It's good for all of us—like love."

Teagan shook her head. "I think it's better if we see each other as little as possible." She walked to the door and opened it. Sister Anne nodded as she stepped into the hall. Sorrow engulfed her as she walked down the steps and into the humming throb of the laundry.

Teagan kept to herself the next week. Her emotions were raw; she had no desire to relive her pain. As she worked at the washbasins, she thought about how to legitimately leave the convent. Being only seventeen years old, every idea seemed unrealistic, unworkable; nothing she thought of, legal or otherwise, gave her any confidence that she would be freed. Her father wanted nothing to do with her. The Church, especially Father Matthew, would be opposed to her release.

Nora was walking and eating now. The basic functions of life seemed to keep her alive. The modest recovery hardly cheered Teagan. Sister Mary-Elizabeth, knowing the alternative was an asylum, forced her friend back to the laundry. Nora worked at the sorting bins with Sarah, but said little, only giving Teagan and the other Magdalens a sad look.

Nora lifted the clothes, tablecloths, and bedspreads with stiff arms, letting her body drop with the weight of the dirty wash until her limbs were purple with bruises. More than once Teagan thought an institution might be a better choice for Nora, rather than slowly killing herself in the laundry. No matter how hard she pleaded with her friend to "come back to us," she couldn't break through the wall in her mind.

Lea's body had been taken away by her stepfather for burial. Betty had taken Teagan's place at the lace-mending table, relegating her to the laundry.

A new Magdalen had taken Lea's place, a pretty girl with dark brown hair who had run away from home to be with a boyfriend. Teagan was reluctant to get to know her because the fates of her friends still hung heavily upon her heart.

Sister Anne avoided her, walking silently past as if she didn't exist.

During a stretch of warm days, she and the other girls struggled with the heat. The work exhausted her after a few hours. The smells of bleach and detergent turned her stomach. The work was dull, the daily routine duller; sleep blocked out the pain somewhat, but like Nora, she could feel herself slipping away. Another year and she would be gone—like Sarah, Betty, and many others. She knew it.

She stuck her hands into the hot water. Her body temperature rose even higher. Sweat dripped from her brow. She lifted her soapy fingers from the water and swiped them across her forehead.

Shouts and angry voices filtered down the stairs. The Magdalens stopped to listen to the commotion, which could be heard above the hum of the machines. Sister Ruth gave the signal for the girls to shut off the laundry equipment. An eerie silence fell upon the room.

The shouts continued in the hall above. She tensed when she heard Cullen's voice call her name. The Mother Superior was shouting, too, shrill and biting, above his calls.

"Don't move," Sister Ruth ordered. "I'll see what's going on."

If anyone could stop Cullen, it would be Sister Ruth. Teagan had no intention of obeying the nun's command and she ran to the stairs, following the rustle of the habit.

When she rounded the corner, she found that the Mother Superior and Sister Ruth had blocked the stairs. Mr. Roche held Cullen back. Her boyfriend was pushing toward the two nuns.

When Cullen saw her, his face shifted from anger to desperation.

"Me pal here climbed the gate and forced his way in," Mr. Roche shouted at Teagan.

"I knew you were keeping her in the laundry," Cullen said. "Let go of me. I won't cause trouble."

Sister Ruth, seething with rage, turned on Teagan. "I told you to stay put. Did you have anything to do with this?"

The Mother Superior raised her hand. "It's all right, Sister. Let's hear what the boy has to say. Mr. Roche, release him." She glared at Cullen. "What do you have to say that's so important?"

Cullen focused on Teagan. The color drained from his face as he walked toward her.

"Your parents are dead."

Her body stiffened.

Sister Ruth shook her fist at Cullen. "If you are making this up—I'll—"

"Are you calling me a liar?" Cullen shouted. "Why would I make up such a terrible joke? Read the evening papers. Cormac Tiernan worked for the government." He held out his hands to her.

Sister Ruth stepped between them, but Sister Anne pulled her back. "Let him go," she said.

The convent was slipping away. It didn't matter anymore. Words caught in her throat. Death had mocked her again with its brutal surprises; her body reeled in pain. "They're . . ." was all she managed.

"I'm sorry," Cullen said and grasped her hands. "Both gone. The car went off the road into a canal. They drowned. Your da had been drinking."

She looked at him. His lips moved, but the words he spoke didn't seem real. Memories of the house, her parents, flooded through her. She collapsed on the top step and covered her eyes with her hands.

Cullen knelt beside her. "I'll keep trying. For your sake, I'll keep trying."

She couldn't think about the future when the present seemed so dead.

Someone touched her shoulder. She looked up to see Sister Anne standing over her. "Thank you, young man, but I think you'd better go now."

Cullen backed away. "Yes, I'll go." He stopped at the door. "But I'll be back. I promise." He pulled the door open and stepped outside. Mr. Roche followed him.

Sister Anne pulled her up. "Sister Ruth, go ahead with the work. We can't falter. . . ." The nun disappeared down the stairs to the laundry.

The Mother Superior put her arm through Teagan's and led her to the chapel. "We must pray. We receive our strength from God."

She sat in the front pew as Sister Anne gathered votives and lit them at the small altar dedicated to the Holy Mother.

Time stopped as she sat looking at the chapel walls. The burning wicks reminded her of the orphanage fire. Death was too close, an entity who had grabbed her and wouldn't let go. Perhaps the Reaper had even more surprises in store.

She clasped her hands. The murmuring voice of Sister Anne, who prayed on the kneeler next to her, made no sense. How could she believe that the Mother Superior, her aunt, the woman who hated her, now shared her grief? She wondered whether her mother had read her note before she died. She hoped so. The tears came and she fought back sobs.

She prayed in the chapel until there were no more tears left.

CHAPTER 18

Nothing could have prepared her for the shock of losing her parents.

She was an orphan again on the cusp of adulthood, but not yet of legal age. Her parents were gone. She had no idea whether the house was hers or someone else's, but it really didn't matter since she couldn't leave the convent. Every avenue had been closed. Such thoughts were numbing.

The funerals were held at St. Eusebius three days after the accident. Father Matthew, the old priest, conducted the funeral Masses. Still harboring his prejudice, he never looked at Teagan. The Mother Superior and Sister Mary-Elizabeth accompanied her to the church.

A large contingent of government workers turned out to pay their respects, in addition to all the current and former bridge club players in her mother's circle of friends. Mrs. Bryde, the woman who had discovered her in the house a few weeks ago, spurned her. Teagan assumed the woman now knew the "truth" about the Magdalens and wanted nothing to do with her.

Cullen attended with his mother and sat a few rows behind her. They only gave their condolences. They had no chance to talk privately with the nuns hovering nearby.

The funerals brought up painful memories of her parents and of the many days she had spent at the church, including her introduction to Father Mark at the parish house. She couldn't help but fixate on the Sunday the old priest had called her father aside to chastise him about her meeting with the handsome priest. Getting her jumper back was a simple and innocent act; yet so much had happened because of it. After she had been sent away, her father's depression and drinking had deepened, leading to the deaths of her parents. As she sat wedged between the Mother Superior and Sister Mary-Elizabeth, she wanted to get out of the church as quickly as possible, even if it meant returning to her life at the convent. Too many hurtful memories stung her.

When the Mass ended, she noticed a man sitting at the back of the church near a holy water font. He turned away from her, but there was something familiar about the face, shadowed in a full black beard.

She turned her head for a moment to acknowledge sympathy from a neighbor. When she looked back at the man, he had disappeared. She walked to the car with the nuns. Mr. Roche drove them back to the convent.

Sister Anne was standing in the hall the next morning. Teagan was on her way from breakfast to the laundry. She tried to judge the Mother Superior's mood. The nun stood stiffly upright, her lips pursed to a narrow slit. Her eyes seemed black, like the dark orbs of crows. She motioned for Teagan to step inside her office and closed the door behind them.

A man was sitting in front of the Mother Superior's desk. As Teagan drew near, he turned. She recognized him as the man with the beard who had been sitting at the back of the church.

He got up from the chair. "Hello."

Teagan knew Father Mark's voice. No wonder she hadn't recognized him at the funeral Mass. The full black beard grew high upon his cheeks, hiding his handsome features. He wore a white button-down shirt—one any working-class Irishman would wear—and dark pants. His shoes were scuffed, his pants and shirt somewhat wrinkled. The crisp style he had once displayed was gone.

An awkward silence grew between Sister Anne and Father Mark. Teagan refused to sit next to him.

Finally, Sister Anne spoke. "Father Mark wants to talk to you. He has already told me what he intends to say, so there are no secrets between us."

He faced her, his eyes sullen and heavy. "I've come to ask for your release from The Sisters of the Holy Redemption."

She understood what Father Mark had said, but, oddly, the words rang hollow, without substance, in her head. How could he rescue her? He had come to release her when she had no home to go to? Her face reddened in anger.

She looked at his sad face. Maybe he was suffering, but his penance was nothing compared to what she had been through. She had lost her parents because of him. How could she trust him after what he had done? How would she make her way in the world with no parents, no money, and little chance of employment? Nothing like joy or elation filled her. She stiffened as these questions occupied her thoughts.

"I know how hard this has been for you," Mark continued. "I want to make it up to you. I'm no longer a priest."

She stared at him, hardly able to believe her ears.

He didn't take his gaze off her, despite the tears brimming in his eyes.

"I've come to ask for your forgiveness, because for more than a year, I've lived with a lie." He brushed away a tear. "Let me tell you what happened from the beginning. After much soul-searching, I told Father Matthew I'd developed feelings—sexual fantasies—after our meeting. It wasn't a confession, just a conversation with my superior. In the Church, a priest can do no wrong and his mentor stands up for him. Father Matthew took our talk and made it his own. My admission grew like a hideous beast; you became the sinner who could cause me to fall into the devil's hands. Once our talk was over, it took on a life of its own. Father Matthew was intent on saving me from my own 'destruction.'"

Sister Anne frowned and looked down at her desk. Her mouth worked silently as if muttering a silent prayer.

"I've been weak, a disciple of the devil, living a lie," Father

Mark continued. "I knew what Father Matthew had done—telling your father—but I didn't have the strength to confront him. Later I told him what he had done was wrong, but I didn't fight for you. He told me everything would be better this way; that life would be easier. It was better to get sin out of the way, he said.

"After seeing you at Christmas, knowing the horrible rumors that had been spread, even by people in our own parish, I suddenly realized I couldn't go on as a priest. It took time for me to act upon this decision. All the while the lie was eating me up inside. I had to leave the Church because I'm not a worthy person. I have failed myself, my priesthood, my parish, and most of all, you."

Something deep inside begged her to forgive, but a stronger feeling told her to remain calm, consider what Mark was saying and disregard his plea for absolution.

"Go on." Her voice was dull and flat.

"I want to atone for this sin. I want to support you while you get back on your feet. I can even apply to be your guardian until you attain legal age. I'll get you a flat of your own."

Sister Anne gasped. "Do you think that's wise, considering the realities of this unpleasant situation? Such an arrangement would only make things worse for both of you."

"I'll leave that for Teagan to decide." He nodded, awaiting a response.

"How could I trust you?" she asked, never averting her gaze.

Mark sighed. "That's a fair question. You'll have to take my word for it—as a reformed man filled with compassion for those he has wronged."

Sister Anne shook her head. It was clear to Teagan what the Mother Superior thought of Mark's offer.

Teagan knew his offer was false comfort, although she was somewhat cheered by the possibility of getting out of the convent. A bit of hope had appeared out of the blue.

"I can't accept your offer," she said. "It would be wrong after all that has happened." She stopped, considering whether to ask a question of the ex-priest. After a brief internal debate, she decided she wanted an answer. "Did you get a girl pregnant? Is that the real reason you left the priesthood?"

Mark looked as if he was going to laugh out loud. Instead, he sneered. "See what rumors and lies can do? They have ruined you and me." He shook his head. "No, I never got a woman pregnant—at least not in Ireland."

Sister Anne rose from her chair. "I think you've said enough. I'm sure Teresa—Teagan—has much to consider."

He stood and looked at Teagan. "I mean what I say. If I can help you, get in touch with me. I've left a number with Sister Anne where I can be reached." He walked to the door without looking back, opened it, and vanished into the hall.

Sister Anne reached for her *LOVE* blocks, picked them up, and held them tightly between her palms. The message faced Teagan, a mocking salute from the Mother Superior. "Certainly, this admission puts a new light on your situation."

"Certainly," Teagan replied. "I should get to work." She walked toward the door.

"Wait." Sister Anne put the blocks back on her desk.

She turned.

The Mother Superior fumbled with papers. "You don't have to work; in fact, I'm not sure The Sisters of the Holy Redemption can hold you here—if you want to go."

Teagan smirked. "No, I belong here for the time being. For the past year, you've made me what I am. I want to be with the other Magdalens—the other 'sinners' who may be as unjustly confined as I've been."

She closed the door and left Sister Anne to consider her words.

The next day Teagan worked in the laundry, but said nothing to the other Magdalens.

Nora was still in a world of her own, aloof, her sarcasm and humor obliterated by the death of her baby. Her friend slept, ate, worked, and fit into the routine as comfortably as Patricia, who was on her way to being a nun.

As she worked, she thought about Mark's offer, but after a few minutes' consideration she brought her mind back to the washbasin. Leaving the convent wasn't as simple as just walking out. Her freedom was complicated, a confusing matter filled with uncertainties.

She thought of calling her aunt Florence in New York, who hadn't been at the funeral mass. Did her aunt even know that her parents had died? She'd have to get back to the house to get the telephone number from her mother's address book and make the call. Maybe Florence could help her get back on her feet. Making that call would open a world of possibilities, maybe even an opportunity to move to New York City.

As the workday ended, she spotted the Mother Superior near the Penitent's Room. Sister Anne kept her distance—Teagan knew Mark's confession had disturbed her.

A few days after the ex-priest came, Teagan was up to her elbows in suds. Sister Ruth put her stout fingers on her back. She turned to find not only the nun, but a woman in a stylish blue suit standing behind her.

The woman's face, so familiar and kind, struck her immediately, yet she had no idea who she was. Her hair was the color of her mother's, almost a perfect match. She was rounder than her mother, but not plump. The woman looked around the laundry, observing the girls who took as much notice of her as she did of them.

"This lady wants to see you," Sister Ruth said. "The Mother Superior said to bring her down."

The woman extended her gloved hand. Teagan wiped the suds from her fingers and swiped them across her apron.

"You don't know what I've gone through to find you," the woman said. "I'm your aunt, Florence Korman."

Aunt Florence from New York. She did bear a resemblance to her mother, who had been a few years older. When Teagan was about seven, her aunt had flown from New York to visit the family in Ballsbridge. She vaguely remembered the experience as an uncomfortable time. Her mother rarely talked about Flor-

ence, because she was a married to a man her father disliked—
"a rich New York Jew who'd take your last dollar," he had
declared. He made it clear that Florence's husband was persona
non grata in his house.

Teagan shook her hand and admired the attractive woman.

"I'm sorry I didn't make the funeral," Florence said, and shed
her gloves. "It's quite hot in here. Is this where you work every
day?" She had no trace of an Irish accent.

"Mainly," Teagan said, unsure how to respond.

"I came as soon as I could, but with the rift in the family—
we didn't find out until after the funeral was over. A solicitor's
office contacted us." Florence fanned herself with her hands. "Is
there somewhere we can talk that's less noisy?"

Teagan pointed to the chair in the far corner. Sister Ruth was
watching them, but didn't seem too concerned about what they
did. Teagan led her aunt to the seat. Florence sat delicately and
crossed her legs, while Teagan stood. She felt like an ungainly
and embarrassed girl who had just come in from playing in the
mud. She was ashamed of her dirty apron and ugly shoes, and
unable to look Florence in the face.

"Teagan, I have an offer to make. Please look at me."

Teagan acquiesced.

Florence leaned forward. "A nice man who seems very concerned about your well-being told me where you were, after I
inquired at the parish church. I met him at his flat. He told
me everything. His name is Mark. He used to be a priest." She
paused. "He seems very sorry for what you've gone through. He
even cried when I told him what I have planned. I'm sorry, too,
that you've had to go through this. . . . I've talked with Sister
Anne. I can have legal paperwork drawn up for a guardianship
within a few days. I know Dublin is your home, but what's to
keep you here? I'm offering you a home in New York City—you
can live with my husband and me. We can afford to take you in,
and we're more than happy to do it."

Teagan leaned against the railing that separated the laundry
from the expansive windows. She looked out on the grounds,
taken aback by Florence's offer. The breeze rocked the leafy

oaks. Shadows scattered across the grass. "I don't know what to say."

"Say 'yes.'" Florence folded her gloves and put them in her purse. "My husband is a doctor. We can offer you a home you could never make for yourself here. We can send you to the best schools in America. Later, if you decide you want to come back to Ireland . . . well, I might hate the idea, but it's up to you. Harold and I want to make sure you have a fresh start."

"So you know everything?"

Florence didn't flinch. "I believe Mark told me the truth. I'm sorry—your father was bent on his own destruction. Unfortunately, he took everyone he loved with him, and, for that, I find it hard to forgive him."

Her aunt was here in answer to her prayers, but America seemed so far away. "I'll have to think about it. Dublin has always been my home."

"I understand, but know that keeping the house would be throwing money away. I'm here to settle the estate, sell the house and its contents. Your father may not have been fond of my husband and me, but Shavon was able to dictate the beneficiary because Cormac had no siblings. It was recorded so many years ago, I don't think he even remembered or gave it a second thought. People don't like to think about their deaths." She clutched her purse. "The proceeds from the sale will go into a trust fund whether you decide to come to America or not. The money will be yours when you're of legal age."

Florence stood and smoothed her dress. She hugged Teagan and gave her a kiss on the cheek. They walked toward the washbasin.

"Getting the final details straightened out with the solicitor and the estate agent will take about a week. After that, we'll be free to go, once you get your passport. The legalities can all be handled from New York. Let me know your decision within a few days, if possible. I'll be staying at the house—in your parents' room. You know the phone number." She grasped Teagan's hands warmly. "Come live with us. Be good to yourself, especially after what you've been through."

"There's a spare key under the garden gnome," Teagan said. Florence smiled, then walked past Sister Ruth and up the stairs.

Teagan stuck her hands back in the soapy water. Florence, although not by blood, was her real aunt—not Sister Anne. She trembled with joy as relief flooded through her.

How could she tell Nora? Would Nora even understand?

She pondered those questions that night at tea and evening prayers, and for the first time in more than a year, she prayed in gratitude, because she felt God was looking after her.

That evening, Nora crept into bed in the old library, as she had done every night since the fire, and rolled onto her side, her face turned away from Teagan.

Teagan waited until all the Magdalens had settled in, then lifted the sheet and slid next to her friend, whose mattress was still next to hers. Teagan touched Nora's shoulder. Her friend started and jumped up in bed. After a few moments, Nora lay back down but didn't speak.

Teagan held her hand and whispered, "Nora, I want to talk to you." A few beds away, Betty snored. The sleepy breaths of the Magdalens filled the library. "I've been praying this evening about what I should do. I'm going to America, which means I'll be leaving the convent soon—and leaving you." She squeezed her hand. "We made a pact we would help each other—one for all, and all that. I haven't forgotten. Once I get my feet on the ground, I'll come back and get you. I hope you understand I'm not deserting you, but I have a chance for a good life—better than I could have ever imagined."

She threaded her fingers through Nora's, hoping for some kind of response, but there was none. The room was lonely without Nora and Lea, as if she were sitting in it alone.

"Please, Nora, let me know that you'll be all right if I leave. Let me know that you'll hang on."

It was no use. Nora was as unresponsive as the day Seamus died. Teagan withdrew her hand from her friend's. She brushed her fingers against Nora's cheek and felt the cold sting of tears.

Somewhere in that hard shell, Nora was alive. She kissed her and slid back to her own mattress. She prayed she had made the right decision.

She waited until after the nuns had left for their morning duties before heading up to the garret. The Sisters were still sleeping in the girls' old beds. There was nothing in her locker she needed to take, but it warranted a last look. She wished now she had kept the blue dress she'd put on at the house. She opened the locker and found it buried under the personal items of a nun, along with the shirt and jeans she'd arrived in.

Below, hammers pounded and saws buzzed. She looked out the barred window. Workmen crawled over the blackened granite arches, securing beams for the orphanage's new roof. Parts of the structure were salvageable, according to Sister Mary-Elizabeth. In only a few months, Sister Immaculata and the others would be able to return. At least, that was the expectation.

A nun now slept in her old bed, but it no longer mattered. She took off her uniform and peered out over the roof and spotted the corner where she, Nora, and Lea had sat, Nora smoking a cigarette and all of them enjoying the fresh air and night stars. In a way, leaving the convent made her sad, and she wondered how she could have such feelings about a place she despised. Did prisoners feel the same way when they left gaol? She took a deep breath and put on the blue dress. It was the only decent thing she had to wear. The money from Cullen was still in the pocket.

As she walked down, the faint whir from the laundry drifted up the stairs. Her hands were scaly and red from the bleach and detergent. She wouldn't miss the heat or the smells. The room where she had spent so many hours dining in silence, eating horrible meals, was deserted. She took a final look out the broad windows that opened to the trees. The doors to the chapel and the Penitent's Room were closed. There was no reason to look inside either of them.

Florence was in Sister Anne's office when she arrived. Her adoptive aunt wore a white blouse covered by a handsomely cut beige jacket and matching skirt. The Mother Superior bent over her desk, adding her signature to a sheaf of papers. Sister Anne looked at Teagan and then resumed her writing.

"Well, that about does it," Florence said and hugged Teagan. "We're free to go. Are you ready?"

"I guess so," Teagan replied. "I don't like long good-byes."

Sister Anne raised her hand, unwilling to speak. She opened her desk drawer and took out an envelope that Teagan had long forgotten about. The nun pushed it across the desk. Teagan picked it up and then remembered what was inside. It contained the pearl jewelry that had been the seed of an argument between her mother and father. "These are yours, as well." Sister Anne withdrew the transistor radio and the silk scarf her mother had given her last Christmas. She hadn't seen them since Sister Mary-Elizabeth had confiscated them from under Lea's bed.

Teagan gathered the items in her arms and stood looking at the Mother Superior, uncertain what to do next.

"Come now, let's go," Florence said. "I'm sure the Mother Superior has important business to conduct."

Her aunt smiled, but Teagan didn't think the sentiment was sincere. Florence probably couldn't care less about the nun. Her aunt was happy to whisk her away from the convent.

Teagan nodded.

Sister Anne stopped at the door and took hold of Teagan's arm before she could leave. The Mother Superior was trembling. "You've changed me—you may find that hard to believe."

Teagan looked at her skeptically.

"All the prayers," the Mother Superior continued, "all the emotional strife I had created faded when Father Mark confessed his sin to me. I admitted mine, too."

Florence stood in the hall, waiting. Teagan didn't want to hear a confession from Sister Anne. She had lost more than a year of her life, and nothing could bring that back. The emotional torture, the feelings of worthlessness that the Church had systematically laid upon her couldn't be erased by a simple "*I was wrong.*" In fact, the Mother Superior's admission jolted her, causing her face to flush in anger.

The nun continued, "I don't expect you to forgive me now, but perhaps you will in the future. I shed my hatred when I realized you were not the demon I had created in my heart." She pointed to the *LOVE* blocks on her desk. "I'm going to try very hard to live by that rule."

Teagan drew away from the Mother Superior. "I have many to forgive. I pray that when you levy punishments, you'll remember the words you've spoken."

Florence held out her hand. Teagan took it and they walked toward the large doors. She had only been past the imposing threshold a few times since her confinement, but now she was free to breathe, to savor her new freedom.

Sister Mary-Elizabeth stood at the door, her hands clenched at her side. She looked concerned, as if she had lost one of the flock. "Good luck. Forgive us," she whispered as Teagan passed.

Florence and she stepped out on the stone terrace and the door closed behind them. The warm August breeze swirled around her. She could hardly believe how alive she felt as she took in the sensation of the air against her skin, the smell of the pine trees in her nostrils, the sunlight falling upon her face. But she felt exhausted, too, as if she had been running for more than a year and never stopped.

Her aunt walked to the taxi. The driver opened the door.

"One minute, Florence," Teagan said and thrust her belongings into her aunt's hands. She ran along the front of the convent, then turned west toward the corner where Lea had seen the ghostly children. Her heart pounded, and a lump formed in her throat as she rounded the corner and turned north. The laundry's broad expanse of windows came into view. She knew Nora would be inside, maybe even waiting to wave good-bye.

She crept close to the railing. The stone pit opened precipitously in front of her. Past the windows, the Magdalens, who had been part of her life, worked. Betty was tending a washer, Sarah stood at the washbasins. They were all there, except for Patricia, who had started her instructions as a novice.

When the Magdalens saw Teagan, who was staring at them like animals in a zoo, they responded in kind. They dropped their work and came to the windows. Sister Ruth sat in her chair, but the nun didn't object—Teagan thought she might hear her rough bark over the cacophony inside—but instead, Sister Ruth joined the others. Nora stood near the back, working at the sorting bins. A nun came through the door, took Nora by the shoulders, and guided her to the windows. When the nun turned, she was surprised to see Sister Anne. The Mother Superior had come to the laundry to find her friend. They stared with the others.

Nora stood, immobile, with the Mother Superior behind her. The Magdalens raised their hands one by one. A few wiped away tears.

Teagan's breath caught, and her eyes clouded over with emotion. She concentrated on Nora, but saw no sign of recognition. Her friend looked like a broken doll with its owner hanging over her shoulder.

Teagan pointed to herself and then to Nora, using the sign language they had devised, then mouthed silently, *"I'll come back for you."*

Nora didn't appear to recognize what she said. Her friend trudged back to her station.

The Mother Superior was still watching when Teagan left the railing. In the southwest corner, where the dead children lay buried, a voice caught her ear. She stopped—not sure she had heard it—and shivered in the sun.

Good luck, Teagan. I'll miss you.

She rocked on her feet, convinced she had heard Lea's voice. In the corner, something shimmered in the light. Rippling waves, evanescent, melted like a rainbow obscured by clouds.

"I'll miss you, too," she said to the air. "I'll make sure someone knows about the children. They won't have died in vain."

She returned to the taxi and slid into the backseat with her aunt. Florence clutched her hand as the vehicle accelerated down the driveway. Teagan hardly gave a glance to Mr. Roche, who opened the gate. She looked back over her shoulder in time to see the iron enclosure swing shut.

* * *

Little had changed in the house since she had been there. Florence had shifted a few things around, and marked a few plates to be sent to America. This time Teagan was determined to stay in her own room. It felt different, not as threatening as before. It would be her last night there.

Her aunt took her out to dinner at a neighborhood restaurant, where Teagan spotted several of her parents' friends. Most didn't recognize her. The few who did came by and offered condolences, adding that they had "missed her." They had wondered where she had been. She thanked them, but didn't want to talk about the past. In fact, she had a hard time talking about the present.

She was exhausted when they got back to the house. She plopped down on the living room couch. Nothing seemed real. Most of her mother's decorative items, the bric-a-brac, the furnishings, the plants, the house itself, would soon belong to someone else. What was it all for? Why had it ended this way?

"Why so quiet?" Florence asked, sitting in a chair across from her.

"I can't believe I'm going to America, and that our house will belong to someone else. Ballsbridge is all I've ever known, except for—"

"Don't think about it. It's over now." Florence leaned back. Her aunt seemed so composed compared to the nervous anxiety that tied Teagan in knots. "I suppose you could back out of going to New York, but I hope you don't. Where would you stay? What would you do?"

Teagan shook her head. Her life had been turned upside down because of a priest. Nothing made sense since her father had ripped her away from home. "I don't know." She paused. "I hate those words. Life should be more than *not knowing*."

"Well, tomorrow's flight reservations have been made." Her aunt's voice vibrated with excitement. "You'll love New York. There's so much to do—to see. There's a little Catholic church in the neighborhood. You can go to temple with us if you wish, but we certainly don't expect it." Her eyes brightened. "Harold is very excited about your move."

She hadn't even considered religion. She'd had her fill of it. In the past, her father had grumbled about Florence's conversion to Judaism, but it wasn't an issue with her. In fact, she didn't want to think about it. *No more religion. Only making friends and going to school.* Cullen flashed through her mind, and she blanched.

"Everything's taken care of," Florence continued. "I'll handle it all from New York, with your consent and advice, of course. It'll give us something to do." Her aunt explained how the sale would be handled through the solicitor and his agents, how the funds would be wired to the trust in New York, what needed to be done to complete the guardianship, even how she had arranged for a "rush" passport to be issued tomorrow morning.

It all seemed too good to be true—but as if it was meant to be—something that she had experienced little of during her life. The feeling that everything was falling into place was foreign to her. But as her aunt spoke, a dull ache cradled her heart.

"I've got to phone Cullen," she said when her aunt finished.

"I'm going to get ready for bed," Florence said. Teagan knew it was an excuse to leave her alone for the call. Her aunt kissed her on the forehead. "I'll see you in the morning. We have a lot of packing to do before we get on that plane."

As Florence headed upstairs, Teagan made her way to the kitchen. She sat at the small table near the window and admired her mother's plants. She hoped they wouldn't die from neglect after they left, but her aunt had assured her that the smallest details would be handled with care.

The green wall phone stared at her. She reached for it several times, her heart pounding, before getting up the nerve to actually dial the number. A man answered—Cullen's father. When she identified herself, a chill spread over the line. Despite his frosty reception, he called out for his son. In a few seconds, Cullen, excited and eager, was on the line. He greeted her.

"Hello," was all she could say.

A rocky silence grew between them.

"What's wrong?" he asked.

"Nothing's wrong."

"I know you, Teagan," Cullen replied. "At least I think I do. Are you at home? I heard the rumors."

"Yes," she said, dreading what she had to tell him.

His voice dropped. "When can I see you?"

"It'll be a while."

He was silent.

"Cullen? Are you there? Cullen? Please don't do this."

"You're going away, aren't you?"

She nodded, even though he couldn't see what she was doing. A tear rolled down her cheek. "I have to. I need some time away from Dublin—to sort things out. Things are too raw right now. I hope you understand." She wanted to say something to ease Cullen's pain. It resonated through the line. "I'll be back soon."

His breath caught; she heard it clearly and pictured the anguish on his face. "No, you won't."

She swiped another tear away and tried to laugh. "Don't talk like that. You know I keep my word, especially when it comes to friends."

"When are you leaving?"

"About nine, tomorrow evening. We land in New York the same night."

Cullen coughed and his voice tightened. "Listen, I've got to go. Da doesn't like it when I spend too much time on the phone."

"All right. I'll call you in a couple of days, after I've had a chance to settle in."

"Sure," he said and hung up.

She sat at the table for a half hour brushing away tears, thinking of Cullen and contemplating a life-to-be. She hoped the nightmare that had been her life was evaporating like fog in the sun. Finally, she'd had enough moping about. She turned off the lights and climbed the stairs. Her parents' door was closed. She stepped into her room and left the door ajar. She didn't want to be shut in; that feeling of claustrophobia was too much like the convent. Rain fell outside. A cool breeze brushed through the window.

She lay on the bed and stared at the ceiling. The textured

plaster, in various places, reminded her of objects: the surface of the moon; a cathedral; a building at Trinity College, where she had hoped to go. When she blinked, they popped into focus as the swirls, circles, and lines they were.

The transistor radio her father had given her lay near the pillow. She turned it on and listened to several current tunes before an "oldie" came on. It was a big hit before she had been whisked away. She'd first heard it in the bedroom where she slept tonight. Somehow, it meant more in this moment.

"I Can't Stop Loving You."

EPILOGUE

———◦——

From her aunt and uncle's penthouse balcony on the East Side, she could look north toward the Queensboro Bridge and the gray-green expanse of the East River. To the right, the glittering tower of the United Nations Headquarters came into view.

She had been introduced to Florence and Harold's friends— all nice and all more than willing to welcome her to New York. A world of shopping, galleries, museums, restaurants, practically anything she wanted to do day or night, opened before her.

Her bedroom was half as big as the first floor of the Dublin house. Her aunt had placed a wide desk before the window that looked out over the East River. There she could read, study, decide upon schools, think about the choices she had to make, and forget about the past. For once, the tension that had permeated her life seemed to have lifted. She no longer had to deal with her father when he was drunk, her mother's slavish obedience to her father, the Church, or grapple with her feelings about men—Cullen and Father Mark included.

A withered rose sat in a cut-crystal vase on her desk. The yellow petals had turned brown. Cullen had given it to her when she and Florence were about to leave the house. He had unexpectedly shown up with the rose in hand and apologized for being upset on the phone. He understood her decision to leave, to sort things out, and wanted her to know he would be in Dublin if she needed a friend. She kissed him on the cheek. Florence seemed impressed and called him a "handsome young man."

They parted with no tears.

When the runway disappeared beneath the 737 and they were thrust into the air, Florence breathed a sigh of relief. Teagan watched Dublin drop away. As they jetted west over the countryside, she thought of Lea and her Celbridge home. The last she saw of Ireland were the high cliffs jutting above the coast and the thin lines of cresting waves that crept toward the shore in slow motion.

At her desk in New York, she took pen in hand to write to Cullen. It had been several weeks since they had corresponded. She wrote a few words and then looked out the window. A fast-moving line of clouds approached from the northwest. Teagan had never seen anything like it in Ireland. The storm clouds in America were different: sharper, linear, brutal. She stepped out on the balcony to take a look. The weather reminded her of the turmoil she had left behind—Sister Anne, her parents, and Nora and Lea. The wind wrapped its cool fingers around her. The warm days of fall were vanishing. Winter approached, but she was settled and comfortable in her aunt's New York apartment.

Several blocks away, a patch of grass grew between two high-rises. A leafy tree stood encircled by lush green. The verdant sight dimmed, obscured from the sun by flowing clouds.

That was the way of life, she thought, bright one moment and dim the next.

She left the terrace and shut the sliding doors, closing out the chill.

It was green in that little patch of New York, and still green in Ireland, despite their differences in location.

Someday she would see green Ireland again. Cullen might be waiting, and Nora needed her help. Nothing mattered more than a promise to a friend.

AUTHOR'S NOTE

The history of the Catholic Church has been fraught with war, religious intolerance, and scandal, yet in fairness, the institution has been tempered throughout the centuries by its charitable actions, the lives of its saints, and the devotion of its faithful. In recent years, the Church has been scrutinized for financial malfeasance, priestly overindulgence, and sexual abuse. The story of the Magdalen Laundries has only come into the cultural spotlight within the past two decades.

Perhaps this story has not been as exploited as something so overtly inflammatory as the sexual abuse scandal of priests because of the nature of the Magdalens' "crimes." The girls and women under servitude were mostly categorized as "fallen women." Could our own cultural biases have served to favor their punishment? They deserved what they got, many might say. Girls and women were sent to the laundries for being mentally unfit or too pretty, too attractive, inducing sin by the very nature of their looks. Others ended up there because of promiscuity or their involvement in prostitution.

The Magdalen Girls is set in Dublin in 1962. It should be noted that the laundries were not confined to Ireland. In fact, the asylums, as they were also known, existed in England, Scotland, the United States, Canada, and elsewhere. They were also not solely under the province of the Catholic Church. Secular interests, as well as other religious entities outside Catholicism, developed laundries to rehabilitate prostitutes.

The first reported laundry opened in 1758. The last closed in 1996. Once incarcerated, a woman's reputation was often ruined. Many stayed in the institution for years, calling it home, because there was no other option for the "penitent." Through its strict doctrine, the institution often managed to make the Magdalen unfit to adjust to a normal life outside the laundry. They were, in effect, prisoners both inside and outside its structure.

In 1993, a mass grave of children was found on the grounds of a Dublin laundry. This led to a formal state apology nearly two decades later. As far as I know, no compensation or formal apology has ever been given by the Church. The history of the laundries remains a contentious subject on both sides of the debate, one calling the actions criminal, and the other portraying them as beneficial and rehabilitative.

Despite the arguments, there is no doubt that the lives of many thousands of girls and women were changed by their time in servitude. Some lived, some died, but their stories continue to touch us all.

ACKNOWLEDGMENTS

Debts are owed to many people who made this book better than the author ever could have. Thanks go out to my beta readers, Michael Grenier, Bob Pinsky, and Charlie Roche; my critique partners, Heidi Lynn Anderson and Lloyd A. Meeker; and the literary talents of Traci E. Hall and Christopher Hawke of CommunityAuthors.com. This novel would not have been possible without the vision of John Scognamiglio, my editor at Kensington Books. And, finally, thanks to Alyssa Maxwell and my agent, Evan Marshall, for believing in me.

The Magdalen Girls

V. S. ALEXANDER

About This Guide

The suggested questions are included
to enhance your group's reading of
V. S. Alexander's *The Magdalen Girls*.